MW01517971

WINTER TIDE

RUTHANNA EMRYS

WINTER
TIDE

A TOM DOHERTY ASSOCIATES BOOK

NEW YORK

WINTER TIDE

Copyright © 2017 by Ruthanna Emrys

All rights reserved.

Edited by Carl Engle-Laird

A Tor.com Book
Published by Tom Doherty Associates
175 Fifth Avenue
New York, NY 10010

www.tor-forge.com

Tor® is a registered trademark of Macmillan Publishing Group, LLC.

The Library of Congress Cataloging-in-Publication Data is available upon request.

ISBN 978-0-7653-9090-5 (hardcover)
ISBN 978-0-7653-9091-2 (e-book)

Our books may be purchased in bulk for promotional, educational, or business use. Please contact your local bookseller or the Macmillan Corporate and Premium Sales Department at 1-800-221-7945, extension 5442, or by e-mail at MacmillanSpecialMarkets@macmillan.com.

First Edition: April 2017

Printed in the United States of America

0 9 8 7 6 5 4 3 2 1

While I was writing *Winter Tide,* my wife, Sarah,
completed a more difficult and rewarding project.
This book is dedicated to her—
and to Miriam, the result of her hard work.

Year after year I heard that faint, far ringing
Of deep-toned bells on the black midnight wind;
Peals from no steeple I could ever find,
But strange, as if across some great void winging.
I searched my dreams and memories for a clue,
And thought of all the chimes my visions carried;
Of quiet Innsmouth, where the white gulls tarried
Around an ancient spire that once I knew.

—H. P. LOVECRAFT, "THE BELLS,"
Fungi from Yuggoth

At last, though, my hope was fading gradually away. Except for a few of
the opening lines of certain books, from which there seemed to flash upon
me the face of the friend whom I had been longing to behold, a momentary glimpse, dim through distance, or, rather, the sight of his streaming
hair, as he vanished from my view—except for this . . . I had no hope of
being able ever to see you face to face.

—FRANCIS PETRARCH, "TO HOMER"
(TRANSLATED BY JAMES HARVEY ROBINSON)

WINTER TIDE

CHAPTER 1

September 1948

I shut the door of the old Victorian behind me, and the stuffy atmosphere closed in: overheated, dry, and redolent of mothballs. Remnants of cool mist clung to my skin, already transmuting to sweat. A whiff of old paper cut through the miasma. I focused on that familiar, beloved scent, and steadied myself.

Charlie, clearly untroubled by the warmth, took off his fedora and looked around the estate sale with a practiced eye. Choice artifacts adorned a table in the foyer—an antique globe and a few Egyptian-looking statues of uncertain vintage. The newly dead patriarch had been not only well off, but a professor emeritus of ancient history at the university. That combination was sufficient to draw us both away from the bookstore on a busy Saturday morning.

A woman approached us, frowning. She wore a floral dress and pearl necklace, but the black veil pinned over her curls marked her as part of the family hosting the sale. A daughter, perhaps? I was never good at estimating ages. Her eyebrows drew together as her gaze lingered on me. I smoothed my plain gray skirt—the color of storms and of mourning—then forced my hands still. She might not like the shape of my face or the pallor of my skin, but I wouldn't give her any reason to complain about my composure. In the privacy of my chest, my heart beat faster. I tried to reason with it: beyond my chosen family, almost no one in San Francisco could know how to interpret my bulging eyes, thick neck, and receding hairline. She'd see an ugly woman, nothing more—the disquieted frown would likely be her worst reaction.

Charlie frowned fiercely back at her. Silence lingered while she twisted her strand of pearls between ringed fingers. At last he said: "I'm Charlie Day, and this is my assistant, Miss Aphra Marsh. We're here to look at the books."

"Oh!" She startled back to some semblance of her script. "Yes. Father was quite a collector. It's mostly old academic junk. I don't know that you'll find anything interesting, but you're certainly welcome to look. All the books and magazines are downstairs." She jerked her head at the hall beyond the foyer.

Charlie led the way. The wooden stairs, hollow under our feet, shook with our steps. I held out an arm to help Charlie down, but he waved it off.

"Cheer up," I murmured. "If she's dismissing them as junk, she'll likely sell cheap."

"If she's kept them in a damp basement, they *will* be junk." He gripped the rail and descended, leaning a little to favor his right knee. I stared at his back, wondering how he could expect any part of this house to be damp.

The basement was not only dry, but hotter than the entry hall. A few books had been laid out on shelves; others remained piled in boxes and crates.

Charlie huffed. "Go ahead, Miss Marsh."

Embarrassed, I picked up the nearest book—a thirty-year-old encyclopedia, *Cartography to Curie, Pierre*—and inhaled deeply. My pulse slowed. Over two years now since I'd gained my freedom, and above all else it was the scent and touch of printed paper that assured me of safety.

He laughed. "Let's get to work. And hope she's too busy sucking lemons to bother us before we're ready to haggle."

I immersed myself happily in the crates, laying aside promising volumes for Charlie's approval while he started on the shelf. His store had no particular specialty, serving discerning antiquarians alongside anyone willing to pay three cents for a dime novel. The dead professor, I discovered, had maintained an unacademic taste for gothic bodice-rippers, and I amassed a stack of the most promising before moving on to the second box.

Here I found more predictable material. Most were histories and travelogues mere decades old. There were a few fraying works dating back to the 1600s—in languages I couldn't read, but I set them aside anyway. Then, beneath a reprinted colonial cookbook, I found something unexpected, but very much desired.

I probed the clothbound cover with long fingers, confirming that the volume would stand up to handling. I trailed them over the angular letters embossed on the spine, laid the book—perhaps two hundred years old, and clearly a copy of something much older—on the floor, and opened it. My Latin was far from fluent, but I could make out enough.

"Mr. Day, take a look at this." I set the book on the table where he could examine it without squatting.

"Something for the back room?" he asked hopefully.

"I think so. But your Latin is better than mine."

"*De Anima Pluvia*. The soul of the rain." He turned the pages slowly, touching only the edges. "It looks like the author, at least, thought it belonged in our back room. We've had no luck trying . . ." He glanced at the stairs, confirmed them empty, lowered his voice anyway: ". . . to affect the weather, with everything we already have. Do you think this'll be any better?"

"I've seen it before. That was an older copy, and translated, but from what I can make out this is the real text, not a fake with the same title. It's supposed to be one of the best works on the subject."

He nodded, accepting my judgment. And didn't ask where I'd seen it.

For two years now, Charlie had granted me access to his private collection in exchange for my tutelage in its use. And for two years, he'd never asked where I got my first training in the occult, how it had ended, or why a pale, ugly woman with bulging eyes lived in Japantown with a family clearly not her own. I'd never offered to tell him.

After two years, I willingly called Charlie a friend. But I told him nothing of my life before I walked into his store, and he told me nothing of his. We shared the secrets we'd created together, and respected each other's privacy for the rest. I didn't even know whether he kept his own counsel out of pain or shame—or both, as I did.

But I did know that I couldn't keep my own secrets forever—not if he kept studying magic at my side.

De Anima Pluvia, if we were able to make use of it, would allow a ritual that I'd long missed—and that, done right, would surely require me to reveal my nature. I tried to imagine his reaction. I didn't think he would flee; he valued what I had to offer too much. But I feared his disgust. I would still trade my knowledge for his books, even without the camaraderie. I valued them too much to stop. But it would be a harder bargain, and I could taste the sting of it already.

The people of the water have always hidden, or tried—and suffered when we failed.

Spring 1942, or possibly 1943: My brother Caleb sits on the edge of Silas Bowen's cot, while I keep watch by the cabin door. The older man thrashes and moans, but stills as Caleb tilts a bowl of water between his thin, protuberant lips. The water is alkaline and without salt, but seems to help. It's been years since the camp guards allowed salt at our tables—with only the three of us left it's a wonder Caleb was able to sneak water out of the cafeteria at all. It's a wonder, in fact, that no one has checked Silas's cabin since he stopped coming to meals over a week ago. The guards are distracted. We speculate, knowing the reason can't be good.

Motors growl through the still desert air. Truck engines, unmuffled, and many of them—more than I've heard since they brought the last of Innsmouth's straggling refugees to the camp fourteen years ago. Or perhaps thirteen years; denied a scrap of paper or coal to mark the walls, Caleb and I disagree on how long it's been. My breath catches when I think of what this new incursion might bring. The sharp inhalation turns into a sharper cough, hacking that tears at my lungs until I double over in pain. Caleb stares, and his free hand clenches the ragged mattress.

Silas pats the bowl clumsily. "Aphra, child, drink." Membranes spread between his fingers, but even this new growth is chapped and flaking.

"You need it," I manage between coughs.

"What?" he rasps. "So I can die slowly enough for them to notice and kill me more painfully? Drink."

Caleb brings me the bowl, and I haven't the strength to refuse it.

Usually at estate sales, we were lucky to find even one book for the back room. So when Charlie called me over a few minutes later, it was a shock to hear him sounding out Enochian with his finger hovering above brittle, yellowed paper.

He broke off as I came near. "Good—maybe you can make this out better than I can. Damn thing's too faded to read all the words, not that I know most of them."

Dread warred with yearning as I approached the journal. In the years since the 1928 raid, a stolen diary could have made it from Innsmouth to San Francisco. If so, this would be the first trace of our old libraries that we'd managed to retrieve.

But as I examined it, I realized that we'd found something far stranger—if anything at all. I blinked with difficulty and swallowed, surprise making it easier to ignore the dry air.

"What is it?"

"I'm . . . not sure," I said. "Or rather, I'm not sure it's real. If it is what it appears . . . it purports to be the notes of a visiting Yith."

"Borrowing a human body?" Charlie sounded doubtful, and I didn't blame him.

"That's usually the kind they wear, during humanity's span on Earth. But when they end the exchange of bodies and cast their minds back to their own time, they try to destroy this kind of record."

I'd told Charlie about the Yith, as I'd told him about all Earth's species whose civilizations and extinctions they traversed aeons to document. For me it was vital knowledge—at my lowest, I found comfort remembering that humanity's follies marked only a brief epoch in our world's history. But for Charlie I suspected that those species, and the preservation of their memories in the Great Archive, might still be a half-mythical abstraction: something he tried to believe because I did and because it served as foundation to the magic that he so deeply desired. He'd never said otherwise, and I'd never been certain how to handle his unstated doubt.

"And one of them just happened to leave this journal behind?" He pursed his lips against the unsatisfying explanation.

"It seems unlikely," I agreed, still trying to make out more of the text. If nothing else, the manuscript was the oldest thing we'd found that day. "I suspect it's a hoax, albeit well-informed. Or the author could have fallen into delusion, or intended it as fiction from the start. It's hard to tell." The fact that I recognized most of the vocabulary, alone, suggested an entirely human origin.

"Should we buy it?" His eyes drifted back to the page. I suspected that he, like me, was reluctant to abandon anything in one of the old tongues.

"It's beautiful. As long as we don't expect to gain any great use from it . . ." Further examination confirmed my guess—the all-too-human author had dropped hints of cosmic secrets, but nothing that couldn't be found in the *Book of Eibon* or some other common text. I suspected a real member of the great race would have been more discreet and less boastful—and made far more interesting errors of discretion. "If it were real, it would be priceless. Even the fake is old enough to be worth something. But our host doesn't seem the sort to know its value either way."

The door creaked, and Charlie jerked his hand from the journal. I flinched, imagining what my mother would have said if she'd heard me judge someone so in their own home. At least it was a young man in army uniform, and not the woman in the floral dress, who came down the stairs. He nodded briefly, then ignored us in favor of the vinyl albums boxed at the far end of the room. He muttered and exclaimed over their contents while I tried to regain my equilibrium. His uniform kept drawing my eye—making me brace, irrationally, against some punishment for my proximity to the books.

"I hope her father did," said Charlie more quietly. It took me a moment to recapture the conversation: our host's father must have seen some connection between the journal and his studies, or he wouldn't have owned it. "I hope he got the best use he could out of the whole collection."

"You wouldn't want to waste it," I agreed.

"No." He bent, wincing, to rub his knee. "It makes you think. I'd hate to have someone go through my store, after I'm gone, and say, 'He had no idea what he had.' Especially if the Aeonists are right—no heaven where we can read everything we missed and ask the authors what they meant."

I shrugged uncomfortably. "I can offer you magic, but only in the universe we've got. Except perhaps for the Yith, immortality isn't a part of it."

Though he might not see it that way, when he learned more about who I was. I really couldn't put it off much longer.

My brother was very young when they forbade us paper and ink. "The scollars," Caleb wrote,

> *refuse my evry effort to beg or bargin entre. I have not yet resorted to steeling my way in, and in truth don't beleev I have the stelth to do so nor the skill to pass unseen throu Miskatonic's alarms.*

*Sister deer, I am at a loss. I do not kno wether they forbid me do
to knoing my natur or in ignorranse of it, and wether it is malis
or uncaring dismissel. Pleaz rigt. Yors in deepest fondness.*

"He should come home," said Anna. "He should be with his family."
Mama Rei nodded in firm agreement.

"He is home. As close as he feels he can get, anyway." I put down
my fork, half-grateful for the distraction from the hot dog and egg mixture that clung vertiginously to my rice. The Kotos had somehow developed a taste for hot dogs in the camps, where we ate the same surplus
rations for days at a time. To me they tasted of sand and fever-dry air.

Mama Rei shook her head. "Home is family, not a place. It does not
help him to wander through his memories, begging books from people
who do not care about him."

I loved the Kotos, but sometimes there were things they didn't understand. That brief moment of hope and fear at the estate sale, when
I'd thought the journal might have been written in Innsmouth, had
made Caleb's quixotic quest seem even more urgent. "The books are
family too. The only family we still have a chance to rescue."

"Even if the books are at Miskatonic—" began Neko. Kevin tugged
at her arm urgently before sinking back in his chair, quelled by a look
from Mama Rei. It was an argument we'd gone through before.

"They didn't take them in the raid. Not in front of us, and so far as
Mr. Spector can determine from his records, they never went back for
them. Anyone who'd have known enough to . . . scavenge . . . our libraries would have passed through Miskatonic, to sell the duplicates if
nothing else." Even books with the same title and text weren't duplicates, truly, but few outsiders would care about the marginalia: family
names, records of oaths, commentary from generations long since passed
into the deep.

"Caleb's a good man," said Neko. She was perhaps the closest to him
of us all, save myself. He had been just enough older to fascinate her,

and her friendship had been a drop of water to cool his bitterness, the last few years before we gained our freedom together. "But a group of old professors like that—I'm sorry, but what they'll see is a rude young man who can't spell."

"Nancy," said Mama Rei. Neko ducked her head, subsiding under the rebuke of the given name she so disliked.

"They will, though," put in Anna defiantly. "She's not saying it to be mean. He should come back to us, and learn how ordinary people make friends, and take classes at the community center. Aphra is always talking about centuries and aeons—if Caleb takes a little time to learn how to spell, how to talk nicely to people who don't trust him, the books will still be there."

That much was true. And it was foolishness to imagine our books locked in Miskatonic's vaults, impatient for freedom.

May 1942: It's been years since the camp held more prisoners than guards, months since I've heard the shouts of young children or the chatter of real conversation. Over the past three days, it seems as if thousands of people have passed through the gates, shouting and crying and claiming rooms in long-empty cabins, and all I can think is: not again. *I've done all my mourning, save for Silas and my brother. I can only dread getting to know these people, and then spending another decade watching children burn up in fever, adults killed for fighting back, or dying of the myriad things that drive them to fight.*

When they switch from English, their language is unfamiliar: a rattle of vowels and hard consonants rather than the slow sibilants and gutturals of Enochian and its cousins.

Caleb and I retreat to Silas's bedside, coming out only long enough to claim the cabin for our own. Most of the newcomers look at us strangely, but leave us alone.

The woman appears at the door holding a cup. Her people have been permitted packed bags, and this stoneware cup is the most beautiful made object that

I've seen since 1928. I stare, forgetting to send her away. She, too, is a different thing—comfortably plump where we've worn away to bone, olive-skinned and narrow-eyed, confident in a way that reminds me achingly of our mother.

"I am Rei Koto," she says. "I heard you coughing in the next room. It is not good to be sick, with so many crowded together and far from home. You should have tea."

She hands the cup first to Caleb, who takes it automatically, expression stricken. I catch a whiff of the scent: warm and astringent and wet. It hints of places that are not desert. She starts to say something else, then glimpses the man in the bed. She stifles a gasp; her hand flies halfway to her mouth, then pulls back to her breastbone.

"Perhaps he should have tea also?" she asks doubtfully. Silas laughs, a bubbling gasp that sends her hand back to her mouth. Then she takes a breath and retrieves the confidence she entered with, and asks, not what he is, or what we are, but: "You've been hiding in here. What do you need?"

Later I'll learn about the war that triggered her family's exile here, and crowded the camp once more with prisoners. I'll learn that she brought us the tea five days after they separated her from her husband, and I'll learn to call her my second mother though she's a mere ten years older than me. I'll be with her when she learns of her husband's death.

CHAPTER 2

December 1948

Charlie, shivering beside me on the San Francisco beach, looked doubtfully at the clouds. "Do you think we can do this?"

"I've ignored Winter Tide for too many years." Not precisely an answer. We'd done our best with *De Anima Pluvia,* but our biggest challenge had been finding a place to practice. The Tide itself was worth the risk of discovery, but any pattern of larger workings would draw notice. We'd managed a few small pushes to mist and rain, but couldn't be certain we were capable of more.

"Ah, well. If it doesn't work, I suppose it just means we're not ready yet." He wrapped his arms around his chest, and glanced at me. He wore a sweater to bulk out his slender frame and a hat pulled tightly over his sandy hair, but still shivered in what to me seemed a mild night. When I left the house, Mama Rei had insisted on a jacket, and I still wore it in deference to her sensibilities. California was having an unusually cold winter—but I'd last celebrated, many years ago, in the bitter chill of an Innsmouth December. I would have been happy, happier, with my skin naked to the salt spray and the wind.

"I suppose." But with the stars hidden, there would be no glimpse of the infinite on this singularly long night. No chance to glean their wisdom. No chance to meditate on my future. No chance to confess my truths. I was desperate for this to work, and afraid that it would.

We walked down to the boundary of the waves, where the cool and giving sand turned hard and damp. Charlie's night vision was poor, but he followed readily and crouched beside me, careful not to put too much weight on his knee. He winced only a little when a rivulet washed over his bare feet.

I glanced up and down the beach and satisfied myself that we were alone. At this time of night, at this time of year, it was a safe gamble that no one would join us.

I began tracing symbols in the sand with my finger. Charlie helped. I rarely had to correct him; by this point even he knew the basic sigils by touch. You must understand them as part of yourself, no more needing sight to make them do your bidding than you would to move your own legs.

Outward-facing spells had been harder for me, of late. To look at my own body and blood was easy enough, but the world did not invite close examination. Still, I forced my mind into the sand, into the salt and the water, into the clouds that sped above them. I felt Charlie's strength flowing into my own, but the wind tore at my mind as it had not at my body, pressing me into my skull. I pushed back, gasping as I struggled to hold my course and my intentions for the night.

And it wasn't working. The clouds were a distant shiver in my thoughts, nothing I could grasp or change. The wind was an indifferent opponent, fierce and strong. I fell back into my body with cheeks stung by salt.

Charlie still sat beside me, eyes closed in concentration. I touched him, and they flew open.

"It's no good," I said.

"Giving up so soon?"

I shivered, not with cold but with shame. As a child we had the archpriests for this. Not a half-trained man of the air and me, dependent on distant memories and a few scavenged books. "I can't get through the wind."

He tilted his head back. "I know *De Anima* likes to talk about 'the great war of the elements,' but I've been wondering—should it really be *through*? When we practice other spells, at the store . . . I know these arts aren't always terribly intuitive, but 'through' doesn't seem right. When we're working on the Inner Sea, or practicing healing, you always tell me that you can't fight your own blood."

I blinked, stared at him a long moment—at once proud of my student, and embarrassed at my own lapse. My eyes felt heavy, full of things I needed to see. "Right. Let's find out where the wind takes us."

I closed my eyes again, and rather than focusing on *De Anima*'s medieval metaphors, cast myself through the symbols and into the wind. This time I didn't try to direct it, didn't force on it my desires and expectations and memories. And I felt my mind lifted, tossed and twisted—whirled up into the misty tendrils of the clouds, and I could taste them and breathe them and wrap them around me, and I remembered that I had something to tell them.

I knelt on the strand, waves soaking my skirt, and gazed with pleasure and fear as the clouds spiraled, streaming away from the sky above us, and through that eye the starlight poured in.

"Oh," said Charlie. And then, "What now?"

"Now," I murmured, "we watch the universe. And tell stories, and seek signs, and share what has been hidden in our own lives."

My last such holiday, as a child, had been a natural Tide: the sky clear without need for our intervention. They were supposed to be lucky, but my dreams, when at last I curled reluctantly to sleep beside the bonfire, had been of danger and dry air. Others, too, had seemed pensive and disturbed in the days following. Poor omens on the Tide might mean anything—a bad catch, or a boat-wrecking storm beyond the archpriests' ability to gentle. No one had expected the soldiers, and the end of Tides for so many years to come.

That past, those losses, were the hardest things I must confess tonight.

We lay back on the sand. Cold and firm, yielding slightly as I squirmed to make an indent for my head, it cradled my body and told me my shape. Wet grains clung together beneath my fingers. The stars filled my eyes with light of the same make: cold and firm. And past my feet, just out of reach, I heard the plash of waves and knew the ocean there, endlessly cold and strong and yielding, waiting for me.

I said it plainly, but quietly. "I am not a man of the air."

Charlie jerked upright. "Truly."

"Yes."

I was about to say more when he spoke instead. I had not expected the admiration in his voice. "I suspected, but I hadn't felt right to ask. You really are then—one of the great race of Yith."

"What? No." Now I pushed myself up on my elbows so I could see him more clearly. He looked confused, doubtful. "How could you believe I . . . no. You would know them if you met them; they have far more wisdom than me."

"I thought . . ." He seemed to find some courage. "You appeared out of nowhere, living with a people obviously not your own. You found your way to my store, and my collection of books, and acted both singularly interested in and desperate for them. And you know so much, and you drop hints, occasionally, of greater familiarity in the distant past. And sometimes . . . forgive my saying so, but sometimes you seem entirely unfamiliar with this country, this world. I'd suppose shell shock, but that wouldn't explain your knowledge. I didn't want to pry, but after you told me about the Yith—how they exchange bodies with people through time—it seemed obvious that you must have somehow become trapped here, unable to use your art to return home. And that you hoped to regain that ability through our studies."

I lay back on the wet sand and laughed. It was all so logical: a completely different self, a different life, a different desperation, so close and obvious that I could almost feel what I would have been as that other creature. My laughter turned to tears without my fully noticing the transition.

Charlie lifted his hand, but hesitated. I struggled to regain self-control. Finally I sat, avoiding his touch, and scooted myself closer to the waves. I dipped my palms and dashed salt water across my eyes, returning my tears to the sea.

"Not a Yith," I said, somewhat more dignified. "Can't you guess? Remember your Litany."

"You sound like a Yith. All right." His voice slowed, matching the chanting rhythm that I'd used to teach it, and that I'd taken in turn from my father. "This is the litany of the peoples of Earth. Before the first, there was blackness, and there was fire. The Earth cooled and life arose, struggling against the unremembering emptiness. First were the five-winged eldermost of Earth, faces of the Yith—"

"You can skip a few hundred million years in there."

His breath huffed. "I'm only going to play guessing games if you *are* a Yith, damn it."

I bowed my head. I liked his idea so well. I briefly entertained the thought of telling him he was right, and placing that beautiful untruth between us. But ultimately, the lie would serve no purpose beyond its sweetness. "Sixth are humans, the wildest of races, who share the world in three parts. The people of the rock, the K'n-yan, build first and most beautifully, but grow cruel and frightened and become the Mad Ones Under the Earth. The people of the air spread far and breed freely, and build the foundation for those who will supplant them. The people of the water are born in shadow on land, but what they build beneath the waves will live in glory till the dying sun burns away their last shelter."

And after humans, the beetle-like ck'chk'ck, who like the eldermost would give over their bodies to the Yith and the endless task of preserving the Archives. And after them the Sareeav with their sculptures of glacier and magma. I could take this risk; even the worst consequences would matter little in the long run.

I raised my head. "I am of the water. I am ugly by your standards—no need to argue it—but the strangeness of my face is a sign of the metamorphosis I will one day undertake. I will live in glory beneath the waves, and die with the sun."

His head was cocked now—listening, waiting, and holding his judgment checked. As good a reaction as I might expect.

"I will live in glory—but I will do so without my mother or my father, or any of the people who lived with me on land as a child. Someone lied about us, about what we did in our temples and on beaches such as this. The government believed them: when I was twelve they sent soldiers, and carried us away to the desert, and held us imprisoned there. So we stayed, and so we died, until they brought the Nikkei—the Japanese immigrants and their families—to the camps at the start of the war. I do not know, when the state released them, whether they had forgotten that my brother and I remained among their number, or whether they simply no longer cared.

"You thought that I hoped, through our studies, to return home. I have no such hope. Our studies, and my brother, are all that remain of my home, and all of it I can ever hope to have."

"Ah." The unclouded stars still burned overhead, but his gaze was on the water. At last he fell back on: "I am sorry for your loss."

"It was a long time ago."

He turned toward me. "How long were you imprisoned?"

That figure was not hard to call up. "Almost eighteen years."

"Ah." He sat silent again for a time. One can talk about things at the Tide that are otherwise kept obscure, but one cannot suddenly impart the knowledge of how to discuss great cruelty. It was hardly a piece of etiquette that I had learned myself, as a child.

"Aeonist teachings say that no race is clean of such ignorance or violence. When faced with the threat of such things, we should strive as the gods do to prevent them or put them off. But when faced with such things already past, we should recall the vastness of time, and know that even our worst pains are trivial at such a scale."

His mouth twisted. "Does that help?"

I shrugged. "Sometimes. Sometimes I can't help seeing our resistance and kindness, even the gods' own efforts to hold back entropy, as trivial too. No one denies it, but we need the gods, and the kindness, to matter more anyway."

We talked long that night, memory shading into philosophy and back into memory. I told him of the years in the camp, of the sessions with my parents where I first learned magic, of my brother's quest, far away on the East Coast, to find what remained of our libraries. I told him, even, of my mother's death, and the favor I had done for Ron Spector, the man who gave me its details.

I knew nothing of Charlie's childhood or private life, and he told me nothing that night. Still, as much as I had learned of him in our months of study, I learned more through his responses now. Charlie was a brusque man, even uncivil sometimes. He was also an honest one, and more given to acting on his genuine affections than mouthing fine-sounding words. And he had been entirely patient with his curiosity until the moment I made my confession.

Now that I had shown my willingness to speak, his questions were thoughtful but not gentle. He would pull back if I refused, but otherwise ask things that drew out more truth—a deftness and appropriateness to the season that I might have expected from one of our priests, but not from even a promising neophyte.

At last, worn with honesty, we sat silent beneath the stars: a more comfortable silence than those we had started with, even if full of painful recollection.

After some time had passed, he asked quietly, "Are they out there?" He indicated the Pacific with a nod.

"Not in this ocean, save a few explorers. There are reasons that the spawning grounds were founded in Innsmouth—and in England before they moved. I am given to understand that the Pacific sea floor is not so hospitable as the Atlantic."

This led to more academic questions, and tales of life in the water beyond the Litany's gloss of dwelling in glory. Few details were granted to those of us on land, as children miss so many adult cares and plans despite living intimately alongside them. Still, I could speak of cities drawn upward from rock and silt, rich with warmth and texture and luminescence in lands beyond the reach of the sun. Of grimoires etched in stone or preserved by magic, of richly woven music, of jewelry wrought by expert metalworkers who had practiced their arts for millennia.

"Is that what you'll do down there?" he asked. "Read books and shape gold for a million years?"

"Almost a billion. I might do those things. Or consider philosophy, or watch over any children who remain on land, or practice the magics that can only be done under the pressures of the deep. Charlie, I don't even know what I'll do in ten years, if I'm still alive. How can I guess what I'll do when I'm grown?"

"Are we all children, on the land? I suppose we must seem like it—I can't even think easily about such numbers." He glanced back toward the mountains. "And such badly behaved children, too, with our wars and weapons."

I grinned mirthlessly. "Be assured that the atomic bomb is not the worst thing this universe has produced. Though no one knows the precise timing of the people of the air's passing, so it may be the worst thing that *you* produce, as a race."

"I suppose it's a comfort, to know that some part of humanity will keep going."

"For a while," I said.

"A billion years is a long while."

I shrugged. "It depends on your perspective, I suppose."

CHAPTER 3

December 1948–January 1949

Christmas followed close on Winter Tide. The Christian holiday first filled Charlie's store with customers, then drew them all back into the seas of their families. Even he closed shop for the day and went to church services—awkwardly, I gathered, given his current beliefs. The Kotos, being Shinto, celebrated neither holiday, though Mama Rei and Neko surprised me after my post-Tide rest with a fish stew, studded with dried cranberries and salted almost to the traditional level for Innsmouth feast days.

To my relief, Charlie's treatment of me didn't change. The days between Christmas and New Year's were quiet, and we spent most of our time studying in the back room. When we returned to the public area, we found that the gift-seeking customers had left it much in need of straightening. The pervasiveness of the foreign holiday had left me jittery: I fell to with a will, and spent happy hours sorting genre from genre and author from author.

Even the most ill-formed words, set to paper, are a great blessing. Still, I was not indiscriminate, and when I found a truly execrable passage in *Flash Gordon and the Monsters of Mongo,* I decided I'd enjoy hearing Charlie's opinion. I drifted forward with one long finger marking my place, stopping occasionally to retrieve a book from the floor or straighten a row of spines. As I neared the counter, I heard Charlie's raised voice:

"I don't need you in here bothering my employee. Take whatever folders and files you've brought this time and get out."

I toyed with the idea of letting Charlie drive him away. But as always, I could not feel safe turning my back.

I stepped out from my haven among the shelves. "It's all right, Mr. Day. I'll speak with him. Hello, Mr. Spector."

He ducked his head. "Miss Marsh." His eye caught on the book, and his lips quirked. I clutched it tighter, then forced my hands to relax. I let my finger slip from the page I'd meant to share.

A year and a half earlier, Ron Spector had walked into Charlie's bookstore and asked for my help. The FBI had heard rumors of a local Aeonist congregation, doubted the group's intentions—and wished to consult someone who wouldn't condemn them merely for the names of their gods. For all his talk of better relations between the state and my people, and for all my acknowledgment that some people might use any faith to justify evil deeds, I refused to work for him. But I could not turn my back on the dangers of the state's renewed interest in me—or resist the lure of meeting others who shared my religion.

It ended badly.

Afterward Spector had sent sporadic notes from Washington, checking on my well-being. Perhaps it was some misguided sense of responsibility. I wrote back briefly, in minimal detail, not daring to ignore his missives entirely. He had not suggested any further tasks. There were, I feared, no other Aeonists in San Francisco, suspicious or otherwise. The rarity of my faith was the precise reason why he had approached me in the first place.

Over the past few months, these letters had dwindled, and I'd thought that he—or his masters—had given up the idea that I might be useful. I hadn't been sure whether to welcome their apathy, or see it as an indication that my fellows were well and truly vanished from the land.

"You have something you wish to ask me. Ask it." I braced myself, praying quietly for anything other than another 'cult.' I didn't think I could bear another room of my fellow worshippers chanting familiar words and phrases that would turn out to be another mask for suicidal delusion. Or worse, for something more malicious than that self-proclaimed high priest's desperate and contagious yearning for immortality.

And yet, if Spector told me of such a group, I didn't think I could stay away.

He shuffled, glanced at Charlie. Charlie glared back.

"He stays," I said. Then added: "He knows."

Spector looked away, his skin reddening. I was not sorry to see his shame. He shook it off quickly enough. He took out a cigarette, tapped it on the counter, but didn't light it. "I suppose you've heard about what's happening with the Russians."

One could hardly miss the papers—and I shared with the Kotos a fervent desire to see coming, early, the storms that might rile people against us. "Yes, the blockade in Berlin. Your allies are fickle."

He shrugged. "They don't see the world as we do. They expect everyone to think alike, act alike—and they'll fight for it, if we let things get that far."

In spite of myself, I shivered. The idea of another war . . . The World War—the first one—had taken so many of Innsmouth's young men into the Army, returned many of them to sit blank-eyed and frightened on their porches—and perhaps triggered the paranoia of those whose libel brought the final raid on our town. The next war had stolen the Kotos from their lives and forced them to rebuild a community almost from scratch.

He continued. "We're working to stop them as best we can. There's the new defense department, and the new agency for collecting foreign intelligence. I'm not involved with that directly"—he patted his suit pocket, as if I might forget the badge secreted there—"but we all work together, when we have to."

"Of course," I sighed.

"And the Russians have what, exactly, to do with Miss Marsh?" demanded Charlie.

"Nothing at all," said Spector. "Except that someone's gotten it into their heads that the Russians might use magic against us. And they've consulted with the FBI's experts on—er—our domestic arts, to learn what they ought to do about it."

I set the book down on the counter. "Mr. Spector, you don't need me to tell you that magic makes a poor weapon. It's not a tool for power, but for knowledge. And a limited tool, at that, unless you appreciate knowledge for its own sake. If your Russians are such scholars, you have little to fear from them."

"We have little to fear from the magical arts that were legal in Innsmouth."

Charlie's glare faltered. He knew the stories about what spells were forbidden, and why.

Spector pulled out a lighter and lit the cigarette. I stepped back discreetly. Charlie normally took his pipe outside in deference to my lungs, but I could hardly expect the same from others. Spector took a drag, and seemed fortified. "In short, they're afraid that the Russians will learn how to force themselves into other people's bodies—and use it not for personal immortality, but to take the place of our best scientists, our most influential politicians. The potential damage is staggering."

"It is," I said faintly. I thought about the bombs that had been dropped on Japan, and the potential for sabotage or theft in the secret places where they were kept. And I thought, too, about subtler things—words that could turn neighbor against neighbor, or government against citizen. "But I'm afraid I don't have anything that can help you. To the best of my knowledge, there are no Deep settlements in the Pacific. If the Russians learned these arts, they didn't learn them from us." And while I could imagine one of our criminals deciding that switching with a Russian would put them sufficiently far from home to avoid capture, we would certainly have noticed if a bitter old man started speaking in a foreign tongue. Not to mention that most human versions of the art required direct contact, and Russian tourists didn't generally visit Innsmouth.

"The Yith?" asked Charlie quietly.

"They don't share their methods," I said. "That's why humanity's versions of the spell are less powerful. But they all stem from imitations of visiting Yith. Russians could have learned that way as easily as anyone else; magic is no harder for men of the air than for us, merely less well known. And no, Mr. Spector, I know of no defense against body theft, nor any reliable way to detect it."

He shook his head. "That's not what I'm asking for—though I wouldn't turn down a defense if you surprised me with one. The analysts believe they didn't re-create the art on their own—but they may have sent someone to study at Miskatonic, some years back."

While I stared, he went on, "I know you don't like working for us directly. But I also know you have your own reasons for wanting to study that school's records. We've persuaded them to accept a research delegation from the federal government. I would hope—that is, we wish to sponsor you to come along as a research assistant and language specialist. You're more fluent in Enochian, and I suspect many of the other relevant languages, than anyone we can provide."

I put a hand on the counter to steady myself. "Answer one question for me. Are you responsible for my brother's inability to access the Miskatonic libraries, these past months?"

"No, of course not." He shook his head vehemently. "Though we were aware of it. You must know that the, ah, activities of everyone released by Public Proclamation number 24 have been—kept abreast of—" Seeing my look, he hurried on. "But we've left him alone." His lip quirked. "It might be better not to ask how we persuaded Miskatonic to offer our chosen scholars access, names unseen."

"It might be better to tell me." I crossed my arms. "Mr. Spector, I do want to see that library, very badly. But I will have no blood on my hands."

He stepped back and held up his palms, a warding gesture echoed in a trail of smoke. "No blood, I promise." He paused. "Miss Marsh, I wish you would give us some benefit of the doubt, however small."

"I am willing to speak with you. To listen. It will take a long time for your masters to earn more."

"The lady asked you a question," Charlie said.

Spector sighed. "If you must know, there's a particular dean with a penchant for carrying on with the maids. Not always entirely to their taste. His most recent girl works for us, and is a bit less easily cowed than the previous ones. He does us favors, sometimes, in exchange for keeping it all from his wife. And from the papers; Miskatonic prides itself on being a respectable school, after all."

It was certainly as distasteful as he'd implied. I could hardly blame the woman for what she'd done—not given some of the favors Anna had won for us, when she was new to the camp and the soldiers grateful to suddenly find pretty, untainted girls under their charge. "Did you order her into that?"

"The girls get a certain amount of discretion in these things. You have to understand, she was already . . ." He trailed off, seeing something in my face, or Charlie's. "She likes it better than her previous job."

Not blood, then, on my hands. I swallowed and thought of the books. Spector was still good at making offers that I couldn't find a way to ignore. And this time, I couldn't refuse his offer and inquire on my own: without the state's support, we'd remain as we were, with my brother hopelessly rattling Miskatonic's gates.

If he needed us, I could at least set terms. "I won't go alone. I'll need my brother. And Mr. Day as well." When Mr. Spector looked doubtful, I added, "His Enochian is coming along nicely," though I suspected that was not where his questions lay.

April 1947: Much as I'd prefer to speak with Spector in my own territory, I meet him at the FBI's local office. This conversation shames me, and I'd rather Charlie didn't hear it.

The office is just outside Japantown, and shows signs of having lost staff in recent years. Spector, on loan from the East Coast, pulls chairs over to one of the empty desks with an apologetic shrug. Behind him, I see dusty file cabinets labeled in tiny, faded print.

"I visited the congregation," I begin.

"I wondered if you might. If you're willing to tell us about it, we could—" He stops himself. "Never mind. You found something you thought was important. Please go on."

I try to guess what he didn't say—was he thinking of offering payment? Should I be angry that he thought of it, or grateful that he thought better?

"They're no threat to anyone else," I start. "I want to make that clear. If you don't believe me there's no point in going on."

"I believe you." He sounds sincere enough. I wish I didn't have to second-guess every word.

"They believe that they're beloved of the gods, and that if one of them walks deep into the Pacific, unafraid and unflinching, Shub-Nigaroth will grant them immortality. Two of them went through the ritual before I got there. The others are convinced that their old friends are 'living in glory under the waves,' but I can assure you these people are entirely mortal—and the gods are not so attentive to human demands as they insist. Mildred Bergman, their priestess, is next. And—soon."

"I'll set something up," he assures me. "We'll keep them safe. And Miss Marsh—I'll do my damnedest to make sure no one treats them like the enemy."

Neko came to me after the washing up, while I was working on a letter to Caleb.

"I want to go with you," she said.

"Neko-chan, what for?" It took a moment for me to realize the source of my startlement: I still thought of her as the thirteen-year-old new come to the camp, and all too much like myself at the same age. But in fact she was nineteen, through with her schooling, more than ready to seek a husband or help support the household. She had been slower about both than Mama Rei would have wished, but that did not make her less an adult.

She twisted her hands together and stared at the floor. "I could go along as a secretary. You'll need someone to take notes, and keep track of what you find."

"I think the FBI already has secretaries." I thought of the woman who'd paid for our entry with her own flesh, and shivered. I owed that woman something, though I doubted she would accept it even if I could figure out what it was.

"Your G-man would bring me along if you asked."

"G-man?"

She shrugged it away. "Like in the movies. Please, Kappa-sama."

I chose my words carefully, trying to explain something that had barely needed saying in Innsmouth. "Miskatonic University is not a nice place. The professors—they are old men, proud of their power, frightened of anyone who might threaten it. They care nothing for responsibilities or obligations outside the school. They are not evil, but nor are they good to be around unless one has a truly important reason."

Her eyes slid toward the kitchen, where Mama Rei still remained sweeping. "You go out in the rain, without an umbrella or a coat. And you come home wet and happy."

I smiled in spite of myself. "The water is good for me."

"But it's not just that." She glanced at me, suddenly shy in a way that reminded me more reasonably of her younger self. "It's a thing you couldn't do, and now you can. Mama doesn't understand, but—please forgive me, but when you were my age, you were still there, but I'm here and I don't want to waste my freedom just taking dictation from old men—and there are plenty in San Francisco, too!"

"Old men who love power are everywhere, I'm afraid," I admitted.

"I know. But I think that travel could be the rain, for me. And Mama will never let me try it, not if we had to pay, even if we could afford it.

But if I'm going along with you, if you asked, she wouldn't argue. And then I would know. If it's what I should be doing."

Few enough of us get to do what we should be doing—assuming that such a thing even exists. I would not be the one to forbid her the rain.

We live in a world full of wonders and terrors, and so I cannot entirely fathom why my first aeroplane flight struck me so. Or perhaps I can: it was the first time I had left San Francisco since following the Kotos there. I felt vulnerable amid the cloying smoke and the crowd of well-to-do strangers at the airport. The women especially, with their makeup and store-bought dresses, watched us with unsympathetic eyes.

I dared not forget how we looked: a herd of odd and lame animals passing cautiously among predatory apes. Neko pressed close to me, and Charlie and Spector walked ahead to either side. I was grateful for their protection. Spector had a better gait for it, and a sturdier gaze. Still, I caught snickering whispers from a few who had picked out some Jewish aspect of his features, and I was grateful when at last we settled into our seats, away from the eyes and opinions of the susurrating crowd.

And then to go from that to the great machine gathering speed, leaping into the air and slipping through the clouds and into unexpected sun. Normally I prefer rain and fog, but somehow I felt safe, knowing that those things still caressed the city below—and behind, as we traveled swiftly onward. It was a perspective akin to meditating on the space between the stars, or the rise and fall of species over aeons. I saw more truly than ever that even a single day, on a single world, can contain both atrocity and kindness, storm-tossed seas and burning deserts. On such a world, lives may never touch and yet still give solace by the reminder that one's own troubles are not universal.

I yearned to share my thoughts with Charlie, but he sat farthest from me, across the aisle. I considered trying to explain it to Neko, but even that would attract Spector's attention. So I stared out the window as we soared over snow-brushed cyclopean mountain ranges, lifeless desert, and endless stretches of cleanly pressed farmland shadowed by dusk, before I fell asleep dreaming of the unfathomable lives of strangers.

The landing in Chicago was rough. The little plane shuddered down through a wild wind, bumping at last onto the tarmac while I considered whether it was worth drawing a diagram on the seat-back in front of me to try and calm the gale. Once we landed, I could see the softly pattering rain around us, barely blowing at an angle, and realized that the apparent storm had been an illusion of our speed, or of the plane's own fragility.

As we milled in the terminal, waiting for our connection, I found myself oddly at ease: the predators all looked as tired as we were, and paid us little attention. I slumped on a chair, glanced over, and found Spector settled next to me. The skin below his eyes darkened with fatigue, but the eyes themselves flicked constantly. I realized that he, too, noticed every person who came within a few feet.

Of course, he caught me watching him as well, and smiled ruefully. "My apologies, Miss Marsh. Whenever I'm up late, my instincts start telling me I'm on watch. It doesn't seem to do any harm, and it keeps me awake."

"Ah." Of course, he'd fought in the war. Most men had.

"European theater," he added, giving me a considering look.

I nodded, quietly relieved that he'd never been in a position to kill any of the Kotos' relatives. Or more likely, given his specialties, provide intelligence to those who did.

He leaned back and rubbed his eyes. "Miss Marsh—when we get there . . ." He hesitated.

I waited for him to go on. "Yes?"

"Just bear in mind that this kind of mission can accomplish more than one thing."

Fatigued, I could just resist giving him an extremely impolitic look. "Mr. Spector, I can be discreet. But my talent is not in working ciphers."

His eyes returned to their watchful rounds, then focused on me once more. "It can wait, I think."

He looked uncomfortable enough that I was tempted to let it go. But I found myself equally uncomfortable allowing him to decide what I'd think urgent. "I'm not fond of answerless riddles, either. I don't want to walk into Miskatonic with my eyes closed, if there's any alternative." I added, lowering my voice, "I have good ears. Speak as softly as you like, but please tell me what I need to know."

He hesitated another moment, and I was afraid I wouldn't be able to push him further. But at last he relaxed and tensed at once, in the way of someone who's made an unpleasant decision. "You know I was out of touch for a few months, before I contacted you."

I nodded. "I assumed you realized there wasn't much more I could do for your masters. They didn't want you speaking with me?"

"We usually refer to them as Bureau leadership, but no, they didn't. It wasn't anything to do with you, though. I don't know how much attention you pay to the news, but when Israel declared independence last May, our higher-ups started worrying about the Jews in service. I got a whole interrogation about whether I was planning to leave the country, whether I considered myself an Israeli citizen. A couple people quit over that, and one did emigrate. Said he might as well fight for someone who appreciated him . . . anyway, they took me off anything active for a while. Not officially, but they obviously wanted to keep an eye on me."

"Oh." I vaguely remembered reading about the new country, but I hadn't made the connection somehow. His own people, half slaughtered in the war, had gone without a home for a significant chunk of the recent millennia. "So now they've decided to trust you again?" I almost asked why, but realized that it would be both rude and unnecessary.

He shrugged, gave a rueful smile. "They're giving me a chance, let's say. Because I'm the one with a reputation for talking to the people they need."

I frowned. "So you . . . need us to find *something*. For your career."

He shook his head. "They aren't stupid enough to encourage false alarms like that—and frankly, I'd rather go back to New York and work in my father's deli than betray them that way. I've seen enough of the files to think there's a real chance that something's going on, but even if this turns out to be a false lead I don't think they'll hold it against me. Whatever we find, the work needs to look good—and it needs to *be* good. I need to show that what I do still matters, even when the threats they care about change."

I considered, pushing through fatigue to see what he was driving at. "What you do—is talk to me. To us. To Aeonists and people of the water. You need to prove that *we're* still useful." And therefore, from the state's perspective, that we still had a right to exist. I wrapped my arms against a chill that had little to do with the winter draft creeping through the plate windows.

He nodded. "I'm sorry, but yes. There are people higher up in the Bureau who've argued that Aeonists, as threat or resource, are no longer relevant. Like Nazis"—he didn't quite keep the bitter irony from his voice—"a sociopolitical relic of the first half of the century, when we need to worry about the threats of the fifties."

"Until 1928," I said, "we thought we could survive by being ignored. We were wrong."

"I don't intend for you to be ignored," he said firmly. "And I don't believe that whole peoples and religions become irrelevant. It still matters that we can work together, and I plan to prove it." He ducked his head, suddenly diffident. "And yes, I know it isn't right for that to be necessary. For what it's worth, I'm sorry."

On the next flight, I slept particularly badly.

CHAPTER 4

Even as my mind hadn't quite compassed Neko's growth from nervous adolescent into restless young woman, so had my image of Caleb regressed, in his absence, to a child eager for adventure in the bogs, anxious lest I should receive the larger share of honeyed saltcake after dinner.

What met me at Logan Airport, after a long night of fitful sleep and exhausted transfers, was instead a gangling man in a suit that hung loosely over his long legs and arms. Like me, he still dressed in mourning grays. We embraced, then he held me at arms' length.

"Aphra, you look wonderful. It's good to see you."

"And you." He did not look entirely well. His hair remained ragged at the ends. I was minded that he'd been eating boardinghouse food of doubtful quality and stingy quantity, while Mama Rei tried her best to make up all our lost meals at once. (Except for the hot dogs, our mother would have entirely approved her table.) And where I had spent these past months in a set routine, with work for both mind and body, he had been shifting through Morecambe County, seeking in vain some way to influence Arkham's academic elite.

His appearance could not have helped his quest. He shared with me the bulging eyes, the flat nose, the broad chin, and long fingers that marked our origin. We both fell on the paler end of our people's range— unhealthily pallid to outsiders' eyes. What he could not hide, he had made a shield of; when well-dressed passengers came too close, he loomed taller and thinner and they shied away from his gaze. I had always sought my mother's dignity when I needed to appear sure or powerful. I wondered how much he remembered of our childhood, and of our parents' strength.

I introduced him to Charlie and Spector. He shook hands with Neko, shyly. Then she laughed, tugged at his sleeve, and informed him that if he needed a suit he should have sent her his measurements. They bickered comfortably as we sought out the car and driver provided by Spector's masters, more easy with each other than I yet felt with him.

It was over an hour's drive to Miskatonic, and we passed it in fits of conversation that fell swiftly into silences. I could think of few topics that would not exclude either Charlie, Neko, or Caleb. All three were precious to me, but I knew them in different spheres. Nor did I wish to tell them of my worries where Spector might intrude with unwanted intimacy.

It was a small problem, and distracted me from what we were soon to encounter.

The Massachusetts winter was wet and cold, a shock of familiarity as we stepped out onto the great arching drive in front of the house of the mathematics dean. Snow deliquesced into slush beneath our feet, with a peculiar splash that I had not heard since I was twelve. Neko drew her jacket closer and shivered. I thought of cracked ice in the bog, and snowball fights. My eyes darted to Caleb, but I saw no humor in his stance, and decided against recalling our old pastimes in any active fashion. Besides, there was Spector.

A young negro woman met us at the door, took coats, showed us to a sitting room, offered tea. A clip pulled her hair tight at the nape of her neck, where it puffed out beneath her hat. Fire crackled in the hearth, exuding the smell of birch sap. I sat up straighter, and folded my hands in my lap. Caleb prowled the edges of the room, shuffling his hands from pocket to chest to the small of his back. The maid nodded at Spector and gave a half-smile, nothing like her otherwise deferential demeanor, before withdrawing.

A tentative throat-clearing in the doorway marked Dean Skinner's belated entrance. Spector rose smoothly to meet him. Skinner hesitated before darting in to shake his hand.

"Well—welcome—that is, I didn't entirely realize you were bringing such a—crowd." He surveyed us with an air of grave doubt. "Are these your—scholars?"

"They are." Spector took on the confident, knowing air with which he had first attempted to persuade me to his cause. "These are our linguistic specialists, Miss Aphra Marsh and Mr. Caleb Marsh, and Miss Marsh's student, Mr. Charles Day. And Miss Nancy Koto, our note-taker."

"Ah. Yes. Marsh, you say." He adjusted his glasses and peered at Caleb more closely. "Well, that does take one back. Not a name one hears much, these days. You are originally from Innsmouth, then?"

The question was directed to Caleb, but he only frowned in response. I drew myself up in my chair. "I am still *from* Innsmouth. However, I currently make my home in San Francisco."

"Ah—yes—well. I'm sure some of the anthropology students will wish to inquire of you regarding Innsmouth's famous—or infamous—folklore. It is still a topic of interest among those, ah, interested in eso-terica." He waved the matter aside before I could respond, and turned back to Spector. "I suppose you must know what you're doing, hiring people with such a—distinct—background. But where on earth are we to put them all? You know that we're always happy to support federal research, though of course we'd do better with more details about what you're looking for. But you made no mention of, ah, students of the female persuasion. It certainly wouldn't be proper to—that is—or—perhaps we could board them at the Hall School?"

"It's almost an hour away," said Caleb quietly. His hands were clenched at his side.

"Yes," I said. "We're here for the library, not the roads."

Miskatonic's ostensible sister school was not a well-kept partner like Radcliffe or Pembroke. My mother, never one to gossip, had spoken witheringly of the Miskatonic professors' beliefs about female intellect. They held Hall at a well-chaperoned distance on the far side of Kingsport, and it lived off the dregs of the more famous school's materials and collections.

Dean Skinner glanced between us, blinking rapidly. "Well. Then I suppose we must—hmm."

I considered suggesting that he and his wife might host us without impropriety. But it would have been cruel, and perilously close to a threat. When he was not so off-balance, the dean must be a formidable predator. And he would not be pleased at having been seen so vulnerable.

At last, his face lit. "Ah. Just the thing. Professor Trumbull has room in her house, I'm sure. She's Miskatonic's first lady professor, you know. Multidimensional geometry. Stunningly brilliant of course—although she—well—they do say that study interferes with the development of feminine faculties—and she is certainly—" He glanced at me and trailed off. "I'm sure you'll get along splendidly. Yes, just the thing."

"That sounds promising," said Spector. A touch of exasperation crept into his voice. "Now, perhaps we might begin our explorations of the library?"

"Let's get you settled in, first," said Skinner, and this time I caught a glimpse of the predator behind the civilized words.

Spector caught it too, and raised an eyebrow. "Briefly," he conceded. "We're eager to get to work."

After wandering the slushy maze of the grounds, I suspected that Skinner had sent us to Trumbull, in part, due to her inaccessibility. Eventually, however, we rounded a corner and came to the Mathematics Building. It was one of the smaller buildings on campus, but rather than being dwarfed by its neighbors it suggested a sanctum for the elite.

Columns rose to either side of carven mahogany doors. All were covered in complex, abstract designs—not symmetrical, but constrained by some formula or ratio that made them by turns either pleasing or disturbing to the eye. Gargoyles on the cornice pieces draped stone tentacles around the rainspouts. I saw no recognizable gods. Still, they reminded me of the statues in Innsmouth's central temple, or the cemetery that memorialized those lost in the cradle or at war.

The short lifespans engraved on the churchyard stones—and the paucity of those stones—loomed often in the rumors against us. I shivered as we walked between the doorposts.

Trumbull's office door stood ajar, and through it drifted a woman's voice, low, even, and calm, and a man's tenor rising and falling in distress. I caught mention of ten-dimensional equations and void matrices—the jargon by which Miskatonic's academics girded themselves against entropy. A moment later, the young man in question stormed out. His hair was shaved close, and he walked with a military stamp made irregular by a missing arm.

"G.I. Bill," commented Spector approvingly. I gazed after the soldier, wondering which front he'd fought on and what he would have thought of Neko, had he noticed her. Then I wondered what he'd seen, to make the university's coldest mathematical studies seem appealing.

Trumbull did not look up as we entered, already engrossed in a clothbound textbook. She was thin and without curves in either body or face, and she wore her hair clipped back severely. Her dark gray dress was well-tailored but extremely plain. She appeared no older than me—she might even be younger, if she'd moved quickly through her schooling.

Skinner ahemmed. "Miss Trumbull."

She looked up, and her eyes were *not* young. Miskatonic's studies are said to leave scars—but I was unaccountably reminded of my paternal grandmother, who had gone into the water before I was born. Here, though, was neither recognition nor fondness.

Skinner did not quite flinch under her gaze, but he did correct his address: "Professor Trumbull. We have a party of visiting scholars from the government. The gentlemen can stay in the visitors' quarters in the dorms, of course, but we need some place to put the girls. You should be able to fit a couple more into your household easily enough." He smirked.

Trumbull swept him with cold eyes, then deliberately turned back to a passage in her book. "Dr. Skinner, if you wish to hire a hostess, then by all means hire a hostess. It is not one of my native talents, nor is it one I care to develop."

"Miss—Professor Trumbull. Hosting visitors is one of the burdens we must all take on from time to time. We can hardly send Miss Marsh and Miss Koto to the Hall School if they are to concentrate on their work at the library."

She marked her place in the book, and this time I was the one who winced under her focused attention. With effort, I avoided checking the tidiness of my skirts. After a moment her gaze turned to Caleb, then flicked back to me.

"Innsmouth?"

I sighed inwardly—I could expect to repeat this conversation many times during our stay, but had hoped to avoid it with the younger professors. "Yes."

"Was it not . . . 1928, yes? I have not misremembered."

"Yes," I said stiffly. "The town was destroyed in 1928. I'm here to find artifacts that might have survived."

"Ah." She seemed struck by this. "Yes. You and your colleague may stay in my house. As Dean Skinner has implied, however, you should not expect much from it. The college sends someone to clean once a week; I do not employ servants, nor guarantee regular meals."

"That's fine," said Skinner, tension leaving his shoulders. "They can eat at the faculty spa. That's settled, then; I'll leave you to it."

Trumbull raised her eyebrows after his passage. "He's not pleased by your presence. I hope he doesn't expect me to show you gentlemen around the dorms."

Spector shrugged. "Now that we're here, I imagine we can find our way."

"We'd really rather get started in the library," added Caleb.

She snorted. "You wouldn't be the only scholars sleeping there." She set aside her book. "I don't suppose any of you are experts in the most recent theories of algebraic topology? Or have access to obscure texts on the subject?"

We all shook our heads. Charlie said, "I have a nice edition of the *Book of Eibon* with R'lyehn and Latin opposing pages. But I imagine Miskatonic has one as well."

"Nine. They assign it in graduate level anthropology classes. In any case, you might as well come and see what else they have. I would certainly be intrigued to learn what survives of fabled Innsmouth. One never does know what one will find in the collections."

"I see their temples are still standing," murmured Caleb.

The Crowther Library was a temple indeed—and not Innsmouth's, where flickering lamplight glinted off statues and icons, making them seem at once intimate and unknowable. This was more like the Christian cathedrals I'd heard of, where the priests face away from the congregation, murmuring in tongues unknown to their listeners.

On entering, we found ourselves in the grand foyer. Light filtered through stained glass windows depicting obscure allegorical figures. A young man fainted against a pile of books, with abstract shapes floating above him. A woman knelt by a pool of water, dangling a pendant from a chain above the moon's reflection. Beneath the windows ran, in Latin: *The world offers its secrets to the willing mind.*

No bookshelves marred the expanse of stone and marble. Around the walls, arched doorways opened into shadow, promising the world's secrets to whoever could negotiate the mazes and barriers placed in their way.

Trumbull frowned at the windows, and led us through the far archway and into the central reading room. This chamber was somewhat more welcoming in furnishing if not scale, and both the central desk and the tables with their padded chairs were peopled by students and staff. Relatively few, since classes hadn't yet started for the spring semester, but enough to mitigate the forbidding impression of the entrance. Caleb drifted closer, and I put my hand on his arm.

"Should we . . . ?" I started to ask. But Trumbull was already striding toward the desk, and the rest of us perforce followed. Once again I was aware of our motley appearance, as students peered above their texts and ashtrays to track the strangers passing through their midst.

I tried to imagine the books we sought, somewhere in this very building, that might lie beneath our hands if only we could ask the right questions. They seemed as vast and wondrous as the Yith's own archives—and I feared that they might be near as inaccessible.

The reference librarian, a middle-aged man with thinning hair, took a deep breath and squared his shoulders. Trumbull started in before he could speak: "We're looking for a collection of rare books, esoterica, accessioned about 1928 or '29. Probably including duplicates of some of the common texts as well as more obscure volumes."

And annotated throughout in the hands of my family, my neighbors, our ancestors. Some might still contain childhood essays or exercises secreted between pages. But Trumbull did not seem inclined toward such personal details, and the librarian's face was already clouded with irritation.

"You'll need the rare books section, and special permission from the collection manager. Second door on the right as you come in the foyer, go through the 100 and 200 stacks until you get to the Second Supplementary Annex."

As soon as we were back in the foyer, Caleb swore. "Special permission? Those are our books!"

Neko put a hand on his shoulder. "Keep your voice down, they'll hear."

"The void I will. They stole them, and now they want to keep them from us."

"Perhaps we will try showing our credentials to the collection manager, and being polite." Spector looked at me wryly. "I hear that works sometimes."

"Your presence here is an abomination," Caleb told him.

I winced, but Spector merely ducked his head. "I hope it's a helpful one. I'm not sure anyone is in a position to apologize for the Innsmouth raid, but I can at least make some small reparation."

"Because we're useful to you. Would you still make 'reparations' if we refused to track down your Russian?"

"Caleb, please," I said, but he shook me off and strode forward into the stacks. Charlie looked uncomfortable. Trumbull pursed her lips as if studying a mildly interesting equation. I caught up with my brother. "Like the government or hate them, a Russian who could switch bodies could do terrible things. Drop all the atomic bombs anyone's built on all the cities they can reach. Start another war. That wouldn't be good for anyone."

He shrugged. "As far as I'm concerned, the land can burn. We've made as much use of it as we can. Let the ck'chk'ck have their turn."

I drew back. "Let's go find out what they've done with our books."

It wasn't as if I'd never thought such things, in dry moments. But perhaps Caleb had more than one reason to live apart from the Kotos.

The Special Collections librarian was not sympathetic.

"Certainly we have the Innsmouth collection," he said. "Students must show scholarly necessity. Non-students—there have been incidents. Those are dangerous books."

Already I retreated into a stiff-held spine and a face that would show only the most necessary anger. "I started reading them when I was six years old."

"Indeed?" He shuffled back a half-step.

Caleb leaned across the desk. "Those books belong to us—to our family. Whether or not *you* can handle them—" I touched his wrist and he subsided. The librarian looked on, implacable, from his chosen safe distance.

Spector stepped forward and flashed his badge. "Sir, if you won't listen to these fine folk, then perhaps it will change your mind to know that we need the books for national security purposes."

"Sir, this is a privately held library. If you want to see collections that we judge dangerous, you'll need specific scholarly justification for specific volumes, like everyone else—or a warrant."

I closed my eyes, attempting to gain some measure of calm, opened them again. "What, precisely, constitutes scholarly justification?"

"A note from the instructor of a class you are taking, or your thesis advisor." His lips compressed. "As I said, we've had incidents with non-students. And with students, when our rules were more lax."

Trumbull glided forward from her post by the door. "I am an associate professor in the Mathematics Department. I wish to explore the collection."

He braced himself—without awareness or intention, I suspected. "Are they—are some of the volumes—relevant to a class you're teaching?"

"I am planning my syllabus. I wish to see all of them. These people will assist me." She put her elbows down on the desk, bringing herself closer to him. I would not have expected her to be the sort to take advantage of manly weaknesses, especially given her insistence on dignity in front of the dean. Or to be willing to play such a card for our sakes—and now it occurred to me that she, too, might have some use in mind for us. Anger rose within me, overpowering as hunger, so that for a moment I could not focus on what was happening.

The librarian blinked rapidly, and licked his lips. "I can't—that is—" Trumbull straightened, and he recovered somewhat. "We have a policy. I must have the names of specific volumes." He held out a sheet of paper, and pushed pen and ink across the desk. Trumbull stepped aside and flicked a finger at me. Dumbly, I took her place, and began writing such titles as I could recall. Caleb, and occasionally Charlie, murmured additional suggestions.

My hand shook, spattering ink. I trembled with the knowledge that I must inevitably forget titles, leave out obscure pamphlets that had failed to attract my childish interest in the houses of distant cousins.

"All the copies of each that you have, if you please," I said, amazed that I could get the words out.

The librarian blanched. "If you insist on multiple copies, this is a substantial portion of the collection!"

I flinched, but Trumbull looked at him calmly and he turned away. "Perhaps if I brought out five at a time? They will be easier to track."

"That will do," she said, sounding indifferent once more.

We waited while he gathered assistants and retreated into the library's further caverns. Once he was gone, I sank into a chair and buried my face in my hands. I did not cry, only tried to find my way through the maze of fear and longing that the conversation had raised around clear thought. Behind me I heard Caleb pacing, heard the swish of skirts and muffled click of patent soles as Trumbull and Spector stepped out of his way each in their turn. Air displaced on either side of me, whiffs of dusty paper and peony, and twin chairs scraped against the wooden floor. I let the world back in, cautiously, as Charlie grunted into a seat on one side of me and Neko took the other. Neither spoke, but in their presence the maze faded. I sat in an ordinary mortal building, recently built and soon to crumble, and I could face whatever awaited me here.

Caleb still paced, and I saw that his hands were shaking. At last, he pulled a pack of cigarettes from his pocket, lit one with a match.

"Caleb!" In Innsmouth, men had enjoyed their tobacco as they did elsewhere—though at some point during our incarceration, the outside world had judged it proper to smoke in mixed company. But the desert had left its mark on our lungs, and I could hardly imagine that Caleb found the stuff any more comfortable than I did.

He took the cigarette from his mouth, let it dangle. "What of it? Why should they take *this* from me, too?"

So it was another defiance, and one I could not entirely begrudge him. "Not near the books, though. We've nowhere to get replacements if you let loose a stray spark."

It was a full half hour before the librarian returned pushing a pine-wood cart—the metal wheels shrieked protest—bearing five leather-bound volumes. I half rose, then forced myself back down. As if in the grip of ritual, tiny movements and expressions filled my attention. Caleb put out his cigarette—his seventh as I'd counted them—and came at last to rest in the seat opposite mine across the long reading table at which I sat. Spector and Trumbull almost sat on either side of him, but then Spector hesitated and moved to Trumbull's other side instead. Derision crossed her face, quickly masked. Neko flashed Caleb a smile, but he only grimaced in return.

The books were unloaded one by one: three copies of the *Book of Eibon,* one children's text—never one of my favorites, more focused on moral platitudes than true history or ritual—and a *Necronomicon.* This the librarian placed on the table with some hesitation, and I recalled that it had a particularly infamous reputation at Miskatonic.

Trumbull immediately snatched up a *Book of Eibon.* Caleb and I drew startled breaths, but did not argue, only craned our necks to see.

To her credit, Trumbull treated the volume with respect once she had claimed it. She opened the front cover, and ran a delicate finger down the inscriptions within. Even upside down, I could pick out names: Horace Eliot, Felix Eliot, Eliza Gilman Eliot. Neighbors, but all I could remember of them was Mrs. Eliot's cross-stitched bonnet, dangling from her hand as she tested the morning wind, and a bowl of salt taffy that they kept on the parlor table.

I mourned, but did not look away.

CHAPTER 5

We left the library late, and with a promise that my list of books would remain available on the morrow. At Spector's plaintive query, Trumbull led us to the faculty spa, which even in the intersession served food well after the ordinary dinner hour. Tall men hunched in corners, gesturing with pipes and murmuring in low tones over wine and steak.

The books all bore marks from the families that had owned them. Even in the moral primer, a young Waite had drawn tentacles and mustaches on illustrations previously lacking either, signing "OW" proudly in the corners. Obadiah Waite had died of heatstroke our first summer in the camp, at the age of six.

As of yet, we'd found no Marsh records. I was ashamed at my gratitude for the delay.

I'd forgotten hunger easily in the mausoleum of the library, but now discovered myself ravenous. As warm clam chowder recalled me to the living world, I considered Trumbull. My subconscious had marked her as a predator from the first—she had a strength and viciousness almost certainly necessary to survive Miskatonic's academic and political grottos. She ate as deliberately as she did everything else, but gave no sign of noticing the quality of either the food or the company. The others stole glances at her as well. She looked at none of us, but when I turned away I felt her attention like the barrel of a gun.

Spector's motivations, the danger he presented, I was learning to understand. I did not know what drove Trumbull, and her interest in my people frightened me.

As I considered that fear, a draft of cool air hit us. I looked up to see Dean Skinner stamping snow from his boots as he took off his hat. He saw us and smiled, an unpleasant expression considerably more confident than any he'd shown earlier.

He moved through the room, stopping at several tables to converse quietly. Laughter drifted from shared jokes, and a couple of people glanced in our direction as they spoke with him.

At last he came over and clapped Spector on the back. "Mr. Spector. I trust you're settling in well. Does it look like you'll be able to find what you wanted?"

Spector stiffened, then returned an answering smile that seemed a deliberately transparent mask. "Too soon to tell, I'm afraid. But thank you for asking."

"You're my guests on campus. Miss Marsh, Miss Koto, I trust Professor Trumbull is seeing to your needs. It's good to have more ladies here, from time to time—brightens the place up." I worried that he might try to touch one of us as well, but Trumbull gave him one of her dry looks, and he stepped back. "Excuse me, it looks like they have my drink ready. I'll catch up with you later, I'm sure."

I didn't get a chance to talk with Caleb before we dropped the men at Upton Dormitory, where the door guard confirmed that guest rooms had indeed been reserved. Neko and I continued on with Trumbull, and Neko walked closer to me than the frigid night warranted. My breath escaped in bursts of warm fog. Though I knew it was foolishness, I mouthed a prayer to Yog-Sothoth, keeper of gates, for safe passage through this season.

Trumbull had been honest about the state of her house. It was neat enough, and well-dusted, but still gave an impression of staleness and disuse. She directed us to sheets and guest beds, and left us on our own to combine them. We did so without complaint.

Sometime after the lights were out, I felt Neko's weight settle on my mattress.

"Are you awake, Aphra?"

"Entirely. How do you like travel?"

"It's exciting, but cold. And I wish you had books in English. Or Japanese."

I laughed in spite of myself. "You'd have needed to meet us much earlier, for Innsmouth to have books in Japanese."

"Would it have made a difference, do you think?"

I shook my head. I could see easily in the cloud-dimmed moonlight, but suspected she could not. I put my arm around her. "Two despised peoples, together? We'd have ended up in the camps a decade earlier."

She shrugged. "It still upsets people now, and I don't think staying apart would help. Being out here on his own hasn't helped Caleb."

"No, it hasn't."

We curled together in the narrow bed, sisters sharing warmth. I breathed the remains of her floral perfume, the mammalian sweat beneath it, and eventually fell asleep.

Recently, Charlie and I had been practicing wakeful dreaming. He looked forward to the more advanced skills of walking between dreams and gleaning knowledge within the dream world—for me it was sufficient that when I woke in endless desert, throat too dry and hot to breathe, I knew it for illusion. I forced back the panic, the desperation for air and moisture, and imagined breath until it came to me, harsh and painful. I did not yet have the strength to change the desert to ocean, or even to the comfort of snow or fog.

I do not need to dream. There is a real body, a real bed—and by repeating this mantra I awoke at last, gasping.

Neko still slept beside me. I slipped out from the corner of the bed where my struggles had carried me and went in search of water.

Eye-stinging electric light burned in the dining room. I halted on my way to the kitchen as I saw Trumbull bent over a spread of books and papers. She cocked her head.

"Bad dreams." She stated it as a fact, and not a particularly interesting one.

"Yes," I admitted. "Sorry to disturb you; I was only going for a drink of water."

"The salt is beside the sink."

I had my first blessed sip of water, and poured a little salt in it to wet my face. Only then did it occur to me how much she must already know, to offer me salt water as casual comfort. I considered what I had seen of her so far, and considered also the courage it must have taken Charlie to hazard his guesses about me.

If she were something worse than I suspected, it would be best to know quickly.

I stepped back into the dining room and asked in Enochian, "How far have you journeyed?"

"Space beyond measure, aeons beyond understanding," she replied in the same language. She turned around. "You've been slow, water child. Memory should be a guide, not a distraction."

I knelt, placing my glass on the floor beside me. "I'm sorry, Great One. I had not expected to find you here."

"One of us is frequently in residence at Miskatonic," said the Yith. "Too many of this era's records pass through their gates to neglect the place. And they offer resources for travel and study that are otherwise inconvenient to seek out."

She turned back to her papers. Waiting for a member of the Great Race to ask me to rise might be a good way to spend the night on the floor; doubtless she had already forgotten it was not my natural posture. I took a seat at the table.

She ignored me for a few minutes, then looked up. "Do you plan to ask me for an oracle? Hints of your future?"

Probably I should. "Do you enjoy doing that?"

"No. It's tedious."

I considered what I might learn from her, given the opportunity. But it was late, and when I cast about I found only the past that I should *not* ask about, and trivial concerns. "When the original Trumbull gets her body back, will she be startled to find that she has a professorship at Miskatonic?"

"Don't be foolish." She ran a finger down her sleeve, as if suddenly noticing the body she wore. "Our hosts must possess great mental capacity, or the exchange would be much less fruitful."

"It takes more than intelligence for a woman to gain such a position."

"This is true." She smiled at her hand, almost fondly. "I find that hosts with a degree of tenacity and"—she paused, considering—"resilience, yes, resilience, make for a more comfortable exchange. Such minds are less likely to waste their time in the Archives on distressed mewling. Also, they are less likely to flood one's home body with stress chemicals. I don't like to find my limbs twitching at every statue."

"That makes sense."

She looked at me pityingly. "Of course it does."

I cursed myself for tediousness. "Excuse me. I'd best get back to bed."

"Certainly. You are young, after all."

"Isn't everyone, by your standards?"

She frowned at a manuscript and moved it to a different pile. "Your subspecies lives to a reasonable age. Long enough to learn their arts with some proficiency."

I made it almost to the hall before I gave in to the question. Turning back, I demanded: "Did you know what would happen to my people?"

"The generalities, certainly. If there are specifics you wish recorded in the archives, you might write them up for me."

"That's not what I meant. Would some warning of the raid have been too *tedious* an oracle for you to give?" I winced even as I said it. My parents would have been appalled to hear me take such a tone with such an entity.

When she turned around, she did not appear appalled or even startled.

"I met the last sane K'n-yan, after her people became the Mad Ones Under the Earth. She demanded the same thing of me. Her name was Beneer."

It was neither explanation nor excuse, yet the anger drained out of me, to be replaced by all-too-familiar mourning. At this time of night I would gladly have traded it back.

"Iä, the Great Race," I said tiredly. "Please don't use my name as an object lesson for the last ck'chk'ck. It will not please her." And I returned to the guest bed, as I ought to have earlier. When I dreamt of lying parched on a bed amid empty desert, I did not bother to wake myself.

CHAPTER 6

Trumbull had a morning faculty meeting in preparation for the coming semester—her teaching style, I suspected, would be frightening to behold—but the rest of us were due to gather in the library after breakfast. As much as I'd wanted to be here, I couldn't yet face returning to that darkened building and reading our own books under the librarian's judgmental eye. Instead, seeking strength in the manner that had become my habit since leaving the camp, I went for a walk. Neko, after a long look at the snow, offered to meet the others and give them my regrets and my promise of a later reunion.

As Neko had said earlier, I walked because I could. The air smelled clean and crisp. It would have been too dry save that gusts periodically tossed snow aloft from the branches and drifts. I plucked an icicle from Trumbull's fencepost and sucked on it as I walked.

Arkham was not much larger than Innsmouth save for the college buildings, but it was more urbane and attracted more visitors. The streets seemed full of strangers, not only to me but to each other. As I put space between myself and the campus, I witnessed few casual encounters. People shuffled briskly, chins buried in thick coats.

In San Francisco, I had neighbors who knew my name and did not despise me, friends and adoptive family who knew and loved me. But I had no one who understood what I was, where I came from. The gambrel roofs and sagging Victorians of Arkham, the streets hemmed in by snow, invoked memories of Innsmouth, where we required no effort to understand each other's ways.

I wandered for some while. I knew my self-pity for indulgence, and yet the walking was itself a comfort. The rhythm of my steps, the feel of breath and muscle, drew me slowly from my ruminations to a more meditative state. My awareness spread, or narrowed, so that I now saw the houses beside me, the people hurrying on purposeful errands, the snowbanks and trees and parks, and not the imagined houses and people and snow and trees of Innsmouth.

I became aware of the rumble and hiss of flowing water. Following the welcome sound brought me to the Garrison Street Bridge over the Miskatonic River. Here, clapboard houses lined the precipitous bank. Porches jutted over the water, leaning downstream. Just past the bridge, the river widened and slowed, and a small island marked where the calmer flow had dropped detritus over the years. It was a spot of pure white land and charcoal-sketch trees amid the kaleidoscope of bobbing ice.

The river smelled less welcoming than it sounded. Acids and lye from the upstream textile mills assaulted me, and some inner instinct warned me that they would burn gills and clog lungs. My neck muscles clenched in as-yet-useless protective reflex.

At the cusp of the bridge, one old house had installed a waterwheel. It no longer turned, but it had been brightly painted in blue and orange, like the wheel of the steamboat in my childhood copy of *Huckleberry Finn*. (Which I had forgotten to put on the list.) A wide porch, sturdier than most, wrapped around the building, laid out with tables and chairs. These now stood empty and slick with icemelt, but the entrance marked the place as The Book Mill, and Open.

A bell sounded as I entered: chimes, deeper and more somber than the usual jangle. I inhaled the familiar scent of old paper and leather and the vanilla-edged whiff of pipe smoke. The bones of whatever had been here before were brighter and more spacious than Charlie's store. It still felt like home. I realized that what most distressed me about

Miskatonic's library, what had kept me away all morning despite my love for the collection entombed there, was the absence of that expected comfort.

Voices rose on the far side of the shelves. I followed them to an alcove jutting over the river, where a portion of the store had been given over to a small café. Clusters of sleek young people sat amid coffee cups and half-eaten pastries and cigarette stubs and open books. They leaned close or tilted their chairs, avid in their discussions.

One of the boys saw me and grinned. "Hi! What's this?"

I froze, and put a hand on the nearest shelf to steady myself.

"She's not from Hall," said one girl. Turning to another, she added, "That's a face you wouldn't forget."

"You work in one of the factories?" asked the boy.

I let go the shelf. "I'm Aphra Marsh. I'm visiting Miskatonic for research in the library."

"Woo! They let you in?" The second girl hooked a free chair from a nearby table and patted it. She waved her hand expansively, trailing acrid smoke. "I'm Audrey Winslow. I took the special Introductory Folklore course last summer, but they wouldn't let me near anything interesting. What're you studying?"

I took the chair with some trepidation. "Mathematics. And folklore as well, perhaps."

"Ah," said the boy. "You mean magic." He shot a look at Audrey, who rolled her eyes.

"If you want to call it that," she said while I was still deciding how to respond.

"If," said another boy, "you want to remain mired in superstition instead of acknowledging that ancient wisdom might merely be another form of modern science."

And they were off, arguing lightly about the fundamental nature of the universe.

During a collective pause for breath, Audrey asked me: "What do you think, Aphra?"

I considered the wisdom of a serious answer, and shrugged. "If magic violates the fundamental laws of nature, they clearly weren't all that fundamental."

"But do you think they connect?" asked the first boy, the one who had called magic by name. "Maybe there are things we can never learn through science. Things beyond understanding in any rational way."

"Like why Sally won't go steady with you?" asked the other boy, and the first girl—Sally, I presumed—blushed.

Audrey leaned in and whispered to me: "That's Jesse Sadler, Leroy Price, and Sally Ward. Don't mind Jesse—he wants everything to be fathomless mystery. That's fine for him—he can get into the stacks."

"But it's true," I said, drawn in despite myself. "There are different ways of understanding the universe, and you learn nothing by running an experiment if a spell or a sculpture is what's needed. And there are things we'll never understand because we don't have the time, or the right sorts of minds."

"Defeatist," said Leroy. He preened a hand through slick hair.

I blinked. "You have a narrow definition of victory."

Jesse smirked and took a sip of coffee. "Lady has a point. The universe is vaster and stranger than we can know. Maybe than we *should* know." He intoned this with the confidence of someone to whom the universe had so far denied nothing. I stared out the window at the tainted river.

"Say," he continued. "Where are you from?"

"San Francisco," I said, still distracted.

"Are you sure? You sound local." I barely had time to catch my breath before he continued. "Marsh? Like the Innsmouth Marshes? My mother used to talk about them; I thought they all left."

"Yes," I said faintly. "They left."

Sally was already leaning forward. "Innsmouth? The old ghost town? I heard it's haunted."

"Going to be some upset ghosts, then," said Leroy. "Someone bought up the land, and they're building new houses."

She pouted. "You're no fun."

"Don't blame me, blame the developers. And all the soldiers who want nice places to settle with their sweethearts."

"You should drive us there before they knock everything down. See if we can find any ghosts."

Leroy preened again. "Sounds like a gasser."

I stood. "Pardon me. It was a pleasure to meet you all."

"Aw, don't be like that," said Leroy. "We were just—" but I fled to the shelter of the aisles with my eyes dry.

I had known that Miskatonic's scholars did not see the world as we did. In the pews and streets of Innsmouth we'd mocked them as dilettantes and power-seekers, godless, prurient, exploring Aeonist philosophy and practice as others might take a safari.

It was harder now.

I thought of seeking out the store's occult section, which must have some worthwhile content to attract the university's tourists. But more of their kin might be there, gossiping over clever interpretations of the *Necronomicon* and squealing over Innsmouth's picturesque ruins. My courage failed me. Instead I hurried out onto Garrison Street.

Arkham felt less of a refuge now. I sought my bearings. If I followed the river upstream, I must eventually return to campus.

"Hey, hold up!" I whirled at Audrey's voice. "I'm really sorry about those guys. They can be drips sometimes."

I tried to slow my racing blood. "I will not disagree." I walked, as briskly as I could without giving the appearance of fear, back toward the street that paralleled the river.

Audrey, sleek in her A-line skirt and heels, scurried to keep up. "They didn't mean—are you really from Innsmouth?"

I turned, as I always found myself doing toward danger. With a jolt of fear I realized that I had left just such a risk behind in the Mill: Audrey's friends might even now be polishing old rumors, salivating over blood libels that had grown dull in our absence. "What of it if I am?"

"Makes no difference to me. It just seems creepy for them to be wandering around your old house looking for ghosts, that's all."

"Creepy. Yes, that's one word for it."

She didn't seem inclined to leave me be. I looked her over: narrow nose and small eyes, limp blonde hair, not a drop of Innsmouth blood in her. But she watched me eagerly, with the familiar curiosity one might offer a newly met relative.

"What do you want of me?" But even as I asked, I realized. "You think I can get you into the library. I barely gained permission myself."

"It's not that." Although from the slump of her shoulders, that must have been part of it. "They still talk about Innsmouth at Hall, you know."

I sighed inwardly. "And what do they say of us?"

"That the Innsmouth girls were always snobs—but that they knew what they wanted, and went after it, and didn't let anything stand in their way. That they could get things out of the school that no one else could. A real education, not just enough to nod in the right places when Miskatonic boys want to feel smart." She swallowed visibly.

I blinked. "They say different things about us at Hall than they do at Miskatonic." And Hall, I recalled, had always been more willing to let us through its gates.

"We say different things about Miskatonic, too."

Startled, I laughed. "Yes, so did we. I don't suppose you know whether this street leads back to the college?"

"It does, but there's a safer neighborhood about two blocks farther from the water."

More sanguine about her company in spite of myself, I went where she directed. She chattered about her "Bohemian" friends, their comings and goings and forays into new areas of study, glancing at me from time to time with that same watchful curiosity. Fortunately little response on my part seemed required.

My wanderings had been as circuitous as I suspected, and in less than a quarter hour I began to recognize the area around the school.

I attended to her stories as best I could, knowing that the school's politics might prove vital, but I could capture only part of the fluent stream of names and events that washed over me.

As we neared the school's main gate, she continued a complicated explanation of how the group pooled their resources when texts proved difficult to acquire. "And when Barinov went back to Leningrad, there was a whole argument over his books, too. He was so mad, he ended up gifting them to the Hall library out of spite."

"Wait," I said. "You've got a Russian in your group?"

"Had—like I said, he went back home my first year. Kirill Barinov. Lost his permission to study abroad or something. Why?"

It had been easy to ignore Spector's formal mission, in the previous day's bittersweet frustration. But I must not neglect it: both because it might represent a genuine danger, and because it was all that allowed us any intimacy with our books. "I was just surprised. It makes sense that he would have gone home, I suppose, given the news out of Russia. What did he study?"

She grinned wryly. "Math and folklore, same as you. You could probably see his materials, if you came over to Hall. Our collection isn't so impressive, but our library makes it a lot easier to check out books."

"I might do that. Thank you."

I found the others in the Special Collections reading room, and settled myself among today's pittance of books. Trumbull wore a faint smile as she perused a rare volume of Falconer's *Cryptomenysis Patefacta*—I remembered it as a pride of our uncle Sidrach's collection, one that I had felt very grown-up for being permitted to handle. A dog-eared copy of *Song of R'drik and Ghak-Shelah* still lay on the table. I was grateful to see that it was in R'lyehn; I wasn't sure what Spector would have made of the old and rather explicit epic. Caleb motioned me over.

"Here," he said quietly.

It was a copy of *Mens Pelagium,* bound in red leather and printed on alternating pages in Latin and R'lyehn—not a rare edition, and there had been many like it in Innsmouth's libraries. But when I looked over his shoulder, I inhaled sharply. I recognized our mother's handwriting.

"I read it correctly, then?" he asked quietly.

"Yes. This one is ours."

Mens Pelagium has much to say on the pedestrian life of the land, how someone keeping house or catching fish should best prepare themselves for a life of glory beneath the water. Kezia Marsh, like many, had added her own notes in the margins: meditations and frustrations and responses to the book's suggestions.

"The land does not ache so much," she had written beside a passage comparing a pregnant woman to the land that gives us over to the water. And in messier handwriting, below: "But birth may be much like the metamorphosis. Such a tiny creature, it is wondrous and terrible what she will become." I could scarce read the words to Caleb. He balled his fists and closed his eyes, and I wished for seawater to offer him.

Charlie, caught by some explication of Trumbull's, didn't notice, and Neko had retreated to a corner chair with a less consequential volume. But Spector saw that we'd found something of interest, and came over.

"May I?" he asked. Before I could say anything, Caleb whipped around and hissed. Spector flinched. My brother's already bulging eyes went wider.

"I would like you to know my mother as she was in life, too," I said carefully. He'd been the one to track down and share the government's all-too-detailed records of her death—something for which I still owed him, though he'd never say so. "But this is not the time."

"No. My apologies."

And of course I must needs tell him what I'd learned from Audrey, and Caleb would not be pleased at the reminder of why the government wanted us here. When we adjourned at last, I sought to pull Spector aside. But Caleb trailed behind me, and I ended up explaining Audrey's tenuous lead while Spector eyed him nervously and rubbed his wrists.

Trumbull drifted over. Charlie came along with her and stood next to me, his nearness reassuring and familiar.

"You've found relevant material elsewhere, I take it?" asked Trumbull. "May I come along? I find this line of inquiry fascinating."

I cocked my head at Spector, who frowned. Of course, he didn't know why her input would be so relevant to what we sought. I doubted it was my place to inform him. I looked at her, hoping she would give me some indication of what to say, but apparently she had not gained quite so much fluency in the human dialect of eyes.

I settled for telling him, "Her expertise might be relevant." It sounded weak, and he frowned again.

As we left, I managed a moment with Trumbull far enough from the others to murmur, "If he knew where you were from, he'd want you along."

"Mm. He is a representative of the local governmental authority, is he not? I do not care for such attention."

"Neither do I," I admitted. "But Spector is reasonable, for a . . . representative of the local governmental authority."

"Dominant humans are rarely trustworthy. And I have seen how he reads; he is no scholar. Your brother, your student: they may know my nature if you think them capable of discretion." She tapped fingers against her side. I wondered if the tic was hers, or native to the host body. "Spector concerns me. What does he want with these books, if not to study them?"

Spector, like Trumbull, would not be pleased if I shared his secrets without permission. So far as I could tell, even Skinner knew only that the government had an interest here, not what it was. But my interest wasn't the government's. I wanted only to prevent the body theft spell from being misused, and to keep my surviving family from at least that one danger. "You know that the United States—the local governmental authority—just came out of a war."

She shrugged. "Humans are always at war."

"Yes. It looks like we might be getting into another one soon, this time with Russia. There's . . . apparently there's some reason to believe that a Russian scholar might have learned the art of body switching. And brought it back to their government . . ." I trailed off. The dangers of sabotage between nations, the specter of city-destroying weapons, could not be compelling to someone who so easily dismissed the deaths of species.

But she frowned. "Our arts are not meant for petty politics."

"We know. Our laws have always said as much." That was another thing: if the Russians used such an art, it would be incumbent on me, and on Caleb, to enforce the ancient prohibitions. Oblivion take Spector, for always managing to find places where my own obligations and desires so neatly aligned with the needs of the state. I could easily wish that I shared Trumbull's indifference.

She tapped her fingers again. "Tell me what you find. It may be of interest to us."

I ducked my head. "Thank you." I thought of something else. "Great One, do you know where I might find a chapel on campus?"

"The campus church is ostensibly nondenominational; in fact it is extremely Christian. But there is a shrine in the back that is . . . discreet." She said the last word with some distaste.

After getting directions, I drifted forward and touched Caleb's elbow. He turned from his conversation with Neko.

"Professor Trumbull says there's a shrine on campus. Come with me?"

"Why would—" He swallowed, and then more gently. "Aphra, you know I don't—"

"Believe in the gods. I know. We've been"—I switched to R'lyehn—"surrounded by the flesh and minds of strangers, and I wish to speak with my sibling." In English again: "Come anyway?"

His face darkened, and I thought for a moment that his grasp of the tongue was too meager and too distant. But then he nodded fractionally. Neko, of course, caught the nuances if not the words, and let us go off on our own. I would talk with Charlie later.

Crowds of young men passed us, boisterous in the cold night. To my relief, they gave us a wide berth.

"We need to get our books back," he told me once the others were out of sight. He pulled out his cigarette pack. I kept my reaction in check.

"I know," I said. "This agreement where they ration them out . . . but I don't have a good idea for how to get them back. I don't think Miskatonic would take payment, even if we had it, and there's no trade I'm willing to offer that they'd be interested in."

"Payment! We should take the books—it's no crime to steal from a thief."

"Keep your voice down. It's no crime, but they'd lock us up all the same. And we'd get Professor Trumbull in trouble for giving us access in the first place."

He waved long fingers dismissively. "We'd be careful. And what of it if she gets in trouble? She's just a mortal, and a rude one at that."

I started to answer, took a deep breath, saw the steeple peeking from behind a low brick building. "Let's talk inside."

We made our way to the church. From the outside it was Christian in its entirety, though very gothic. It was not suited to its own scale, but looked rather like the childhood form of a cathedral. The doors, solidly built from plain dark wood, were closed against the cold but unlocked.

We slipped in. I kept a wary eye out for priests who might waylay visitors, but the interior was still, lit only by flickering gas lamps. Columns like great petrified trees lined the center aisle, branches entwined in the shadows above. Above the altar hung a grotesque statue of their god, bleeding. Caleb stared at it a long moment, expression unreadable.

At the outskirts of the room, we found the shrines: alcoves filled with saints and mythic images. Some appeared to be perishing in worrisomely imaginative ways, but others laid gentle hands on sick supplicants, or stood alone against soldiers and monsters. Winged figures hovered over all, bearing silent witness.

As promised, one shrine was more discreet. A stone altar stood empty except for a single candle. If I let my eyes unfocus, the half-abstract carvings resolved into great tentacles reaching from the altar to enfold the little grotto. The artist, I realized, had placed those who knelt there within the god's embrace, while making the god invisible to any who did not know to look.

I settled before the altar. I wanted to compose myself, as I might before ritual. But Caleb hovered at the edge of the space, a lightning jag of impatience at the edge of my attention.

"Aphra, if you came here to beg favors of the void, I don't want to watch."

I turned with a sigh. "I'm not begging anything of anyone. I'm trying to calm myself. It would do you some good as well."

"I have reason enough to be angry."

When I found myself endlessly circling my own bitterness, the old litanies and prayers still brought me comfort. They were stark reminders of entropy's even hand. But Caleb had given them up long ago. "You can be angry. You should be angry. *I'm* angry. But I think we'll do better by being angry and patient, and calm enough to plan. Please sit."

He sat, leaning against the organic curve of the wall. He looked at me narrow-eyed. "Do you want to plan, or do you want to avoid upsetting your government friend?"

I took deep breaths, several of them. "Do you want to plan, or do you want to mock me for every choice I've made in the past two years?"

He turned his head, giving that same doubtful and disappointed gaze to the altar. "I want our books back."

I let out a breath that turned into a cough. Caleb waited unmoving while I recovered. "Good," I said when I could talk again. "So do I. But I also want to protect the Kotos. And yes, Trumbull. It's not right to speak as you did out there, to dismiss someone's pain just because it's briefer than ours. We're mortal too."

"I never dismissed the Kotos." His shoulders slumped. "You know

I love them. But they can't understand, they haven't lost as much as we have—"

"They lost what they had to lose. You just did exactly what I said. You think the gods are judging some contest of loss?"

"If they existed, I doubt they'd care. No one cares but us!"

Footsteps cut through our rising voices, and we both stilled. I pushed myself, silently, to the shrine's edge. I balanced, half kneeling, on the balls of my feet, ready to attack or flee as our tracker's identity dictated.

A querulous, half-familiar tenor called, "Miss Marsh, is that you?" I said nothing.

A young man came into sight, tall and thin and well-dressed. After a moment, I recognized Jesse Sadler from the bookstore. He spotted me and smiled. "Hey. I've been looking around for you, since you said you were doing research at the library. This is a great spot, isn't it? You seemed like someone who didn't just *study* the old ways."

I stood and pulled away from the wall, hoping he hadn't seen us prepared for a fight. "Mr. Sadler. Hello."

I had been about to introduce Caleb, when Sadler saw him and blinked. He stuck out his hand. "Hello. Are you Miss Marsh's, um, fiancé?"

Caleb ignored the hand. "Sister dear, have you become engaged without telling me?"

I gave him what our mother would have called a fish-eye. "Caleb, allow me to introduce Jesse Sadler. We met in town earlier. Mr. Sadler, my brother, Caleb Marsh."

"Ah." He let his hand drop, as Caleb still had not taken it. "Pleasure to meet you." He glanced between us. Clearly he had expected to find me alone, if he found me at all, and I wondered what he'd hoped to gain from the encounter.

"Were you seeking me for some particular reason?"

He eyed Caleb again. Caleb turned and knelt before the altar. Sadler continued to watch his back for a moment, then forced his attention back to me. "No particular reason. I just—" He gestured at our sur-roundings. "Not many people actually use the temple. I come here sometimes, to think more carefully about the things I've been study-ing, to try and understand them."

"I see. Are you planning on joining that expedition that your friends were discussing earlier?"

"Sure. If you want to come along—"

"I do not. If you will please excuse us, my brother and I were in the middle of a private conversation." I touched Caleb's shoulder. "Brother, dear, let's go."

Outside, Caleb sang out, "Sister dear!" I punched his arm, but I was shaking.

"I don't like walking away," I said.

He glanced behind, but Sadler had apparently stayed in the church as requested. "From what? I could tell he displeased you from the start. Did he insult you, this morning?"

"After a fashion. He was with the group of students in the bookstore, talking about magic—or what they think of as magic. They're organ-izing an expedition to Innsmouth. Supposed to be haunted, you know."

He tensed beside me. "We ought to go down there and talk to our grandparents. Give them a haunting, if that's what they're looking for."

"You haven't yet, have you? Talked with them, I mean."

He shook his head silently.

"Caleb—Professor Trumbull."

"Leave be! Haven't we had enough rude mortals for the night?"

I looked up, but winter clouds obscured the stars. I would have liked to see where we stood in the cosmos. "She's not mortal. She's one of the Great Race. We talked last night."

"How do you know?"

I was surprised at the doubt in his voice. "The usual ways, I sup-pose. I asked the right question, and she gave the right answer. She knew more about us than I expected. I think she pushed the librarian, mentally, to make him give in about our books."

He shook his head. "She may know enough magic and lore to do those things. That doesn't make her an ancient, all-remembering intelligence."

I had been worried for Caleb's well-being. Now, I worried for his sanity and his own memories. "Doubt the gods as much as you please. People do. But to start doubting things that our people have seen throughout history, and recorded in those books you want to rescue . . . you have to believe in us, even if you don't believe in anything else."

When he turned to me, I saw in his eyes both the bitter man and the frightened boy. "I haven't forgotten our history, I promise. But trust me, it's better for Trumbull if I think her an arrogant mortal, rather than something that might have real answers."

I thought of my own conversation with her, and how he might react to the story of Beneer. And I let it lie.

CHAPTER 7

The next morning, Spector insisted on stopping at Dean Skinner's house before we left for Hall. His black government car waited in the drive while Trumbull idled behind in her own older model.

"We need to borrow Miss Dawson for the day," Spector informed the man with a cheer that bordered on malicious. Skinner blustered, and eventually disappeared into the house without inviting us in. A few minutes later the maid appeared, demure in a blue day dress and matching hat that set off her dark skin.

"This had better be worth it," she told Spector after the door closed. "The dean doesn't like to be reminded about my other duties."

"We've got a lead," he said. "We may need you to look at some notes."

She looked back at the house. "Well, it's a day off. Later's later."

"What's she doing here?" asked Caleb. I glared at him—I'd been wondering the same thing, but hadn't been about to ask.

She looked him up and down. "Vy govorite po-russki?"

He blinked, and suddenly grinned. "Cru, Vharlh nge R'lyehn. Th'dyn Zhucht."

She said something else in the other language—I presumed Russian—and he laughed. It was astounding to see Caleb laugh at his own ignorance, though I supposed this was an easier lack to swallow than most. They continued to trade phrases as we walked back toward the cars, and I realized that we were now two seats short in the original vehicle rather than one.

"I'll ride with Professor Trumbull," I said, because the thought of anyone else doing so unnerved me.

"I'll go as well," said Charlie. "There's no reason to be crowded in."

The others agreed, and before I could come up with an objection, we were standing alone on the icy walk while Trumbull tapped the steering wheel in annoyance. Charlie rubbed his knee as he eased into the front passenger seat, and it occurred to me that he might have physical as well as curmudgeonly reasons to prefer some space. I joined him, taking the seat behind Trumbull.

She seemed to feel no pressing need to fill the drive with chatter. We passed quickly down the streets that had made a comfortingly long walk. The sun broke through the winter haze, and houses and yards that had been picturesque white were now pocked with slushy gray and the black residue of exhaust.

"I miss California," said Charlie.

"So does Neko," I said.

"You don't?"

"I do. I miss the store. I miss the rain and the fog. I miss Mama Rei and Anna and Kevin. But I've missed snow, too."

He glanced at Trumbull, clearly waiting for her to throw in some comment about the virtues of Massachusetts, or the weather. This didn't seem like the appropriate place to explain her reticence, though holding back closed off many things we might otherwise have discussed.

We drove around the outskirts of Kingsport, a kaleidoscope of buildings from every era since the colonial, winding up toward the distant central hill with its sprawling hospital. The Hall School lay at the town's southwestern tip: a series of low-slung brick buildings with none of Miskatonic's flourishes. Bare-branched oaks and spreading pines lined the walkways, sheltering the girls who hurried between classes. Their semester apparently started earlier than Miskatonic's. Black and red uniforms peeked from under heavy coats.

We pulled up in front of the library—considerably smaller than the Crowther. Trumbull stepped out with alacrity, tilting her head with the slightly-less-distant interest that she turned on most things scholarly.

"Where are the others?" I asked.

Trumbull wrinkled her nose. "Perhaps they got lost on the way. It is quite a distance."

Charlie hugged himself; even with the sun out the day was chilly. "Shall we go inside? I'm sure that once they find the building, they can figure out the rest."

Nervous of our reception, I would have been just as pleased to wait outside. Nevertheless, I followed. I trod carefully on the ice and slush, testing each step for a steady landing.

I was right to be cautious: Charlie yelped as his bad knee went out from under him. I rushed to help. He pushed himself up slowly, cursing. I checked his head, but he waved me off.

"It's fine, it's fine. I landed on my arm. I'll have a hell of a bruise. Excuse me. Ow." In spite of his protests, I steadied him as he got slowly to his feet. He grimaced as he put weight again on the knee, and glared at Trumbull. "Let's get inside."

With me steadying his elbow, we managed the path without further incident—though another spotter would not have been amiss.

Trumbull waited inside. I found myself shivering, unsteady, not from cold but from instinct.

"Not a very social people, are you?" I asked. She raised an eyebrow, and jerked her chin at the librarians behind the information desk, the students wandering among the shelves. I was not being sufficiently discreet.

Charlie seemed distracted by his knee. I found him a chair, saw him settled and comfortable, and went to find a reference librarian. Trumbull could follow, or not, as she saw fit.

The librarian, shockingly, was entirely cooperative. I explained that we were looking for Barinov's donated notes, probably from a year or two ago, and she told me that they would take a few minutes to track down. She scurried off with the pleased air of a woman on a quest.

I returned to find Spector kneeling by Charlie's chair, palpating his knee. He glanced up as I arrived. "Don't tell me. Dawson and I are the only people here who know first aid."

"Where would I have learned?" I asked lightly, but saw it hit home.

"I'm fine," said Charlie again. With a look of apology in my direction, he took out his pipe.

"I suppose you can afford the pride," said Spector. "Don't need your legs much, running a bookstore."

Dawson said, "I'll find something to wrap it properly."

"No, you won't." Spector smiled wryly. "You read Russian; I'm just here to look useful. I'll find what we need."

"Do we have something to read in Russian?" she asked me.

"In a few minutes," I said. At Caleb's look of surprise, I added, "One could get to like the Hall School."

"Shall I at least get some snow?" asked Dawson. Spector nodded, and they both left on their own missions.

"Practical woman," said Caleb approvingly.

Dawson returned shortly afterward with snow packed into a scavenged bag, which she made Charlie hold against his knee. A few girls looked at her oddly, but she ignored them. Or rather, she drew herself straighter, held her neck proud and tense, and did not look.

"I'm sorry," I told her.

"For what?"

I looked down. "For what they're making you do. For what you did to get us into the university."

Her expression became bland. "It was nothing."

Fortunately, the librarian returned before I could say anything to worsen the insult. "I have a room set up for you. This way, please."

Charlie put out his pipe, and leaned on my arm as we followed her into a back room. The logistics of helping him gave me an excellent excuse to avoid looking at Dawson. I imagined apologizing to Anna the same way, and felt my face flush. She would not have appreciated it either.

Charlie must have mistaken my blush, for he tried to draw away. "I can make it on my own."

"Mr. Day," I said, keeping firm hold of his arm. "I assure you I can take the weight. In spite of which I don't intend to carry every book box that comes into the store for the next several years; please listen to Mr. Spector on this one." He subsided reluctantly.

Thankfully the room to which the librarian led us was not far: one of a row behind the reference section, each with a long reading table and several chairs. Three neat piles of books awaited us, along with an intriguing stack of black leather-bound notebooks.

"These are all the notes, and the books cited most often in them according to our record. If you need to see other books, or the cross-reference list, find me and I'll track them down."

"Thank you." I was too startled to say anything else. Trumbull nodded at her with what might have been respect. She sat down immediately and claimed the top notebook.

I took a moment longer to ensure Charlie's comfort, and both the cold pack's survival and its distance from any materials vulnerable to the melting ice. When I finished, I saw the librarian still hovering by the doorway, watching me nervously. My stomach felt hollow; clearly this had been too simple. I went to her side.

"Is there some difficulty?" I asked quietly.

"No! I'm sorry, miss, I . . ." To my surprise, she blushed. I've never been good at judging ages outside of Innsmouth, but with her gray-specked hair and skin beginning to wrinkle and thin, embarrassment looked incongruous on her. "May I ask—I know it's a strange question but—are you a Waite?"

I blinked. My lids felt tight and painful over my eyes. "Marsh, actually. But the families are related."

She smiled, a little sadly. "I thought you might be. You look so much like Asenath."

I blinked again. "You knew Asenath Waite?" I could not put a face to the woman who had left town when I was still a babe in arms, but her fate had been the subject of much dark rumor.

Some of those rumors were related to our topic of study. And this woman was the first I had met since the camps with memories of my town, my people. "Please tell me about her?"

We drew chairs away from the table. "She had your look, but that same—she carried herself well, attracted people to her. She frightened a lot of people, too, but I always admired her drive. She had an . . . audacity about her, and we always expected great things." She sighed. "Then she got married, like any ordinary girl. He was a Miskatonic graduate, years her senior but still spending all his time with the college students, and he brought out everything that was worst in her. And then, well, you know how badly it ended."

She wiped her eyes. "I'm sorry. It was a long time ago, but she was a friend."

"You hardly need to apologize for mourning," I said. Neither of us had a handkerchief, and no one at the table had noticed, so she made do with her sleeve.

"Did she ever offer you salt water?" I asked, suddenly curious whether she had held to our customs even after leaving.

"Yes!" She laughed shakily. "We always thought that was strange, but she said it was a potent tool." Her eyes slid to the books on the table.

"A magical one," I said, and she nodded.

"She was very . . . she had quite a reputation." She watched me carefully, and I did my best to look like someone who would not mock her past. "She seemed a magician sometimes, and she was certainly a hypnotist. She could catch you up with her eyes and make you feel that you were someone else, something else . . ." She trailed off wistfully.

I swallowed hard, because that certainly fit the rumors. "You liked it?"

I saw on her face first the fear that she had said too much, then the determination to bear witness to the truth of it. "This school can be confining, sometimes. Asenath made us feel free."

And yet, here she was, a quarter century on, still in the place of her confinement.

Spector slipped in, bearing bandages and what appeared to be a scavenged cane. Our conversation stilled as he passed, and we waited until he bent to more properly dress Charlie's knee, murmuring reassurance in exchange for grunted protests.

"From what I heard when I was a child," I said reluctantly, "Asenath may not have been as free as she seemed."

"Certainly not after she married Mr. Derby. Or after they got involved with that Upton fellow." She regained some of her composure, and a proud tilt of her chin that made me ache so much for home that I thought she must have picked it up from Asenath. "I hope he rots another twenty-five years in that asylum, for whatever role he played in that sordid situation."

"Wait—he's still alive? The man who—" I broke off, uncertain with what version of the story I ought to finish my sentence.

She grimaced and fussed with her sleeve. "They never gave us a straight story, but either Upton or Derby murdered her." She met my eyes, now that she had spoken it aloud. Spector's head jerked up, and I waved him back to his notes. "Then Upton killed Derby, and blamed her for it. I always assumed there was an affair; she can't have been happy. And yes, he's still alive, locked up because of how he ranted about her." She shook her head. "I never married. A woman with a brain who marries is a fool. Men will eat you alive."

That was almost certainly true of Asenath, though I didn't think it would be a kindness to share what I knew. "I'm sorry for your loss. She left town when I was very young; I'm afraid I don't have any memories to share. I knew some of her closer cousins, but they died years ago."

She nodded. "I heard rumors about what happened to Innsmouth, too. I'm glad to do anything I can to help a relative of Asenath's, even a distant one."

"Thank you," I said faintly.

After she left, I joined the others at the table and took a free notebook. I wanted time to think over what she had said, and to decide what I ought to do with it.

Spector stood and checked the now-closed door. "I'm sorry," he said, "but when I hear the word 'murder' it attracts my attention."

"And when I hear the name of 'Waite,'" added Caleb. He and Dawson had been murmuring together over marginalia, but apparently not loudly enough to block our conversation. In the camps, I'd grown used to the absolute fiction that people did not hear when there was no room for physical privacy. Apparently the habit had not taken with my brother.

I sighed and put down the scarcely opened notebook. "It's a very old case," I told Spector.

"With a Waite . . . ," said Caleb thoughtfully. Then, eyes unfocused as if summoning old memory, he chanted: "Old Man Waite will steal your eyes, Old Man Waite will steal your soul. Better run to the sea by the count of five, if you don't want to pay Old Ephraim's toll." He reddened at the others' looks.

"Caleb, where did you get that?" I asked.

"It was a song the kids used to sing. Don't you remember? You have to run from the street to the porch of the old abandoned Waite house and back before the chant is over, but some people count way too fast."

"They hadn't turned it into a song when I was young enough for that sort of game." Of course the others would not be dissuaded now. "You all understand that this . . . this thing we're researching— Body theft is a grave crime. The last suspected case in Innsmouth took place when I was very young. If I remember the details right, Ephraim Waite supposedly stole his daughter Asenath's body, but was somehow dissatisfied with it. So he left Innsmouth as Asenath, and went to the Hall

School. He seduced and married someone from Arkham, and then moved into *his* body, or tried to."

"Hold a moment." Spector looked both queasy and as if he were having difficulty keeping up. "How many bodies at a time?"

"Just one at a time," I said, "unless he knew a whole different version of the spell from the one people talk about—I certainly hope not. I'm sorry—I'm trying to reconstruct something I overheard—"

"—eavesdropping from the top of the staircase," put in Caleb.

I ignored him and went on: "—so I could be wrong on the details. But as I understand it, once Ephraim Waite had the husband's body and forced the husband—'Derby' is the name the librarian gave—into Asenath's, he killed Derby. And then a friend of the family killed *him*, in Derby's body. That's all I know, except that the elders seemed dissatisfied about whether they'd been able to do justice." I took a deep breath, drawing in air rich with leather and old paper. "That librarian"— and I realized we'd never exchanged names—"was a friend of Asenath's. Or rather, a friend of her murderous father, unknowing."

Charlie and Spector spoke nearly at the same time. "I'm sorry." They looked at each other, then away.

"So am I." Asenath herself had lost whatever voice she might have had in the whole complicated story, dead before anyone noticed. I glanced surreptitiously at Trumbull. She was unlikely to mourn Asenath Waite as a person, but I wondered whether she regretted the lost perspective, the little piece of history fallen away into the trench created by Ephraim's crime. Reluctantly, I added, "Mr. Spector, the librarian did tell me about a living witness. If you think it might help. It sounds like he's the one who killed Ephraim, and probably knew what he was doing."

To his credit, Spector took the moment to think about it. "I believe it would," he said slowly. "If he could suggest signs that distinguish a body thief . . . It could help not only to track down actual cases—if there are any—but also to avoid unnecessary paranoia. Unless you saw it yourself?"

I did not look at Trumbull. Even if one dared judge the Yith, their art was not the same thing. I shook my head. "I was young, as I said. And my understanding is that Asenath—Ephraim, I mean—left town soon after the first switch, presumably to escape notice."

Spector glanced at Dawson, and she nodded. "Do you have a name?" she asked.

"Upton," I said.

"There are a lot of Uptons in Morecambe County."

I looked helplessly at Caleb. "He's in an asylum . . ."

"I'm sorry," he said. "I never heard any skip rope songs about Uptons."

Neko leaned forward, as intrigued by Caleb's childhood as by Ephraim's old crime. "I thought you said it was for playing keepaway with a haunted house."

"For the boys. The girls used it for skip rope." More color in his cheeks suggested that he'd sometimes played the safer game as well.

Dawson gave Caleb an amused look, but her tone was all professional confidence. "I'll find him."

Kirill Barinov's notebooks did not provide any hints of body switching that day—nor indeed of any magical mastery beyond the dilettantish. According to Dawson's translation, he'd speculated wildly about the powers one might develop through proper study, but ultimately showed a deeper fascination for the legends of otherworldly creatures and gods. Like many at Miskatonic, his great hope appeared to have been finding secrets of physics and mathematics hidden in ancient lore, or the reverse. He seemed to take great enjoyment in the play of ideas with the rest of his crowd, whatever the topic. Certain names cropped up frequently in the English sections of his marginalia, including a few instances of "Sadler says" and "Miss Winslow made an intriguing observation." As Dawson pointed out, the only possibility precluded by these entries was Kirill as an *incompetent* spy. It would have been easy enough to keep two sets of journals and leave one behind, or hide meaningful observations in some cipher that Dawson hadn't yet detected.

The helpful librarian had left by the time we were ready to go, but her evening replacement assured us that we could continue our work when we returned.

Spector pulled me aside on the way out. "I wanted to warn you: Dawson says that Skinner is acting suspicious about you and Caleb. He's not happy that we haven't explained what we're after, and he seems to have latched on to the idea that it's something to do with"—he shrugged, looking embarrassed—"old rumors about dark arts and destructive powers that were hidden before Innsmouth was . . . before the raid. He seems to think you're using us to go after . . . whatever he imagines you want to find. She's trying to redirect him, but you may want to be careful."

"That, I'd figured out." I tried to hide my discomfort. The rumors about Innsmouth had always included fantastical stories about everything from sacrificing our neighbors' children to hoarding artifacts that threatened all humanity. Simply for Skinner to recall those libels, discuss them with others, would be a grave danger. "Wouldn't it be better to tell him? I know he doesn't cooperate willingly, but he might, if he knew what danger you were really after." And it might distract him from his worst guesses as to why Innsmouth's survivors were involved.

But Spector shook his head. "Skinner is discreet only when his own reputation is at stake. I'm not authorized to explain the details of our mission to him, and I don't think his inevitable curiosity is sufficient reason for headquarters to change that. I just wanted you to know—and to let me know if you see reason for greater concern."

Dinner passed with the usual awkwardness—although thankfully without Skinner's personal presence. Afterward, I suggested to Charlie that we find a private spot to continue our studies. Caleb declined to join us, somewhat to my relief. Trumbull surprised me by offering the use of her workroom, "provided you do not interfere with my studies there."

We walked slowly back to the faculty row. The cane seemed to help—Spector had found a good one—but Charlie did not object too strenuously to my staying within reach of his elbow on the night-frozen sidewalks.

Trumbull's second-floor workroom had once been an ordinary study, with built-in bookshelves and a bay window overlooking the snow and moonlit shadows of the campus.

"The knives are purified. Salt them when you're done," she told us before shutting the door.

Trumbull—or rather, the entity that now inhabited her body—had pushed the desk to the side and stacked it with papers handwritten in miniscule but impeccable Enochian. Another table bore, along with a rack of knives and a water-filled glass bowl, a half-built machine that looked like some obscene hybrid of a chemistry set and a home radio kit. It did not appear to be on, but the open flasks gave off a faint, noxious odor only partly masked by the remnants of incense and melted candles. A series of hand-drawn diagrams studded one wall. She'd covered the open part of the floor with a thin slate slab, now a palimpsest of old chalk.

A cushioned chair remained in concession to human comfort, and Charlie sank into it. He rubbed his knee gingerly. "I don't know what to make of her."

"Well." I leaned in to examine the diagrams more closely. They seemed related to astral travel, but beyond that I could tell only that they were far beyond my expertise. "That's probably because she isn't human."

"She's not one of your people. You would have said."

"I'm human, Mr. Day. We share the world in three parts."

He ducked his head. "I'm sorry, Miss Marsh. I didn't mean it like that."

"I know. But remember."

"So then she's . . . is she a Yith?" He leaned back. "Of course she is. You did warn me."

"I did. But it's different, meeting one in person." I settled cross-legged on the slate and looked up at him. "It's one thing to say that humanity is ultimately unimportant in the face of the cosmos. It's another to stand before someone who believes, deep down, that your pain is trivial."

"I felt that. When she doesn't care about something, she's like a personification of the whole universe not caring." He started to bend down, grimaced, and sat back again cautiously. "But they do important work—you've said so. And there were other humans there who did care, who helped me out—even if I was an ass about it."

"You were, rather," I told him, and was rewarded by the quirk of his lips. "Charlie—" His given name slipped out without my thinking about it, and he didn't object. "It's cowardly of me, but I don't want to think about the indifference of the universe tonight. I want to go through the Inner Sea, and see what we can do to encourage your healing, and then perhaps talk a bit about summoning."

"That all sounds fine to me." But he hesitated and asked, "Not more dreamwalking?"

"I'd rather not. *She* might be asleep."

His eyes widened and he made no further objection. I gathered up the necessary materials—the bowl proved to hold salt water—and drew the first-level seal, occasionally quizzing Charlie on the symbols. We centered ourselves—I on the waves and tide, he on wind and breath—and began the chant. Our voices entwined the room, calling on our own bodies and the rhythms they shared with the changing earth, the rush of wind, the water's rise and fall through the ocean. As the words filled us, I washed the blade and pricked our fingers to let blood mingle with salt water. Even before the magic took hold, I began to feel calmer, to gain, not indifference to the day's shocks of fear and sadness and hope, but some measure of equanimity. The tide sweeps in, the tide flows out, and you learn to accept the ocean's inconstancy.

And then the tide swept in. I felt how my body carried my mind, how it held my selfhood enmeshed in the weave of eyes and veins, bone and skin. I felt my blood: a river, a torrent, a reminder that my body had not forgotten the ocean in which it would someday dwell, or the form it would take there.

But our ritual had another purpose, tonight. I surfaced and reached out to Charlie. I must see through his flesh, if we hoped to heal it. I touched his hand, and dove into the weaker, dryer currents that flowed through a man of the air. Through them I sought the signs of his injury, and the tools of healing.

"I'm sorry," I said when the ritual was over. "Maintaining health is always easier than repairing injury. Usually a new injury is simpler, but this one is so tangled in the old damage . . ."

"I know. I saw." He glared at the seal. "My knee's been a problem for years. It shouldn't be more frustrating now, just because I have some control over other things."

"We thirst more for water just beyond reach." The old saying felt facile; I had known for a long time that it wasn't true. "I'm sorry. There's too much we can't do."

He shook his head. "I think you had the right idea, earlier. Tell me about summoning."

So I did. We could not go far beyond the theoretical tonight, not without the appropriate books convenient to hand—Trumbull might have some, but this wasn't a good time to ask her.

Summoning spells would at first be more useful to Charlie than to me. It was possible to call on a specific individual, but far easier to summon by kind. A call to Chyrlid Vhel—the people of the air—would likely bring whoever was in the next room. A call to Chyrlid Ajha would bring either me or Caleb, unless we were very close to the Atlantic in just the right spot. A call to Chyrlid Fazh did not bear thinking about. It was always possible that some wayward Mad One might choose to answer.

"Could we summon a Yith?" His eyes darted to the door, lids crinkling at the presumably entertaining image.

"Unfortunately, no. Both because physically she's a perfectly ordinary woman of the air, and because someone stronger-willed and more skilled in magic can always resist a call. Or follow it under their own power to find the source of the presumption."

"That sounds unpleasant."

"Yes. Miskatonic has a reputation for producing the sort of fools who try to summon the gods themselves, or their close servants. Fortunately for the school, they don't usually get any response."

"Usually?" He leaned forward.

"The gods have never responded to summons. But Earth is warm, and wet, and full of life. And there are things that care even less for our well-being than the Yith, and who have more dangerous interests. They wait for the opportunity in a badly used word, a misplaced symbol."

"I might do better to ask around until I found out where you were. It seems safer, somehow."

I smiled in spite of myself. "I can assure you, Mr. Day, that the symbols that call my people are not conducive to the things that wait out in the cold. It's the attempts to summon things that you *can't* get to any other way that carry the true danger."

We sat in the study, with its warm browns and crisp papers, and I felt at my back winter creeping through chinks in the window. And I spoke to my friend and pupil of colder, vaster reaches, and tried to hold between us a little space of warmth in which we could take our comfort.

CHAPTER 8

After some discussion, we decided to alternate days at Miskatonic and Hall. Should Spector's masters require some justification for the Miskatonic days beyond the possibility of new leads, and the promises made to me and Caleb, the alternating schedule also gave Dawson time to track Upton. But the morning paper carried new reports of Russian aggression, and I worried that they'd pressure Spector for fast results, rather than complete ones. They might not be entirely wrong, either—if Russia did have agents who could wear any body, at some point they must use them.

I did not try again to apologize for Dawson's duties with us, or Skinner's presumed reaction. Their relationship must be all claws and blades: law and custom gave him a thousand types of power over Dawson, while she had only the one, pointed firmly at his heart. She'd made it clear that it was not my place to discuss this with her, nor to try and help her free of their well-honed tangle.

Charlie and I spent a relatively quiet day in the Miskatonic library, pouring over a copy of *On the Calling of Kinds* that I'd managed to finagle from the librarian in lieu of yet another *Book of Eibon*. Orne wrote in engaging style, alternating his slightly eccentric taxonomy of creatures that could be summoned, and "receipts" for doing so, with cautionary tales of impromptu methods gone wrong.

Spector chatted with the Special Collections librarian, apparently trying to overcome his poor first impression. I heard him sympathize, casually, with the man's worries about the wrong sort of people accessing dangerous books. He didn't—yet—press for stories about specific people who might have tried to do so.

During a break, Charlie procured a phone and made a long-distance call to the store, checking with the colleague he'd left in charge, and I started on a letter to Mama Rei. I left it unfinished, though, distracted by an all-too-vivid image from Orne's book—a story of uncontrolled summoning in battle. I feared it would make an easy addition to my nightmares. The unnamed war seemed to have been part of the Roman Empire's early expansion. Perhaps the specifics would have been obvious to a man of the air, better versed in the details of European history. Orne described in detail the defending tribe—"barbarians," as he would have them—who knew their territory and way of life lost, pressed to desperation against the wall of surrender. They, or perhaps merely a single skilled magician among them, chose instead to beg help from any creature that might hear.

In the first minutes, it seemed their pleading would bear sweet fruit, for monsters arose from the caves and streams to fall on the legions: Creatures of claw and diaphanous wing flown from far worlds, willing to take the barbarians' part in exchange for later favor. However, the call never paused at the boundaries of this world, but carried into Outside Realms, to beings of hunger that know nothing of human borders and fears. Where they entered, they made a field of peace: blackened grass, corpses cold and still, and dust where the wings of Yuggoth had descended to join the battle.

It was the desperation before the call that plagued me now: if the swords and spears of the Roman Empire could drive people to such lengths, how much worse the threat of absolute destruction? What might the people of Hiroshima have called to avenge their memory, if they had known what was coming?

That day, Dawson confirmed that one Daniel Upton, an architect, had been institutionalized following a murderous scandal in the mid-'20s. She had not yet managed to identify the asylum, but there were few in the area that would have made appropriate oubliettes for the son of a respectable family. She would soon find our quarry—assuming he was still alive—and I considered what I ought to say to him. It seemed an awkward situation, and a small scrap to offer Spector.

So just as I had been grateful for the respite of our day at Miskatonic, I was now grateful for the trip to Hall that would give me additional time to plan for meeting Upton. For what I ought to do, if he were still sane.

Mid-morning there came a knock on the door to our reading room. Expecting Asenath's old friend, I got up to answer it, and was surprised to find Audrey Winslow waiting nervously outside.

"Hi," she said. "I'm sorry to bother you when you're working. I heard you were here. I could help if you like."

"I don't think—not unless you read Russian, I'm afraid."

"Oh. No. Mr. Barinov taught me how to write my name, that's all." She peered over my shoulder at the others, still engrossed in their texts.

I put on my best voice for confused customers. "Miss Winslow. How can I help you?"

"Oh." She craned her neck further to look at the others, looked at me again, took a deep breath. Then she curtseyed somewhat awkwardly and dropped her voice. "Miss Marsh. I wish to serve you, and learn at your feet as your apprentice. If you'll have me. I'm smart, I do well at school, I'm the fastest reader in our group, and I've even managed to make spells work a couple of times, almost, little ones, but I know I could do it!" This last said with a defiant air, eyes still downcast. "I would serve you willingly and absolutely, I only wish to join your"— her eyes flicked up and past me—"retinue."

I could only stare. I heard rustling behind me, and Caleb whispering something snide to Dawson. At last I found my voice, strained with shock. "You have me mistaken. Where did you get the idea that I have a retinue? Or take servants?"

"Jesse said he went to the chapel and found you leading a service before the altar, with your brother serving behind you. That you were speaking of deep secrets, and dismissed him from your presence. And everyone in our group knows a little about the Cult of Dagon. He said you were a high priestess."

I ignored the choked sound from my brother. He could afford to think this funny. "Jesse . . . Mr. Sadler. Didn't you say that he likes to make everything seem more mysterious than it is?"

She shrugged. "He uses fancy words. But he usually knows what he's talking about."

"And didn't you say you don't believe in magic?"

"I don't think it's the right word for what we do—for what *you* do. But I know you can do things with it that aren't possible any other way. I'll call it whatever you like, if that's what it takes to learn."

I checked over my shoulder. My brother now sat with an innocent, wide-eyed expression. Dawson looked between the two of us, her expression exceedingly dubious. Neko put down her book to watch in fascination. Spector appeared entirely too amused. Trumbull continued reading, blandly.

Charlie came to my rescue. "Miss, I think you're very confused. And bothering Miss Marsh."

She curtseyed again. It fit her just as poorly the second time. "I'm terribly sorry if I've offended you, miss. My lady? But I do want to learn this, more than anything. I'll prove myself however you want, take on any task. Please, I beg of you."

A part of me wanted to slam the door or let Charlie drive her away. But amid her errors and desperation, she had asked a real question. I took a ragged breath. "If you promise to cease bowing and begging and giving me titles I haven't earned, I will"—I thought on how many witnesses this needed, and whether one of them really had to be my brother—"go for a walk with you. Charlie, if you can spare a few minutes, I'd appreciate the company."

As he rose I realized that he was still using the cane, and the sidewalks were still slippery. "I beg your pardon, I ought not to have asked. Maybe . . ."

"No," he said. "I'll be fine." And there was no way to gainsay him without injuring his pride. I would go slowly.

"Sister dear—" started Caleb. I did the only thing I could think of to short-circuit the act, which was to stick out my tongue at him. He laughed and let be.

We made our way cautiously out into the cold. I was grateful to see a bench nearby, and led the way to it. I swept away the patches of snow on the seat, and took a wet spot for myself.

"We don't really need to walk," I apologized. "I just didn't want the others staring."

Audrey's eyes darted between us. "All right. I'm not bowing." She lit a cigarette and took a defiant drag.

Charlie frowned fiercely, and I took strength from his protectiveness. "Thank you. I appreciate that. I'm sorry that Mr. Sadler gave you the wrong impression, but I'm really not a high priestess. The people with me—some of them are friends, and some are family, and some are studying the same material for their own purposes. Mr. Day is my student, but he isn't my servant. I work for him. At his bookstore. We help each other learn; I don't know much more than he does. I'm sorry." I held back any further apologies for not being that which I did not wish to be.

"But you do teach. Magic."

"I learn magic. And he learns alongside me."

"I would learn. Regardless of what you call it."

I heard in Charlie's silence that he was, like me, unwilling to simply dismiss her. He knew too well what it was to yearn so strongly.

I trailed my hand through the snow on the back of the bench, and composed myself. I asked the traditional question, which had no traditional answer: "Why do you wish to learn?"

"Power," she said simply. She put the cigarette to her lips.

"Ah." Charlie knew this one. I nodded at him.

"Magic isn't for power," he said. "That's the first thing Miss Marsh taught me. If our studies brought power, I wouldn't need this." He tapped the cane on the ground for emphasis.

"And I would still have . . . more family than I do now," I said.

She looked between the two of us. Now that she had determined not to cringe before me, her eyes grew colder. "Do you remember what I told you the other day? About Innsmouth girls?"

I thought back to our conversation. "That we know what we want."

"And you go after it. I'm sorry for whatever happened to your family. I can guess from some of the rumors. I don't expect to turn into Superman. I just want a little more control over my own life. Everyone else thinks that's unreasonable; do you?"

"No. I'm just not sure magic is the best way to go about it."

"Oh? What is, then?"

I looked at Charlie, at a loss. I'd been free for all of three years; I barely knew how to rebuild my own life.

"That's what I thought," she said. "Magic is good enough for you. Why are you learning it, if not for power?"

There had been no mentor to ask me that, when I restarted my studies. I could no longer remember whatever foolish answer I had given my father, when he first asked. "It's my birthright. I want it back from those who stole it."

"And that isn't power?"

Still I hesitated. "It would slow us down," I said to Charlie. "We'd have to go back to some of our early practice."

He didn't look entirely pleased, but said: "It's up to you, Miss Marsh. Not my place to say how much we share."

I could tell, even from a few minutes in her presence, that Audrey had been granted a relatively easy life. Little had been denied her—

and yet, in the thing she *had* been denied, I heard echoes of my own desperation, held tight through the years in the camp.

Turning to her, I said: "All right, we'll try this. I'll take you on as a student. But we don't know how long we're in Arkham for. It could be weeks or months. If things go very well, or very poorly, it could be days."

Audrey lifted her chin. "A start is more than I have now."

"Then we'll begin. Tell me what you know—or what you think you know."

≈≈≈

May 1943: The guards are distracted again, as they were before the Nikkei came to the camp. Outside the warden's office, I hear raised voices. The next day, they begin calling prisoners inside in pairs. There are over two thousand Nikkei now, and the rotation takes a long time. Rumors swamp true reports.

They call me and Caleb into the office together. Soldiers stand in the corners, guns trained. But that's not what captures my attention. On the desk are two sheets of printed paper, two pens. My eyes feast on the words without even trying to interpret them. Letters, not traced secretly in sand, but gathered in an impossible abundance of sentences and paragraphs.

The warden's voice draws me back. His hair has grown gray and grizzled during his time here, and he glares with well-worn dislike. "Fill out the forms. Don't make any mark other than 'yes' or 'no.'"

The first question: "Are you willing to serve in the armed forces of the United States on combat duty wherever ordered?" The second: "Will you swear unqualified allegiance to the United States of America and faithfully defend the United States from any or all attack by foreign or domestic forces, and forswear any form of allegiance or obedience to the Japanese emperor, to any other foreign government, power or organization?" I can barely suppress laughter. But the unvoiced hysteria dies as I consider: whoever ordered these questions to the camp made no exception for us.

I glance at Caleb: "You could." The rest goes unspoken: he could get himself drafted as a soldier. Get away from this place where he's lived since he was six, to fight and perhaps die for a country that's done nothing to earn his loyalty—far away from walls and wire and dry air, with a better illusion of freedom.

But he smiles at the warden, takes the pen, and scrawls "NO" twice in unpracticed, childish handwriting. Unwilling to risk separation—and in truth, unwilling to give over whatever remains of my self to such an oath—I do the same.

Still, I let the pen go with reluctance, and leave clutching a new and secret hope: they are starting to forget why they were afraid of us.

Audrey turned out to be familiar with a certain amount of theory, though intermixed with a great deal of nonsense. When she forgot herself—or rather, when she forgot her exaggerated ideas of my station—she was also prone to wild speculations about the "rational" foundations of the art.

What she truly lacked was any practical experience. After a few of her stories I decided that the essential problem with her "wild" college set was that they expected the cosmos to provide human-scale drama. They'd bought a sheep from a local slaughterhouse and sacrificed it on Hallowmas, hoping thereby to earn visions. There had been visions of a sort, but there had also been much drinking. Another time, they'd painted themselves with a paste of dead tarantulas—these stolen from a Miskatonic biology lab—in an attempt to summon a thankfully imaginary spider god.

"Sally got a rash all over her belly," Audrey told us in disgust. "She claimed she was 'spiritually pregnant.'"

"Miss Winslow," I said hesitantly. I did not wish to become like Spector's masters, automatically suspicious of anyone who dealt in magic. Nor did I wish to assume, as did some of our elders, that short-lived men of the air must invariably misunderstand and warp the ancient texts. The "wild" students with their risqué reputations were probably harmless. But I could not bear the thought of being further disappointed later on. "Has anyone been hurt in these rituals? Worse than a rash, I mean, or against their will."

"Not that I know of. You hear stories about how intense things were in the old days, but I think it's just people trying to sound daring. The sheep is the only time I've even seen blood."

"Ah. Well, that will change." And I told her about the Inner Sea.

Spector cornered me after dinner. He'd acquired a cigar from somewhere, and I had to breathe shallowly. "Miss Marsh, I don't mean to pry. But what arrangement did you come to with that student?"

It had been close to noon by the time we returned to the reading room, so I could hardly deny that something had transpired. "And yet you are prying."

He sighed. "I have to report, and justify, anyone who learns about the mission. I have to fill out ten duplicate copies of a five-page form for anyone who learns about the mission. What you do on your own time is your own business—I just need to know whether I ought to fill out that paperwork. Please say no."

I smiled in spite of myself. "No. She is naturally curious about our interest in her friend's papers, but I haven't told her why we want them."

"Ah." His eyes narrowed. "She knew him?"

I hurried to forestall this line of thought. "I don't think she knows any more about what he was working on than the interests he shared with all of her cohort. They don't appear to have been at risk of accomplishing any legitimate magic, let alone anything you need to be concerned with."

He looked at me a long moment and nodded. "I trust your judgment."

"Good."

But the conversation shook me, and I wished for a fleeting moment that I had what Audrey had supposed: a retinue of pliable followers whose judgment I need not fear.

Trumbull, of course, didn't quiz me about Audrey, an unlikely source of either occult wisdom or historical documentation. Neko teased me gently about my would-be acolyte, but that I could withstand.

Once we were alone in our room, she turned more serious. "What's going on with Caleb?"

I turned off the lights and sat on the bed. Electricity probably wasn't dear for Trumbull's budget, but it was a hard habit to break. "He's angry. And frustrated, even now that we have access to our books."

"I don't mean that. He's always been angry and frustrated. He was angry and frustrated in the . . . in the camp . . . but he didn't hold me at arm's length."

I stared, though I doubted she could see. "He's more comfortable with you than he is with me."

"And more comfortable with Deedee than with me."

"Deedee?" I asked.

"You know, the negro girl. Dorothy. Dean Skinner's maid."

"Oh," I said. "Miss Dawson."

"Well, he was calling her Deedee on the way home."

"Was he, now?" I thought about them leaning together over a book, and frowned. "Does she like that?"

"He didn't say." She threw herself on the bed beside me, claiming a patch of moonlight. "He teases me, but he doesn't really tell me anything. I think he's hoping I won't notice."

"That does bode ill." I ran a finger along the bright square in which she lay. "I'm sorry he's pushing you away too. I know you were close."

"Going out behind the cabins wasn't even a big part of it. It was . . ." She trailed off.

"I know you were courting. Casually. It's all right." In fact, I had backed my brother into a corner and demanded to know whether he was planning to breed with her. But he'd known, as well as I did, how our captors would have leapt on a mist-blooded child and its mother.

"Do you think he's courting Deedee? Miss Dawson?"

"I don't know," I said. "But maybe I should ask." After all, we were no longer in the camp. And we had what our elders would consider duties. I felt a sinking nausea at the thought.

She rolled over onto her stomach, making the mattress bounce. "I don't even know if I'd want to—to be romantic with him. When we came out here, I was hoping. But I don't want to *stay* here. I like Arkham, but what I like is being in a new place. Everything looks different. The houses are different, the food is strange, everything smells new. I was right, I want to keep doing that."

I dragged my thoughts away from my own concerns. "And you want someone who will travel with you?"

"Or at least understand why I'm going. Or maybe I don't want anyone at all. Maybe there aren't any men who would put up with me. Men want a wife like Mama . . ."

"Innsmouth men want—wanted—a woman who could keep impeccable house, but also knew her texts." A clever woman, like my own mother, who could track the myriad traditions that held a proper home together. That wasn't an option for Caleb in any case.

I leaned over, awkwardly, to hug Neko's shoulders. We didn't often discuss either of our fathers. Talking about their lives came perilously close to talking about their deaths.

"I'm so grateful that Mama Rei is who she is," I said. "But not everyone . . . can or should be of the same kind." *Not everyone's gills grow in the same,* my mother would have said.

"I can just eat hot dogs and frozen food from boxes," she suggested. "Or become a glamorous star and eat all my meals at the fanciest restaurants."

"You cook perfectly well."

"Not the point. It's not what I want to spend all my evenings on."

"Dive for fish and eat sushi every night," I suggested, and we both giggled. Having raw fish on a regular basis still felt presumptuous: at home such treats had been offered only occasionally by my elder relatives. And I loved Mama Rei's stories of her own grandmother, who dove for abalone in the deep waters off the Japanese coast.

"I'm just the opposite," I said. "I thought I would be pleased to be back in Massachusetts, and I am. It's been so long since I've seen a proper winter. But I miss San Francisco constantly." The feeling had been growing in me all day. "The store and Mama Rei and Anna and Kevin, the shape of the hills . . . It's all right to travel a little, but that's where I want to stay. Life there feels so comfortable. Safe. I suppose I'm more attached to comfort than I should be."

Neko flipped onto her back again. "Aphra, you've dealt with more discomfort than anyone I know. Well, you and Caleb, but he handles it differently. You've . . ."

"I've what?"

"You've never gone back anywhere, have you? We aren't living exactly where we were before the war, but we did go back to San Francisco, and Mama Rei does the same tailoring work she did before."

"Innsmouth wasn't there to go back to. Even though Caleb has tried." I lay back beside her. "You're right. A part of me assumes that I've left San Francisco forever."

She put a hand on my arm. "You do get to go back, you know."

"You're right. Thank you." My eyes widened to drink the moonlight, and I closed them to hold it in. I imagined the steep streets, the rocky beach, the well-organized shelves of westerns and cookbooks and dubious esoterica, all waiting for me as surely as the ocean. And in good time, I slept better than I had since getting on the plane.

The next day Dawson met us at the Miskatonic library, and let us know with a sort of demure smugness that she'd found Upton. He had originally been placed in the Arkham Sanitarium, but later moved to a more isolated asylum in the countryside where his apparent disturbance, if not exactly improved, at least exhibited a less desperate shade of distress. There he remained. On Friday, after only a week in Massachusetts, we would put aside our books in favor of a less pleasant and more personal form of research.

CHAPTER 9

Pickman Sanitarium dominated the surrounding cornfields and pastures: a gated compound of crumbling brick edifices with gabled roofs. Fallen shingles protruded from the snow like gravestones, and the smell of manure pervaded all.

We made a more imposing party than I would have liked. While Neko and Miss Dawson had chosen to stay behind, pleading a need to organize our notes from Hall, no one else could be dissuaded—even Trumbull, whom I would have preferred to leave behind for this particular expedition. But Spector's ID elicited a flurry of excited cooperation from the attendant, who led us to a solarium. He evicted two patients who'd been attempting a tryst and promised that he'd bring Upton shortly, adding with a sharp look at Spector: "A sweet old gentleman, never tried to harm anyone."

None of us took a seat. The chairs had been luxurious once, but looked like they'd been here considerably longer than Upton. Cold seeped through the plate windows; drafts crept among their frames. I ran a finger along the glass and came up with a grimy film that smelled of cigarettes. Spector came up beside me and repeated the test, frowning at the dark smear.

"Mrs. Bergman's place is nicer," I murmured. Mildred Bergman had been priestess of the congregation whose activities first caused Spector to contact me. The one who'd believed herself beloved of

Shub-Nigaroth—and believed that if she walked unafraid into the Pacific, the deity would grant her eternal life. Spector's raid on her congregation, at my behest, had forestalled her attempted apotheosis. When last I visited her, in the asylum where the state had placed her, she still hadn't forgiven me.

He wiped his finger on a handkerchief. "I did some research. A lot of these places have gone downhill in the past few years. The best ones are staffed by conscientious objectors, Quakers mostly. People who take on the work as a calling rather than the best of poor choices."

I blinked. "Thank you." I hadn't realized that he'd done anything beyond bringing Bergman to the nearest available facility; his masters certainly hadn't required it. He shrugged uncomfortably and handed me the handkerchief.

Footsteps in the hall distracted us, and the attendant's voice: "See, Danny, there are some people here to see you." And an old man's querulous response: "I keep telling you no one's come for months. They don't want *me*—"

The attendant stood at the door behind a man who must be Upton. His white hair was cropped short but poorly kept, and an age-stooped back took only a little off his height. Gray pants and shirt hung loosely on his gaunt frame.

He stared at me, small eyes wide, then tried to back away. The attendant held fast. "You! No, I promised, you said—it was you! You said it would be safer, and it wasn't, was it?" He surged forward suddenly into the room. "Don't you blame me for it! I was here, I didn't say anything! Leave me be—" The attendant grabbed his arms before he could throw himself at me.

"I'm terribly sorry, miss, he gets these fits sometimes. Been a while since the last one, but they pass. Danny, you calm now? You won't make more trouble for us, will you?"

Upton slumped in the attendant's grasp, and remained so as the man cautiously loosened his hold. "No, sir. No trouble, I promise. Probably for the best." He twisted to look over his shoulder, wincing. "Maybe you'd better leave us alone, sir. For the best."

"He's right, sir," said Spector. "I realize it's irregular, but if we could have a few minutes."

It wasn't something I'd expect in any respectable hospital, but this attendant was no conscientious objector. One of Trumbull's bland gazes was enough to decide him. He backed into the corridor, and we heard him leave, footsteps a little fast.

Upton drew himself up as well as his spine would allow, and looked first Caleb and then me in the eye. The others he ignored. When he spoke, he no longer sounded angry or afraid, only tired. "All right, then. Let's get this done with."

I held out my hands and tried to soften my voice. "Mr. Upton, we mean you no harm—"

Caleb interrupted. "That remains to be seen. What's the 'this' that you think we came to finish?"

He looked around as if he'd forgotten something. Spector found him a ratty chair. "Innsmouth." He gave a hacking laugh. "Wanted to protect your reputation. And you couldn't. I was still here, called mad for what I said. And now you're back to take revenge."

I put a hand on Caleb's arm. "Are you claiming responsibility for what happened to Innsmouth?"

This time his black laughter descended quickly into a coughing fit. When he recovered, he said, "Of course not. I was here. But why should that stop you?"

I felt Caleb's muscles soften beneath my hand. I knelt, bringing myself back to Upton's level. The others did likewise, or found more-or-less acceptable chairs—save for Trumbull, who remained silent by the window. I began to have an inkling of why she had come along, and could not decide whether I was grateful for her witness.

"Mr. Upton," I began. "We're not here for any sort of vengeance. Caleb and I were—" And here I paused, for he certainly hadn't sounded sorry about Innsmouth's destruction. "You carry a piece of our town's memory. Something that we missed, because we were children and the elders would no more than drop hints when we were around. We know what Ephraim did to Asenath, and then to your friend—but not what happened afterward."

"Ah. Just innocent children, then, are you?"

I bristled. "Not for a long time."

"Heh. Well, I shot her. Him. Avenged Edward Derby, for all the good that it did. And tried to tell what I'd seen. The authorities had no other explanation, but they sent me here anyway—better that than believe such things possible." He peered at me closely. "But they burned Ed's body. Didn't believe, but they did what I asked." Another bout of alarming laughter, but then he turned serious again. "They put me in Arkham. I couldn't bear it. She died there, he died—whoever died, they all did it there. Even with the body gone, the place was haunted. I begged my family, anywhere else or I'll go mad in truth, and finally they sent me here. And then forgot about me."

I tried not to let my flinch show. For all that it had been more kindly meant than ours, Upton's imprisonment had still stolen half his life. But he would not appreciate the comparison and I did not care to share it.

"Well, then, I had a few weeks to think about what I was going to do, how I could convince them I'd recovered from murderous insanity and get back to my wife and my work. And then *your* family came. Some of them had your look." Unnecessarily, he put his fingers around his eyes, and stretched the skin so that they appeared to bulge. "And some of them were worse."

For the first time he gave attention to the others. "Don't know if you've seen their relatives yet. Ought to get out while you can. Horrible creatures, like great walking frogs, or fish. Big mouths. Scaly. Gills." He wiggled his fingers beside his neck, and I put my hand back on Caleb's arm. "They wore cloaks to hide themselves, till they had me alone. They asked me about old Ephraim, about Asenath and Ed. I told them—why not. And they thanked me for carrying out Ephraim's just sentence. Thanked me! Then they talked with each other, some strange burbling, barking tongue, and then they said—" The manic energy faded from his speech, and when he resumed he sounded only a tired old man. "They said that it was safest to leave me here. That people were spreading terrible lies about their children—I suppose that's you—and that if people believed me, they wouldn't understand that Ephraim was a criminal, it would just be one more bloody rumor about Innsmouth.

"And then they left."

Caleb's mouth was set in a grim line. Charlie and Spector looked at us with near-identical expressions of sadness. I wished I had sent them away before hearing the story; I wished I could leave now. Trumbull had at least dropped her usual sardonic air for a more focused look, breathing slow and even as if preparing for ritual.

When no one else spoke, I took it on myself. "I'm sorry for what our elders did. It was wrong. If you'd like us to help get you out of here—"

He cut me off with another braying laugh, this time managing to swallow the cough at the end. "Don't be ridiculous. My family is glad to forget their mad murderer, and they certainly don't want to take in a dying old embarrassment. Better here than on the streets."

"Really?" said Caleb. His voice held an edge of mockery. "That's not how I felt."

That gave Upton pause, but only for a moment. "You're young, boy. You've all the time you could want to take advantage of your freedom."

"So I've come to learn. But when I came out here, I expected to die."

My hand tightened on his arm. "You said you wanted to find our books."

His laughter sounded healthier than Upton's, but just as bitter. "Of course I did. But I expected our old Arkham neighbors to shoot me on sight. What else should I have done? A grown man who can barely read and write, no trade and no family to feed with one, and the ocean dried out of my blood—what else was there for me to do?"

My breath caught. "You know that I've been studying with Charlie, relearning our old arts. Our blood *hasn't* dried. We still carry the tide in our veins—the ocean is still waiting for us." I should have told him before—it was obvious to me now. But somehow, it had never occurred to me that he didn't already know. My stomach clenched at the realization of what I'd just revealed to Upton, even Spector. But I could not regret it, for my little brother's sake.

His eyes widened and he stared at me a long moment. Then he drew away and wrapped his long arms around himself, head tucked into a small sphere of private emotion that I dared not break.

Upton looked between us. "It's true, then. Innsmouth's leaders really did make some terrible deal with demons under the water. And you actually want to turn into one of those *things*."

"No," I said, still sick at having to speak in front of him at all. "It's not true. And yes, I do. Those 'things' are my family."

Spector came closer and tilted his head at the door. "Miss Marsh, do you want to . . . ?"

It was an offer, not a hint, and I shook my head. "Go ahead and ask your questions." I hoped Spector liked his answers better than I had. I retreated and sat near my brother. Charlie leaned down from his chair to put a hand on my shoulder, and I accepted the comfort mutely.

Spector squatted and proffered his card to Upton. "I actually came here today on more immediate business. We have reason to believe someone may be attempting to replicate Ephraim Waite's crime. As one of the few witnesses who's seen a body swap, and knew it, I was hoping you might be able to share your observations—so that we can do the same if it becomes relevant." He spoke smoothly, half-truths falling easily from his lips with no hint of rehearsal.

Upton's whole frame tensed. His hands shook—I was suddenly unsure whether this was new, or whether I'd failed to notice it before. "Kill him. Shoot him as many times as it takes and burn the body. He can survive—just a scrap of flesh to cling to, that's all he needs."

"Yes, sir." Spector lit two cigarettes and handed one over. "But how do I recognize him?"

Upton took the cigarette and slumped back. "He wanted a weak mind, a weak will. But smart. Lots of room to stretch, and no way to resist him taking over. Poor Ed. He couldn't hurt a fly—not able, not willing, it wasn't in his nature. He was nervous and scholarly and so frightfully poetic you could listen for hours when he got into a state. But when she was in his body—when Ephraim was there—Ed didn't look like himself at all. Not just the determination, or the burst of will and confidence. Something dreadful and alien, looking out through my best friend's eyes. Even people who'd never known him could tell something was off. He didn't act like the person who shaped that face. Asenath always disturbed people." He looked at me with narrowed eyes. "But everyone just assumed it was because she was from Innsmouth."

He waved the cigarette at Spector. "Now, see, I look at you: you're not just a confident man, a strong one who's used to people listening to you. Your body fits, it's got muscles where you move the most and a face that's used to your expressions. Or him, he sits down like someone who's used to favoring a bad leg—but maybe the cane is new? I watch, you see, I always have to watch in case he tries to come after me. Those two, they've got Asenath's horrible eyes and the heads that don't look quite right, but they don't act like they think it's funny, the way she did. And they don't look at everyone else like they're thinking how they might taste."

And now, of course, he turned his attention to Trumbull. She was back to her usual sardonic look; individualized observations of human physiognomy were apparently not something that needed preserving for the ages. Upton looked her over, frowned more deeply, looked again. His hands shook harder, and he sucked on his cigarette to steady them. "You—you don't look right. Not like he did—but not right." He tried, I thought unconsciously, to push his chair back, but his strength wasn't sufficient. Suddenly he whipped around to the rest of us. "Her! I don't know what she is, but she isn't a woman!"

"So my colleagues at Miskatonic always tell me," Trumbull said dryly. "But I've checked, and overstudy hasn't yet made me completely masculine." Charlie and Spector colored, and even Caleb raised his head.

"I assure you she's been at Miskatonic for some time," said Spector, recovering. "And with no reports of abrupt personality shifts, I gather . . ." This last said with less certainty, but she nodded firmly. It was true that while Skinner had made nasty intimations, none suggested any loss of memory or nervous breakdown that might have cast doubt on her qualifications. I would have to ask how she had managed that.

"Anyone who knows me can confirm that I'm much as I've always been," she said. "I'm afraid your detective abilities are not all that you might have hoped."

As the rest of us failed to support Upton's near-panic, he seemed to doubt his own senses. He subsided in his chair, muttering to himself. I was grateful when Spector started to make our excuses.

As we reached the door, Upton craned his neck to follow us. "Funny you should come asking this now," he said abruptly.

"Why is that?" asked Spector.

"Well, twenty years and more with no interest. And then a year ago, those 'scholars,' and now you. Something must be happening out there." He shivered. "It makes a man glad to be inside someplace safe. I hope it's safe, anyway." He grinned suddenly, incongruously, ghoulishly. "It'll be waiting for you, too, when it gets to be too much out there. It always waits."

CHAPTER 10

We weren't able to get any useful description of Upton's previous visitors from the staff—nothing that couldn't describe any random handful of gentlemen dressed for business. Spector seemed disgruntled, and begged leave for an immediate private errand, so Charlie and my brother and I squeezed into Trumbull's car. She moved papers from the back seat to the trunk to make room for us. Caleb rebuffed my attempts to converse, not with his usual sullen anger but with a rawness that encouraged me to give him what space I could.

Charlie twisted around from his seat, and I leaned forward. "Miss Marsh—are you well?"

It took some doing to get such a direct expression of concern from him, although less than it once had. "I'm just . . ." I tried to put words to my roil of emotion, and failed. "Irked at my family."

That brought Caleb out of his silence. "They were trying to protect us."

"They could have done any number of things. Gained his promise of silence, or blackmailed him. Brought him to live in Innsmouth where they could watch over him. Instead they left him imprisoned, when he'd done nothing but the justice the law required."

"And thought it a sign of all our corruption, not just Waite's. You know as well as I that it was outsiders living in town who brought the raid down on us. Don't be absurd, sister dear." The usual wry term of endearment turned against me like a slap, and he dismissed me in favor of the countryside racing by out the window.

"I suppose we *are* all human," said Charlie. I nodded mutely, grateful for the reminder that he at least thought so.

"Sapient," said Trumbull. Charlie and I both started. "No thinking, feeling being survives by being entirely gentle. Your family is in a greater company than humanity alone."

Charlie looked at her sideways, but said nothing. It was no surprise that she'd picked up on his awareness of her nature. I found our shared imperfections more reassuring than I would say, but: "I still question their judgment."

She nodded, not arguing.

"Did you get what you were looking for, this morning?" asked Charlie.

Trumbull nodded again, eyes fixed on the road. "Oh, yes. And then some."

It occurred to me to ask her, "Are *you* all right?" In the same breath as I said it, I felt extremely foolish. Of course she wouldn't answer such a puerile question.

"Yes—although somewhat disturbed to discover that my grasp of this body is so noticeable. I must explore the connection more carefully."

"From the records," I said, "people often notice discrepancies when your people make a switch—or simply find the results inexplicably disturbing."

Trumbull snorted, unladylike. "Some of my people have no subtlety. If every one of our visits were taken note of—outside of the people we deliberately make aware, of course—then such records would be considerably more common."

I checked Caleb for signs of an oncoming diatribe, but while he glowered a little he didn't seem inclined to argue. This was a far more comfortable conversation than the previous topic, and I therefore gave in to the question that had piqued my curiosity earlier. "How did you hide the amnesia? I'm sure Dean Skinner would have said something if they'd noticed."

She chuckled, seeming equally eased by the change of topic. "None of the people here actually know Trumbull, or care to know her. Her family disapprove of her studies and take no interest. And I was fortunate enough to arrive during the summer intersession, so that no classes were interrupted and I had ample time to study her notes and her journals. There was only one servant to witness the faint, and one discreet doctor. I reassured the doctor that even I am sometimes prone to feminine weaknesses, and dismissed the servant with a generous allowance so she need not notice the inevitable changes in habit and personality that might be visible in intimate quarters."

It was a clever answer, but one particular aspect stood out for me. Ignoring his mood, I grabbed Caleb's hand, and he turned to me, startled. "Journals! I didn't think to ask for private journals, but they'll be right there in the collections. Not just the spellbooks and theology and philosophy, but records of our lives."

"Oh." He gaped, and then leaned close into my arms. So quietly I struggled to hear, he murmured, "You keep reminding me that we haven't lost everything." I felt my shoulder wet, and held my little brother tightly.

The librarian very nearly demanded that I give the full name of every person whose journal I wished to read. However, he surrendered with surprisingly little argument. Perhaps it was our eagerness—or Trumbull's, which was palpable—or that Miskatonic never inculcated its staff against our private diaries as it did against our more overt theology. He brought us an eclectic stack: pocket daybooks and easel-sized sketchpads, bound in cloth and leather and paper. Some were carefully inscribed with their authors' names; others went entirely unlabeled.

The collection was not well-sorted, and I got the impression that

Miskatonic's historians had not yet so much as organized them by common script. Charlie took on this task, looking inside covers or reading a few pages and sharing with us the names he found. Trumbull, of course, delved in without shame, which I did not this time begrudge her.

Caleb had been squinting at the same page for several minutes, marking his place with a finger and a fixed glare. "Can you read that?" I asked gently.

He turned his mute glare on me. I came round the table, abandoning my own journal to share his. "We'll look at it together, if you like." He grimaced, but moved his chair to the side.

What he held was a thin, factory-made notebook bound in cheap leather. Memory washed over me: the five-and-dime where our mother had taken us for school supplies every August, the smell of dusty tools and crisp paper and the jar of salt taffy by the register. Stacks of neat lined notebooks like this one, alongside pencils and nibs and ink and chalk, and a disordered row of used novels tucked incongruously at the end of the aisle.

The handwriting was not that of a child: it had the confidence and irregularity of someone who no longer labored over penmanship. Caleb had barely started his cursive when they forbade us the written word altogether; of course he wouldn't be able to interpret. I read to him quietly. The entries were dated from autumn of 1903, and belonged to a cook for one of the Gilman households—there have been many Patience Gilmans with fisher husbands, so it was impossible to know which one. Still, the household's rhythms made me ache with familiarity. Meals and tutoring sessions and children begging sweets, shopping at that selfsame grocer and the other markets that lay behind the dunes. Saturday evening services, where distinctions of mistress and servant fell away in the glimmering darkness.

> *Reverend Eliot spoke to me again after services last night, asking of my visions. I was fearful to confess that I've had none since before last Winter Tide. He was quick to reassure me on the matter,*

but still I fear that disappointment will attend my metamorphosis. Perhaps I am trying too hard to force the gods. When Alydea Bardsley's air-born lover ran away with their son, I prayed all night for a glimpse of the boy's whereabouts and received not so much as an allusive dream.

I must try to do as Archpriest Ngalthr bids, and focus on the duties of the land. Yet this morning while picking herbs, I was struck near as strong as vision by imagining what bolder and stranger duties might attend my life in the water. It is not right or proper, and I must put such dreams aside until it is time—if these half-fantastic abilities strengthen with my blood.

Caleb put his hand over the passage. "I know who she is! Do you remember Archpriest Ngalthr's acolyte? Who helped with the midsummer ceremony when I was five? Chulzh'th was her water name, but someone said she'd been a servant on land, and she put up with old Charis Gilman being very familiar."

I wracked my mind, but to no avail. I could recall the archpriest easily, but not the woman attending him that one year. "I don't remember. I'm sorry."

"She had almost black scales all down her back and legs, but with purple highlights like quahog shells. And a sort of spiky crest." He traced its outline in the air over his scalp.

I shook my head. "I'm sorry. I don't think I paid her much attention. But I'm glad to know who this is, anyway." And to know too that she'd changed young, before the raid. I dropped my voice. "We're going to have to talk with them, I think."

Caleb lowered his voice as well. We knew from long experience the safe range between our hearing and that of ordinary men. "So you can complain to them of Upton's treatment?"

"Possibly. But we've been talking about getting our books back, and we still don't know how. And these journals—no one at Miskatonic is even reading them. Maybe the elders will be able to help. I'm scared too, but we literally can't avoid them forever." And beyond that—though I wasn't sure how Caleb would respond to the idea now—they needed to know how dangerous the wars of the land might become. When last they'd been involved, poisonous gases and torpedoes had been the gravest threats armies could muster.

Caleb let out a breath and nodded. "We'll need someone who can drive. Trumbull, I suppose, is the best option we have. I wish there were some way to distract your . . ." He failed to find a suitable term. ". . . Mr. Spector. Or maybe we ought to introduce them." He bared his teeth.

"That sounds like a terrible idea. But it might be best to tell him outright that we're visiting our family. It's not as though he's ignorant of their presence. And we could bring Neko and Mr. Day. The elders ought to know that we've found kind people on the land as well as cruel."

"Huh. Yes, they'll want to know the Kotos. And I suppose it's best to get their approval of your students before you start a whole school. Are you going to bring your newest devotee, too?"

It was surprisingly tempting. Sharing my ancestry felt less terrifying now that I'd done so with Charlie. And unknowing, she would hold our studies back even further. But when I thought of telling the elders I'd revealed them so casually, I quailed. They might still question my knowledge of Charlie's integrity after a mere two years' intimacy. I did not care to think how they would judge someone who learned after two days. "No. It's too early."

Plans made, I was about to return to Chulzh'th's journal when I heard footsteps at the doorway. Audrey herself leaned against the frame, a little out of breath but apparently pleased. I got up to meet her, hoping—now that I'd made my decision—that I could dissuade her from inquiring too closely into our reading material.

"I'm sorry we didn't come to Hall today," I said. "Something new came up—we had another errand in the morning, and then some specific volumes we needed to look at here. We should be back there Sunday, or Monday at the latest."

"I know you've got some deeper goal here," she said. She straightened and brushed off her skirt. "Though I wish you'd tell me how I could help. I was hoping I could still join you for lessons tonight?"

I withheld a sigh: imagined hours of summoning practice, much needed before an Innsmouth visit, would have to be saved for later in the day. I toyed with the idea of refusing her—but I had promised. I wanted to be a good teacher, not the sort who put off my students until convenient times that might never come. I remembered the urgency of my own first days of study in Charlie's back room, and could not bring myself to leave her so frustrated. "Yes, I think we could do that. I can spare you an hour or two."

I glanced at Trumbull, and considered advantages to getting an early start on our studies. She still sat immersed in a diary, a small pile of those she'd read through set to one side and a larger stack waiting at the other. She turned the pages steadily, capturing each with avid eyes before flicking to the next. While she remained here, her house would feel a more relaxed place to work.

Charlie needed little persuasion. When I asked Caleb if he cared to join us, he hesitated. At last he nodded fractionally. Trumbull passed me her house key without looking up from her reading.

Neko and Dawson sat at Trumbull's dining room table, notes spread around them.

"You're back early," said Neko. She paused. More gently: "Did you find what you were looking for?"

"We learned many things," I said. "How are you doing with the notes?"

"We're learning many things." They shared a smile—Dawson's a fleeting thing, quickly hidden.

"In that case, we'll just go upstairs to study," Caleb said. His cheeks flushed. "So everyone can keep learning."

That drew a real smile from Neko. "I'm glad. Call us if you need us!"

As we went upstairs, Audrey asked him, "So they're your . . . are they both sweet on you, or have you been making up to both of them?"

Caleb blushed. "Audrey!" I said. She flinched a little, but seemed to have mostly gotten over seeing me as an unapproachable priestess. Opening the door to Trumbull's study distracted her nicely.

"Wow. This is just . . . wow." She peered closely at the diagrams on the walls and craned her neck to read titles on Trumbull's bookshelf. She leaned over the half-built machine, but sensibly pulled back before I could warn her not to touch it.

Caleb stood by the door until I pulled him inside.

"Audrey," I asked, "do you want to help me draw the diagram for the Inner Sea?" I'd told her what to expect during our previous session, but had given her little preparatory reading. I knew I was rushing her. When we finished in Arkham—however that happened—she might be able to gain access to Miskatonic's stacks, but would no longer have teachers with practical experience.

And if I sated her desire for wonders swiftly, I could send her downstairs with one of the easier books so that Charlie and Caleb and I could practice more advanced and urgent arts.

I drew out the lines slowly and carefully, explaining their logic as best I could. Caleb knelt across from us. When I offered him the chalk, he drew one tentative sigil from memory before handing it back. My face heated, and I corrected his effort with as little fuss as I could manage. Audrey surprised me with a couple of accurate guesses and a fine hand—she had apparently picked up something amid the dross of her friends' studies.

"This is the simplest of spells, and foundation to all others. Magic seeks to better understand, and eventually to build on, the connection between minds and bodies. Even to calm a storm, you treat the wind and rain as if they were alive and corporeal. That is why blood is part of the spell, along with words and symbols."

"So that we may better know that even the cosmos, vast and seemingly eternal, is in truth a mortal form," said Caleb. "I remember that."

"Yes," I said. "All things fade and die. Magic makes their momentary glory tangible—but it also makes it impossible to hide how small and temporary they are. How temporary *we* are." I would not insult Caleb by asking—mortality was one lesson he had well learned—but I asked Audrey: "Do you still wish to go on?"

"Of course I do."

"All right, then. Today we'll look more closely at our own bodies. You'll only be able to see briefly, at first—when you come back to ordinary awareness, just wait for the rest of us. Don't try to touch anyone else." I'd forgotten that last instruction when I first tried this with Charlie, and remembered belatedly the effect of physical contact. He'd been too pleased with his first taste of magic to properly interpret the difference between my blood and his, but I didn't want to take the chance with Audrey.

For this ritual, I did play at priestess—and Charlie at priest, for we were the only two who knew the necessary chant by heart. I washed the blade, pricked fingers, and we each let our blood into the bowl. My confidence grew with the rhythm of my words. Even as I settled on my heels to let the spell take hold, I found my awareness stretched as it had never been with Charlie alone.

There was my own blood: my river, swift and sure and wild. But beyond that—even without physical contact—Charlie's familiar trickle and the aching love I felt whenever I touched it. I knew its courses, and knew too how to read the unwelcome signs they carried of my friend's mortality.

But then there were other waters. Caleb's torrent ran twin to mine, so similar that it took a moment even to see it. I wanted to dive in, to revel in the truth of another like myself. It was ridiculous, for I'd been beside him a week now, but I did not fight the absurdity.

Audrey, by contrast, showed what Charlie must have been only scant years ago. Her stream ran slow and silty and rich, muddy banks not yet sliding in to choke it. The loamy, fertile scent of swamp water rose in my mind.

I could feel the others reaching as well, more tentative but eager. In the throes of the ritual I saw no reason to resist their pull. We explored the tangle of rivers, of roots and channels shaped by the lives we had lived.

Time passed, and at last the connection began to slip. I let go easily, certain that we could find it again when we wished.

And came back to the study with a gasp of indrawn air. The others looked at me, and at each other, with wide eyes.

"I recall now," I said, a little unsteadily, "that a group of people who practice together is called a confluence. Are you sure you wouldn't rather find a teacher who remembers that type of thing *before* it comes up?"

"Not a chance," breathed Audrey.

We stood—except for Charlie—stretched, moved our newly familiar bodies. I found myself hyperaware of the others, coordinated as if in some well-practiced dance. Caleb touched my elbow, and his eyes were bright.

"You're different, the two of you," said Audrey.

I froze, caught between imperatives. I had warned her against touching us precisely to avoid this, and Charlie had seen my blood for months with no such recognition. I found myself impressed anew by Audrey's perceptiveness. Newfound intimacy, and the desire to nurture her clever instincts rather than quash them, argued against the entirely logical decision I'd come to earlier.

"We're family," I said at last.

Her eyes narrowed, but her voice was mild. "What kind?" Before I could answer, she added, "I *have* heard the other rumors about Innsmouth."

Caleb bristled, and the newfound comfort drained from his stance. "You shouldn't believe everything you hear."

Charlie leaned forward. "I think we've just done something precious. And terrifying. And I don't think it's something we can undo."

So he thought I should tell her, too. I took a breath, dry with winter air and tinged with the salt of our mingled sweat. "What have you heard?"

"Oh, you know. Dark rituals—I always assumed that someone rubbed dead tarantula on themselves and talked it up at the college." She rubbed her pricked finger against her palm. "But that Innsmouth was destroyed because the people there made deals with some sort of water demon, and had children who were half demon. Or half mermaid, or half fish. People are more interested in not-talking about the details of demonic marriages than in the details of the kids. But your blood felt—I'm not accusing you of anything! Even if you did marry demons, they're probably more worthwhile than most human boys. It's just that your blood doesn't feel like mine at all. It feels like running toward the ocean as fast as I can go."

I shared a glance with Caleb, but knew already that the conversational undertow had us. "No demons. And no dark deals—our people have always been like this. We're human, just a different kind than you. The people of the water don't age as the people of the air do. We change, as we get older, to live out our lives deep in the ocean. That's what you felt." I shook my head. "I'm doing this all backward. There are things you should hear." I motioned her to sit.

I recited the Litany, sketched for her the vastness of the cosmos and the abundance of lives and minds that strove to survive it. And knew all the while that I had bound myself to something unknown. In my ignorance, I had made Charlie and my brother—perhaps my whole family—vulnerable to any least failure of understanding or empathy or discretion on the part of a near stranger.

Now I must make her vulnerable in turn.

"I told you that we do not age," I said. "But twenty years ago, when the state raided Innsmouth, they found every other way we could be harmed. Caleb and I are the only ones left that I know of—on land."

"But your family . . . ?"

"We're in Arkham for two reasons: to try to get Innsmouth's books back, and to let our elders know we're alive. Will you help?"

She took my hand. "This is what I've been looking for since I came to Hall. Of course I'll help." She paused. "Um. I hate to ask, but your friends downstairs. Do—I mean, I suppose all humans must look alike to you."

Caleb snorted. "You don't have a problem with fish-faces because we're exciting and magical, but you've got a problem with Japs and—"

I put up a hand. "Caleb, names have meaning even if you're mocking them—please don't use false ones. And Miss Winslow, you bear that in mind as well. We were in that camp for decades, and most of our people dead, when the government decided it would be a convenient place to stash some of their new batch of prisoners. If the Kotos hadn't come when they did, if the government hadn't been vague in their order to close the camps, we'd be there still—or dead ourselves. They're family, and we owe them our lives. And Dawson's the one who got us library access, so I don't care to hear whatever you were thinking about her either."

She shrank back, releasing my hand. "I'm sorry. I was just curious, that's all. They're not studying with us, though?"

"Neko's never been interested. And Miss Dawson hasn't asked. If she asked—I would teach her. If that bothers you . . ." Then, I supposed, I would have to learn some way to cut the connection that I'd made with Audrey. I'd heard of such things, but nothing to indicate that they were easy or pleasant.

She wound her fingers together, then placed them firmly in her lap. "You may not claim any title, but as far as I'm concerned you're in charge. You say who joins us and who stays away."

Caleb looked doubtful but didn't argue. Charlie nodded firmly. I bowed my head, accepting the weight.

"So—now what?" asked Audrey.

"Now—" I checked the window and found the night grown dark. "If we want to speak with our elders, we need to learn how to call them. You won't be able to help much, but if you want to stick around?" She nodded eagerly. "Mr. Day, if you could tell them what we talked about the other night, about how summoning works, I need to get my notes."

I tarried in the doorway long enough to hear that he remembered our discussion well, then went downstairs. Neko and Dawson were frying eggs with the minimal supplies in Trumbull's kitchen.

"Margarine and salt," Neko told me in disgust. "No spices at all. Do you want some?"

"Not just yet. But if you feel a sudden urge to go upstairs—don't."

Dawson flipped one of the eggs and looked at me over her shoulder. "We'll leave you your privacy, don't worry."

"Not like that. You should *expect* a sudden urge to go upstairs. There's no need to follow it. There's no particular need to not follow it, either, it's just not a requirement even if it feels like one."

Dawson shook her head and slid the egg onto a plate. "Dinner, that's what I'm doing."

I found my notes from *On the Calling of Kinds,* and returned upstairs. Caleb stood to meet me.

"Aphra, I know it's going to be easier for them to summon us, regardless, but I'd feel more comfortable if we learned to summon them first."

I considered. It was true that the spell to summon men of the air was practically useless, but it was the foundation for summoning individuals, so not a complete waste. And he was right—I was not ultimately willing to offer this vulnerability without demanding it as well. "All right."

I wiped the previous diagram and started again. The new one required a central sigil—though a small one—drawn in blood, for which I nicked another finger. I hesitated before pressing it to the slate, but Trumbull wouldn't need my blood to take advantage even if she cared to do so. Caleb apparently came to the same conclusion, and added his own to the spiraling sign.

"Blood of the kind being summoned is also helpful—if they have blood—but not necessary," I told them. "The same for individuals. We'll do without tonight, since we want a relatively weak summoning. We're not calling anything that would be inclined to do us harm, or to leave as soon as it arrived. This version will let everything of the right

kind in range"—and I had shortened that range as much as I could—
"know that we're interested, and then settle at random on one to call.
There, that's done."

I went over the chant with everyone, but raised my voice alone. I
felt silly, sending out a summons for people in the same room. But absurdity, like awe and fear, is a layer of meaning we impose, one of an
infinite number of possible ways to interpret the world. I let it fall
away. What I felt in its place was not so intimate as our earlier meditation, but still a reaching: a growing awareness that the thing I sought
existed, was near, was even now being drawn to me. The pattern came
more easily than I expected: even in their silence, the others now added
strength and direction to the working.

The call swirled through the house and settled, as promised, close
by. Charlie stood abruptly, and I reached automatically to steady him.
He stepped into the diagram, and set his cane abruptly to catch his
balance. I was about to apologize, to help him back to his chair, but
paused at the expression of distracted joy on his face.

"Mr. Day?"

He twitched, and his eyes flew wide. "Miss Marsh! I'm sorry—this
is odd." He looked uncertainly back at his seat. "Ought I . . . ?"

"It's probably best for your knee," I said with some reluctance.
"What's it like?"

He made no move to sit. "Like . . . someone who loves me calling
my name, someone I didn't expect to see at all. You want to go to them.
And my damned leg hurts. Excuse me, miss." This to Audrey, who
didn't look offended. I swiped a break in the blood sigil holding the
diagram together. He slumped and turned his head, as if seeking the
person who had called, then surrendered to the chair.

I redrew the diagram, this time with Charlie's blood to line the sigil
for my own folk. He tried the chant, halting at first but steadier as he
went on.

I felt the words immediately, but it was a moment before their pull
became as Charlie had described: the wondrous certainty that some-

one was looking for me, and that I very much wanted to find them. The words promised love, promised reunion—and more than that. I felt my identity, my sense of self, fundamental to the structure of the world: as real and whole and vital as a star. I realized that I stood in the little triangle I'd drawn for myself moments before, and wanted only to stay there, immersed in what I still dimly knew for a comforting illusion.

Charlie finished the chant, but the effect remained. "Miss Marsh— are you well?"

"Mmm. Yes. I ought . . ."

The door opened, and I felt a faint embarrassment as Trumbull looked us over. "Ah. I thought I felt something like that when I came in."

Audrey leapt to her feet. "I'm sorry, Professor! We were just—"

"Practicing an elementary summons, yes, I know what it looks like. Reverend Orne's version, I believe, from *On the Calling of Kinds.*" She knelt to examine the diagram. "Planning to contact your family, I suppose?"

"Yes," said Caleb, his voice rough with irritation.

My knees buckled as she wiped away the sigil. I managed to catch myself before stumbling against anyone, and blinked away the fog of the ritual. I swallowed against the feeling of unreasoning loss.

"A perfectly effective method," she continued, "but the side effects can be irksome to those who wish only to have a conversation. A strong mind can resist, of course, but this version is more polite." She sketched a slight change in the arc of chalk. "With the angle adjusted, it calls but does not flatter. Orne was always over-nervous of first impressions."

"Thank you." I knelt to examine the changes more closely, and to cover my still shaky balance. "We haven't spoken with our elders in some time, and certainly don't wish to offend them."

"Yes. You ought to practice your own resistance, however; it's not good to be susceptible to the blandishments of so common a spell." She stood, brushing chalk dust from her skirt. "I would speak to them as well."

It took me a moment to follow. "Good. We need a ride to Innsmouth."

"Tomorrow? Classes begin on Monday, and I expect Sunday to be extremely tedious."

I traced the revised lines of the diagram. "I wanted longer to practice"—and perhaps to prepare myself—"but we do have it working. Tomorrow, yes. Thank you."

~~~

Charlie and I walked Audrey to the bus stop. Caleb begged off, and by the time the other two had their coats on he and Dawson were engaged in some sort of verbal sparring, or perhaps a grammar lesson, in mixed R'lyehn and Russian. I glanced back at them, considering.

The winter clouds colored pink behind the trees. The air was still pleasantly brisk by my standards, and Charlie and Audrey walked with their chins up rather than tucked into scarves. We went slowly for Charlie's sake, in silence that I didn't yet feel ready to fill.

A group of young men marched past, wearing papier-mâché masks with distorted animal faces: snarling cats and long-nosed dog-things and a toothy crocodile painted in garish blue and gold. They sang something loud and boisterous, in which I made out "days of olden kings" and "draughts of strength" and "Miskatonic will go on." They blew kisses to Audrey, who laughed and curtseyed.

"It's Museum Night," she explained after they passed. "First Friday before classes start, the university museum stays open till midnight, and the boys who stuck around for break dress up and do sort of a scavenger hunt to find specific stuff in the collection."

I stopped in the middle of the walk. After a moment, I said, "There's something I ought to look at in the museum. But maybe another time would be better."

Audrey shrugged. "I wouldn't mind. They put cookies out, and you're less likely than most days to get funny looks or questions about how long your kid's been at Miskatonic, because people bring dates.

Leroy took me last semester, but I think he's doing something else tonight."

The museum was more self-consciously a temple than the church itself, though strangely sterile. The classical columns and marble floors had never been intended for worship—only to let visitors imagine that they trod someone else's sacred space, long since given over for their edification. Portraits lined the entry hall: men who'd played some role in the college's history, or purchased this memory with a substantial donation. Well-lit cases in the center showed off artifacts gathered on university-sponsored expeditions. As promised, incongruous plates of cookies lay on a folding table.

The boys we'd seen earlier clustered around the food, masks pushed back, and argued over a sheet of paper. Another set, this one including a pair of girls, came in from some more distant part of the building and went directly to one of the display cases, where they pushed and laughed as they read the labels. Whatever they were looking for, they clearly found it, for they exclaimed happily in a ragged chorus and ran out through another archway.

Audrey grabbed a handful of cookies and offered us each one. I took it, though I wasn't feeling hungry, and nibbled a mouthful of oats and sweet raisins.

"You know this place," I told her. "Do you know where they keep local artifacts?"

She laughed. "I'm afraid the place doesn't have quite that much organization. It's all set up with objects they thought would be interesting together. If you tell me what you're looking for, though, I might have seen it."

I hesitated. I'd never seen the thing, only heard about it. "It's a gold necklace. Large, probably carved with bas-reliefs. It was all they had of ours that they had before the raid."

She looked me over, perhaps trying to imagine what sort of jewelry would go with my appearance. "That sounds familiar. Let's see if I know what I'm talking about."

She led us back into the exhibit rooms, and I saw immediately what she meant about organization. The place was a jumbled cabinet of wonders, with detailed landscapes of the Miskatonic sharing walls with murky and disturbing abstractions, all hanging above vases and rings and statues and arrowheads: calculated to intrigue the eye, and to prove that generations of Miskatonic explorers and artists and curators had claimed the world for their own.

Eventually we came to a room that did have a theme: treasure. In the artificial dusk, spotlights focused on gold and silver, sapphire and emerald and polished lapis.

Charlie looked around with the critical eye of a collector who collects something else. "Do they keep a flock of ravens on staff?" he asked. But I'd already seen what I was looking for.

At the back of the narrow room, on a pedestal and covered by glass, lay a circlet of gold plates, each as wide as my hand. Light gleamed from the sculpted surfaces as I approached. My hand rose of its own accord to hover near the case, though I didn't dare touch.

Charlie leaned over my shoulder. "Oh! There are thirteen of them— it's the Litany, isn't it?"

"Yes. One for each species." Each panel was carefully wrought: the shoggoth seemed to writhe in the midst of changing form, and the ck'chk'ck's chitin verged on iridescence. In the center, a half-changed human lay amid perfectly textured waves, new gills flaring as the water washed over her. "This is a masterwork. No wonder they tried for so long to get it back."

Audrey read the label: "Donated by Malcolm Clark. Necklace: Innsmouth Massachusetts, 17th century."

I snorted. "A lot older than that. And he *sold* it, after an Eliot girl stole it and ran off with him in the mid-1800s. She came back, but we never managed to retrieve the necklace."

Audrey laughed. "Guess that sort of thing happens everywhere. But it's gorgeous. Is this yours too?"

I followed her gaze. "Yes. It must be." The statue of Hydra was carved from onyx, and doubtless here for that and the inset ruby eyes rather than its relation to the necklace. Tentacles spread mane-like around the goddess's face and swept back along Her sides. I wanted to see the statue's presence as a promise for tomorrow's expedition, perhaps pray for guidance, but could not. In the library I felt that the books were still ours, even stolen. The museum sucked meaning from things that ought to be sacred, or bound it too tightly to sense. Looking at the image, I saw nothing but stone. Charlie moved to stand next to me, silent comfort.

I heard voices before I saw them: three boys wearing foil-covered masks with long beaks, and feathers dangling from their hair. They looked like metallic crows, perhaps the sort to gather a collection like the one before us. One of them spotted Audrey.

"Hey, sweetheart! Someone leave you here?" He waved the list of clues in what I realized was his only hand. He looked older than the usual run of college students, though it didn't show in his demeanor. *GI bill.* "Have you seen a 'blood-soaked rose'?"

"I'm fine, thanks." She pointed at a case with a garnet pin carved in the shape of a flower. "That's probably what you want."

"Thanks, sweetheart!" He caught sight of me and frowned. "Hey, come over here."

I didn't enjoy such orders at the best of times; I gave him my best withering look. "I beg your pardon."

He strode over, and I braced myself rather than back up against the statue's case.

"That's a fishface for sure! I haven't seen one of you since I was a kid. I heard rumors you were around again, but I figured someone was pulling my leg. I thought they put you all away for bootlegging!"

Charlie looked like he was ready to deck the guy. I put a quelling hand on his arm and repeated, "I beg your pardon."

He glanced at Charlie and backed up. "I didn't mean any harm. Just funny to see a fishface lady visiting her things, is all. That really your tentacle god there? They always said Innsmouth folk kept some pretty creepy stuff in their churches, but that takes the cake!"

The other two were watching now, looking nervous, and one of them said, "John, don't bother the lady. Either back off or take it outside with her boyfriend." Charlie tensed under my hand.

Audrey stepped forward, drawing their attention. "Why don't you boys leave now? You're not going to look smarter if you stick around."

John glanced at Charlie's cane, and our would-be defender grabbed his arm and chivvied him into the next room. The third guy gave us an apologetic shrug, bent over the rose brooch, and scribbled a quick note in his pad.

"Um," he said. "Sorry about John—he gets kind of excited but he doesn't mean any harm. Are you really from Innsmouth?"

I was getting extremely tired of this. "Clearly not, since they killed us all for bootlegging back in '28."

He blanched, but said, "I'm sorry. It's just, I'm doing my thesis on local history, and Innsmouth is this huge hole—no one really knows what happened there."

"Of course they do. They've been telling me about it all week. Ask anyone."

It was Charlie's turn to put a hand on my arm. The history student started to say something, then shook his head, muttered an apology, and left.

"Would it be so bad to tell people?" asked Audrey. "About what happened, I mean, not the other stuff. It might shut them up."

"I don't like the company he keeps," I said. And didn't like what he'd suggested about rumors. Skinner must still be talking about us, trying to learn the reason for our presence—and reawakening old stories in the process. "Besides, people have studied us more than enough."

As we left, I glanced back at the statue, and wanted very badly to go home.

CHAPTER 11

On Saturday morning Spector seemed distracted, more so when I mentioned the disturbing conversation at the museum, and acquiesced easily to our suggested plan. I supposed visiting Innsmouth followed logically from what he'd witnessed. He pled errands of his own, freeing me of the need to discourage him from joining us. Neko was pleased to come along: magic might only interest her in as much as it mattered to me and Caleb, but family was another matter. Audrey, when she arrived, looked as nervous as I felt, and I couldn't blame her.

The old Innsmouth road had grown jagged and pockmarked. And yet, as we drew closer, we found crews repairing holes and sealing all with blacktop. The scent of tar mixed with the tang of salt. Gulls circled and occasionally swooped to retrieve the workmen's abandoned crumbs, announcing our approach with harsh cries.

At last we entered the town. The old ring of dilapidated houses, long used to discourage tourists, had fallen into even greater decay. A few had been cleared entirely to make way for foreboding new foundations. Where once the true town stood within that ancient protective ring, now were broken windows and sagging porches, slumped chimneys and walls fallen away to reveal crumbled remnants of kitchens, libraries, nurseries. I knew every street. I hesitated, but did not direct Trumbull down the turns to what had once been our house. And of course, she did not ask.

Though I did not seek mementos, sometimes a glimpse of half-rotted fence or vacant lot, or the screaming of the gulls, would call a trivial childhood moment into vivid awareness.

At last we came to the row of waterfront markets, stalls now collapsed into piles of salt-eaten clapboard. Trumbull parked, and we clambered over the dunes. Patches of snow clung to the sand. Wind rattled the stalks of dry beach grass, the sound so improbably loud that I could imagine not only the town, but the ocean beyond, become lifeless in our absence. Audrey, Charlie, and Neko pulled their coats tight and tugged their hats low around their ears.

I had forgotten how much San Francisco's rocky beach, embraced into the larger landscape by mountains and the shining reach of the new bridge, differed from this. The dunes hid all the land beyond, making a world of ocean edged only with a ribbon of damp sand. I slipped off my shoes and stockings, let my feet recall the feel of the sand, how it shaped itself around my skin and slumped in after, leaving shallow outlines to await the tide. Near the horizon, the thin black line of Union Reef lay bare and uninhabited. Behind it and far below, I knew, the outpost town of Y'ha-nthlei marked the true boundary between the civilizations of land and sea.

"You don't actually get cold, do you?" asked Charlie. He leaned heavily on his cane.

I spread my arms to the ocean. "What do you think?"

The waves slid onto the waterline and retreated, but I could see that the tide was rising. Beside me, Caleb shed shoes and jacket and ran down to the water.

Audrey rubbed gloved hands together and ducked her chin against the wind. "Is that necessary? For the ritual, I mean?"

"I imagine that for people of the air, it would largely result in frostbite. I don't recommend it."

Trumbull wore coat and hat, but acted less affected by the cold than the others. She gazed out over the water, holding herself very still. It occurred to me that for all she affected indifference, the ocean was one of the few things to survive all her tenure on this world. It must mean something to her, to see whole remembered continents shaped into unrecognizable new forms.

I, too, would see such change. I tried to imagine not only Innsmouth gone, but the dunes and beach eroded into a wider ocean, or crushed up into new mountains. I could not, and yet in the deep cities of the Atlantic architects already planned how they would adapt to aeons of seismic metamorphosis.

I found a fragment of driftwood, and with it began to draw the summoning signs. I made certain to include Trumbull's alterations. The world still felt deserted save for the six of us, a response to our summons as unimaginable as the drift of continents. At last I called the others to join me. Trumbull checked my work, Audrey and Charlie asked after the details, and all added their own blood to the central sigil. Caleb and I were most careful; we did not know the variant signs that would focus the summons on our elders, and the spell must recognize us as callers rather than targets lest we waste our efforts entirely. I recalled rituals where the blood of dozens blackened the sand, but today the ground soaked up our scant sacrifice without darkening.

As we began our chant, the rhythm of the waves and the steady roar of wind forced us to raise our voices, and still drowned them out more often than not. Air and ocean sang another chorus, descant to our human tongues.

The last of the chant died away, leaving only that descant. "Now we wait," I said.

Minutes passed, shading toward a full hour. My impatience grew, alongside a fear not yet fully acknowledged. Caleb and Neko wandered down to the water and began flicking tide-smoothed pebbles into the waves. Audrey fidgeted, closed her eyes and tried to breathe evenly, fidgeted more, took out a cigarette. I stood and checked the progress of the ocean's advance, worried whether we had placed the spell high enough.

At the tideline, tiny holes washed shut as the waves covered them, appeared again as they were exposed to the air. My father had said they were burrows for some manner of mollusk; I crouched to watch them, trying to reclaim my youthful fascination. Eventually I wandered back to the ritual site, trailed by Neko and Caleb.

"Maybe," said Audrey hesitantly, "it's not working?"

"You are remarkably impatient creatures," said Trumbull. "Do you think they've been sitting out on the reef for twenty years, ears cocked to respond instantly to your first call?"

"No," said Caleb. "But they might have given up on us by now. If they've all returned to R'lyeh to await the death of the sun, they're well beyond our reach."

"Impatient," Trumbull repeated. "And with no sense of how time scales. Your elders may be young, but after even a few millennia, twenty years is nothing. Certainly not long enough to give up on their remaining spawn." Her voice turned steely. "Wait."

Caleb's gaze hardened. "I apologize, Great One." He hunched his shoulders to look up at her, mimicking a child's fawning cadence. "Please, Great One, will you tell us a story to help pass the time?"

I winced, and braced myself for either scathing reply or equally scathing dismissal. Instead she leaned back and stretched, digging fingers into cold sand. "*That* is a tradition of proper age and sense. Although if you prefer mockery, I need not."

Caleb affected nonchalance. "Go ahead, by all means."

"Hold on a moment," said Audrey. She glanced between Caleb and Trumbull. "I'm missing something—what's *she*? If she's not one of you?" Neko, who would never have asked, stilled to hear the answer.

Trumbull looked at me, amused. "Haven't you told her?"

"You didn't say I could."

"I admire your discretion. You didn't seem the sort to keep things from your students. After all, she is here."

I sighed. "Audrey figured out my nature on her own. Or came close enough that it made more sense to tell her than to let her speculate."

"In two days? Impressive." Trumbull turned dark eyes on Audrey, who met her gaze defiantly. They locked stares, and then Trumbull's eyes widened in shock. Only a moment before they returned to their usual bland amusement, but it was enough.

I pushed between them. "Professor, I'll thank you to leave my student's mind alone."

"Calm yourself. I am perfectly content with this body; I was merely testing. Your student has a strong will. I would have had to work much harder to hold her."

Audrey's breath had quickened, but she managed to match Trumbull's own sangfroid. "That tells me what you can do—and it's impressive—but it doesn't tell me what you are except for three inches taller than me and in need of better glasses."

Trumbull smiled, an incongruous expression. "I am an archivist. I record and remember the history and knowledge that would otherwise be lost."

"And not human. Not even like them." She jerked her elbow at me and Caleb.

"Most of those who live and die on Earth are not human. Best accustom yourself."

I forced tension from my shoulders. "Needless to say, this requires discretion as well."

"I'm not Jesse," said Audrey. She leaned back on her elbows, letting the wet sand cling to her sleeves. "I want to *do* magic, not boast about it. And I want to hear that story."

Trumbull nodded, and I relaxed further. This, at least, we had survived. And Audrey's reaction made me feel again that I'd chosen well.

Trumbull wove her fingers together and apart again, a not-quite-human mannerism that brought to mind the tentacles and lobster-like pincers of the Yith's best-known form, the legendary "cone-shaped being." Yet that, too, was a stolen body. I wondered in what ancient form she first heard this story, what she recalled as she translated the words for a human tongue.

"It is written in the Archives," she said, "that the human species in its infancy came perilously close to extinction. An incursion from beyond the solar system—its nature doesn't matter, for it did not find these worlds congenial and passed on swiftly—left plague in its wake, and the young species reduced to only a few chance survivors.

"Less than a thousand all told, they gathered near the mouth of a great river. There they huddled, pooling their resources and trying to protect themselves from the mindless but deadly forces that the invaders had left in their trail. Of course, being young and inexperienced they could not agree on what form that protection ought to take. Over weeks of argument, three factions arose."

The wind blew a fine cold spray off the ocean. I blinked salt across my eyes and imagined the African warmth of that river delta, and humans so rare that they must put aside all disagreement beyond the immediate crisis.

"This is, necessarily, an oversimplification. There were more than three opinions—probably there were a thousand. But it is true that three of the most powerful priestesses put forth plans, and that most of the survivors eventually aligned behind one of these leaders."

Audrey leaned forward. "Just priestesses? No priests?"

The look Trumbull gave her seemed almost fond. "Of course there were priests. But in those days humans had not yet learned how to magnify the power of a single drop of blood. Even the simplest magic required males to bleed themselves to weakness, or take blood from a wounded enemy or a successful hunt—and as humans hunt and fight in packs, often the blood would dry while those who laid claim to it squabbled. A female, however, could build much power from her monthly courses. And while she could do no working when pregnant, many spent the full period of gestation preparing a single powerful spell to draw on the blood and pain that attend childbirth. Most would simply use that power to protect themselves and their offspring—but those who sacrificed that safety for some greater goal were much admired."

I caught quirks of movement, amid her twining fingers, that might have been language with different limbs. "As it happened, these three priestesses each carried offspring near to term.

"One priestess, a traditionalist—in so far as such a young species can be said to have traditions—called on humanity's old allies of wind and fire. This was a good choice and an easy one. Fire has been tool and traitor for every earthly intelligence. Air, too, is a familiar force: one that grows from life and feeds it in turn.

"The second priestess called on the solidity of stone, the shelter of caves, knowledge that forms like jewels deep in the earth. It was a dangerous choice, but it served her followers well for a few millennia.

"The third priestess thought on the gods who are said to sleep in the deep ocean, the strange forms and ageless predators that thrive there, and she called on the protection of the sea. This was a good choice but a hard one, for while humans already lived on land, breathing air and huddled around fire pits, the sea did not know them and they did not know the sea. To accept its protection—" She paused and cocked her head.

I turned to follow her gaze, and saw the waves break in a surge of iridescent shadow. A rush of scale and crest and talon, and a dozen tall, well-muscled elders bared needle teeth at our little group. They brandished tridents and wands and naked hands ready to ward or attack. Dark eyes looked coldly down.

CHAPTER 12

Charlie scrambled back in a panic, stopping only when he realized that the elders pressed close behind as well. Neko shrank against me. Only Trumbull and Audrey, along with Caleb, kept still—though Audrey's stillness felt a brittle thing.

It had been a long time. "Grandfather?" I asked.

The tallest of the elders, a broad man with green scales shading into purple along his arms, bent and flared his nostrils. Neko squeaked. "Aphra Yukhl Marsh," he said. His tone pitted delight against anger. He continued in R'lyehn: "And Caleb Nghadri. Are these mortals your captors? Say the word and we will rend them."

"No!" I put my arm around Neko, doing my best to make my affection apparent. I switched to English. "Grandfather, these are friends and allies. Allow me to introduce my students: Charlie Day and Audrey Winslow. My sister-in-adversity Nancy Koto, called Neko. And"— I paused as I sought and translated the appropriate R'lyehn title, which I'd never before had cause to use—"a member of the Great Race of Yith who prefers at this time to be called Professor Trumbull."

Obed Yringl'phtagn Marsh looked them over slowly, then nodded. The others lowered their weapons. Two trident-bearers whirled on their heels and dove back into the waves. I could no longer resist, but disentangled myself from Neko and leapt up to throw myself against him. He wrapped his arms around me and I buried myself against the smooth scales of his chest. Their complex patterns—barely perceptible beneath my fingertips—the strength of his embrace, the scent of salt and algae and oil, all enveloped me, familiar and welcome.

He sniffed my hair. In our own tongue: "You've been sick, but your blood is healthy now. Where have you been, child? Where are the others?"

I shook my head against him. "Dead." R'lyehn was not a language for circumlocution. "Unless you found survivors after the raid."

"No—we only found signs of battle, and soldiers left to guard Innsmouth's skeleton. They shot at us, and we killed as many as we could. We tracked them far inland, but lost the trail."

"They took us a long way away, into the desert, and kept us there for a long time. Most died, of illness or dehydration or not being able to go into the water when they changed." I told him how Neko's people had come at last to the camp, when it was only the two of us and one old man in the throes of metamorphosis—how they had kept Caleb and me sane, kept us working to survive. How we had gained our freedom at last, alongside the survivors from our newfound family. Out of the corner of my eye, I saw the other elders passing Caleb among them, taking in his scent and touching him to be sure of his existence.

He pulled one of them over, speaking as he did so. "Look, it's Acolyte Chulzh'th." To her: "We found your journals at Miskatonic—we need to get them back."

At her heels came another: slender for an elder, and midnight blue save for a hint of green around the eyes. The webs between his fingers were pierced with emeralds, and he wore an ornately wrought gold necklet.

I pulled away from my grandfather to go properly to one knee. "Archpriest."

He put his hand on my forehead, the backs of the piercings tiny droplets of ice against his cool skin. I closed my eyes as he prayed. His hand fell away at last and I looked up.

"Aphra Yukhl," he said. "Have you truly taken dry men as apprentices to learn our ways? What have they done to earn this thing?"

I tried not to bristle; it was a fair question. "Shared their own knowledge, and in Mr. Day's case books that allowed me to continue my own studies. And done their part to help me preserve wisdom and stories that would otherwise be lost to the land."

"They're afraid."

"You came rushing up with tridents drawn—you wanted them so."

"True. We did not know who added your blood to a summoning diagram, but we could only assume that they meant to lure us." He clicked his tongue. "Bring me your students, and your battle-sister."

I gathered them and they came, hesitantly.

"This is Archpriest Ngalthr. One kneels." I demonstrated, then added belatedly, "I apologize. Mr. Day has a bad knee."

"Fragile creatures," he said in English. "You may sit more carefully, then; we are all mortal."

He touched our foreheads one at a time, tracing a sigil on each. Neko had calmed since her initial fright, but I could still smell Charlie's hidden fear. Audrey, by contrast, looked almost drunk on the sight of the archpriest. She tilted her head to take him in, and the tip of his claw drew a pinprick of blood. He lifted it to his lips and licked it clean.

He spoke to Neko first: "You have seen our children through many trials. You understand their nature, and it does not frighten you."

"No, Ngalthr-sama." She stumbled over his water name but otherwise spoke clearly. "She and Caleb helped us in the camp, as we helped them. She's a good sister and daughter to us, and we knew she had other family. It won't stop us from taking care of each other."

"And you," he said to Charlie. "You fear us still."

He shrugged—bravado, I thought, not indifference. "You're frightening. And you were scared too, or you wouldn't have come charging up full force."

The archpriest looked at him a long moment, nostrils flared, then gestured to Audrey. "Were you afraid, child?"

"No," she said. "You're strange and beautiful, and I've never seen anything like you before."

"Charlie," he told me, "has sense. Even if he is insolent."

Chulzh'th, who had been standing quietly to the side, spoke up. "Aphra Yukhl would hardly be the only teacher here to prefer students who speak their minds."

Ignoring this, he continued. "The other one will become lost in some outer realm, if she does not learn fear."

Before I could craft a response, he turned to Caleb. "Now you will tell me of your work at Miskatonic. Come," and he drew him away.

Charlie pulled himself awkwardly to his feet. "Is he always so polite? And long-winded?"

I laughed shakily. "One doesn't look for either of those things from someone of his age and rank. Wisdom, however abrupt, and judgment, however nerve-wracking, are the realm of an archpriest."

"He didn't pass any of his instant judgments on you."

"I brought him my students," I pointed out. "Everything he said was aimed at me as well as you." More at me, in fact. Upton had reminded me, uncomfortably, that the elders thought of outsiders in terms of their value to *us*. To judge my air-born protégés was to judge how I'd used my freedom. At least the archpriest approved provisionally, even of Audrey—else he would have said more.

Audrey interrupted my rumination. "How old is he?"

"I haven't asked. But I know that he came to the Massachusetts Bay Colony under the boat, not on it."

Several of the other elders clustered around Trumbull. From their deference and the expression of annoyance on her face, I suspected a request for oracles. Now, having embraced my grandfather and paid my respects to the archpriest, I could pick out faces and forms dimly recognized: some I knew by name, others I merely recalled from ceremonies and meetings and chance encounters. It eased my heart to see, as Caleb put it, how much we had not lost.

Archpriest Ngalthr and Chulzh'th made their way back to us, along with Caleb and our grandfather. The archpriest spoke for them: "Aphra Yukhl, tell me more of this government man who seeks your aid."

I could have wished to bring the topic up before Caleb mentioned it—but then, Ngalthr was old enough that he wouldn't simply accept whatever view of a situation he heard first. "Ron Spector serves the state, but he doesn't share the ignorance that caused the raid. He'd have us as allies." I paused, collecting my thoughts. "I wouldn't argue for anything so close, yet, but what he's doing now should matter to all of us. War is brewing again, and some of the enemy may have learned the arts of body theft at Miskatonic. And there are new weapons, worse than those from the last war we fought in, weapons that can destroy whole cities. The combination could be catastrophic."

If Innsmouth still stood, the elders would have seen the newsreels: miles of flattened buildings in Nagasaki, where Mama Rei told stories of visiting her cousins. Operation Crossroads, and the cloud rising like a massive alien fungus above splintered test ships. Self-satisfied announcers describing everything in calm tones. I hoped that my inadequate description gave some idea of the danger so viscerally carried by those images.

"His cause seems worth aiding," said Ngalthr. "Though I see little we can do here. I know of no likely enemy who could have learned such arts from us—but I'll spread word and find out if anyone does. This Spector, though. You didn't bring him to meet us. Does he know of our existence?"

I thought of the file he'd shown me, the pictures of my mother's body. "Yes. But I don't trust him that far yet."

Ngalthr nodded slowly. "Caleb Ngadri says that he's granted you some access to the old libraries, in exchange for your aid. But he fears that your access is temporary, and doled out on sufferance. He worries less about this oncoming war, and more about reclaiming that inheritance. Do you also wish our aid to retrieve these books?"

"They're ours," I said, letting the darker topic pass with mingled worry and relief. "Miskatonic stole them from our deserted homes, and now they mete them out in trickles to those they deem worthy. Our histories, our canons, our spellbooks, our own diaries—don't you want them back?"

"Where I live, they cannot go. What do you intend to do with them?"

I glanced at Caleb. "Take them with me. With us."

Chulzh'th chuckled, a bubbling sound. "Do you have what's needed to protect thousands of books from wind and rain and fire? Miskatonic may show little respect, but they know how to keep paper and leather clean and dry—for an age if not an aeon."

"I do run a bookstore, actually," put in Charlie.

Her nostrils flared. "Ah? How large is it? May our people enter freely to read what's within?"

"It's in California," I admitted. "On the other side of the continent. As am I, most of the time."

"You ought not be," rumbled my grandfather. "You ought stay here, by us."

"I'll come when it's my time to change, I promise. But I'm learning now, with Charlie, and aiding the Kotos as well as I know how." I ducked my head, tried not to look like an abashed child. "I'll have a long time to learn in this ocean."

"It is not only the learning," said the archpriest. "The two of you are all our remaining youth—either the last and the youngest of us, or ancestors to all further generations who might join us in the water. If you wish our aid to retrieve the library, do you also intend to rebuild the spawning ground that it served?"

"That's what the others are asking the Great One about," said Chulzh'th.

"They are asking *it* for advice. I am asking *her* for her plans. Even with these greater weapons, men of the air have a little time left: perhaps a hundred years, perhaps a hundred thousand. The Great Race were ever poor at sharing precise intervals. We must determine whether this is the time to cease breeding and retreat fully into the water."

"While there are still Aeonists on land of any race," said my grand-father, "our spawning ground is worth rebuilding, even with half-breeds. I have always said that mistblooded children, when they change at all, cannot be distinguished beneath the waves. A generation or ten would give us greater strength, greater understanding, greater memory. In the face of death and diminishment, the gods would have us make life."

"They'd have us live," said the archpriest. "What that means remains to be determined. Do not preach to me, Yringl'phtagn."

"Archpriest," said my grandfather stiffly.

In the pause that followed I felt the pull of duty—and shame at the fear it raised in me. "I'm sorry, Archpriest. I don't have a mate, and I have no desire to take one from the men of the air. Or to bear a child who could easily age and die on land . . . I've lost too many people. I'm sorry."

I felt a stinging pain in my cheek. I put up my hand and realized that Grandfather had slapped me, fast as only an elder can. Charlie lurched at my side, then visibly held himself back. "Have you not just told me of my own daughter's death?" Grandfather demanded. "It's too painful for you to risk passing on her blood? I did not raise a family of dry-hearted cowards."

I winced and rubbed my cheek. "I survived to speak with you now by courage as well as luck. But if you want to persuade me to take on more mourning, bring me a woman who loved a man of the air and bore his child. Few enough have dared, even with their parents and cousins awaiting them in the water." I'd never spoken to an elder so, let alone my grandfather. I did my best to hide the way it made me tremble.

"Your sister-in-adversity will bear children, will she not? Don't you expect to mourn your nieces and nephews? And what of this one?" He ran a finger along Charlie's cheek, knuckle bent to avoid scratching him. Charlie pulled back and glared. Grandfather bared needle teeth in a predatory grin. "He nearly leapt on me when I slapped you, and yet he held back—courage *and* will. He's lame, but it oughtn't run in his blood. And you've bound that blood to your own; you can hardly mourn him more if you mate with him."

"I beg your pardon!" said Charlie while I blushed furiously.

I looked to Archpriest Ngalthr in hopes of some reprieve. He shook his head. "Regardless of whether you rebuild a true spawning ground, the two of you ought not be the last of us. A few seeds, so that we are not fully lost on land . . . That would be wise. But if you are not rebuilding, the books are not needed."

"I'll think about it," said Caleb abruptly. "It's less difficult for me."

"Both would be better. One line may easily fail."

"Are there—" I started, then froze as all the elders went still as scenting hounds. Grandfather's arm rose, pointing to the dune path.

"Strangers!"

In a rush they were up the beach, tridents raised. Audrey pelted after, calling, "Don't kill them! They didn't mean any harm!"

"Don't—" I shared a look with Caleb and we gave chase.

CHAPTER 13

J ust past the peak of the dune, two people stood shivering, already penned in by the elders' tridents. Leroy Price had an arm
around Sally Ward, and he shifted defensively as he tried to get
between her and whichever assailant drew nearest. Audrey danced
around the outside of the cluster, alternately cajoling the archpriest and
yelling at her two friends. I caught the latter as I came up behind her:

"I told you two not to come today! Didn't I tell you the cops were
out? Why don't you ever listen to sense?"

"Those aren't cops." Leroy's voice was almost too soft to hear. Then,
clearing his throat: "You're not cops. You've got no right—you get away
from my girl!" That last distracted Sally long enough for a startled
glance before her eyes were drawn back to the unfamiliar forms surrounding them.

Archpriest Ngalthr spared Audrey a quelling gaze. "Are these *your*
family? Aphra, if you are going to teach dry men, you must ensure that
they give their relatives sufficient excuse for their absences. Otherwise
one inevitably invites these inquiries."

Audrey rocked back on her heels. "They're not my family, they're
just friends. Very stupid friends."

"Why didn't you tell me they were coming today?" I demanded. "We
could have tried another time."

"Because they *shouldn't* have come today. I thought I talked them

out of it." She glared at Leroy and Sally. "I guess Jesse showed some
sense and stayed home. What's going to happen to them?"

"I don't know." I thought again of Upton, whose fate I'd yet to ask
about. To my grandfather, in R'lyehn: "What do you plan now that
you've captured them? They're students at Miskatonic and Hall. They're
well-known and deeply entangled socially."

Leroy's knees bent a fraction. My grandfather—along with several
others—hissed. Leroy bared his teeth, anger masking fear I could smell
from the circle's edge, but he did not leap.

"Twenty years ago," my grandfather told me, "we had one or two
people at Miskatonic to handle those who saw more than they ought.
To scoff at their reports and demand impossible evidence until they
doubted their own memories. Sometimes we bound intruders' tongues,
but that's easy enough to break for someone who knows even a little
spellwork—or is in a position to learn it. Sometimes . . ." He hissed
again, this time thoughtfully. "Perhaps a binding that they would not
seek to break. They seem young and healthy—fine thralls, if you treat
them well, and you might make use of the boy's seed without becoming overly attached."

"Grandfather!"

"You would hardly be the first magician, of any human kind, to take
as servants those who stumbled across your secrets."

It would not do to sputter at my elders like some Victorian grandmother at a flapper. And it would miss the point. I took a deep breath,
let the sea-touched air settle in my lungs. Then another, while I sought
to assemble my words. For now I kept to R'lyehn, even though I saw
Leroy and Sally grow more nervous as they failed to follow our conversation. "I am aware that it's a tradition. It's not one that I care for. I've
spent too long as a prisoner to hold anyone captive, and I've seen too
many forced to serve their captor's pleasure. It nauseates me to think
of doing likewise."

His head whipped around. "Did they try that with you?"

"No—they thought we carried the metamorphosis like plague.

Should it matter that it was only my beloved friends and never children of the water? Or that they starved and tortured and killed us, but never raped?"

"I did not suggest that you do any such thing to them, merely—"

I held up my hand. "Enough. I will consider breeding with a man of the air, if that is what we decide is truly best. But I won't force them to it, and won't hear any more suggestions that I do so."

Grandfather frowned. "You've grown insolent in your isolation, Aphra Yukhl."

Chulzh'th turned. "If she hasn't had our voices to guide her, be glad she's made her own worth listening to. But Aphra, if you will not have them killed or bound, what would you have us do? If they call attention to our presence, Innsmouth will be in grave danger. Especially now, when men of the air have weapons to reach the deeps."

Audrey hovered, gaze darting from person to person. I glanced at the dunes—Charlie and Neko and Trumbull had not yet arrived with whatever wisdom they might offer. And Leroy and Sally's tension had grown. At any moment they might break into hysterics or try to force their way free, and drive the elders to something irreversible. For now, my people held their tridents steady, immobile except for tiny movements that showed they were tracking our conversation and each other. They stood ready to maintain their siege for aeons, and yet the whole fragile situation would likely shatter within moments. I pushed my way between two guards, Ph'tngul and another whose name I could not remember, into the circle of their weapons.

"What do you intend to do?" I asked the prisoners in English.

Leroy tightened his arm around Sally. She squirmed a little in his grip, and glared at me. "What do you mean, what do *we* intend to do?" she demanded. She loosed an arm to gesture at the elders. "What are *they* going to do? What *are* they? What are you doing here? What's Audrey doing here?" She paused, gulping air.

"This is our beach. This is our town. You came to see if it were haunted, didn't you?"

"Yes, but . . ."

"Did you expect the ghosts to hover tamely for your delectation? Perhaps hoot a few times to make a good story? Did you even believe in magic, or read those books in the Miskatonic library?"

"I told you," said Audrey from outside the circle. "They never let *us* in. Why do you think she followed him for a taste?"

I resisted a look at Leroy, and sighed. "And do you like your taste of forbidden lore?"

Sally bit her lip. "Don't make fun. If you're going to kill me, I'd appreciate it if you'd answer my questions first."

One of the guards laughed, and she flinched. "A Miskatonic student to the core," he said.

"I beg your pardon." She pulled away from Leroy. He tried to reclaim her hand and she shook him off. "I am a *Hall* student."

I smiled in spite of myself, aware that it would not be reassuring. "Audrey is here with me. I'm here to speak to my family, whom I haven't seen since 1928. These are my family, and what they're going to do depends on whether you can convince me—and them—that you won't bring down the National Guard on us." Spector might well be able to curtail such a thing, but it wasn't something I cared to gamble on, and certainly nothing I could persuade the elders to take into account.

Leroy broke in—from the look he gave Sally I suspected he wanted to regain control of the conversation almost as much as he wanted to survive it. "Why shouldn't we? Shouldn't they know about you?"

Before I could find a response, Chulzh'th stepped between us and grabbed him by his starched collar. "We keep to ourselves. You are the intruders here—do you really think to threaten us?"

The sharp stink of ammonia told an end to any chance of rational negotiation. Leroy kicked and swung at her with unscientific punches. I pulled Sally to the side. "Say something sensible—anything!"

"We won't tell. I promise we won't tell!" She tried to pull away toward Leroy and Chulzh'th, but I held fast to her arm.

"That's no guarantee—you can *say* anything."

"What do you want?" Her breath came quickly, stinking of fear. "We tried a ritual last year. Some sort of crazy tantra thing Jesse found. One of the teachers caught us, caught me with Jesse and Leroy all together. Leroy's dad paid to keep it quiet and there, a nice bit of blackmail, are you happy?"

Leroy froze in the midst of his struggle with Chulzh'th. "She's making that up—I never!"

"Mammalian rutting," said Archpriest Ngalthr. "Is what she describes truly forbidden? It has been a little while since Puritan mores held sway on land."

"Sodomy, and interfering with the virtue of a young lady of quality? Yes, those are still scandals." Chulzh'th grinned and lifted Leroy a little higher. "Are you sure you don't want this one as a mate, Aphra? He sounds lively."

"Quite. Thank you." I gritted my teeth against the sudden memory of a soldier in my parents' foyer, lifting me just so, mugging for his fellows, goading my father to his death. *Hey Jack, check out my ugly girl.*

Leroy rolled his eyes wildly and flailed in Chulzh'th's grip. She caught her balance easily and tried to grasp his swinging arms—but one unlucky blow landed in the vulnerable soft tissue of her eye. She roared, slashing out blindly, and Leroy fell to the sand, shirt and chest shredded by four parallel furrows.

Chulzh'th gasped and clutched her hand. I let go of Sally, who threw herself to the ground beside him, Audrey close behind.

"You killed him," wailed Sally. Chulzh'th backed further, holding herself tightly.

"She didn't," observed the archpriest. "His blood is still flowing." But he made no move to intervene.

I wished for Spector or Dawson, and their knowledge of mundane first aid. I had a vague idea of bandages, and that salt water might clean a wound. I had neither skills nor supplies. Instead I knelt at Leroy's shoulder and dipped my finger in red arterial blood. Sally shrieked and tried to push me away, but Audrey grabbed Sally's hands and shook her head violently. I drew a quick and dangerously messy glyph in the sand, muttered the chant as swiftly as I could pronounce it, and hoped the salt left in Leroy's wounds from Chulzh'th's talons would be sufficient.

I'd never done this variant on the Inner Sea before—trying to ride someone else's blood without using my own as a foundation—and could tell immediately that I'd done it wrong. Blood is one of the three foundations of magic, but it is not a foundation of *control*.

The spell tore me from awareness of my own body and plunged me into Leroy's. His blood was of the air, and fragile. But he was young and strong and knew his final form only vaguely; everything in him fought desperately for survival—not a torrent but a flood overflowing its banks. I floundered, seeking the flood's source, but could not direct my own consciousness, let alone the vital forces surrounding me: the pulse, too fast to ease the flow; the natural guardians that staunch wounds, too slow at their work.

I began, dimly, to feel my own body again. Something touched my shoulder, and a familiar pulse echoed Leroy's. I grasped at the familiarity, found Audrey's muddy river bank, dragged her into the spell as a drowning man will seize a hand without regard for sense or safety. As our connection flared I felt Caleb, drawn forward to touch my other shoulder in spite of deep reluctance, and Charlie, out of breath from the climb and sitting abruptly in the soft sand of the dune, reaching out and sharing strength.

And none of that was enough. I sensed them all, knew they could sense me, knew they swept into the same flood that bore me along. But the spell had no less power, no more control, than before. If we had practiced longer, knew one another better, I might have been able to push my students to pronounce our intentions in clearer Enochian or trace better-formed symbols. But my vague sense of Caleb's unease was the closest thing to thought that passed among us.

I clung to their bodies. I heard Neko's urgent questions through Charlie's ears, saw out of the corner of his eye Trumbull survey the scene and start down the dune. In strange offset harmony—Caleb's hearing a fraction sharper and faster than Audrey's—Ngalthr said to Chulzh'th: "Your wound. Your choice."

Long silence, and flood waters rising—and then Caleb's eyes following Chulzh'th as she knelt to mark a diagram around our bodies. On her claws, Leroy's blood had already begun to dry and darken. She moved slowly, trying to draw lines that would hold in the shallow sand. Sally cringed and glared as the acolyte came close. Further symbols crowded around us.

As Chulzh'th built word and symbol atop my rough foundation, our path through the floodwaters began to take on form and meaning. Now I could find the wound, sense the places where it sought to knit together and the purpose in Leroy's blood as it strove to find a healing hold. I worked to strengthen those capacities, channeling the power that had almost drowned me. There were ways to draw on the support of my confluence, but none that I'd studied. Still their presence anchored me against the temptations of fear, as I worked with tools I scarce understood to save a man who'd likely turn on me if I succeeded.

At last I felt the floodwaters recede. They settled slowly, still far too high. I continued to push until Audrey shook my shoulder. "Aphra, it's stopped healing. That's all we're going to get."

I awoke to my own body, shaking my head with the shock of the transition. I gathered my courage, then took in what lay before me. Leroy breathed, a victory in itself. His wounds had grown shallow, blood begun to thicken and clot. Some seeped around the edges, though, and his breathing was labored. A hand to his forehead found it covered in clammy sweat: both wounds and their repair had taxed him, and further illness might threaten. But he was alive. Now we would need to figure out what to do with that.

Charlie came down the dune, faster than he should with the cane, close-spotted by Neko. She hurried to my side: "Onee-san, are you okay?"

Neko rarely used the Japanese honorifics that came so easily to Mama Rei; she must be shaken as well. I realized I was trembling. I put my arm around her. "I will be, I think."

"What happened?" asked Charlie. Trumbull knelt to examine the healing sigils, and I resisted the urge to shout at her.

"Leroy tried to fight the acolyte," I said instead. "She lost her temper."

Chulzh'th ducked her head. "I was not angry. I was startled." In R'lyehn: "For one on the clerical path to so easily be caught unawares, and to shed blood in surprise, is inexcusable. I might have chosen to harm him if he would not promise silence, but I apologize for doing so without intention."

"You might have? He's barely spawn, surely there were other ways." Now I was losing my temper—fully aware of it, but unable to resist the need to release the pent-up fear and frustration and the sight of a boy I disliked lying unconscious in the sand. Every blade-sharp R'lyehn phrase I'd ever heard from my mother, in her rare moments of anger, came pouring out. "Have the pressure changes addled your mind? Are you a mayfly to make thoughtless choices in a second's time? Is this what you wish written of you in the Archives?"

"Aphra Yukhl," said Grandfather. "Speak respectfully to your elders."

"We do what we must to protect our people," said Archpriest Ngalthr. "Sometimes it must be done quickly. Long life does not mean having forever to choose."

"Is that what happened with Upton?" I demanded. "You had no time to decide what to do with him—no time to reconsider this past quarter-century?"

"Wait, who?" asked Chulzh'th, startled into English.

"He avenged Asenath Waite," I said. "And you left him in a mad-house for it."

"*I* did that," said my grandfather. "No one would have sent a new-made acolyte against Ephraim. And if you had heard his killer ranting against us, or seen the destruction wrought by mere fear of body theft, you would not question our decision. *You* must learn patience, child."

"Which brings us to the current question." Ngalthr's bass cut through our escalation. "We still must decide what to do with these children. And they *are* children, as Aphra Yukhl says. Can they be trusted, having given us their own secrets as surety?"

"And . . ." Chulzh'th trailed off, but her glance at Leroy's chest made their concern clear. His body might tell what his tongue would not.

"The Miskatonic Monster!" said Audrey. She shrunk back as a dozen heads turned her way.

One of the elders I didn't recognize shook her head. "Regardless of rumor, if there were still wolves in this part of the state we'd have smelled them."

"Hasn't been a sighting in twenty years anyway," said Sally.

"We're not trying to *catch* it," said Audrey. "Look, we carry him up closer to the construction site, everyone who can vanish vanishes, and I get hysterical about how we were exploring the marshes outside town and this huge wolf thing jumped us, and it was the Miskatonic Monster, and just keep being hysterical so they bring him to the hospital without asking too many questions. Jeez, Sally, if you guys knew how to do a cover-up story right, maybe you wouldn't have gotten *caught* trying to summon demons under your skirt with the boys!"

"The girl's plan is sound." Trumbull spoke at last. "If you do wish to continue your connections with the land for another few decades, I suggest *not* standing around in endless argument over a bleeding body. This area is open, and sound and sight carry information a long way. The men in town are bored and cold, and will investigate the least anomaly soon enough."

A pause while everyone considered this, and then Archpriest Ngalthr ducked his head. "As you say, Great One. Yringl'phtagn?"

My grandfather nodded. "Jhathl and Khr'jhelkh'ng, bring the body closer to the marshlands, and make enough tracks to support their story. Don't let anyone see you. Child"—this to Sally—"come here."

She crouched beside Leroy a moment longer, then hesitantly stood and approached. She cast her gaze up and down, taking in my grand-father's form.

"I apologize, but we must have surety for your word. Hold out your arm."

This time she looked to me, and when I nodded she did as he bid. Her hand did not tremble. Audrey slipped up and touched her shoulder. Slowly, so as not to startle her, my grandfather took Sally's hand and nicked her palm. She shivered but did not pull away. A drop of blood welled to the surface. "Aphra Yukhl." At his direction, I rolled up my sleeve. He sketched a sigil on my forearm with the blood-dipped claw. I winced at the blossom of pain and the dim echo of Sally's corporeal fear in the sigil, clear in my mind for a moment before it faded. "There. With that, you will practice tracking, and you will know if she be-trays us—and do what's needful."

The look in his dark eyes dared me to argue further, and I ducked my head. "Yes, Grandfather."

"Good." He gathered me close again, and I wished that I could for-get all the day's fearful demands in the circle of his touch and scent. He gestured Caleb over, embraced him, held him at length. "Study with your sister, and do not be frightened away by the ignorance that was forced on you."

"Yes, Grandfather."

"And both of you, think on the duties we've discussed. We'll talk further when you return—do not wait so long this time."

In moments, we were alone—save for the two elders that my grand-father had assigned to move Leroy.

"All right." I squared my shoulders, tried to focus on practicalities. "Who will have been exploring the marshlands with you?"

"I'll go," said Audrey. "I'm usually with them when they do stupid things, and I can do believable hysteria at the drop of a hat. Anyone else'll get more questions. You've got a car, right?" Sally nodded shakily. With the promise that Audrey would report back that evening, they left, trailing Jhathl and Khr'jhelkh'ng and their burden.

"Have you other errands here?" asked Trumbull.

I looked back at the dunes. "No." I considered asking if she had learned what she wished, realized that I wouldn't be able to ask politely.

"Your family . . ." Charlie trailed off.

"We'll talk about them later. For now, let's go back to the university."

When we returned, we found the campus invaded.

CHAPTER 14

At first it seemed natural that, on the Saturday before classes began, we should find a long line of cars wending slowly through Miskatonic's wrought iron gate. However, as the line moved forward I saw a barrier across the road, and five tall men in well-tailored suits who spoke to each driver before permitting passage.

"They've got guns," said Neko quietly. She was right. The bulges under their jackets were unmistakable—nor, I thought as I saw one man flash his badge at a recalcitrant chauffeur, were they intended to be mistaken.

Caleb grimaced. "We should turn back. Something's happened."

"Don't be absurd," said Trumbull. She gestured at the cars. "Can you think of anything more suspicious? Look at how they all conform."

So we remained. "Puritans," I murmured to Caleb, and he nodded. They were all of the type that we'd grown up calling by that name, and that I always had trouble distinguishing: tall and uniformly pale, with small eyes and aquiline features and chins that looked half cut off.

"Puritan soldiers," he said. And indeed, they wore the close-shaven haircuts of the camp guards. I tried not to look frightened, and I tried not to look like someone masking fear. But then, how would an ordinary person react? I watched the drivers and passengers in the other cars, tried to hear them above the rumble of idling engines. I caught snatches of curiosity, irritation, respect—a couple of boys, presumably returning students on the G.I. Bill, snapped salutes and passed easily. In others, though, I caught a hint of fear. Perhaps I could let some of what I felt show without marking myself as their rightful prey.

Neko pulled up the hood of her coat, and buried her face in her scarf.

"Hello, ma'am," one of the men said when Trumbull rolled down her window. He sounded bored, though he peered curiously at the rest of us. The returning students did not, as a general rule, have nearly so many females in their cars. "What's your business on campus?"

"I'm a professor of mathematics. I'm returning home to do a great deal of course preparation."

One of the others frowned. "Miskatonic has girl professors?"

Trumbull's tone chilled. "It has one."

"And these folks," the second man continued. "What are they, research assistants?" He motioned for us to roll down the back window. "She's got a Jap back here. I don't know what these other guys are, except the ugliest couple I've ever seen."

I held myself very still, and hoped Caleb could do likewise.

"Now see here—" began Charlie from the front, but Trumbull held up a hand to silence him.

"The aesthetics of my guests can hardly be your concern." She pulled her scarf away from her eyes. "Why don't you let us pass? There are many waiting behind us, and regardless of our looks, we're no threat to you."

The man who'd insulted us nodded and stepped back. But the first man, the one closest to Trumbull, put his hand to his heart. He frowned and squinted down at the spot he touched. Then his eyes flew wide and his hand leapt to the lump beneath his suit jacket. Glancing at the line of cars behind us, he did not quite draw. "Ma'am, I need you to pull your car to the side so these other people can pass. And then I need you and your passengers to step out of the car. Keep your hands where I can see them—and your eyes where I can't."

"That's really not necessary," said Trumbull.

He pulled the gun an inch further out of its holster. "Ma'am, I told you, do *not* attempt to look anyone in the eye. Now please pull over."

"Do what he says," said Neko quietly. "Please, Professor, do what he says." She kept repeating the demand, holding herself tightly—"do what he says, do what he says"—as Trumbull steered the car through the gate and to the side of the road. Several times she started to turn her head, then forced her gaze forward again. Her hands clenched white around the steering wheel.

"What do we do?" Caleb whispered. He sounded young and frightened.

"For now, what they tell us." I tried to keep the fright from my own voice—not to fool the soldiers, or whatever they were, but to reassure him and Neko.

Trumbull found a resting place for the car, and looked back at us. I sensed her fear so clearly that I couldn't be certain whether she had deliberately sent the impression into my mind, or whether it was merely that I had never seen that expression on her face before.

We all got out, slowly and with our hands plainly visible. White flakes drifted down around us, broad and slow, lighting weightlessly on hair and hats and suit jackets. I stared at the ground, so that the fog of my breath rose to cloud my vision. It was terrifying, a claustrophobic pressure against my thoughts, not to be permitted to see what had trapped us. Polished shoes, entirely inappropriate for a Massachusetts winter, shuffled in and out of sight.

A faint movement of air behind me, and the scent of anger-sweat surging over the putrid smell of exhaust, warned me of the man's approach so that I didn't lash out when he touched my wrists. Then the ice-cold steel of cuffs against my skin. As he ran his hands down my light jacket and patted my pockets, I reminded myself that I had dealt with this many times. I regretted every one of those memories, but I could—would—survive one more.

Neko continued to repeat, so quietly I doubted the men of the air could hear: "Do what he says, just do what he says . . ."

He pulled my dagger from my belt. "Not much of a weapon."

I gritted my teeth. "It's not intended as one."

There was some fuss over Charlie's cane, which they let him keep though I couldn't see the exact arrangements. At last they began herding us in toward the campus proper—only two, I thought, but couldn't be certain. I knew that if we fought or ran, there would be more of them.

The administration building stood just around a bend from the gate. I was startled, when we passed through the brick archway, to realize how short the walk had been. High heels and dress shoes stepped hurriedly back as the men directed us through, and murmurs followed our wake. At last, having paraded past several witnesses—presumably so they could attest to our dangerous natures—we entered a whitewashed room with broad windows.

It must have been until recently an ordinary office—the metal desks pushed to the side still held test papers and framed photos scooped into rough piles. Now larger tables bore neat stacks of files and an official-looking phone. Before I ducked my head again, I saw several more well-dressed men and a secretary look up in surprise. I heard clicks as our captors drew and aimed their guns.

"What's this, damn it?" demanded one of the new men. "Sorry, Mary." The secretary murmured reassurance.

"A mistake," said Trumbull. "I'm a professor—"

"It sure is a mistake," said one of our captors—I thought the one who'd first taken issue with Trumbull. "I wasn't expecting our Ruskie spy to try and hypnotize us at the gate. She didn't manage it—that talisman worked a treat."

There were so many things they could have accurately accused us of being. It would have been funny, if I thought they'd believe any reassurance I offered.

Scent of wood polish, soap, sweat—and fainter, paper and leather and ash. Footsteps around us, more shoes. Fabric rustling. "You're right, it's gone all black. Impressive. Mary, a replacement ward, if you would. Why are they all staring at the floor?"

"I told them not to make eye contact, sir. She seemed to need it, when she tried to roll me."

"That's reassuring. Means she hasn't found what she's after yet. Peters, get them some chairs. Who are all these others?"

"Her 'research assistants,' she said. They seem like a motley bunch."

Charlie broke in. "This is absurd—we're American citizens, we have rights—"

"Are you now? That remains to be seen."

I wished I could tell Charlie to stay quiet, not make things worse—but speaking would make it worse as well. He seemed to figure it out on his own. I wished, too, for claws, strength, greater magic. I knew from painful experience that those wouldn't help either.

They brought in old wooden chairs, sat us down, clipped our cuffs to the slats. My arms ached already, as much from fear as from the awkward angle. The bottom of a crisp-ironed suit jacket appeared in front of me, and the owner tied something around my face. Folds of fabric dug into my skin and instantly started to itch, an irritant all the greater for my inability to ease it. It smelled of wax and dust.

"Now, ma'am." The man's voice stood a little way off—closer to Trumbull. "Why don't you make this easy on yourself? It must be hard to get a position at a place like Miskatonic. Any offer of a way in must have seemed tempting. You're hardly to blame for wanting to get a little something for yourself, but you could be in more trouble than you realize. Tell us now what you're doing here, and we might be able to help you."

A long pause. "I'm teaching multidimensional geometry."

"Don't play coy. You burned out Peters's protective ward. Are geometry professors usually familiar with advanced methods of hypnosis?"

"Of course we are. What do you suppose multidimensional studies are *for*?"

A different voice. "I doubt every math professor would try and mind control our gate check."

"It depends how rude your people are, and how patient the professors. But I assure you, it's not an unheard-of skill on campus."

The first interrogator. "Let's try this again. Who are you working for?"

"Dean Skinner. Whom you should perhaps contact."

"We already have. Mary, there are other talismans we might try testing. Get the box for me, there's a love."

Heels clacking against hardwood floor. Papers rustling; something heavy dragged across the floor and lifted with a dull thunk onto a table. Metal against metal, and the muffled click of a lock turning.

And Caleb's voice: "Leave her alone. It's me you want."

A sole scraped against hardwood, and the first interrogator spoke. "What?"

"Caleb, no," I said, and heard the same cry from Neko.

"I've been trying to get into the library for months. She had the access I needed, so I offered to help with her research. She doesn't know anything."

"Why speak up now?" asked the second interrogator.

"I don't like to hear a woman scream. Gives me bad dreams."

I didn't know whether to laugh or scream myself: it was a line from one of the pulps I'd read aloud to Charlie while we were cleaning the store. A dime novel: Caleb must have used a copy to practice his reading. I didn't blame him for thinking of it—though to real agents, the melodrama might not ring true. At least it had distracted them.

"So you're working for . . ."

"Russia, obviously. Not directly, of course. There are people everywhere who'll pay good money for the secrets in Miskatonic's library."

A woman's voice this time, low and clear—the kind of voice some people put on like makeup. "I don't believe it, sir. He's too smooth, and she's too scared."

"Yes. Better try the talisman on both of them."

A door slammed heavily, and a sudden draft spilled cool air over my face. Spector's voice rang out: "What do you think you're doing here?"

The first interrogator, sounding unperturbed: "Hello, Ron. Questioning the suspects you didn't manage to find during all your poking around the library."

"Suspects?" Spector's voice turned dry. "They're my team. If you take off the cuffs and—blindfolds? What the hell, George?—I'll introduce them to you, though I don't think they'll be much inclined to shake hands at this point."

"Yes, I actually did guess that these might be your 'irregulars.' I heard you'd picked up some . . . odd characters. We took them in because they were acting extremely suspicious."

"They may be irregulars, but they're my team nevertheless. Whatever 'suspicions' made you pick them up—and leave me out of the loop—I can assure you that they aren't Russian, or German, or any of the other monsters you think you'll find with that parade at the gate. Take off the damn blindfolds."

"This one tried to hypnotize Peters. And this one claims to be a Russian spy."

"I have no idea why Peters would accuse a respectable professor of any such thing, but I promise you she's working with me. And—Mr. Marsh, why did you tell the man you were a Russian spy?"

I felt warmth near my face, smelled cigarettes and the faint lemon of Spector's cologne, and then I blinked against sudden light as he pulled the blindfold off. When I opened my eyes I saw Caleb, too, shaking his head against the change.

"He was threatening Professor Trumbull with some sort of . . . talisman, he said."

"I see." Spector continued to pace, removing the others' blindfolds. Neko's face was streaked with salt water. Spector held out his hand to George. "Key? If you don't like the people I'm working with, take it up with our superiors and go through proper channels. I can assure you they've seen everyone's files. *This* just looks like a grade-A illustration of why we aren't supposed to send independent teams to the same site. It's embarrassing."

"I don't expect the details of either investigation to get in the papers. Or don't you trust the discretion of your irregulars?"

"I'm perfectly capable of being embarrassed when we screw up, even if it doesn't go public. I don't know about you." Spector bent to fiddle with the key behind Charlie's chair, helping him to his feet before unbinding Neko. He handed her a discreet handkerchief, and came next to Trumbull. "My apologies for the inconvenience, professor, on behalf of the U.S. government."

As soon as the cuffs dropped away she pushed herself to her feet. She wound her hands together, then forced them to her sides. In Enochian, she said to our captors, "May your eldest ancestors die childless in a tarpit; I hope never to see your eyes again." She strode out into the hall.

The men all looked at Mary. "I *think* that was extremely rude," she said. "Where did she learn to swear in R'lyehn?"

"This is Miskatonic," said Spector. "Perhaps you should all research its history before continuing your inquisition." No one bothered to correct her identification of the language.

"Your concerns are noted," said George. "And I can assure you I'll look into them. Why don't you take your team home now?"

"I certainly will." He strode over to what I could now see was a small wooden chest, polished in plain style but with ornately carved metal latches. He poked his finger delicately into the interior. "Some sort of talisman . . . Miss Marsh, what do you make of these?"

I had no interest in posturing at a roomful of armed soldiers. But he'd rescued us, and it seemed wise to follow his lead. And to get some idea of what he'd rescued us from.

The chest held a series of charms: stones carved in the Enochian alphabet with a mix of Enochian, R'lyehn, and doubtful nonsense, as well as wholly unfamiliar sigils. A few were bound with herbs or bits of wood. Putting my hand near them felt like standing too close to a bonfire built too high: sparks and hot ash against my skin. I drew back, but not before I sensed, along with the physical illusion—I checked my hand and found it unburnt—the intimation that someone watched me with great suspicion.

I had not the faintest idea what their diagrams entailed or how they got their effect, or what it would do in close quarters and at length. I tried for Professor Trumbull's best expression of bored irritation.

"Very creative," I told them. "Your grammar is poor, but effective."

"No surprise," said Spector. "George's team is noted for their creativity. Shall we?" And thankfully, finally, he led us out.

Trumbull paced the hall, hands writhing. As soon as she saw us she whirled and stalked outside. We followed and found her standing with eyes closed, face upturned to catch the snow. Spector rounded on her.

"All right. I risked my career to get you out of there along with everyone else, because I trust Miss Marsh's judgment and she seems to trust you. But before this goes further I need to know who you are, and why you're here."

Her eyes flew open. "I am a math professor. As I have said far too often today."

He stepped closer. "Not good enough. You've thrown yourself into our research with no apparent motive. You went with Miss Marsh to meet her family, which suggests something well beyond ordinary academic curiosity—and she brought you along, which suggests something well beyond the historical relationship between Innsmouth and Arkham." He paused. Trumbull had not backed away, as a human would, and I saw his foot lift as he nearly retreated himself. But he continued: "There may be other professors who can hypnotize with a look—though I've gathered that Miskatonic's reputation is exaggerated on that count—but few who'd try it with officers of the law. You were either remarkably confident in your superiority to them—or not at all confident in your right to enter the campus."

"Perhaps I'm just strange. Everyone says so."

Spector sighed and turned to me. "Miss Marsh? You'll forgive my unwillingness to continue blindly. Either I understand what she's doing here, or she's out of this thing entirely and we find you bunks at Hall."

Around us students passed, nonchalant as if their home had not been violated. Many went with heads down in deference to the weather, but others paused to observe our altercation. "We'll talk. But somewhere private."

CHAPTER 15

In the end we went back to Trumbull's house—it wasn't far, and I doubted my ability to persuade her anywhere else. The house not having any proper parlor, we settled in her living room. In contrast to the office, I suspected this room more reflected its original owner. The unadorned couches and chairs looked as inexpensive as a new professor might reasonably get away with, and rubbed thin in the centers of the cushions. A bookshelf held a few choice literary classics along with works of philosophy and esoterica. The paintings were of good quality but somewhat mismatched: a pointillist impression of the Miskatonic River from Meadow Hill alongside a pair of swirling abstracts and a surreal dreamscape of fabulous birds flying through a star-studded abyss. I examined this last more closely while the others settled into their chosen seats, and was not entirely surprised to read "C. Trumbull, '46" boldly scrawled in the lower corner. The others had the same mark, with dates ranging from two years to a decade past.

Neko headed for the kitchen, but returned quickly. "Professor, don't you keep anything on hand to offer guests?"

"It isn't usually an issue. If the two of you keep inviting people over, I suppose something will need to be done." Her posture and aspect sharpened. "Mr. Spector, will you accept my word that I do not represent any polity of interest to you, and hold no political opinions relevant to your concerns?"

He leaned forward on his blue velvet chair. "I'm afraid you'll need to be more specific."

She sighed heavily. "Miss Koto, I do believe there to be tea in the cabinet above the sink. The social prop might in fact be helpful." She examined her hands, then Spector, with an air of displeased unfamiliarity. "What do you know of Earth's history?"

He frowned. "More than most. Would you like a textbook?"

"Perhaps the question is too broad. Try instead: how much do you know of the history of Earth's future?"

He sat back. "I know that the Marshes' religion includes prophecies and promises of what is to come. My religion includes others. I wouldn't call either 'history.' Beyond that, I suppose I can guess—or fear—as much as anyone."

"Hopeless." Her bored irritation was still more impressive than mine. "Miss Marsh, you explain, since he insists. I shall be curious to hear how you manage."

I was curious as well. I must not only explain, but satisfy Spector's concerns. And I had questions of my own for *him,* that I suspected he'd be reluctant to answer. "Humans aren't the only intelligent species to walk the Earth," I began.

"I know," he said, nodding at me.

"I'm as human as you. Just a different kind." And truly sick from having to repeat that assertion to people who supposedly respected me. "Civilizations have risen and fallen on this world since the surface cooled. After humanity dies, or destroys itself, people like giant beetles will build in our ashes. After them, five more species in Earth's own evolutionary chain will rise and fall—and a dozen others who come and go from distant stars, or who last aeons and never learn the art of writing, or who are lost when plagues wipe out their first attempt at agriculture. These races are not prophecy and myth, but recorded history— and Professor Trumbull's people are the ones who record it."

Neko returned bearing a tea tray. Spector snatched a cup and busied himself with sugar and cream. I gave him the moment to consider. At last he took a sip, winced at the heat, and said: "That's a remarkable claim."

"The universe is a remarkable place," I said. "What do you suggest I do about it?"

"Evidence would be nice. There are whole corners of the government that go haring off after unlikely prophecies and passages of the Bible. I am not on any of those teams."

"A demonstration might be in order," said Trumbull. "If Miss Marsh will permit, of course."

"He's not my student, but I suggest you ask him directly."

She pursed her lips. "Mr. Spector, you have my word that I'll make no permanent alteration to your state, and do nothing to change your thoughts or beliefs—other than the changes that occur naturally through encountering new information. Or so one hopes." She put down her teacup, and locked gazes with him.

Audrey had not only pushed back against Trumbull, but also appeared singularly unimpressed—though I began to suspect that she was not as forthcoming with her thoughts as she sometimes appeared. Spector was more vulnerable. His jaw went slack—then for just a moment, I saw shock in her eyes and cold mockery in his. The moment passed, and their expressions returned to their accustomed faces.

"That's . . ." He trailed off. "You didn't feel Russian. When we . . . passed each other."

"I should hope not," said Trumbull. "But the spell that they supposedly seek is a lesser version of my race's art. I object to it being used for petty ends; that is the beginning and the end of overlap in our interests."

"Petty?" He ran his hands over his body, rumpling his suit worse than hurry and weather had already managed.

"The Yith apparently take a long view of history," said Charlie.

Spector retrieved his tea. "I can see why you were reluctant to explain."

I took a deep breath. "Along those lines . . . you were quite eager for us to leave you to your 'private errands.' And then, on our return, we were besieged by soldiers. *What did you do?*"

His shoulders tensed, and he stared down at his cup. "I assure you, I didn't mean to do *this*. Upton's suggestion that others were looking into the body theft spell worried me, and I called in to request help following up. What I wanted was a warrant that would let me examine the asylum records in more detail, and a report on any anomalous tips from the area around that time. What I got . . . I'm afraid we've run afoul of . . ." He put down the cup and straightened. "Not everyone in the federal government agrees on how we should handle supernatural issues. My superiors think, as I do, that we need a better working relationship with those who already have long experience with magic. Others agree that the . . . the purges . . . of the '20s were a mistake, but disagree on the appropriate response. The task force that you just encountered is, uh, symptomatic, of those who think we ought to build a more trustworthy understanding of magic from the ground up, without being bogged down by what they see as ancient history and superstition."

Trumbull cocked her head, and a slow smile spread across her face. "That's mad."

"And dangerous," I said. I didn't feel nearly as amused—though I supposed that by her standards, we were all stumbling along, trying to reconstruct what the Yith well understood.

"I agree." Spector pushed himself out of the chair and paced. "In any case, they got wind of my 'difficulties,' and managed to talk some Bureau supervisor into letting them try *their* methods, since mine were working so slowly. And promptly treated the whole campus like a crime scene, as if they were dealing with some ordinary criminal who could be penned in by barricades. Come Monday, they'll try to turn their arrest of *my team* into proof of my mistakes." He paused by the wall, and reached up to straighten one of the abstract paintings. "I'm sorry, you don't need the spillover from our internecine politics. But I'm afraid they've made it your business."

"Do you know what they intend to do," asked Caleb, "aside from accost people at the campus gate?"

"I don't," said Spector. "Officially they're here for the same reason I am. But their roadblock is so visible that any spies or traitors still here when we arrived will be gone by tomorrow—unless they're *very* confident in their ability to stay hidden. Either Barlow thinks he can convince our body snatcher to panic, or they're looking for a chance to practice something in the field that they can't do back in D.C., or they've decided that some of the 'old-fashioned' resources at Miskatonic are worth their time. Or all those things at once—George Barlow isn't a man who does things for only one reason."

We discussed further—but in frustrating fact, this didn't change any of our plans. We didn't know enough to make such changes. Even though it was increasingly unclear to me what we could do about our books, other than continue to read them as they were doled out to us. Even though it made the tea turn bitter in my stomach that to get to and from Hall, even to wander the streets of Arkham, we must again risk Miskatonic's self-appointed guards.

"Are they going to eat dinner in the faculty spa?" I asked abruptly.

"I don't know," admitted Spector. "I don't know for sure who arranged for their presence here, but I think it may have been Dean Skinner. They called him to say they had Professor Trumbull, and apparently—I'm sorry, ma'am—he didn't sound surprised. He said you could cool your heels for a while. Made reference to the rest of you as well. Dawson overheard, and called me right away, but it was the first she knew of the team's presence."

I leaned back and closed my eyes. "Maybe I'll skip dinner tonight."

"Eggs?" offered Neko.

"How many do we have?" asked Caleb.

"I'll tell you what," said Spector. "I hope they won't give you trouble again so soon, but I *know* they won't take that risk with me. It's still early—I'll go into town and get something that isn't eggs, and you can eat in tonight. If the professor doesn't mind."

Trumbull shrugged, but said, "Frankly, I don't care to encounter them again today either."

"We could *cook*," said Neko dreamily.

I nodded with real enthusiasm. "Do you know where there's a fish market?"

Spector bore the transformation of nervous relief into shopping list with good grace, and departed with the promise that Trumbull's kitchen would soon be better stocked.

Trumbull went upstairs to work on her notes—whether documenting the afternoon's events, or recording what the elders had told her, I didn't know. Perhaps I ought to have written down my own experiences for her collection, as she'd suggested.

I suspected us all in need of private conversations, and not quite ready for them. Caleb and Neko found a checkers board and settled into a game with one of their many sets of variant rules. Charlie and I drifted to the bookshelf.

"Are you okay?" I asked.

He shrugged, winced, leaned more heavily on his cane. "My shoulders hurt. My knee hurts. I feel like an idiot for being so angry about what happened."

"Anger . . . seems like a pretty reasonable reaction."

He pulled out a copy of *Exercises in Descriptive Geometry*. After a moment I took it, and held it open so that he could examine the pages with one hand. "With all that happened to you, and to your brother and Miss Koto—I can hardly complain over losing an afternoon."

Careful diagrams showed warped planes intersecting to produce ever-stranger shapes. "Is that really what's angering you? The time it took?"

He shook his head, traced one of the diagrams with a thick finger. "I think it's the power that they have. The way they used it. I could tell"—he checked the game over his shoulder—"they were upsetting you, and her, and if anything they thought it was funny. Humans are awful people."

I could neither argue nor agree. "It's a big universe," I said instead. History was long, and life short, and if I took comfort in the fleeting existence of our momentary captors, I must remember that Charlie too, and Neko and Audrey and even Spector, were ephemeral.

Charlie put the geometry text back, and pulled down a leatherbound edition of *Plato's Republic*. "This one's always good for a distracting argument," he suggested.

〜〜〜

Charlie was right: I'd never encountered Plato before, and he was a good distraction. If I'd never met a person of the air, it would certainly have caused me to look oddly at the first ones I did encounter. I would have to ask Trumbull if anyone had ever tried to put his ideas about "justice" into practice.

When Spector returned I rifled through his paper sacks, and at last pulled out a bag of flour and a jar of honey.

"Would you like to eat with us?" I asked him. The newly stocked kitchen made me feel generous. "I can't imagine you want to break bread with those people either."

"Want, no." He unpacked a box of pierogi, which hadn't been on the list but inspired a pang of nostalgia anyway—I'd never found them on the West Coast. From the look on his face, that had been Spector's motivation as well. He put them on the counter. "For later—I miss New York. It'll go easier for all of us if I don't act fazed by this afternoon. We'll all be very polite to each other, and then I'll go back to the guest rooms and drink scotch. Thank god Barlow's got his people in a hotel; I don't have to deal with them once dinner's over."

After he left we continued to sort groceries. Growing up, a winter meal would involve a great deal of salt cod and tinned sardines, and potatoes and apples from the cold cellar. Spector had found all those things, but also frozen whitefish fillets, neatly packaged chicken, and a bag of peas frozen out of their shells that could be boiled in five minutes. And dried herbs, flour, sugar, oil—even butter, usually a rarity since Mama Rei hated it and I always assumed it a costly luxury.

Neko hefted the whitefish. "Do you want to use this, or can I?"

I thought mournfully of holiday stew, probably too salty for anyone but Caleb—I knew Neko didn't like it. "You go ahead. I want to make honeyed saltcakes. Caleb, do you remember how they go?"

"Do you? I remember how to follow directions, and how to lick the spoon."

"I do. And how to give directions." Cookbooks, I reminded myself, were another thing useless to Miskatonic that they'd have hidden in their stacks. I wasn't sure I remembered a single title, though. Mother's collection I knew by their colors, or by stains on much-used pages.

Charlie settled into a kitchen chair and read Plato, while the three of us rinsed dusty mixing bowls and squabbled over counter space. I sifted the flour, measured out honey and salt by eye, and tried to decide among the abundance of fats for shortening. Oil would probably work best, but I wasn't sure it would taste right without a little rendered chicken fat.

Outside, someone pounded the door knocker. I spun, clutching a wooden spoon. Neko froze in place. Caleb took a step toward the arch to the dining room, but hesitated.

Charlie put a finger in his book. "There are probably plenty of people who want to visit Professor Trumbull. Right?"

"Right." I stalked to the front hall. *I am a Marsh. I have every right to be here.* Nevertheless I opened the door cautiously, ready to slam it shut if our company were unwelcome.

Instead it was Audrey, who looked nonplussed at my expression. "This is the place, right? You haven't all been replaced by mad twins?"

I laughed and let her in. "No, this is the right place. We're just on edge."

"How did you get in?" asked Caleb. "Didn't they want to know what business a girl had alone on campus? Or do they not care about that?"

"Who's 'they'? I climbed the oak by the east wall, same as always when I don't have company or a class for an excuse. There's another at Hall that I use to get off campus when I don't want to beg for a note. You don't think they let us innocent young things wander around loose, do you?"

"Ah, you missed the soldiers then," he said. I herded everyone back into the kitchen, where I could bury my fingers in dough while we explained the events of the afternoon. Audrey was suitably impressed and disturbed.

"How is Mr. Price?" I asked belatedly. "And Miss Ward?"

She sobered further. "Leroy will recover, they say. He'll miss the start of classes, and he'll have a scar. Sally has decided that he's a hero instead of an idiot, but I don't think she's going to do anything stupid."

"I'm glad he'll be okay. Chulzh'th will be glad too."

After a couple of hours' bustle and carefully neutral conversation, we had a motley meal: chicken fried with rice and eggs, spiced fish, boiled potatoes with bits of apple and sage, and the saltcakes smelling of safety and home.

I considered the wisdom of intruding on Trumbull's studies, but she came into the dining room before I reached a decision. Many of the serving dishes probably hadn't seen light since her arrival, and she looked them over as if observing a slightly distasteful foreign custom.

"You needn't have any if it bothers you," I said in some annoyance.

"It's no worse a way of taking in energy than any other, I suppose."

The others accepted their helpings with more enthusiasm. Whatever the faults of the day, it had given us all a good appetite. Caleb bit into a saltcake and smiled, eyes closed. "These were an excellent thought."

"They're good," agreed Audrey. "I wouldn't have expected the sweet and the salt to go together."

Neko tried some. She murmured half-hearted appreciation, but it was clear that she and I still had very different ideas about what constituted appropriate amounts of salt.

"It's a kind of record," I said to Trumbull. "These foods, they're all memories, even if they're harder for a stranger to read than a diary. A honeyed saltcake, the actual thing itself, tells you more about what holidays *felt* like in Innsmouth than the words of any story or ritual."

"That I know." She nibbled the edge of one. I could see her discomfort in the exaggerated way her lips peeled back from her teeth, in how attending to her food seemed to reduce rather than increase her pleasure in it.

I took another bite, closed my eyes, tasted a picnic during the Rites of Dagon, eaten swiftly with a summer thunderstorm threatening.

"Do you have holidays?" Audrey spooned out another helping of rice and cocked her head at Trumbull.

"Of course. Although we don't usually attend to the flicker of solar orbits. Some celebrations mark changes in the Archives; those we carry from world to world. Others observe the rhythms of this planet while we abide here. Great Equinoxes, for example—the people of the water also keep those, of course."

I nodded, then explained for the rest of the table: "Earth's orbit around the sun changes slowly, so the equinoxes and solstices move around the year. A Great Equinox is how long it takes them to come back to the same place. It's a little longer every cycle, but the current one will take a bit under 26,000 years."

Charlie paused with a forkful of potato halfway to his mouth. "That sounds like quite the feast."

"I'm told it is. The next Great Equinox, at the end of this cycle, is in . . ." I paused to calculate, surprised to discover that I did, in fact, remember the relevant figures. "Nine thousand, eight hundred and fifty-three years."

"So the last one was before humans learned to write," said Charlie. "Or build cities."

"Before men of the air learned to write," said Trumbull. "The folk of the water and rock met that milestone considerably earlier. I actually came down to ask a favor."

That was enough to still my own fork. "Go on."

She put down the half-eaten saltcake and splayed her fingers on the table, frowning. "Several times in the past few days, I have failed to conceal my nature. That's a danger, more so with this new power on the campus. I wish to join you in the Meditation on the Waters Within"— it took me a moment to recognize the alternate translation of the Inner Sea—"to better ground my sense of this body and its capabilities. I must restore my control, and this seems like the most efficient way to do it."

I shared an uncomfortable look with the others. "Practicing together has already connected us more tightly than we expected . . ."

"And naturally you don't want to bring this body into your confluence. Nor, I assure you, do I care to involve myself in human family structures. I can show you how to prevent our streams from flowing together permanently—though I'll need a temporary connection. I must compare this body to others, to ensure that I haven't inadvertently deformed it."

We agreed—it was a fair request, and the lesson she'd offered was a useful one—and after cleaning the dishes we went upstairs to the office.

"Do you want to join us?" I asked Neko. I'd asked all the Kotos before, and they'd always refused—though they'd never hesitated, in the camps, to stand guard over my hastily whispered prayers. "This part— it's not religious, or it doesn't have to be."

"You study your way; I'll study in mine. I want to look at that book you were reading earlier—it sounds a lot more interesting without a teacher insisting it's the foundation of all civilization." Charlie handed over the Plato.

CHAPTER 16

Trumbull had clearly been busy—papers on the desk were shuffled, the mysterious device grown larger, and two additional diagrams hung on the walls.

What I knew as a newly reclaimed art was for Trumbull well-practiced technology. She sketched her variant sigils swiftly, narrating as she went.

"The *thng'wy* stands for the blood, but can be altered to represent any vital fluid. This line is made thinner to decrease the strength of connections, and the addition of the *phwl'k* ensures that our wills may overcome such connections as are created during the ritual. It cannot cut connections previously made; that is more difficult and more dangerous." Her terms for the symbols were unfamiliar. The books I knew presented most of these sigils as parts of a whole, to be memorized spell by spell, rather than named components.

But the end was the same as always: the bowl, the blade, salt water, and blood. For that, my experience was not wholly inadequate.

The reunion with my family had shaken me more than expected, and Spector's unpleasant colleagues had been worse. Now I sank into my own body and affirmed my own rhythms.

After a time it felt natural to reach out. Tonight my connection to Charlie and Caleb and Audrey was only physical—perhaps our emotions didn't spill over into our blood without a driving emergency, or perhaps the safeguards provided by Trumbull's sigils made a difference. Experimentally, I sought to change the tenor of the connection. I heard whispers of emotion like voices in a distant room, the edge of something that might have been thought. It felt so faint as to verge on imagination.

Reaching further, I found Trumbull. This too felt entirely physical: waters narrow but unblocked, banks tangled in brambles. But as I explored, I began to sense something hidden amidst the brush. *Predator,* my instinct whispered, but it was not even that. The whole landscape shivered, resolving in a shuddering rush as the thing broke from cover— and then the overwhelming awareness of something not at all physical and not at all human.

It is probably impossible to describe so truly alien a mind in English. Enochian and R'lyehn have better words for strangeness, for thoughts as cold as space, for memories as deep and dense as magma, for minds that know time as intimately as a childhood home.

I recoiled instinctively—but I had promised to look. I forced myself to reach out again. Even braced, its presence burned and froze, but it had drawn the spell to strengthen will and I made myself persist. I could see now how the thing fit itself into Trumbull's form, how it was formed to fold forever into new shapes, to adapt endlessly. How the terrible cold and heat allowed it to maintain identity through all those permutations.

And—harder still—I let the thing look back at me, and sensed the others following my example. I felt it examining joins—invisible even to me—between mind and body, refolding itself to better mimic those connections.

Felt it shrink from something I could not see, then extend a cautious tendril. Felt a hint of Yithian emotion: jagged and vast and faceted with a million associated memories.

And returned to awareness of my own body, Trumbull's inner self fully and mercifully invisible once more. Tenebrous impressions lingered among the rest of us—by our own desire, I suspected. A clutch of mammals, we huddled together for warmth.

Trumbull turned her gaze on Audrey, frowning. "You appear perfectly sane."

Audrey blinked. If she felt any fear or repugnance, she kept it well hidden. "Do people often go mad at the sight of you? That seems like it would be awkward."

"Do you know of anything odd in your heritage? An unidentified grandparent, or an adoption under doubtful circumstances?"

"Of course not. My family's been in Massachusetts for three hundred years, and our records go back even further. Ask the Daughters of the American Revolution if you don't believe me."

Trumbull shrugged. "The interference could be from earlier, I suppose—though the blood is strong."

"I've seen her blood," I said. "It's fine."

"I suppose you've only examined a few people of the air. You should know what you've bound yourself to. Your pupil is unmistakably dust-blooded." She edged away from the rest of us and lifted a hand, as if preparing to defend herself. I resisted the urge to back away from both. Trumbull looked more threatening, but "dust-blooded" was a word rarely heard outside cautionary tales.

Audrey raised an eyebrow. "Maybe you'd better explain what that means. It sounds like an insult."

"It's—" I looked at Audrey, a little nervous myself. I'd made her read the Litany—perhaps it would have been better if I hadn't. "It means you're related to the people of the rock."

"The Mad Ones Under the Earth." Apparently the phrase had stuck in Audrey's mind. I looked at Trumbull, still on her guard against some expected attack, and it occurred to me that for the Yith to lay such a dramatic label on one race out of all those that walked the planet, that race must have made a notable impression.

Audrey's bloodstream didn't look entirely like Charlie's—or Leroy's, now that I thought on it. I had assumed the differences were due to youth and health. "How is that possible?" I asked. "I thought they didn't have children any more, or come to the surface save to guard their gates. It must have been a long time ago."

Trumbull lowered her hand as Audrey continued to appear annoyed but nonviolent. "They do both, very occasionally. For experimental purposes. A female might take a lover of the air to test out some obscure magical theory, or a male choose to sire a half-blood child out of boredom and abandon it later. Either way, the other parent's survival would be remarkable. From the state of your student's blood, I would guess no more than five generations past—though I wouldn't be shocked if it were only a single generation."

"Impossible," said Audrey. "I'd have heard something."

"Not necessarily," said Charlie. "It doesn't seem like the sort of thing people would talk about."

"Or *do*," said Audrey.

"Your air-born ancestors wouldn't necessarily have had much agency in the matter," said Trumbull. "But clearly the Mad Ones didn't have your raising."

Audrey sat back and flexed her nails against the slate. She traced the nearest sigil thoughtfully with her finger. "Say this is true. I've learned a lot this week. It's kind of wild how much. Enough to know that the different kinds of people spread all sorts of rumors about each other, and not all of them true. So what makes you call the people of the rock mad? Am I going to wake up one day gibbering? Will I end up in an asylum?" She took a deep breath. "Is it a bad idea for me to study magic? Everyone who believes in it at all, and some who don't, says magicians risk their sanity, but I always assumed they were blowing smoke."

"It depends what you study," said Trumbull. "The people of the rock started out much like the other branches of humanity. So far as we can tell, their madness isn't carried in their DNA."

"In their . . . what?" I asked, since I suspected no one else would.

"In their . . ." Trumbull counted on the fingers of one hand. "It isn't passed down in their blood. But they studied domains of magic inimical to rational thought, and shared that knowledge with their children. They value the power they get from it more than what they've lost. Or so we infer—the dangers of exposure, and the cruelty with which they destroy suspected outsiders, make it impossible for us to sojourn among them for most of their history."

"Huh. So I shouldn't study . . . ?"

"Transmutation of material forms into energy. Nor should anyone else. Fortunately I doubt those secrets can be found in Miskatonic's stacks."

"Well, that's a relief." Audrey shook her head, smoothed her hair, and frowned. "You sound awfully reassuring. Why did you—" She mimed shrinking away, and made a passable imitation of the way Trumbull had moved her hand.

"As I said, the Mad Ones have children for . . . experimental purposes. Very scientific people, that way. They might easily have attempted to make heritable those things they valued or found intriguing. I must say, you show remarkable skill at magic for someone who has been studying, as I calculate it, for three days and a handful of hours."

"I've only been working on basic stuff. And I think Miss Marsh has been hurrying me a bit." She glanced at me and lowered her eyes. "I haven't taken offense—I know you want to keep going on the more advanced material with Mr. Day. I've been doing my best to keep up."

"Your best has been remarkable," I admitted. "It took us weeks of study to successfully perform the Inner Sea, the first time. And I had already tried it as a child. You didn't have to do it by yourself, but you picked up the principles very quickly."

"Huh." Audrey hugged her knees.

"I don't think this changes anything," I said, as much to reassure her as because I was confident in the decision. "We keep studying, but you let us know if any of it strikes you oddly. We don't try anything that's known to drive whole races to mindless sadism. And we keep an eye out both for signs of trouble in ourselves and for, um, troublesome relatives."

Caleb put a hand on Audrey's arm and looked at her solemnly. "You could follow Grandfather's suggestion and bear my offspring. Children of water and air and rock: they would terrify everyone."

I was about ready to slap him, but Audrey laughed and swatted his hand away. "You are the most improper man I've ever met, and I've met Jesse. Do men of the water always go around making indecent proposals, or is that just one of my special powers?"

"They do *not*," I said to Caleb. "And Mother would have something to say to you *and* to Grandfather."

"That's a relief," said Audrey. She turned to Trumbull. "Okay, enough of that. I know how the story you told earlier ends, and I'm kind of sick of it. What do Yith tell their babies, when they tuck them in at night?" She lifted her chin in challenge.

If I were not careful, I realized, I would start to interpret everything I found admirable and exasperating about her—her skill, her persistence, her refusal to give in to anything stronger and older than herself whether Yith or university—as a sign of her perilous heritage.

"You may be overgeneralizing from your own experience," suggested Trumbull.

"I admit I don't know if you tuck your babies in, or sleep at night. But I'm pretty sure you have kids, and I know you tell stories."

Charlie tapped his cane. "I don't know if any of us will sleep tonight if we hear what the Yith do with their children."

"You disapprove?" Trumbull asked mildly.

"I wasn't under the impression your bodies were immortal. Your kids all go the way of Asenath Waite—you steal their lives so that you can keep going."

"Charlie," I said, my voice low and urgent.

Trumbull laughed. "Miss Marsh, your people are always so politely circumspect about these things. Do you think we're ashamed? Ephraim Waite wanted to live forever, and failed—as all must, sooner or later. What we seek isn't individual immortality, but the preservation of memories. As a child, I would have submitted to that purpose if called on—as most are—and I still will, someday, if I lose the ability to carry my recollections with the respect they're due. But for as long as I can carry them I'll remember the taste of your saltcakes, the sensory impressions that never transmute properly to words, after this world is barren rock. The young mind that nurtures my next body through its development stewards no such store of experience."

Caleb glared at her. "You didn't even like the saltcakes."

"I don't have to appreciate something personally to know that it's beautiful. Or to know that it's an important record." To Audrey: "This is a story I tell my offspring. I was born two worlds before Earth, and on that world I sojourned among a people who communicated by stimulating their bioluminescent symbionts—something like fungi that grew on the surface of their bodies. The symbionts went extinct ten thousand years before the people who spoke through them. After that, they communicated only through writing; they forgot the rhythm of their own songs. But I remember. Song and scent and taste, what it looks like to be conscious of every part of the electromagnetic spectrum, what every sort of sapient body feels like from within—these things matter. And they matter, too, to the children who accept mortality that their ancestors' memories might be carried a little further through the universe."

"Well," said Charlie after a moment. "I suppose if you tell yourself something for a few billion years, it gets convincing." He stood. "If you all will excuse me, I need to get some rest. Mr. Marsh, do you want to come along?"

I put a hand on my brother's arm. "Do you mind staying? I still want to talk."

"Good night, then." Charlie nodded to all of us save Trumbull, and left. I heard the thunk of his cane on the stairs, then the door. I would have to speak with him later, as well.

"I, too, will rest," said Trumbull. She held up a hand, smiled grimly at it. "I must have gotten what I needed from the ceremony, if I find myself trying to explain rather than simply record. It is the place of the Yith to attempt understanding across vast gulfs of experience; there is no purpose in expecting you to do so." With a nod, she rose and left.

The three of us who remained sat silent for a minute.

"I think," Caleb said at length, "that there's a reason most people who meet a Yith in the modern era only spend a few hours in their presence."

"Because that's about how long it takes for their arrogance to overcome your awe at the great keepers of the Archives?" I said. "Or because sooner or later, one feels compelled to pass judgment on them? I have no idea what to do with such judgment."

"There's nothing to do," Caleb said. "She's right—everyone goes out of their way to appease the Yith, but they don't care whether we approve or condemn. I *told* you I didn't want to know her for what she was."

"Hard to avoid, though." I saw Audrey staring quietly at the door, and asked: "Are you all right?"

She laughed. "That's an interesting question. I'm more all right than I was Wednesday morning. Leroy's hurt, but everything else . . . all that's changed is that I know more."

"That's not a small thing," I said.

"Are you gonna keep looking at me that way? Because I promise, I'm no more likely to explode than I was yesterday."

"I know. And I saw this morning what you're like under pressure. You don't lose your mind in a crisis, and that's huge." I paused; I had a feeling it wouldn't do to be dishonest with anyone in my confluence. "I'm sorry. I grew up hearing stories about the Mad Ones, and I suspect knowing one will take a little getting used to. I'll do my best."

"Like I said, if there's one thing I've learned over the past few days, it's to be suspicious of the stories everyone knows."

"The stories of the Mad Ones come from many sources," I said reluctantly. "The Yith, the people of the air, the people of the water. All have testimony from those who stumble under the earth—the few that come back. All those travelers agree about what they've seen."

"Which is what, exactly? If the people of the rock learned their suspicion of outsiders from meeting the Yith . . . maybe they're just a little more willing to pass judgment than the rest of us."

Caleb flinched, but said sharply: "And a little more willing to torture trespassers to death, and breed thinking creatures as cattle for food. Of all people, they'd see nothing wrong in what the Yith do. They might be confused that the Great Race gives any justification other than their own passing desires."

Audrey considered that, then nodded. "Even the ancestors I know about have done some nasty things. However awful my secret crazy relatives were, they did something decent leaving their kids alone. Letting us grow up unburied by duty, or whatever it is they stick on kids in place of duty."

"Duty's not a bad thing, necessarily," I said. "It depends what it is—and who's defining it."

"You gonna have those babies, then?"

I started—not because I hadn't been thinking about the question, but because I hadn't intended to discuss it with anyone but Caleb. "Maybe. After our conversation with Trumbull, having children and doing right by them feels more important. But if some part of my mind thinks I'm going to prove a point to Trumbull that way, it's going to be disappointed."

We talked more: nothing adequate to the revelations of the day. Perhaps it was a flaw in our language, or in our species.

CHAPTER 17

A t last we noted the hour, and Audrey realized that the bus to Kingsport had already stopped running. She asked to stay the night, and we went downstairs to check the idea with Neko.

I was relieved to see that she was alone in the living room. "There you are," she said. "I heard Professor Trumbull go to bed a while ago."

"It's been a long night," I said. "Do you mind bunking with me? Audrey's missed her bus."

"That's fine." She held up the Plato. "Have you read this thing? He wants people to hand over their babies to the state, and have just a few people raise them all!"

It sounded like a horrible idea, and yet. "He could have worse suggestions."

She put the book down on the side table, stood to wrap her arms around me. I returned the hug, grateful.

"Before you share a room with me," said Audrey, looking at her hands, "you should know that I'm part inhuman monster."

"It's okay," said Neko. "We're all monsters here."

Audrey whipped her head around to stare, then came over and embraced Neko.

"Entirely human monsters, to be precise," said Caleb. "Trumbull's the only *inhuman* monster in the house."

"Point," said Audrey. "In the future, I'll try to be more specific about the crazy cannibalistic branch of my family."

Neko took her to find fresh sheets, leaving me alone at last with my brother.

"I want to go to the chapel," I told him. "Walk with me?"

"After a day like this, you want to pray?" he asked.

"Or meditate. Away from Trumbull's house. You don't have to stick around; we can talk on the way."

Outside, there was no sign of the gate guards. Broad wet flakes still drifted through the air. The sidewalks, only partly cleared, were coated in a thin layer of white. I hoped Charlie had made it back without trouble. I scuffed my foot; it didn't seem too slippery.

The aeon that Trumbull came here from was warm: the atmosphere a different composition, the Earth at a hotter phase of her cycles. It would never snow, except perhaps on the highest mountain peaks. The same was true when they stole the bodies of the eldermost, who carved their polar cities from seething jungle rather than the glaciers that buried them now. And it would be hot once more in the time of the ck'chk'ck. How had I never noticed that in the Litany before? The Yith's original world, however far back, must have been a sweltering place.

"It was so good to see our elders again," said Caleb without preamble. "But somehow I'd come to imagine them as— If only I could prove that I'd done *something,* they'd swoop in and make everything all right. Everything that could be made right."

"They could still help. Although I'm reluctant to invite them near Miskatonic at the moment." I thought of the soldiers with their guns and talismans. "I wonder if we should do as Grandfather and the archpriest suggested. If we ought to try and . . . but I don't know if I can bear it. Caleb?"

He cocked his head, and my heart ached with the familiarity of his silhouette, with its similarity to mine.

"What are you doing with Dawson?"

He started, which gave me my answer, then tucked his chin and stuck his hands in his pockets. It made him look younger. "I've taken her as a lover."

"Are you trying to get her with child?"

"It's only been a few days. But I'm not trying to prevent it." He shuffled. "It's not like it was in the camps. She could bear and raise healthy offspring. If it takes after us, she'd have a powerful child to look out for her. And it *is* what Grandfather wants."

"You didn't say anything when he asked."

"I didn't want him to talk about Deedee the way he was talking about . . . other possible mates."

"You have to know," I said, "how these people treat women who have children out of wedlock. It's not right to subject her to that. Unless—you're not thinking of marrying her, are you?"

"Of course I'm not going to marry her. How much mourning do you think *I* want to do? But Deedee's not a fool. She's been made to play mistress to Dean Skinner, because he's useful to the government—it's better than what she was doing before, so she puts up with it. But do you think she hasn't thought about how to get out of it?"

"So you two talked, and she told you to get her pregnant as some . . . ornate letter of resignation?"

"Don't mock. You just sat around pitying her; I'm the one who did something. Of course we haven't talked about it. That would be planning treason, or something like it, on her part. This way she can testify that the inhumanly charismatic Deep One seduced her—she couldn't possibly have been expected to resist."

I looked up at my brother. "You're inhumanly charismatic?"

"They certainly won't believe she wanted me for my looks."

A swarm of boys passed, raucous with shouted plans and friendly teasing. All were clean-shaven, pale, small-eyed, handsome by any ordinary standard.

"Tell her," I said. "It's far better for her to lie to the state about whether she had a choice in the matter than for you to steal that choice. Even if not for her sake—suppose you want to teach the child our ways, later, and she flees inland? A few children who never knew themselves until they changed, or carried a touch of our blood and never knew at all—that was one thing when the bulk of our people were born and raised in Innsmouth, but is it all we want now?"

"Is it?" he said. "Do we want to rebuild?"

"I don't know." My thoughts coalesced: listening to myself, I learned what I believed. "But of the idea of our children *never* knowing their nature, always wondering until the change why they don't fit in— I don't want that. To me, the choice is to have offspring we can raise and teach, or to accept our place as the water's last and youngest children."

What an interesting—terrifying—thing to think.

"She's not the sort of person who wants everything laid out cleanly," he said. "Sometimes it even makes her angry. You saw."

"She might get angry either way—better now than later. I don't care if you lay it out cleanly, or in subtle insinuations, or in Morse Code. Just have an actual discussion about the possibility of an amphibious child."

"I'll think about it." He traced a line in the snow-covered walk with the toe of his boot. "She won't listen to you, if you try."

"I know. That's why I'm not threatening to do so." It occurred to me, seeing his discomfort, that after the camps I'd sought connections, while he'd fled them. Perhaps he needed this kind of baroque excuse to let himself get close to someone new. For all I knew, Dawson did too: in many ways her own brittleness seemed a match for his. "Caleb? Let her know that if she'd rather another way out, we'll find one. I don't want you to be another man she has no choice about."

He hunched his chin into his chest. "We've talked about *that*."

December 1945: In San Francisco, the Nihonmachi—Japantown—regenerates in patches. The Kotos find a one-room apartment in a building shared with a dozen other newly released families, and every morning we scatter looking for temporary work that will let us keep the place, and then for better work that

will let us save for a larger one. We all want something less reminiscent of the camp's confining cabins.

Caleb and I, who wake every day shocked by hills and mist and the scent of salt, vacillate among extremes. I walk for hours with aching feet, testing my reclaimed strength and reveling in streets full of strangers, then in a moment find myself clutched by panic to realize my brother's out of sight. Caleb clings to me all night, drawing Kevin into our tangle when the boy wakes with nightmares, then screams at everyone when he finds an orange going bad in a bowl of precious fruit.

After a month of freedom, Mama Rei has regular business taking in mending. Anna finds work at the laundromat. And I walk into a bookstore with a help wanted sign in the window and stand utterly still, forgetting my purpose entirely amid the heady scent, until the proprietor asks impatiently what I want.

"I have to go back," Caleb tells us at dinner. There's fresh salmon, rolled with rice and seaweed, to celebrate Anna's and my newfound work. It tastes of home and freedom and strangeness, and I push down memories as I eat.

"Back where?" Mama Rei asks. But I know what he's tasted.

"You want to go back to Innsmouth," I say. "Caleb, there's nothing there."

"You don't know that," he says. "Someone must have taken our books, looted our houses. The elders might still be around, too." It's hard to imagine: that anyone would wait for us so long, that they wouldn't blame us for surviving. "Someone needs to go back and look."

"By yourself?" I ask. I put down my chopsticks, suddenly queasy as I imagine things we've lost, things that would be more achingly familiar than the raw fish.

But he nods, and I can see his relief at admitting it. "I need to be alone for a while. I need to find out what's still there."

We were getting close to the church. Caleb craned his neck, blinking rapidly at the white-tipped crenellations. "Whatever we're doing— I still want to save our books. Even if there are no children to learn from them."

"Agreed," I said, though it hurt to think of them going unused.

"We need help. The elders care about the knowledge those books hold, but I don't think they really care about them as artifacts. They're willing to put them aside. Maybe it's Trumbull we should be talking to, if we want someone who cares about the journals, and the marginalia, and the family records inside the covers."

"You want us to ask *that* for a favor?"

"By *that*, do you mean the ancient intelligence who cares little for our petty mortal concerns? Or do you mean the Yith who does what we've always known they do to survive, and has the nerve not to be ashamed of it? Because I don't like those things either, but we may as well use the 'Great Ones' as people always have—deference and indulgence in exchange for legacy. She's the one who got us into the library in the first place—even if only as a means to see the books herself. They must have a place to store records locally. Perhaps with one of their cults. I don't really care, as long as they let us in without reservation, and as long as Innsmouth's books are out of the hands of the thieves who stole them."

I started to speak, trailed off as rebuttals failed to coalesce. All I had was the gut horror of what Trumbull had told us—I did not want to ask her for help.

He switched to R'lyehn: "It shows something about humans that we depend on the Yith for remembrance, but turn deaf to the cost until they say it plainly to our ears. Then we prate of scandal and horror. You don't actually dislike the idea, you just don't like how it tastes. You need to figure out what you really want, and what that's worth." He paused, and said more quietly. "*We* need to figure it out. With Audrey and Charlie. The three of you are all I'm sure of right now, odd as it seems—and if we don't act together, I don't think we'll succeed at any endeavor."

"You . . ." I wasn't going to put it off, as he had with Dawson. "You're right, I think. I'll meditate on it and we'll talk, all of us. And I'll think on Trumbull, too. Maybe it's wrong of me to be repulsed by what she said—or maybe it's wrong not to have been repulsed before."

"Of course we should be repulsed. But we have no control over who the Yith sacrifice. We do have control—a very little—over what redeems that loss. What's remembered and preserved. I won't be forgotten, or have our parents forgotten, because I wish the Yith had found another way."

We stopped outside the church door. "Two days ago you wanted nothing to do with Trumbull, and were ready to let the land burn."

He shrugged uncomfortably. "I'm still angry. But if I'm not dying, I don't have the luxury of letting that anger cloud my judgment."

"Do you want to come in?"

He shook his head. "Not yet."

The church's gas-lit interior was only a little warmer than the snow outside. The air within was still, held in place by stone and stained glass, broken only by a faint trail of cool wind as I passed the center aisle.

No one else moved in the building. Any night in Innsmouth, a priest would have tended the temple: ensuring all was right with the altars and statues, waiting for congregants who might need a thoughtful ear. Dusk brings questions, and when darkness falls it's a poor time to be alone with them.

I was glad enough for the solitude, this time—I would hardly have asked the archpriest for advice on the confusion he himself had raised.

I settled in the god's embrace, and lit the altar candle.

It's common to meditate on the gods and their functions—though any priest would tell you those functions, the personalities claimed for them, the divisions among different species of deity, are simplified for the understanding of the young, with the priests themselves very much included in that category. There's risk in defining the indefinable. Still, the stories serve purposes: guides for worship, mnemonics for virtues and fears, ways to consider the unknowable without being entirely overwhelmed.

Iä, Dagon, guardian of waters, steadfast. And yet absent from Innsmouth when needed.

Iä, Hydra, defender of waters, fierce. And absent too—here I could imagine Her well enough to feel bitter about that, as I could not in the museum. It had been a while since I'd prayed to Innsmouth's presumed patrons at any length.

Iä, Cthulhu, bringer of life and death, ever patient. I'd always felt most comfortable with the Sleeping God, and more so now. Cthulhu listens, and never promises aid that cannot be forthcoming.

Iä, Nyarlathotep, herald of knowledge. A favorite of the Yith. But I considered the psychopomp's customary role: showing the path to what was hidden, ensuring that wisdom could never be fully censored or forbidden or lost. I imagined a black-robed figure treading the echoing floors of the library, entering the stacks that Miskatonic's guardians thought theirs alone, and smiling. Of course, it would as smilingly open those doors for Russian spies as for us. Nyarlathotep doesn't play favorites, or try to protect anyone from the consequences of newfound knowledge.

Iä, Yog-Sothoth, maker and keeper of gates.

Iä, Azathoth, void and melody.

Iä, Shub-Nigaroth, mother of fear. I had never understood that cognomen, had taken it as a joke when Mother simply said that children were terrifying. *Have you not just told me of my own daughter's death?* Now, thinking of Grandfather's raw mourning, I believed her—and feared further understanding. I thought on that fear a long time, and reached out to touch an encircling tentacle.

A whisper of motion, a breath of ice, told me that someone else had entered the church. I froze, but didn't blow out the candle. I stood and faced the nave, ready to argue for my presence.

After staring so long into the flame, the rest of the church appeared dim and deeply shadowed. My nostrils flared, and brought me the scent of snow and musky cologne, some odd chemical astringence, and below that the more natural musk of a nervous man of the air. Boots scraped the floor, and at last my eyes picked out the form of Jesse Sadler. I felt a wave of irritation before recalling that Leroy was a good friend of his. The astringent scent was from the hospital, and he had every right to seek me out.

Although hadn't Leroy and Sally sworn not to mention my family?

"Miss Marsh?" he called hesitantly.

I stepped to the side. "You're welcome to join me."

He trod into the circle of candlelight. "Please don't be angry. I kept pressing them—I knew that Audrey hadn't gone to Innsmouth. Finally, after she left, Sally told me to ask you. I thought I might find you here."

Apparently Audrey's lessons in effective deception went only so far. "Suppose I tell you that what happened isn't likely to be a danger to you and yours again, and that you're better off not knowing? Because both those things are true."

"Then I would agree that you're probably right, and leave."

I sighed. "And promptly do everything in your power to investigate?"

He sank to the floor before the altar, kissed two fingers and touched them to the stone. "I'm a biology minor. I know the track and sign of every animal found in eastern Massachusetts. There are no wolves. If there are monsters, they fall within the scope of my major—and they could carry all manner of infection, or have developed a taste for my best friend's blood. So no, I can't leave be." He shrugged and spread his arms. "I really hope Sally wasn't hinting that I ought to bring some sort of weapon and force you to help. It seemed like a terrible idea— but if you're going to grow claws and attack me, you may as well do it now."

I shuddered and sat beside him. "I'm glad you didn't. I've had a horrible day already."

"I heard those weird government people arrested a bunch of girls earlier. That wasn't you and Audrey, was it?"

"That was me, yes. But not Audrey, who's more sensible than to come in through a guarded gate. They let us go, anyway."

He nodded. "I don't like having those people on campus. Miskatonic minds its own business, and they just come barging in here like they know anything about us. Are they looking for whatever got Leroy?"

194 • RUTHANNA EMRYS

I rubbed my arms as if against the chill. I brushed my hand across my forearm and the sigil that connected me to Sally, caught the echo of tension and boredom in her distant skin. "No. Them arriving today is—not coincidence, I think, but not directly connected, either." I weighed whether to warn him that they were interested in his old friend Kirill. "As for what attacked Leroy . . . he ran afoul of my family."

"Your family have claws?" His eyes flicked downward, and I held out my long-fingered hands with their ordinary nails for his inspection.

"Some of us. Give me a few years." Explaining this to him was a terrible idea—but it was late, and I was tired, and I couldn't see a good way around it. Perhaps I needed lessons from Audrey as well. "Leroy was rude to her. She was rude to him. He hit her, and she was hurt enough to fight back. I don't think she gained any taste for his blood— she helped us save him."

"Huh." He leaned back, and it took me a moment to interpret the expression on his face as a sort of horrified wonder. "I don't suppose they'd talk to me? It must be an amazing thing, going through that kind of change—I mean, I assume you don't *just* grow claws?"

I stiffened. "I thought you believed there were things beyond human understanding."

"Cosmic mysteries that can't be understood through science, sure. But this is *biology*."

"We're not some sort of experiment for your edification."

He held up his hands, placating. "Sorry—I didn't mean to upset you again. But you can't blame a guy for being curious." He reached out and touched my cheek.

I should have slapped him at once for taking such a liberty. Instead, I'm ashamed to say, I froze. He took that as invitation, and drew my face toward his. His breath smelled of burnt meat and a horrid mixture of fear and excitement, and it spurred me into motion. I pushed him back—harder than I intended to, harder than an ordinary woman of my size could have managed. He flung his arms back and managed

to avoid hitting his head against the stone wall of the shrine. He lay
still for a moment, blinking rapidly.

"Mr. Sadler," I said, drawing from script. "I'm afraid you have misunderstood me entirely."

"Yeah." He sat up, rubbing his neck and eyeing me more cautiously—
though with no less desire. "I'm sorry. I didn't mean any offense."

"So long as you keep your hands to yourself, we'll forget that it
happened."

He nodded, and examined his arms. They looked bruised, and I
caught a whiff of blood. "I'm sorry," he repeated. "I won't try it again.
I take a girl at her word. Safer that way—especially with you!"

I tried to reclaim the trail of our conversation. "That may be. I don't
think you'd get along with my family, either, and I hope you'll respect
my not making introductions. As for this afternoon—Miss Ward told
me about your tryst with her and Mr. Price."

He blanched. "She told you about that?" He swallowed, added
quietly: "She was . . . I mean, we didn't . . ."

"As long as they were both interested, it doesn't change my opinion
of you"—*irritating and smarmy, with extremely foolish ideas about magic*—
"but she told me as surety for her silence, and I won't hesitate to tell
those who *will* object, if you start talking to people about my family.
We've suffered greatly when others knew of our presence, and all we
want now is to be left alone."

Jesse nodded hurriedly. "I understand, I really do." He stood, started
to back away. "Uh—is there anything I should know? To help Leroy?"

I shook my head. "At this point, they're just ordinary wounds. I did
everything I could for him before he went anywhere near the hospital."

"Gotcha. Okay. Good. I'll see you around."

I waited until the door creaked shut and I could no longer hear his
boots. I knelt before the altar, curled against myself until my forehead
touched the cool marble floor, and wished for the vastness of the ocean
between me and all men of the air.

CHAPTER 18

I slept poorly. No sickening dreams whose reality I might deny—instead, I startled awake a dozen times, convinced that a particular camp guard loomed in the door to check on our slumber. Once I woke Neko as well, whimpering the man's name, and she shivered and put her arm over me.

When at last I came down to breakfast, Trumbull had covered half the table with syllabi and lesson plans. "The library is a chaos of forgetful students and teaching assistants waiting to use the mimeograph machines. They all smell like chewing gum. The department can't spare an assistant for me, of course."

Her mundane exasperation startled a laugh from me, and eased the fog of fatigue. It was hard to hold on to my revulsion. Neko handed me a plate of fried eggs and a cup of tea. She sat beside Audrey, who'd finished her own breakfast and was reading the Sunday paper with pursed lips.

"Perhaps this isn't a good day to brave the stacks," I suggested. "Or will it be that bad all the time, now that the students have returned?"

"Last semester the bedlam was confined to their first day back," said Trumbull. "If that's typical, tomorrow should be safer."

So, she'd arrived last summer. In four years or so, I'd need to come back to the university and see if I couldn't help the real Trumbull through the shock of her return. For now, I needed to be on this Trumbull's good side if I was to follow up on Caleb's suggestion. "Is there anything I can do to help?"

"If you'd asked earlier, I might have made you brave the crawling crowd. At this point, I just need to look over my notes, and do a last check for anachronistic insights. The same horrible low-level classes every semester—the price one pays for access to the university resources, and I gather the other professors feel much the same."

"Ah." I peered over her notes, sideways, but the last of my mathematics had been the most basic of algebra, two decades past.

Trumbull tapped her pencil on the table. "Well? Whatever you want to ask, it will at least be a distraction."

I glanced at Neko and Audrey—but my desires here were a secret from neither. "We're still discussing what to do about the spawning grounds, but Caleb and I thought—that is, we hoped you might be willing to help us retrieve our books. You're as frustrated with the limited access as we are. Your people must have places where you store records in this era. Followers who help out when you want to do something authorities might not like."

She snorted. "Certainly we have places to store temporary records. We call the local one Miskatonic University."

I dropped my eyes. "Oh. But still . . ."

"Despite its inconveniences, we have long cultivated this place as a shelter and way station for knowledge worthy of preservation. One of our architects helped design the library. Our cultists, we choose primarily for tractability. They don't know the first thing about even primitive archival technique. I have no interest in exposing your texts to the vagaries of amateur storage. And I think perhaps you underestimate the size of the collection."

I let it lie, and wished I hadn't spoken at all. The elders, if willing, could offer gold and magical support—but Trumbull's resources were more suited to quietly moving well-guarded records. Or to keeping records well-guarded. Now that I'd mentioned it, she might well wield those resources against us. Even given a new spawning ground to support, the elders might not dare to gainsay her.

Someone knocked on the door, and Neko went to answer it. Trumbull didn't even begin to rise. Had she ever actually received visitors, before we arrived?

Spector stomped snow off his boots before entering. Charlie followed.

"Where's Caleb?" I asked.

"He'll be along," said Charlie. He eyed Trumbull. "Said he had someone to talk to."

"Oh, good." I hoped Dawson would listen—but was glad either way that Caleb had done so.

"George's people are off the gate," said Spector. He shrugged out of his coat. "That's good, except that I don't know where they are now. Best I could tell from last night's dinner, they're after something besides the obvious, but George didn't drink enough to do more than hint."

"Did he, perhaps, apologize?" I asked.

"George, apologize? Only if you count insinuations about what rock I turned over to find the lot of you. Begging your pardons."

Trumbull shrugged. "You may assure him the low opinion is mutual."

"Oh, I think he knows. Is that more tea? Wonderful—thank you, Miss Koto. I'm feeling a bit under the weather this morning."

Spector reached past me to take the tea. Beneath his familiar lemon-and-soap, and the clean smell of snow still melting in his hair, I caught another odor startling in its greater familiarity: Charlie's scent mixed with his. I frowned. Had Charlie fallen again, or needed help along the walks? But this smelled like a lengthier exposure, and less recent.

Charlie still struggled with his coat and cane, and I went over to help him. I inhaled deeply and found lemon and soap tangled in his hair, and a male arousal not his own. The fear, though—that was entirely Charlie.

"Come outside," I said, abruptly changing course on his coat. "I need to talk."

As soon as the door shut behind us, I put a hand on his arm. "Are you hurt?"

"What?" He jerked back. "No, I'm fine, why?"

More gently, I asked, "Did Spector hurt you?" He seemed disinclined to answer. "I can smell where he touched you."

Charlie's face reddened, and he lowered his voice. "Miss Marsh, you can't just—say these things—in public."

Scattered masses of students passed on the other side of the street, but none ventured across to the faculty row. "No one's in earshot, unless they have ears as good as mine. I just want to know whether you're all right."

He swallowed visibly. "Yes. I'm all right. Yesterday was . . . a long day. He offered to share his scotch, and we got to talking, and—I'm sorry."

"For what? I suppose I could fault your choice of lovers—" I paused and considered Spector. What did I hold against him? That he'd attempted to recruit me, and backed off when he realized the insult. That he made use of me, in ways that benefited both of us. That he worked for a state that had hurt me, and done his best to ease that hurt and to ensure it wouldn't be repeated. "But I don't. He makes me uncomfortable, but he's working, harder than most ever bother, to be a good person."

He looked directly at me for the first time all morning. His cheeks were still flushed, and every muscle drawn tense. "Things must be very different among your people."

Of course the Christian world's disapproval must weigh heavy on his mind, as it did for Leroy and Jesse. I shrugged. "Priests of the air can be hypocrites for fifty years about things that can't be ignored for fifty thousand. We wed in order to breed on land"—and here I swallowed—"but for some, water lovers are a different matter. Of course people of the air can't simply wait."

The color in his cheeks deepened. "You realize we could go to jail. If there were even rumors, Ron—Mr. Spector—could lose his job."

I hadn't thought about that. "You know I won't risk you going through any such thing."

He ducked his head. "Caleb was staring at me this morning. I thought he was just in a poor mood, but . . ."

"I'll speak with him." I paused, still thinking of my own people's strictures. "I wonder if we ought to do as Grandfather suggested after all. Before, I assumed you'd eventually want to take a wife of your own people. You still might, I suppose."

He shook his head violently—and then more so. "Miss Marsh! Your grandfather . . . I couldn't. I wouldn't do that to you. I can't believe he made that suggestion."

I shrugged. "He's right that I'll mourn you. Having a child—and perhaps mourning them as well—frightens me terribly, and I'm beginning to believe I must. But I won't press; I didn't mean to offend you." Now I could feel myself flushing. With a little effort, I could have forced my capillaries to dilate, and looked perfectly calm. That seemed a poor idea. "Your own family must expect children, though?"

He winced. "My family also expects me to move back to L.A. and join my dad's insurance business. I'm used to disappointing them."

"Ah." Snow stuck in clumps to the juniper bushes beside Trumbull's front step. I ran my finger through the greenery, examined the crystals as they melted against my skin. "You were angry at my family, yesterday."

"They expect too much from you."

"Caleb and I are all they have left on land." The snow soothed, melting to clean cold water against the lines of my palm. "If that's a lot of weight to bear, it's no flaw or malice on their part."

He adjusted his feet around the cane, and I knew we ought to go back inside and find him a seat. But I didn't want to break the conversation.

He said: "You told your grandfather and your priest, plain as day, that you didn't appreciate them trying to matchmake. And they kept at it anyway."

I shrugged. "They're right that I have an obligation. I didn't want to admit it, but I also—it's not reasonable; it can't be entirely Caleb's and my choice whether there will ever be more of our people. I don't blame them for having opinions—or for how they expressed those opinions—when they'd just learned we were still alive."

He caught his breath. "I hadn't thought about that part. I suppose if my grandparents believed I was dead, I might forgive whatever they said when they found me."

"All the elders on that beach had just learned, too, who they *had* lost. Children, grandchildren, friends, husbands—we're *all* they have left. That matters, even if I don't like the weight." For a moment, the image of life without that burden washed over me. I pictured an Innsmouth never raided. A husband of my own people, children preparing to come of age. There might still be heartache in such a world: a friend lost to a storm, a child stillborn. "The universe is what it is."

He opened his hand, tilted it as if letting something fall. "I'll do what I can to help." Then he blushed. He'd already said he wouldn't—though I couldn't hold it against him. "Are you certain you're the last? Did all your people stay so close to home?"

It was a fair question. "The soldiers came in the middle of winter, and the boats were all at dock. We had people away at school—but most were brought to the camp in the weeks after the raid. We assumed those who didn't appear hadn't been taken alive. Any survivors would have sought out the elders, if they could. And there are lost children, of course, mist-bloods. Most in whom our blood ran true must have gone into the water long ago, but I suppose it's possible that the youngest are still on land. And those with weak blood might still come together, and have children who can change as their parents cannot. It happens; usually they're impossible to find before their metamorphosis. And then they make their own way home."

"You could look."

I nodded. I wasn't hopeful, but I thought of the stolen child that Chulzh'th had been unable to track, and wondered if he'd ever made it into the water. If not, he'd be old now, but his offspring would still carry strength in their blood. A mist-blooded man could give me children I'd be less likely to lose. "I'll ask the elders if they know of anywhere to look."

Trumbull hadn't so much as gathered wood for her hearth, but the radiators kept her house warm. I found it stifling, though the others seemed comfortable enough.

"Everything okay?" asked Audrey, and I nodded.

The small crowd around the dining room table felt uneasy, interactions edged with sandpaper. Everyone still trod cautiously around Trumbull—Charlie in particular. With luck I was the only one who noticed how he and Spector had grown formal. I ought to try and ease the tensions, as Neko did, but I wished only to run back to the ice and snow.

"Audrey," I said, and she looked up. "You're the . . . sneakiest person here."

She nodded cheerfully. Spector raised his eyebrows and pointed at himself in exaggerated fashion, and she pouted.

I continued over their byplay: "I hope Barlow's people have given up on guarding the gate, but I don't want to count on it. Can you show me how you got onto the campus?"

She shrugged. "Sure." She finished her tea in a gulp, and stood. "Lead on. Or let me lead, since I know where we're going."

Outside, she bumped against me, a moment's comforting touch. "Something's eating you."

"Yith. Or perhaps government agents eager to arrest us? I just felt closed in, honestly—thanks for helping out."

"No problem. I'm feeling a little twitchy myself. And you ought to learn how to sneak, anyway."

"Do you need to get back to Hall?" I asked.

"Eventually. I've missed morning chapel, though—so either I'm already in trouble, or they think I'm at the hospital with Sally. Either way, it can wait."

The faculty row stood on the opposite side of campus from the main gate. Audrey strode confidently through the grounds. I tried to emulate her, but felt terribly exposed. We were the only women in sight—elsewhere there must be secretaries, maids, others who filled the gaps left open by the school's aristocracy, but this morning the quads were full of faculty and students, and of scattered handymen clearing paths through the snow. Some of the boys whistled or called out, and Audrey nodded regally as if they had knelt before her. The difference in our dress made me even more self-conscious: Audrey all fashion in her knee-length blue skirt and a hat that was mostly an excuse for its feather, me in my sedate mourning dress that met neither my own standards nor those of the folk around me. *I am a Marsh,* I thought, and tried to move like a queen rather than like prey.

As promised, we saw no sign of intruders either in the depths of campus or at the entrance. I wished I could believe they'd stay away. From the gate, we followed the winding path that shadowed the fence posts. Well-tended near the facades of the History and Biology departments, elsewhere it grew wild with pine and winter-bare bramble. In these areas the crowd thinned, and those who remained kept their heads down.

"Here we are," said Audrey. We abandoned the main path for a little curve hidden by juniper hedges. A fountain nestled in their arch: a long-dry mermaid spilled nothing from her conch shell. Ivy half-drowned her tail and splashed across her chest and shoulders. Someone had crowned her with a handwoven wreath of vines, long since turned brown.

"Meet Chastity," Audrey said. She laughed. "People bring her offerings when they haven't been living up to her name. See?" She waded the ivy-filled basin, held up a few coins, and tossed them back.

"Do people come here often?"

"Not on a Sunday morning. But she's conveniently located on the way to and from the opportunity for sin."

As promised, an oak spread over the mermaid's nook. She was an old archpriest of a tree, full of twists and splits, bark rich with folds.

One branch dipped low over a marble bench, and standing on tiptoe Audrey pulled herself up.

"It's not dignified," she called. "But it's not a bad climb."

I hadn't climbed a tree in twenty years, and even then Caleb had been better. But my new-grown strength proved useful as I grasped the handholds Audrey showed me, and got my feet into the branch's saddle. I grimaced as twigs tugged my skirt, but moved carefully and did not tear it. Audrey showed me where to place each step. Her route was well-practiced, and I watched carefully to mimic the little shifts of balance that passed beneath her notice.

From the ground Chastity had been a smooth-skinned and well-proportioned woman of the air, only her tail betraying her disinterest in admirers. From above, I could see that her thick marble hair grew from a scaled scalp, and tiny snakes twined within. One pointed ear poked above the tilted wreath of vines.

We crept to the central trunk. Here, where there might otherwise have been an awkward breach in the aerial passage, some thoughtful student had long ago nailed a wooden block as a much-needed foot-hold. The bark curved out around it; in another fifty years it would be only an indented scar. I clenched my fingers tightly above as I stepped from branch to block to branch again. Audrey dropped to all fours and peered cautiously over the fence. She pulled her head back and put a finger to her lips.

Over the whisper of wind I heard voices on the street beyond. Two voices, familiar: they'd made a strong impression while I was blind-folded. I shrunk away and clung to the damp bark. If I moved forward a little, I might be able to understand more clearly, but I was reluctant to take the risk. Words drifted up in isolation: "Doubt . . . ask . . . students . . . stupid to . . ." And then they passed beyond our overlook.

Audrey inched back. "We'd better leave off for now," she murmured. "Normally Garrison Street is pretty deserted."

Back on the ground, I did my best to brush off my skirt and blouse. Audrey picked a few pieces of wet bark from my hair.

"That was them," I whispered. "George Barlow, and one of the soldiers who arrested us yesterday. Peters, I think."

She dropped a dead leaf into the ivy, paused. "Did you hear what they were saying?"

"I couldn't catch it. Something about students and stupidity."

She snorted, and started for the fence. I grabbed her arm and drew her back. "Don't, they're dangerous. And if I couldn't hear them, you won't be able to."

"How d'you know? I might have secret rock powers." She pulled away—I didn't hold tightly enough to stop her—and headed back toward the fence. It was thoroughly draped with ivy: someone on the other side might be able to see through, but only if they pressed close to look. I thought of what they might say, unheard, and went after her.

We followed the path, pausing as I tried to pick out voices across the sounds of wind and wildlife and the more distant babble of conversation within the campus grounds. After a couple of hundred feet I caught their cadences again. But off the path, the snow hid a crackling of dry leaves and twigs. Every time I tried to get closer, I rustled one thing or snapped another. Audrey moved lightly: she occasionally tested before putting her weight down, but more often picked the silent spots by eye and captured them in short, swift steps like a stalking heron. At last she crouched beside the curtain of vines. I watched anxiously, hearing the voices rise and fall. Their location seemed to change, and I thought that Barlow might be pacing.

At last the voices silenced, and Audrey made her way back. I wanted to demand a report as soon as she got close, but refrained. I beckoned her further inward, and we hurried to put distance between ourselves and the fence.

Once we were out of sight, I gave in to temptation. "Well?"

"Well." She bounced on her toes, cheeks flushed. "Secret agents, unfortunately, turn out not to discuss specific plans on public streets."

"I don't think they're 'secret' agents," I said. "We'd all be better off if they tried to keep out of sight."

"Whatever they are, they're cryptic. They were arguing about whether it mattered if 'they' have 'it,' or whether 'we' need 'it' whether or not they have it. It sounded like they just walked out of the same discussion with the rest of their group."

"Ah."

"Ah? You know what they're talking about?"

"Perhaps." I felt sick—I'd already thought about what disasters an enemy might provoke, clothed in the bodies of those in power. I'd somehow managed to avoid considering what Spector's own allies and colleagues could do with the same tool. The next world war would be equally deadly regardless of who started it—and perhaps worse for my own people if the state that still hosted them took the lead.

I really ought to speak with Spector before sharing his concerns with one of Kirill's old friends. That I trusted Audrey—for the most part—didn't mean that her friends were trustworthy, as I had cause to know. Still, while the specifics of what Spector had found weren't mine to divulge, she deserved to know the generalities. "They might be interested in magic for switching bodies. Trumbull's people do that, usually temporarily, but a few humans have also learned how—most often to steal younger bodies for their own immortality."

She pursed her lips thoughtfully. "You were talking about that the other night. Sounds like the Yith do the same thing."

"Yes. But when humans do it, by all the laws of the Aeonist faith it's a capital crime. Normally it's mad old magicians—the sort who're mad before they start their studies, not the sort driven mad by them. If the state starts using this spell as a tool of war, it will go badly for everyone."

"Huh. Why isn't it a capital crime for the Yith?"

I sighed. "Everything that will survive of Earth, survives because of their work. And there's the practical difficulty of trying to execute them, but that hardly matters—humans have chosen to honor the Yith's work, and to believe its cost worthwhile. If any of this world's other species think differently—and there are some who'd have cause—the Archives don't record it."

Audrey hummed softly to herself. "I wish I knew that song she remembers."

I nodded, imagining the symbionts Trumbull had described, their melodies of light and color. In my people's deep cities there were creatures that might be able to sing such a song: bioluminescent squid, and fish that once fluoresced only to attract prey, now bred to decorate sunken streets.

Audrey shook herself. "The spooks are less interesting to think about, but we probably should. Is it illegal, if they don't want to switch permanently?"

"I don't know." I thought about it. "That's not usually how humans do it—most wouldn't learn how to switch bodies at all, because the assumption is that you'd misuse it."

She laughed. "Lots of ways to misuse body swapping without stealing anyone's youth. Or to use it perfectly nicely. I think your body thieves must not have much imagination. Aren't you curious what it's like to have a different body? To be a man, or to be an Olympic athlete? Or just to be taller?" Audrey looked up at me. "If you gave the body back afterward, or if you were switching with someone who wanted to try out your body, that shouldn't be any sort of crime."

"Probably not, but I've never heard of anyone doing that—in all the cases I know about, the thief murdered their victim once they had them stuck in the older body."

Audrey shuddered. "Not enough imagination, that's the problem."

I lowered my voice as we passed closer to a herd of students. "I don't think that's what Barlow's group wants, though. They may not care for immortality. But political authority, or military sabotage—we may not have imagined it before, but we don't want to encourage it either."

"That's for sure. I don't want anyone doing that, even our side." She looked at me sidelong. "Didn't you say that magic wasn't for power?"

I closed my eyes a moment, filtered the world through touch and sound and scent. I imagined what I might be able to do differently with a taller or stronger body, and what would not change. "It's not supposed to be. Listen—when a posse goes after someone who's stolen a body, they bring guns and knives to take them down. And if Barlow's people steal bodies for power, that power won't come from magic. Someone put the power there, manipulated or forced themselves into a position to have that much control, do that much harm."

"Aphra, you're a cynic."

I shrugged. "I was a prisoner for a long time, for fear of my supposed power."

"And what if you'd known how to take the body of someone who had a key?"

Probably they would have recognized the change, and shot me. Probably if we'd run, they would have come after us with their guns—rounded us up again, or just shot us all to be safe. But if they hadn't . . .

I was quiet the rest of the way back.

~~~

When we returned we found Spector away on some manner of errand, Trumbull retreated to her study—and Dawson sitting with Caleb and Neko and Charlie in the living room.

"She wants to join our confluence," said Caleb without preamble.

"Does she?" I asked, surprised.

Dawson stiffened. "You don't approve?"

"If you want to learn, you're welcome," I said. A sidelong glance at Audrey drew no complaints. "But . . ."

"My sister thinks you don't like her," Caleb explained to Dawson.

"I think," she told me, "you maybe overestimate how much time I've been thinking about you."

If I had other concerns, I'd best leave them lie. I'd told Caleb to reveal himself to her, and if I hadn't predicted what intimacy she might demand as a result, I'd no right to complain that I hadn't chosen it.

Still, my chest felt tight. If my breath shortened, I hoped she didn't notice. I ducked my head. "My apologies."

"As far as Spector is concerned," continued Caleb, "she's brushing up on her Enochian."

"I will be, too," Dawson said. "It's a good idea around here. And I may as well start in on R'lyehn, too. They're close enough related that I'll only get confused if I try to learn them separately."

"Two languages at once?" Charlie sounded doubtful—he'd been doing the same, but struggling, and most of his vocabulary was memorized ritual rather than conversation.

Dawson tossed her head. "I didn't get this job for *just* my looks."

"Deedee's good with languages." Caleb's voice held equal parts pride and envy.

She patted his arm. "You'll catch up, boy." He swatted back, and I could see a little of what they had between them.

"Did you already ask why she wants to learn?" I asked him.

He nodded. She didn't volunteer to repeat her answer, and I didn't demand it. The tradition's purpose was to ensure the *student* knew, not the teacher.

Lacking a private space for ritual, I instead shared what was becoming my standard introduction to Aeonism and the study of magic. Recalling Trumbull's disgust with repetitive instruction, I amused myself imagining this lecture as a class in one of Miskatonic's grand halls, well-dressed young men furiously scribbling notes on the order of Earth's dominant species. The image was both wildly unlikely and as disturbing as it was funny. Confident young men with easy lives might memorize the Litany, but could hardly do more than glaze over what it said about their place in the universe.

Dawson showed no such difficulty.

I wanted to have the promised, frightening conversation about children, about what and where and how we might build a new home. But I didn't know how overt Caleb and Dawson's discussion had been, or how much she was willing to say to the rest of us. So we instead discussed history and myth, and practiced conjugation, and kept our thoughts hidden behind our eyes.

Nothing else of note happened on Sunday, save the tension of people trying to avoid events and conversations of note, well aware that they were unlikely to hold off for long.

That night I slept poorly once more, woke again and again persuaded that someone watched us. Neko did not stir. Eventually I curled around her sleeping form; she murmured wordlessly but did not wake. Lying beside her, unable to so much as doze without nightmare, I asked myself why that guard should come so strongly to mind now after almost three years.

Ressler had never treated the Nikkei girls as entertainment, or as perks to ease an isolated posting. He treated his duties as a guard, and the danger we presented to the outside world, with solemn confidence. He didn't want us to feel free to conspire, or confident in any momentary privacy. If you woke and saw him in the doorway, he would continue to watch for a few minutes—no lasciviousness, no pleasure in our fear, simply the assertion of his absolute right to observe.

Barlow's team didn't seem nearly so pure in their intentions, but they were equally confident in their rights. Since Spector's rescue, I'd been hiding from their sight. That choice might be comfortable, but it wasn't safe. And hiding from Barlow acknowledged, implicitly, some rightful power. Though I was grateful to Spector for claiming us as "his" team, in truth the others were mine—save for Trumbull, they'd said as much—and it was as much my place as Spector's to prove the legitimacy of our presence.

Tomorrow night, then, would not be another family dinner safe in Trumbull's dining room. I needed to let Barlow's team see me, see us— and I needed to speak to them like someone who wasn't afraid.

I *was* afraid, but after making my decision I slept untroubled.

CHAPTER 19

With classes in session, the whole feel of the campus changed.
Students hurried with greater purpose, toting stacks of text-
books. Professors donned suits and strode with a confidence
born of the rightful order restored. Women reappeared, smartly dressed
secretaries bearing packets and parcels. Lacking only Trumbull—on
her way to a despised class—and Dawson—caught up in Skinner's
packets and parcels—we made our way to the library. As promised, the
crowds were larger than before but not unmanageable.

The weekend had made one difference—several of us now sought
specific texts from the collection. Caleb wanted more journals, Chulzh'th's
especially, while I asked for the *Cthäat Aquadingen,* an advanced text
that discussed the workings of confluences. Quietly, I hoped to find
more hints of mist-blooded children flown from Innsmouth before the
raid. At Audrey's request, I also recalled titles that might have something more or less reliable to say about the Mad Ones. They were not
common manuscripts, and I was particularly proud of the query that
successfully retrieved a ragged copy of *A Report of the Trials of J. Pyre by
an Admirer and Companion: Concerning the Peoples Underhill, Their Degener-
ate Worship, Their Violations of Natural Order and Wicked Practices Against
Ordained Forms.* With that to hand, along with Bishop's anthology of
shorter reports, Audrey was soon immersed in her studies—though
she kept close by and occasionally brushed against me as she read.

The librarian seemed more relaxed about the five-book limit, but I doubted this would extend to direct storage room access. I watched through slitted eyes as he came and went from the shadowed hall behind the desk, but could only faintly discern the distance and direction of the building's hidden heart.

Late in the morning Trumbull joined us. Her expression of contempt wasn't surprising, but after she sat and plucked a journal from Caleb's pile we learned that no mere undergraduates had roused her distaste.

"Virgil Peters," she said, voice dripping disgust, and Spector looked up with a frown. "He claims to be *auditing* my geometry class. He has a note from the dean." She glanced over the journal's bookplate, opened her own notebook, and began scribbling in quick, neat Enochian. A grim smile passed briefly across her face. "Some of the students recognized him from the gate. They didn't appreciate his inconveniencing their return. A few were quite outspoken on the matter; it does make me feel more kindly disposed to them."

"What does Peters want from your class?" asked Spector.

"I dearly hope he doesn't want to learn geometry. I'd rather he leave disappointed. And quickly."

We returned to our studies, though the reminder of Spector's unpleasant colleagues distracted me. That they thought overt surveillance of his team worthwhile wasn't promising. Was it an attempt to investigate Skinner's suspicions? A threat? Likely both.

My suspicions grew when, an hour later, Peters entered our reading room. He took in the table, and our various looks of displeasure, and smiled cheerfully at Spector. Their eyes danced a brief dominance contest. I shrank back in my chair, then remembered my resolve and forced myself upright.

"Let me guess," said Spector, putting down the *Book of Hidden Things.* "You had no idea we were here."

"I didn't, in fact—hello, Professor Trumbull. George sent me to look up a few specific texts, and they told me I'd find them in the rare books collection. Which I gather is here."

Spector waved his hand at the desk. "Go on then, don't let us keep you." Then added, as Peters took a step past, "You should know that they require professorial permission before they'll grant access."

Peters paused, glanced over his shoulder. "Since it's a matter of national security, I'm sure they'll be cooperative."

Spector looked at his hands. "If only. They've already reminded me that this is a private library. Unless you happen to have a warrant . . ."

"Hm." Peters's eyes drifted first to the books on the table, then to Trumbull. "Professor, you could give me that permission."

She didn't look up from her notebook. "I could. But I won't, because I hold grudges."

Peters's expression nearly matched Trumbull's for blandness, but he turned his attention back to Spector. "Perhaps you might remind your team that we're colleagues—of a sort."

I reminded myself—though I knew I lied—that this man had no power over me. That I had more right to be here than he. I stood. "Mr. Peters." He blinked, looked me over—and I saw in his eyes the usual dismissal of a woman found unappealing. I could not let that hold. I strode around the table, approached him though all my instincts screamed of danger. "You haven't apologized for Saturday. Your—" Calling him their master would be a poor choice of words. "Mr. Barlow has not apologized. The way you treated us was unconscionable, and it is not your place to insist that we let it drop. We had an extremely unpleasant afternoon, and Mr. Spector recognizes that."

He took a step back. "My apologies," he said without feeling. He whirled away without waiting for reply. I remained standing, watching, not daring to turn my back for long enough to reclaim my seat. So I saw him approach the desk, heard him attempt to charm the librarian and traverse the same refusals we had initially encountered.

Movement in the corner of my eye caught my attention: Trumbull had stiffened. I'd thought her face bland before, but now she looked like she'd forgotten to animate it entirely. She reached smoothly across the table and took my copy of *Cthäat Aquadingen,* flipped to a specific page, and made a complex gesture over the symbol thereon. She then found the passage I'd been reading, returned the book to its original place on the table, and resumed taking her notes on the journal.

Peters's voice rose in frustration. He brought it under control, clearly with some effort, and returned to our table. "Miss Marsh," he said. "May I speak with you in private?"

Spector looked up sharply, and Charlie started to rise. But I didn't want to get everyone involved in an argument—not until I knew what he wanted. "Of course."

Out in the hall, he turned to me. "Miss Marsh. You're from Innsmouth." A statement, not a question.

I swallowed the fear that welled up at his words; it was hardly a secret he could use against me. "I'm certain my files say as much."

"And it was Ephraim Waite's old case that brought us out here in the first place. Your people knew the body-snatching trick—and even if the raid in '28 was an overreaction, you were never exactly loyal Americans. The Waites and the Marshes . . . pretty closely related, right? The town's leading lights."

I bit back a fitting response. I needed to tread carefully here. But I could feel sweat on my palms, and the scent of it wafted up like some nauseating incense. "Our families are related, yes. But Ephraim Waite was a criminal, and his studies an aberration."

"Really? It sounded like your leaders were as concerned with covering up his 'crimes' as punishing them."

I sought an answer that wouldn't simply mimic Caleb's excuses— there was all too much justice in Peters's accusation, though none in the smug insinuation alongside.

He went on: "And here you are, coincidentally, at the heart of the investigation despite having no clearance, and no special expertise that isn't itself suspicious." His voice grew honed. "Whatever you thought to get out of this, I suggest you watch yourself." He stalked away.

The librarian came over as I returned to the table. "I presume, Professor, that he did not in fact have your permission to access *On the Sending Out of the Soul?*"

I winced, distracted from my alarming conversation with Peters; if such a book had originally come from Innsmouth it was not a volume I'd been permitted to read as a child. Trumbull said only, "Certainly not." The librarian nodded and left us to our studies.

I fell back into my chair, strength draining from my shoulders.

"Are you all right?" asked Caleb. His voice dropped, and I barely caught the next words. "You sounded like Mom."

"Thank you," I whispered. I bent over my book, biting the inside of my lip. I would not cry; Peters might come back. Examining the section of the book that Trumbull had found so easily, I discovered a series of defensive counterspells with varying strength and specificity.

Trumbull nodded at the page. "Barlow's people do seem to carry quite a range of those little talismans. Fragile things."

I read, and regained a little of my equilibrium. Time passed, and eventually Trumbull stood and stretched.

"'Advanced' Calculus calls," she informed us. She gathered up her notes. "If that illiterate wants to sit in again, I'm going to break his mind into such fragments that the asylum will spend years piecing them back together."

Spector frowned, obviously trying to decide whether she was serious. At last he smiled—a little forced—and said: "First, they will take you in for questioning again, and I will not be in a position to retrieve you. Second, I will make *you* fill out all the associated paperwork."

She blinked, then smiled—not forced. "As you say." She gave a little half-bow. "I'll spare him."

After she left, Spector tapped my shoulder. "Walk with me?"

I stood, but glanced back at Audrey. "Are you certain you don't need to get back to Hall? I'm glad to have you, but surely they'll miss you."

She tapped the trials of J. Pyre. "I need to be here right now. You're all going over to Hall tomorrow, right?" Spector nodded. "I'll get a ride

then. I'll plead hysteria over Leroy's injury, if I need to explain myself."
She added more gently: "There's a sandwich shop at the corner of High
and West that does good business with the townies—not as overrun
by boys as the cafeterias on campus. If the gate isn't awful and you two
are going for a walk anyway, do you mind picking up lunch?"

Grateful to do something more useful than wander the campus
again, I agreed readily—though the thought of passing the gate still
made my stomach clench. Better to go than be imprisoned by my own
fear.

The air was clear today, the walks swept and salted.

We walked a ways before Spector spoke. "The Yith . . ."

"What of them?"

"What can you tell me?" he asked. "More than the little I've learned
already?"

I shrugged uncomfortably. "They are an ancient race—perhaps the
oldest literate civilization in existence. Perhaps the first. They've lived
through the span of at least two worlds before Earth, likely many more.
They cast their minds between bodies and between times, sometimes
temporarily as individuals to learn and record, sometimes permanently
en masse to survive. Over the course of Earth's existence, four species
serve as their faces. And in each of those times, they record and preserve the history of our world—of every species that lives and dies here."
I paused, angry again. "Except for the species that will never live out
their span, because the Yith take it from them. When they've just discovered agriculture and are beginning to imagine cities, the entire
species wakes one day in the distant past, in alien bodies, facing whatever threat the Yith deemed impossible to survive."

Spector swallowed visibly. "That's vile."

"It is. And yet the eight and more species whose memories they
preserve cannot bear the idea of going unrecorded and forgotten.
Without the Yith, all of Earth would be lost, including the eldermost
and the hy-lameae and the ck'chk'ck and the avolorafuno. So for that
boon, we offer our respect."

"Appeasement?" he asked wryly.

"My people will be the only humans ever to overlap with one of their civilizations. Even if we wished to fight them, I doubt we'd do better than we have against our fellow men."

He winced at that. "What about Trumbull?"

"The actual Professor Trumbull will be restored to her body in four or five years, with half-lost memories of the Archives: of recording her life story, exploring the cities of the Jurassic, and conversing with the best minds from six billion years of solar history."

"Ah. That part sounds . . . not as vile." He sighed and looked away. "This is probably a stupid question, but in your judgment, are they a threat to national security?"

I stopped walking, blinked, tried to consider the question. Instead the absurdity overtook me and I bent gasping with laughter.

"I said it was a stupid question."

"I know," I managed. It took me another minute to regain control. "I'm sorry. It's just . . . national security? The Yith don't interfere with the rise and fall of *species,* save the ones they take for their own survival. Their only interest in atomic war would be recording the arguments leading up to it before getting out of the way. This weekend is probably the first time Trumbull has considered the existence of the United States beyond the way you'd think about, I don't know, Atlantis or the Byzantine Empire." Spector probably didn't know the history of Atlantis, but I let it pass. "The Yith have the power to bring down worlds, but they handle violent conflict by not existing in the place and time where it occurs. They're not a threat to your precious state."

He rubbed his temples. "I suppose that's a good thing. I still don't know how to write my report on them."

I put my hand on his arm, and he jerked in surprise. "I would strongly recommend not writing that report. The only way I can imagine them becoming a threat to national security is if the government impedes their ability to record this era."

He made a noncommittal noise and looked deeply uncomfortable.

"The universe is full of powerful things that could crush us with a thought," I said. "Often we survive by remaining unobtrusive and inoffensive."

"Yes," he said. "But the powerful take notice, and take offense, on their own terms. Better to insist on one's right to exist."

I thought of Peters, and the notice he'd already taken of me and my people. But we were nearing the gate, where two buzz-cut men in dark suits stood grimly on either side. They weren't stopping people today, merely watching. I kept my head high. Spector nodded as we strolled through, and they nodded back.

"Taking your irregular for a walk?" one asked. His tone made me stiffen, but Spector smiled easily.

"You can let George know we went to pick up lunch. It'll liven up your report, I'm sure." When we'd gone a block further, his expression soured. "Idiots, trained by badly behaved monkeys. 'Hello, we're the government, we're here to make you horribly uncomfortable. Why won't you answer our questions?'"

"I, ah, overheard them talking the other day. About their plans." I hoped those plans might be enough for him to act on, even if Peters's attempt at intimidation was not.

He grimaced. "Badly behaved monkeys, yes. All right, what did they say?"

"Nothing that could be interpreted without a great deal of context, if that reassures you." Minded of their example, I checked around us: no one was in earshot, nor were there any obvious places for an eavesdropper to hide. "But with context, it sounded like they're more interested in learning to steal bodies than in finding out who's already done so."

"*That* does not reassure me."

We reached the sandwich place. A cheerful awning labeled it Jake's, and the tantalizing scent of fresh-carved meat and pickles seeped through the door. We stood by the window, made no move to enter.

"Mr. Spector," I said, keeping my voice low. "I'm still worried about what Russia might do with the art, however little my love for the American government. But as you *do* love them, you can't want them to claim such a power."

He put a hand against the cool glass. "And as you still despise them, you can't want it either."

Though his own behavior had softened my opinion somewhat, I couldn't deny the accusation.

At my silence, he asked, "Is it a difficult trick?"

"I don't know it personally, but I'm told not—merely rare. Miskatonic may make even commonplace books of magic hard to access, but it's not the only place they're kept. If your colleagues look for this thing, they'll eventually find it." A thought occurred to me, and I added: "But didn't you say they prefer to develop their own methods, free of 'ancient superstition'?"

"A principle they follow whenever it's convenient. Usually they find some minor new twist, and claim it in the name of invention. What they won't do is ask you why something's done a certain way, or whether their change looks like a good idea."

We went into the shop, waited in line with clean-suited boys and laborers on lunch break, women with babies and kids counting dimes.

In Innsmouth, at the butcher shop or the grocer's, I once believed I knew the future of everyone around me. The same people would surround me as I grew, would live with me later among the throng in the deep ocean. The insurmountable age gap between child and storekeeper would dwindle until we could hardly remember which of us was older.

These people had no such illusion of security. I would probably never see them again. Or one might turn around and say some mad thing, and like Audrey become an unexpected and intimate part of my life. Part of my burden of mourning.

I couldn't even imagine that I knew their future. In the morning papers, in the tension that drove Spector and Barlow in opposing directions, I heard murmurs of apocalyptic fear. I could be confident, as they could not, that life would last long on this world. Even men of the air had history yet unformed. The Yith, as the elders complained, were ever stingy with specific timelines, and history told us they had good reason for that. But there were empires named that had yet to rise. Little comfort to be found there: they could rise tomorrow and fall to the great bombs in a scant few years—or could rise long after humanity again dwindled to a thousand individuals huddling around a river mouth.

Endless disasters might overtake the short-lived people to whom I'd bound myself. Plagues and famines, mind-destroying magics, careless or uncaring powers, vast rocks hurtling unseen through the dark. And the little choices, made by people with a little power, that could unravel lives.

A young man laughed, flirting with the woman behind the counter. She moved aside and began preparing his meal: picking the best of the sliced ham, piling it with care, slicing cheese to his nodded approval. I forced my attention to the little island of order, and thought on whether I might, in the face of power and foolishness, make any such refuge of my own.

CHAPTER 20

Dinner at the spa was a tense affair, during which we all affected relaxation. Barlow dined with the rest of his team. He greeted us affably, every word glinting obsidian. At intervals throughout the meal one or another of his people found an excuse to wander over, ask a question of Spector, inquire about the progress of our studies. It was a relief to put aside our plates and go out into the cold, uncrowded night. Spector headed for the guest dorm, while the rest of us went on with Trumbull.

As Trumbull unlocked her door, Dawson slipped up beside Caleb. Trumbull gave her an amused look. "You'll want the study again tonight?" she asked me.

"If you don't mind."

"This is what comes of having guests." But she acquiesced. Neko took out a notebook and settled to her chosen secretarial duties, and we of the confluence went upstairs. Once the door was shut, Dawson dangled a ring of keys for Caleb.

"You got it!" he cried. He grabbed her waist and swooped her into a somewhat improper kiss. She shrieked, but returned the embrace in full. When he set her down, though, she pulled away as if burned and eyed the rest of us with trepidation.

Charlie had looked away, blushing. Audrey's mouth had thinned, but she shook it off. "Boy, you two are cute! What's the occasion?"

"Library keys," said Caleb simply.

My lips parted. "Caleb, you didn't ask her to—but is it safe—and where are we going to—"

He put up a hand to forestall my sputtering. "For now, let's just look. To know what we're dealing with, how big the collection really is. We can plan more from there."

"And it'll be safe," said Dawson, "if we go at the right time." She squatted to examine the palimpsest slate, not meeting any eyes. "The library closes at midnight. Watchmen check in during their rounds, but there's no regular guard—hasn't been a break-in in over twenty years. I'd say 2:30 or so's a good time to slip inside. Should be okay as long as you resist waving flashlights around near windows."

"We see in the dark," Caleb told her smugly. It was a slight exaggeration, but the moon wasn't yet new, the night was clear, and we'd manage.

"I don't," said Charlie. He hefted his cane, frowning. "You'd better do this without me—be careful."

I could see that he wondered whether it was a good idea at all, and I felt much the same. But I could also tell that the others wouldn't be dissuaded, nor did I wish to waste whatever sacrifice Dawson had made for this opportunity.

And I was grateful for those excuses: my heart sped at the thought of standing unimpeded among our treasure. "Can you see in the dark?" I asked Audrey.

"Not that I ever noticed. But I'm pretty good at not bumping into things unless I mean to."

It was well before midnight, and our burglary required minimal planning. Instead—after making sure she understood what she was getting into—we brought Dawson more formally into the confluence.

There were no great revelations in her blood. If anyone was startled to find it much like Charlie's, they kept it to themselves. Afterward, she leaned against Caleb's shoulder. There was something in our connection that transcended propriety. In the afterglow of the ritual my companions felt solid and sure and safe—and while I knew it for illusion, I also knew it concealed more truth than the seductive lies of our first summoning.

"You got pretty blood," she told him.

A blush crept over his sallow features. "So do you."

"That's a new one," said Audrey. "Most guys stick to saying nice things about your outsides."

I forbore from sharing some of the more salacious stories of the Mad Ones. "That's never been an issue for me," I said, keeping my voice light.

Audrey gave me a piercing look. "You have your own way of looking right. It's different when you know what it means."

I forbore, too, from pointing out that men of my own kind—had I agemates other than my brother—would need no such deeper understanding to find me alluring. Or that I'd begun to fantasize about such men, even as I struggled to call up the urges that would let me return their imagined affections. Jealousy of Caleb under the circumstances went beyond unseemly.

We talked of other, easier things. I told Dawson more of the principles behind the Inner Sea, Charlie and Caleb and even Audrey adding explanation as they were able. I wondered whether Spector would notice Charlie's continued absence.

I stifled a few yawns, but when the time came to go I felt wide awake. Audrey poked my arm.

"Have you actually done anything like this before? Illegal, I mean?"

Prayed. Snuck food beyond my ration from the camp mess hall. Drawn letters in dirt for Caleb, though we'd had no texts to show their importance. "I'm alive, aren't I?"

"Just try not to look like you're skulking."

I gave her my mother's best irritated look, and she faltered.

"That'll do," she said.

"You may be the sneakiest person here, but that doesn't mean the rest of us can't manage."

"*She's* the sneakiest?" asked Dawson.

We walked out into the night, doing our best not to skulk. Dawson wore a wool coat with a fine, large hood; the rest of us bundled up as well, and I didn't think the unusual mix of our party would be noticeable in the sliver of dim moonlight. Charlie provided a good excuse should anyone recognize us: we dropped him at the guest dorm on our way.

Crowther Library loomed in silhouette, more obviously a fortress than in daylight hours. Crenellations and ornate towers stretched above bare oak branches. Windows glinted like eyes. The walls looked ancient, malignant, made smug by the hoard of knowledge cloistered within.

I shook my head sharply: I needed to be fully awake and sensible. But I didn't feel caught in the paranoia that sometimes strikes on the boundary of sleep. Instead I felt the alertness that comes in the presence of a feral shark. If seeing the library as a living foe helped me do what was required, so be it.

Dawson led us away from the imposing front entrance to an ordinary steel door in one of the distant wings. The key turned easily, letting us into a cool, plaster-walled corridor shadowed by emergency lighting. There could be no excuse for our presence now. But even straining, I heard no sound other than our own breath and footsteps, and the mindless whisper of ducts and pipes.

Dawson promised that she knew the way: she'd explored every corner of the labyrinthine building as Skinner's research needs (and her own, covered by his) demanded. While she hadn't previously been in after hours, she'd taken advantage of connections among the staff to gain access to less public areas. We stayed out of the common sections, keeping to back halls and storerooms. I did my best not to let unease shape my gait.

We came at last to the dusty heart of the restricted stacks. Dawson's key ring gave us passage through further, older locks, into rows upon rows of plain hardwood shelves. These were filled with antiquarian books, ragged journals, even a few cased scrolls. Endplates coded their contents as long strings of numbers, but more comprehensible handwritten notations appended them: *Orne Bequest, Derleth Collection, University-Sponsored Expedition Records 1890–1915, Eibon copies—reserved by Prof. Peaslee.* At one end of the room, caged in glass, the library's original copy of the *Necronomicon* lay closed on its stand. I drifted closer—not too close, for it was guarded not only by locks, but by complex signs and diagrams and what I suspected was a pressure sensor in the pedestal beneath. The book itself was one of the impressive seventeenth-century editions, bound in ornately etched black leather with silver-edged pages, and doubtless illuminated by hand.

"Here," said Dawson softly. A spiral staircase led to further levels. The iron shook beneath us as we followed her up. We passed a second floor, where wooden doors studded the walls on all sides, and came out in the shadows of the third and final of the library's most forbidden rooms.

Here, at last, we found our books. Along one whole side of the level, the shelf notations read simply "Innsmouth Collection." I stopped in the middle of the floor.

Audrey touched my elbow. "Aphra?"

My eyes felt tight in their sockets. "I'll be all right." Caleb was already among the shelves, and I forced myself to move.

Had the books been in my charge, I'd have organized them by family and household, by books for home or temple, books for teaching and meditation and cooking. This last they'd made a start on: they'd segregated the clearly Aeonist texts from books that could be found in any town, and relegated the journals to the far side of the farthest bookcase. But within that first category, either they had only the vaguest understanding of each volume's contents, or interpreted them through some filter I couldn't begin to comprehend. They had managed to sort by title: copies of the *Book of Eibon* clustered nearest the dumbwaiter, probably the reason we'd gotten three the first day.

When I looked closer, I saw that they'd placed markers in front of the books we'd requested. I frowned. It made sense, but felt deeply intrusive. Did they seek some pattern in our requests that would reveal the books' secrets—or ours? Then again, given the collection's poor organization, it might simply ensure that they could return each book to its assigned spot.

Would they notice if I took one out to look at? Some of the shelves were very dusty. Even the breeze of our passage might leave trails. The journals, though, should already be well-disturbed by our recent requests, and by the librarian's willingness to bring whole stacks to the reading room.

As hoped, I found the journals disordered and the dust around them thoroughly smeared. Caleb stood at the aisle's end, sharing one of Chulzh'th's volumes with Audrey and Dawson. Audrey kept her voice low, but I could hear the suppressed energy as she described our elders to—Deedee, should I call her now? We'd ridden each other's blood, but the remaining barriers between us were hers to preserve or remove.

I checked notebooks carefully, but quickly. I hungered for well-known names, or familiar handwriting. Some of the books, yellow and pungent with age, bore dates from the 1600s and earlier. Sections in English were barely comprehensible; in Enochian and R'lyehn the dialect had barely altered. I found Marshes and Eliots, Waites and Gilmans, along with the more diverse names of the smaller and poorer families—but no one closer than a distant cousin.

And then—in one of the common five-and-dime notebooks, familiar handwriting indeed. My own, my childhood scrawl. I clasped the book against me, afraid to look, then did so anyway. The first entries were from 1923; I'd been seven. My script was still shaky, wavered above and below lines as it complained of Caleb's infant irritations and exulted over classroom triumphs and favored desserts. My spelling was excellent. I wanted to curl around myself or cry; I did neither, though my whole body felt taut with the distance between myself and myself.

Surely one's childhood concerns must be hard to encounter decades later, regardless of the life fallen between. Must invoke yearning and repulsion inextricably mixed.

Caleb saw me standing motionless. "What did you find?"

"My diary," I said. Then added, knowing the absurdity: "It's private, no brothers allowed."

He snorted, but sobered quickly. "I'd just started my first. When the raid came."

"I remember." Caleb was a Hallows child, born while the last brown leaves clung to their branches. As tradition bade, he'd received a fine new journal and pen for his sixth birthday. I remembered him holding them proudly, sitting poised with nib above paper for minutes on end as he considered what words might be worthy. I looked again at the shelf, but didn't see that small leather-bound volume, nor any others of mine, near the empty spot I'd made.

Dawson tapped her watch. "I'm sorry, but the longer we stay, the more risk of being caught. Let's do a quick scan for any unusual security, and then get out of here."

I hesitated over the diary. Wasn't it mine? And the journals were so obviously untracked, uncatalogued. But Dawson shook her head, and Audrey said, "It's not just the risk of them noticing it missing; someone might find it in your room. We'll come back for everything." She took a last look around, eyes wide and bright, as I reluctantly returned my younger self to her place on the dusty shelf.

The building felt no less alive, no less malignant, as we made our way out. I heard it breathe around me, every creaking pipe a sign of pursuit and discovery.

These convictions may have been simple fatigue—for we were well out of the building and a couple hundred yards down the path when the alarm went off.

It shrieked through the night: an old foghorn of a siren, intended to waken and summon all possible aid within a vast reach. I froze, but when no blades materialized in the first second, I began sprinting.

Behind me, other footsteps. Then Caleb, shouting under the clangor: "Vhr'ch! Cru Phlyr ich nafhgrich yp! Aphra, cru linghn yzhuv th'rtil!"

The reminder of the others' vulnerability broke through my panicked flight. I stopped, and turned to wait. Audrey gestured that I should return, and reluctantly I did so.

"Innocent people will be running *toward* the alarm," she hissed.

"Oh. *Oh.*" It was obvious once she said it. She ran her hands through her hair, took out bobby pins, mussed locks too obviously un-slept-in.

We hung back from the path, not wanting to be the first spectators. But soon enough, students and faculty arrived bearing flashlights or stumbling on the darkened walks. Many wore coats hastily thrown over nightshirts, but others were still dressed, especially as the crowd expanded. We joined in, but did not push to the front.

A police car braked hard on the nearest street, its own siren masked by the library's. The whirling red and blue lights made me turn away abruptly; the constant noise already sent spears of pain through my ears. When I forced my head up I saw that the police had been joined by a university guard and two people I suspected were librarians. A taller man arrived, white-haired and gaunt and angry. Two policemen and a librarian went in through the front door, and a couple of minutes later the alarm silenced its wailing. I nearly fell to my knees in gratitude, though the police car still cried over the chaotic babble of the crowd.

George Barlow and three of his men strode toward the other investigators. They moved with grim dignity, but their faces were flushed and their breath hit the air in quick puffs of steam.

The police car raised its voice once more, then wound down into silence. Barlow spoke, voice pitched to carry. "We need to ask all of you to remain here for a few minutes. We want to hear about *anything* you may have seen—once we've spoken with you, you can get back to your warm beds." Both police and guard looked irritated but didn't gainsay his assertion of control. The gaunt man announced officiously that everyone ought to wait and remain calm, and Dawson identified him as the college president.

"Miss Marsh!" Spector's voice from behind, out of breath. He came around and nodded to the others. Charlie hobbled after. "Did you see anything?"

"No one but this crowd," said Dawson. "And I didn't hear anything over the alarm." Audrey nodded agreement. Charlie kept his face impassive.

Peters went inside, and Barlow and the others spread out to begin their interrogation. I fretted silently—invisibly, I hoped—over footprints and fingerprints, a door left unlatched, a brilliant Holmesian sleuth concealed among their team. Students and faculty murmured to each other: some excited, others cold and irritable, few noticeably worried. I focused, trying to stay calm. *My blood is a tide.*

Barlow made us wait just long enough to prove he could. He smiled easily. "Ron. I see you've been adding to your irregulars."

Before Spector could respond, Audrey offered a dazzling smile and held out her hand. "Audrey Winslow—I'm delighted to meet you. I've heard so much about you."

He took her hand and started to bend over it before settling on a businesslike shake. "George Barlow. Charmed, of course." He released her hand, slightly belatedly. "I'm certain Ron's picked out an observant team. I hope you caught something useful?"

Audrey shook her head, managing a blush and a rueful duck of her head. "We only saw the people in the crowd, and the alarm made it impossible to hear anything. I'm afraid we can't tell you anything helpful."

"That's a shame. How quickly did you get here?"

"Before we heard the alarm, we were up late talking at Professor Trumbull's place. We didn't have much getting ready to do, but when we arrived there was nothing to see."

"Hm. And the rest of you?" Barlow tinted his voice with the faintest trace of doubt. We shook our heads dumbly. "Ah, well. One can't expect everything, I suppose."

"It's a large library," suggested Spector. "Whatever—whoever set off the alarm might still be inside. Best if we work together on the search."

Barlow made a show of considering it. "No, I think we'd better handle this one ourselves. But do let me know if you—or your ladies—notice anything that might be relevant. Why don't you get back to your beds; it's a cold night." He tipped his hat. "Good night, Miss Winslow. A pleasure to meet you."

Spector started after the other agent, his face a mask of control.

Audrey put a hand on his elbow. "Wait. Is he likely to listen to any-thing you have to say right now?" Spector shook his head. "Can he make more trouble than he has?"

"She's right, sir," said Dawson. She kept her gaze low. "It might be better to take this somewhere a bit less chilly."

"No," said Spector. "I want to know if they find anything."

"You think they'll tell us?" she asked.

"This is my assignment, damn it. I was first on campus; they can't just run around me. Excuse my language, I'm sorry."

I waved off the apology, but said, "Actually, Miss Dawson was the first of your people here. And they don't seem inclined to keep her informed."

Spector worked his mouth around a grimace, but then sighed. "So she was. My apologies. Still. One of us might overhear something."

Exhaustion weighed on my eyelids. Afraid to remain and be accused of thievery to my face, afraid to leave and be accused in absentia, I stayed, as did the others. The rest of the audience began to disperse as they were questioned and released. A few still lingered, though not enough for us to hide among—not that we were well-camouflaged in any case.

After what seemed an aeon, but was in fact barely a half hour, Peters emerged from the building. He spoke with the librarians, who responded with quiet urgency. My ears still ringing from the alarms, I couldn't make out their words until one librarian raised his voice abruptly: "You certainly may not!" Then more low voices.

Barlow turned to the remaining stragglers. "You're all free to go. We'll be investigating more extensively in the morning, and the library will be closed until further notice."

The college president stalked up to him, a righteous scarecrow. "What's the meaning of this? How dare you make such decisions on my campus, disrupting my students' studies? Their parents will demand an explanation—I demand an explanation!"

Barlow held up a hand and gave a placating smile. "Sir—" His voice dropped, intimate, and I wished desperately for my ears to regain their usual sensitivity. Audrey frowned slightly, then masked the frown with a worried smile. She approached Barlow and the president, a subtle rhythm in her walk drawing the eye. She leaned in, pupils wide, to ask a question. Both men turned to her, and Barlow patted her sleeve and said something apparently intended to be reassuring. She said something more, wrapped her arms around herself, looked small and worried. Barlow spoke further, and her body language loosened. She gave him a grateful smile, ducked her head.

"It'll look better if we retreat a bit now," whispered Dawson. We followed her down the path, back toward the faculty row. Out of sight of the library lawn, we stopped to wait. Dawson shook her head. "You're going to hire that girl, aren't you?" she asked Spector.

"I might have to."

A few minutes later Audrey appeared. On seeing us she produced a more genuine smile. "His brain just turns right off," she said, miming a silent snap of her fingers. We began walking again. "You, now," she nodded at Spector, "if I wanted you to tell me something, I don't know what I'd do. Your brain is always going, even when you're talking to a girl."

"Thank you. I think. Did you learn anything?"

"Oh yes, he was at great pains to reassure me that he had it all under control. He says that someone has stolen books—wouldn't say which ones, but implied they were worrisome choices—and that the case for the *Necronomicon* was damaged. That's what set off the alarm."

I tried to match her nonchalant attitude, but my own brain kicked into high gear as I processed this information. Had another intruder been in the library at the same time we were? Or had Barlow's people somehow engineered the alarm as an excuse to go where the librarians had forbidden?

As Audrey had said, little could induce Spector to be a fool. "That's very interesting. I'm not going to ask why Mr. Day was so distraught when the alarm went off, but if you did see anything, I'd be obliged if you'd get that information to—someone—who might be able to make use of it. Not necessarily Barlow and his self-appointed investigators."

"I'm afraid we really haven't," said Audrey firmly.

I added, finding something I could say without confessional implications: "And I don't know why someone would go after the school's *Necronomicon*—the one they've a right to, I mean—when there are dozens among the Innsmouth books. They can't have all those so thoroughly locked up, can they?"

"That's true," said Dawson. "But their original copy has a special reputation among the faculty and students. The Innsmouth collection is less well-known."

We talked further as we approached the dorms, but we were exhausted, and the conversation turned in circles and skittered into useless corners. So we didn't tarry when the time came to separate out by sex. With Spector as witness, Dawson and Caleb's parting was friendly but impersonal.

Dawson peeled away as we neared the faculty row. A few lights still burned in Dean Skinner's house. I gazed after her a long moment before turning toward Trumbull's place.

"You didn't have to do that," I told Audrey.

A tight frown and a glare passed over her face, swiftly replaced by a more thoughtful look. "It's power. Like magic—however much weaker it may be than what the really powerful people have, I'm not going to turn it down." She glanced over her shoulder at Skinner's house. "I'm lucky. Simpering for a few minutes is a small sacrifice. Haven't you ever . . . ?"

I shook my head. "Men don't think of me that way—men of the air, I mean. I'm an ugly woman to be ignored, or a monster to be feared." I recalled Jesse's hand on my cheek. But I suspected he merely had a different opinion of monsters.

"That has its own uses."

"I know. I've used it." And would again, doubtless, before our time in Arkham was up.

CHAPTER 21

I slept late, only drowsily aware of Neko's rising as I rolled into the patch of wan sunlight she'd vacated among the sheets. Hours later, I woke to the sound of shouting. I lay still, trying to determine whether it presaged some invasion. All I could pick out was Trumbull's voice, furious, and Neko's, placating.

Beside me, Audrey sat up and rubbed her ears. "What the hell?"

"Trumbull's angry." Likely about something related to our adventure of the previous night—and therefore something I ought to know, even if I'd rather slink back under the covers.

I threw on skirt and blouse, padded into the hall in stocking feet.

Trumbull rounded on us as we came into the dining room. "You were out when the alarm started. What do you know? What are these illiterate morons doing to my campus? The library is locked and guarded, and there were government agents waiting outside my classroom asking pointless questions!"

I held up my hands. "What did they ask you?"

"Whether there were books I'd been forbidden in the library. Where I was at 3 a.m. I was here, sleeping, until their alarm went off. It wasn't just me, either—they're keeping all the faculty from their work, and I had twelve students late for the same reason. This place is supposed to be secure, not overrun with ignorant, monosyllabic savages. I can't work like this! I repeat: what do you know?"

Trumbull angry was only a little more alarming than Trumbull at any ordinary moment. Still, I caught my breath. I put up a hand to halt whatever story Audrey might tell; for all that we feared her interference, Trumbull was one of the few people who might do something useful with the truth. "We did go to the library last night, but we stole nothing. We only wanted to see our own books—how large the collection really was, where it was stored. We went in, we looked, and we left. Then when we were well outside, the alarms started. Now Barlow and his thugs claim books are missing and cases broken." I glanced at Neko, to whom this was also new. She nodded, considering. "I think they set off the alarms themselves, to get access to the restricted books. And perhaps to keep them from us."

"They wouldn't let Spector help them search," added Audrey.

"He doesn't know we were inside ourselves," I said. "And is working hard to maintain his ignorance."

"Thank you," said Trumbull. She seemed calmer. "I'm slightly reassured if they're acting incompetent to cover for an actual attempt at learning—even if the results are obnoxious." She wove her fingers together. "Still best to go to Hall today, I think. Staying on campus would only result in useless irritation. But perhaps the right words in a few ears—no need to mention how close your witness was, but a rumor about their motivations could make their work considerably more difficult. Perhaps even drive them off, eventually."

"I can do that," said Audrey. "They seem awfully determined, but I'll give it my best shot. How soon are we leaving?"

"Spector wanted to make some phone calls," said Trumbull. "Perhaps some good will come of that as well. I expect him here within the hour."

"All right." Audrey stood and stretched. "Let me fix up my face, and then I'll just slip out and find someone to talk to. I finally got permission for library access, and I was so disappointed to find it closed. But you'll never guess what I heard . . ."

I looked after her, a little envious. "I have no idea how she does that."

Neko shrugged. "The same way you put on your—" She sat straighter in her chair, folded her arms in front of her in a passable imitation of me trying to look dignified and stern. "Everyone's got their faces. I think hers are more what normal girls pick up." There was a trace of wistfulness in her voice as well.

"Females of this period aren't usually so aware of what they're doing," said Trumbull. She pursed her lips. "Though more aware than the males think they are. I suppose she falls within the normal distribution."

Audrey returned with her hair neat and her lips and eyes darkened; she waved cheerfully and slipped out the door. Half an hour later she was back, looking pleased with herself, and trailing Spector and Charlie and Caleb behind her. They seemed less pleased, but eager to quit Miskatonic for the day.

Audrey slipped off when we reached Hall—to make her excuses, or find out what excuses were needed. The rest of us went to the library. It was open, bustling with students, unnoticed by the outside world.

The reference librarian who'd pointed us at Upton had the desk, and smiled when she saw us. "I wondered if you'd be back. I'll get your room ready."

In short order we had a table full of Kirill's notes, along with the relevant texts and a smattering of other Aeonist material that she thought we'd be interested in. Hall's collection came nowhere close to Miskatonic's, but the difference in attitude made up for it. Especially on a day like today, when I sought refuge as much as information.

I followed the librarian back into the main room. "Thank you for all your help. I'm sorry, I didn't catch your name last time?"

"Birch. Edith Birch. And I'm glad to help."

I realized that everything I wanted to tell her—that we had visited Upton, and why—would still be no kindnesses. But more immediate events might well affect her. "There was a break-in at Crowther last night. Government agents have shut everything down."

She sucked in a breath. "That hasn't happened for a while. It's always trouble, when someone's that eager to get into their collections."

"We're more concerned about the agents." Here, away from Miskatonic's politics, I worried I might sound a little ridiculous, but said anyway: "We think they may have set off the alarm deliberately, to gain access to books they'd been forbidden. Knowing even a little of what they're after, it's possible they might come here as well."

To her credit, she took me seriously. In some ways we'd made a tacit agreement last time, to trust one another's absurd claims. "Oh dear. I'll warn the rest of the staff. But Miskatonic's trouble rarely makes it to Kingsport." Her lips quirked. "They don't consider us troublesome."

"Their mistake?" I asked.

She smiled. "We have our ways." The smile turned thoughtful. "If whatever you're looking for is in those notebooks, I'm sure you'll find it. But I also know you've been exploring the Miskatonic collections. If there's some specific topic you're researching, it's possible we have material here that you don't know about, especially if it's something they might have overlooked."

It was my turn to consider—it was a generous offer, but I had reason to be cautious about taking her up on it. And Spector might not be pleased. Still . . . ultimately, we'd have trouble find anything of use without aid. "You mentioned that Asenath could . . . you said hypnotize people. Make them feel as if they'd changed identity, in some fashion. We're looking for books that claim to know something about that—but more than that, we're interested in people like Mr. Barinov, who might have written commentary on such books."

"I see why you'd be interested in Miskatonic's esoterica. But I'll look."

I settled in with one of the texts—Skinner had claimed Dawson for the day to help deal with his professors' complaints, so our ability to search Kirill's notes was limited. Neko started paging through them systematically, noting down English marginalia, volumes, and pages (which he had numbered intermittently for his own use). After a couple of hours Audrey appeared.

"No problem," she said in response to my query. "Sally and Jesse are still sitting with Leroy. I got reprimanded for staying out overnight without a note, but it was pretty pro forma. Of course, now I'd better spend tonight in the dorm to calm everyone down—I'll take the bus over first thing in the morning." She seemed disinclined to give more details, and I suspected that Hall's guardians had put more effort into trying to bind her than she let on.

After a while, she put down her book, and I realized that I'd misunderstood her distress. "Mr. Spector, my friends have been arrested, and I haven't entirely avoided trouble myself. I know that Barlow and his gang are FBI, and I know you are too. I think there's more going on than I've been told, and I think the reason Miss Marsh hasn't told me is because it's yours to tell. Want to let me know why you're so interested in Kirill's books? Or shall I guess?"

Spector looked at her and put his head in his hands.

"I'll fill out the paperwork," I told him.

He lifted his head slightly. "And what will you list as 'reason for disclosure?'"

I shrugged. "Magically bound blood sister to several people who already know?"

"*I'll* fill out the paperwork." He sighed and raised himself back up. "My apologies, Miss Winslow. It's been a long week. There's some concern that the Russians may be interested in the art of body switching for purposes of espionage. They might have researched the topic at Miskatonic—which is widely believed to hold the best esoterica collection in the world. Kirill Barinov is a Russian who had access to that collection. We have no concrete reason to suspect him."

She leaned back. "That's good, because Kirill knew about as much about body swaps as I know about pig farming. He once claimed to have accomplished astral travel but—actually, I'm not going to tell you how he thought he did it, because it wasn't entirely legal, but it was illegal in an entirely boring way. If you're looking for magical insight in those notebooks, you're looking in the wrong place."

"That may well be the case," said Spector. "But it's a lead, and at the moment it's the only lead we have access to. And even if Mr. Barinov wasn't sent by the Kremlin, they could have pressured him later."

"That's possible. He sure wasn't happy to go back." She reached for a notebook from the stack. "And he didn't even try to bring these. Anything else I should know?"

"Not that you're missing, as far as I'm aware. I'm afraid there's not much to know. We found very little before Barlow and his—team— showed up. I was trying to persuade the Miskatonic special collections librarian to let me look at access records, but that won't be possible until Barlow calms down." He gave me a sideways look, from which I gleaned—or chose to glean—that he wasn't trying to hide our visit to Upton, but thought that piece of mixed Hall and Innsmouth history mine to tell. And so I would, I decided, when we had a moment less surrounded.

Spector went on: "There's nothing unusually suspicious about Kirill Barinov, so far—there are foreign students at every major university, just trying to learn. But the things we look for are high enough stakes that it's worth checking out every possible lead. False trails are ninety percent of the job."

I nodded and took a notebook, and did not say: *the stakes were already high, but we may have raised them too far just by looking.*

We ate dinner at a Polish place in Kingsport—good, solid food, kielbasa and potatoes and soups warm against the winter night. Trumbull returned to Arkham immediately afterward, but Spector we persuaded to wait in the car while I gave the others a short lesson. I delivered Audrey to her dorm just before curfew, hoping that I appeared a reasonable facsimile of a chaperone.

It was late when we got back to campus, but Neko and Caleb tarried long on Trumbull's porch. I half woke, later, as Neko came in. "Is all well?"

"Yeah," she said. She sounded a bit—not sad, exactly, but not happy either. I opened my eyes to see her sitting on her bed, one shoe off and looking out the window in lieu of removing the other.

"Are you certain?"

She offered a little smile. "Just confirmed that neither of us actually wants to pick up where we left off, that's all."

I pulled myself out of the luxuriously empty bed, hugged her, and didn't try to say anything on a topic about which I knew little.

Half asleep again, I woke when she said, "You should talk with him about what you want, too."

"I know," I said. "We should all talk."

~~~

"The library is still barred," reported Trumbull at breakfast. She ate her egg and stale pierogi mechanically.

"I expect it'll be closed for a while," said Spector. "Once George has something he wants, he's not likely to let go until he's done regardless of inconvenience to everyone else."

"They're still questioning faculty and students as well," she added, an afterthought.

Spector grimaced and stood. "I'd better go commandeer a phone. If I can get a few people at headquarters to see sense, we might be able to sort this out. You can do without me today?"

"I need to stay on campus," said Trumbull. "I have the geometry students again—I hope Peters has lost interest. I don't much like paper-work."

I would have preferred to go back to Hall rather than remain in Barlow's web, but nodded and assured them that we had plenty to do. We had much study to fit in, and much planning.

Audrey appeared about the time Trumbull left, and it occurred to me that we could all take the bus over if we wanted to. But Audrey was clearly pleased to get away. Caleb went in search of Dawson, and returned a few minutes later with her in tow.

"I don't think Dean Skinner's as pleased with Barlow as he was a few days ago," she reported. "Little enough he can do about it now, more's the pity."

In Trumbull's office, the stacks of notes had grown, and the strange machine gained a few gears of doubtful function.

"Can you read this stuff?" Audrey asked me.

I looked at the top sheet, careful not to touch anything. "About as well as I could read one of Dr. Einstein's papers. The language is no problem. The words, on the other hand . . ." Atop another pile I caught a glimpse of my own name, and Caleb's. That one, I did not examine too closely.

This time, as we rode our braided streams, we tried deliberately to reach beyond mere shared sensation. People are more than bodies— else the Yith could not travel between them, nor ordinary magicians traverse dreams. But it's also true that emotions are heart and breath and heat.

We were all of a piece, twined together in ritual. But beneath that, as I tried to push through without pushing away, I could sense a particular flavor to each of the people around me. Caleb was full of wonder and fear, still edged with anger. Dawson felt much the same, with brittle suspicion caging the whole. Charlie at his core was all yearning. Audrey remained full of a deep confidence that welled up under her frustration, strengthening it even while constraining its depth.

What did they see in me?

In what was not truly the corner of my eye, I started to glimpse the world outside the office. There was Neko, focused on the surface and vibrating with nervous energy within. And beyond—I pulled back, but not before brushing against the miasma of frustrated prideful joyous anger that was the campus.

I retreated to my own body, singed and abraded and caressed. I wanted a warm bath, or to wash clean amid cold waves, but I also wanted to immerse again in the fascination and comfort of my companions' not-quite-unfamiliar selves.

Charlie rubbed his arms, and Audrey stretched so nonchalantly that it surely masked some other urge. Dawson wrapped her arms around herself, pupils wide. Caleb touched her back, tentatively, and after a moment she relaxed her grip.

"So," she said to me. "Is this all going to be ever more intense get-to-know-you sessions?"

"After a fashion," I admitted. "Magic is about knowing yourself. But sometimes the best way to know yourself is by knowing others, or the world beyond."

"I suppose that makes sense. Is it always this terrifying?" She tried to sound flip. Odd how automatic masks are, even with those who've seen beneath them. Or perhaps not odd at all.

"Yes," I admitted. Audrey and Charlie nodded confirmation. Seeking the steadier ground of didacticism, I continued: "Sensing emotion can be used for good or ill. With a little work, one can learn to calm others' fear, share joy, or ease suspicion. For those who aren't Trumbull that usually requires ritual preparation. Weather control, to the degree that it's possible, is much the same thing—it just connects the mind with patterns of cloud and wind rather than an actual body. They're surprisingly similar. And as with emotion, if you push too hard you just end up stumbling." Charlie smiled at the reminder.

"Hmm." Audrey closed her eyes, and the ritual connection—dimmed but not yet ended—swelled around me. When I felt Audrey gently pushing I gave way—not as one who falls, but as one who allows her partner to lead their waltz. A strange enthusiasm bloomed in my mind. I would have said "alien," but suspected it was merely that the untrammeled anticipation that came easily to my blood sister had long been foreign to me. Slowly, as if it might break, I offered that same emotion to Dawson. Then, tentative, I thought of how I felt during the best moments of prayer, the awe and wonder and fear at the scope of the cosmos. I shaped that feeling and took the lead with Audrey.

Luminous and strange, emotions passed among us in splashes of impossible color.

Wind thrummed against the window, and in this state it seemed another sort of body, another emotion. I touched it gently, felt it move with the rhythms we built between us, felt it whirl up to break apart the winter clouds and let the distant stars light our work. And beyond those stars—or through them—I felt other things, moving to their own rhythms. I breathed slowly, with the wind, trying not to disturb them. But in the clarity of the ritual, it seemed natural to explore this larger pattern of which we were a part. Worlds that once birthed gods, music to guide inhuman dances, intelligences scarcely recognizable as life, all lay just out of focus. At any moment, the draft from our movement might push aside the veil, allowing us to see—

The clouds parted further, and something brushed against me. For a moment, all I felt was cold: beyond the winter ice outside, beyond childhood stories of benthic depths and blackest space, cold too absolute for breath or blood or thought. I recoiled, shocked to discover I could, and realized with further shock how I'd let the ritual lull me.

Outside the haven of our workspace, in our own ordinary world, it was full daylight, and no beach far from the prying eyes of the public. I could still feel the rhythm of our shared emotions feeding the break in the clouds, but further veils lay once more shut and invisible. I pulled away from the wind, gently as I could, and with mingled relief and reluctance felt the whole synchronized spell of mind and nature collapse back within the boundaries of the everyday. I stood and checked the window. Whatever strangeness we'd worked had vanished.

"Lost track, did you?" Dawson asked as I returned to my companions. She looked more thoughtful now, less folded in on herself. Whatever I'd felt, there at the end, hadn't come close enough for the others to share my perceptions. For that I was grateful. The sense of what had frightened me was already fading, as if only the ritual had let me come close to understanding or even sensing it. Such things, our books warned us, lurk always at the edges of perception, and it isn't wise to try and know more of them.

"A little," I said ruefully, and let the disturbing half-memory slide away in favor of my more immediate connection with the confluence.

Dawson looked around. "Funny-looking family, but you could get used to it."

Audrey nodded, but Charlie ducked his head. "What happens after this? These sessions have been . . . this is a bigger, better family than I've had in a long time, but I'm settled in California. Miss Koto, too, I think. Aphra . . ." He trailed off. His eyes flicked to me, but he wouldn't meet my gaze.

"I don't know," I said. I wanted to call Neko to join us, but feared breaking the bubble of honesty. "Having an Aeonist community around"—I broke off, realizing that Charlie and I might be the only people in the confluence who *worshipped*—"or something close, has been amazing. And I don't want to lose any of you. But I'm not ready to leave the Kotos. I love them too, and I love San Francisco. Out here, I'm reminded of everything that's broken. And I want desperately to rebuild, but California has been healing me, and I need that too."

"I'm staying," said Caleb firmly. "And rebuilding. I'd like all the help I can get. But I also think that we can't be as closed off as we were before. Having connections outside of our spawning grounds could make the difference between extinction and survival, next time someone comes after us." He looked at Dawson. "And having other people in town who don't fit elsewhere—in different ways—that could be a good thing too."

Audrey looked at me intently. "Whither thou goest, I will go." I blinked at her sudden formality, and she added. "It's from the Bible. Wouldn't hurt you to know something about your neighbor's religions, either. But I've learned more from you, more of what I've always needed to learn, than from any class at Hall. If you go to San Francisco, I'll go too."

I felt grateful and frightened, and uncertain whether to express either. I settled for: "What's your family going to think about that?"

She shrugged uncomfortably. "That's my problem, isn't it? I could tell them I met a guy, which is technically true. Though they'd rather a Miskatonic brat."

"You could stay out here for a few years while you finish school," said Caleb. "We'll be learning too. And sooner or later, Aphra does have to come back to the Atlantic."

"Wherever we go," I said, "we'll all have things waiting for us elsewhere."

Eventually, the conversation turned from Innsmouth to Innsmouth's books, and whether even our elders might be able to overcome the greater barriers we now faced. We considered probing Trumbull's increasing frustration with the current situation. I hoped that would change her mind, for she could make an even more formidable barrier than Barlow—and one the elders might not willingly cross.

When at last hunger drove us downstairs, Neko curled alone on the couch, reading more of the Plato.

"Did you notice anything odd with the weather?" asked Audrey.

"I was reading. Is the weather broken?"

"Not at all. I'm going to find lunch." Audrey went into the kitchen, while Neko got up and peered out the window.

"Good, you didn't break it," she said. "And you wonder why I don't want to spend my time practicing magic."

I lingered as the others went after Audrey. "Neko, do you know what you want to do after this? I mean, after we're done in Innsmouth?"

She turned from the window. "Caleb and I were talking about that, too. He wants to stay here, I guess he told you? What about you?"

"I'm willing to help rebuild. And I suppose that means children, though I'm not yet sure of the least horrible way to go about that. But I'm not ready to move back to Massachusetts. Our family in San Francisco—that matters too. I wish I could have everyone together."

She perched beside me on the couch. "You're so much better at family than I am. Mama will be happy about that, even if Caleb isn't coming back. I still want to find space for myself, somehow."

"Do you have any idea where?"

"I don't want to go away forever. But I wish I had more good excuses for travel."

"Maybe even to more exciting places than Arkham?"

"Maybe. But I don't need adventure. If I wanted that, I'd go chasing after you *every* time you do crazy things. I just want *different*."

CHAPTER 22

We were still at the dining room table, finishing the last of our leftovers, when Trumbull stalked in.

"I despise faculty meetings."

"And yet," said Audrey, "you went to one."

"If I don't, they assign me extra classes. Or nonsense secretarial work. Or advisees. Today, at least I got to watch Skinner trying to pretend he wasn't upset about the library. And trying to decide whether to pretend he had nothing to do with Barlow's arrival, or to claim more control over the creature than he actually has."

"Are you certain this place is as stable a repository as you thought?" I asked tentatively. "We *have* decided to rebuild Innsmouth."

"No place outside the Archives is truly stable. Nevertheless, this isn't mere unreliability. Oaths were made to keep the records safe and available, and the Miskatonic librarians are violating that trust. If Mr. Spector cannot check his wayward colleagues, we may indeed need to consider alternatives." She fixed me with an amused look. "*After* some other appropriate sanctuary is built, not before. Better that some of our documents should be inaccessible for a few years than that they should be exposed to the vagaries of climate and weather."

It was a start, though Caleb's closed expression suggested he found it less than sufficient. Dawson's hand hovered near his arm a brief moment, before she glanced around and let it drop.

"So what constitutes an appropriate sanctuary?" I asked.

She smiled, not kindly. "We'll send an architect, of course. There are a few decent designers among your elders, but the libraries of R'lyeh and Y'ha-nthlei don't have to hold paper."

I resisted the urge to point out that Innsmouth had held those documents for centuries in buildings of common brick and wood, that they'd been stolen through no fault of those protections. But stolen they had been—and it occurred to me that it might well have been a Yith, nervous over the fate of those abandoned materials, who informed Miskatonic when our books sat unguarded.

And now it was entirely in her power to set the conditions under which we could be trusted to reclaim them.

I was still pondering this, trying not to let it show on my face, when Spector walked in.

"Well, that was useless," he said. He took off his hat, started to hang it on the rack, looked at it a long moment. Then he turned and went back out the door. I hurried after him.

I found him still on the porch, glowering. He looked ready to hit something, if he were the sort of man who lashed out in anger. When we'd first met, when I attacked him in unthinking fear, he'd simply held me off—more self-control than Chulzh'th had shown.

Reminded of the results of Chulzh'th's temper, I touched my sleeve above the cut-in sigil. Elsewhere, Sally changed position, fearful and angry and determined. She itched with frustration. I guessed she was still at the hospital, and hoped Grandfather didn't expect me to divine her precise actions and intentions through this thin connection. Perhaps if I were older and better practiced, I'd get more from it. Presumably betrayal, which it was designed to detect, would be announced in clearer fashion than the background hum of fretfulness over her wounded lover.

"I'm sorry," Spector said, words falling as if strung on wires. "Professor Trumbull—I didn't think I could speak civilly to her."

"Why not?" Though in my current state, it seemed entirely understandable.

"I've spent the morning dealing with enough indifference. A dozen people have reminded me of all the *processes*"—that word pushed through the restraining wire, a hurled stone—"that keep Barlow's team in the field once they're assigned. A half dozen others are trying to break through those processes, but I'm here, and can't do more than I already have to speed them along."

"What Barlow's people are doing . . ." I was no Audrey to find precise and slippery words that would allow Spector to deny their meaning. I forged ahead. "Would your masters—their masters—care, if they set that alarm themselves? Or are they permitted such things for the sake of their research?"

His headshake was half nod. "Technically they're here to track evidence of Russian spies, same as I am. But they could claim just about any research in support of that goal—same as we have, frankly." He sighed. "The fact is, there are people at the agency who see us both as mavericks. Mr. Barlow with his mystical mathematical theories, and that crazy Jew Spector who works with crazy people." He shrugged apology. "We could both end up on short leashes at a moment's notice, if someone takes it into their head—and we both have supervisors who'll go to the mat for our gambles."

Somehow, in spite of my doubts, I'd hoped that Spector represented some fundamental improvement in the state's attitude toward us. Clearly that was what he wished to be. Barlow, if I were lucky, merely saw me as a relic of an outdated tradition. But Peters seemed sympathetic to older opinions. Other factions might back him in that.

"I don't blame you for being upset," said Spector. "But you look like you're thinking about something else."

Gambles indeed. "Suppose we were to rebuild Innsmouth."

His lips parted. "Is that possible?"

"As what it was before, no. As a place for those with even a little of our blood to come together . . . we might be able to make something new. But not if we'd risk another raid."

"Aphra, no, I promise it's not like that. We may have our debates, but no one wants to go back to the persecution of the '20s. No one's even talking about that."

"For how long?"

He pulled out a cigarette, flicked his lighter, inhaled acrid smoke. "How many generations do you expect me to speak for? For all I know, the country could turn around in ten years and decide to lock up all the Jews. We run or fight when we have to, and we rebuild in between. Works a lot better than the alternative."

I hesitated. "Skinner was suspicious as soon as he met us, and he isn't the only one who still remembers the old libels. Peters all but accused us of sharing magical secrets with the enemy."

He frowned. "Peters is a twit. When?"

"In the library. After he tried and failed to get that book." A gust of wind blew smoke across my face. I turned my head and coughed, hoping he wouldn't notice. "I've learned to take it seriously when people threaten me. But I don't know whether he was trying to stir something up, or if he just said what the rest of them were already thinking. I need to know how much Innsmouth would scare them. If it existed." The wind changed again, and I took a grateful breath.

"We really have . . . the raids, everyone's clear on what a bad idea they were. Some on purely practical grounds, because most of the actual nasty cultists went to ground and didn't get caught, and some because they've genuinely realized it was evil. But . . ." It was his turn to hesitate. "You remember what I said about Israel. And how my superiors reacted."

"Yes." His people had lost their own home—and were now fighting to remake it. Seeing that in common between us, I gave in to a question that hadn't occurred to me when he first brought it up. "I hope you won't take this as some sort of accusation, but why *don't* you go? My people—Innsmouth was bad enough, but if R'lyeh and the outpost cities had been destroyed too, and then rebuilt, I'd want to go *home*."

He shook his head. "Israel is building on a myth. I'm not against myths, and I'm glad it's there, but the home of *my* people is New York—a place that wanted us and took us in and where we can live in safety. I'm American, even if some people don't want to think of me that way. Like I said, we build where we are, even if it might not be safe forever."

"I can understand that." And appreciate his bravery, even while I tried to decide whether I could—or should—share it. "They weren't afraid of you as an individual, but they got scared when you had a place to go."

"Better than the alternative." He sighed. "Peters is a twit, like I said. Whatever his suspicions, I think he brought them up to keep you worried about yourself, instead of about whatever he was trying to do—because *that* was almost certainly on orders."

I felt my lips quirk. "It didn't work—I've had plenty of room to worry about both."

He took the cigarette from his mouth, examined the spark at the tip. "You know, if Barlow's playing fast and loose, it's not our supervisors finding out that he worries about. Their reaction could go either way, and he's dealt with it before. But he has to be careful about the university administration and professors. They can't just kick him out, but they could make his life very uncomfortable if they learned things he didn't want brought to public attention. The agency might rein him in to keep them quiet."

He watched me expectantly over his little fire, and I wished again for Audrey's skill at reading people. "I assume he guards those secrets carefully."

"Yes—though I don't know much about what kind of, ah, nontraditional security Barlow uses in the field. I do know that last time he went after a budget increase he wanted to demonstrate the efficiency of 'recursive exponent wards' or some such. You saw more of his methods this weekend than I did." Another apologetic shrug, another drag on his cigarette.

I blinked over eyes that felt suddenly dry, doubtful of what I thought I heard. Was he really implying that I ought to play spy against his colleague? "I told you before that I don't like ciphers."

"I apologize," he said. "They're the best I can offer right now. But you should trust your own judgment on the answers—I do, or I wouldn't have said anything in the first place."

The door opened, and Charlie joined us on the porch. He pulled out his pipe, accepted Spector's offered light. "The professor apparently doesn't want us smoking inside. Sorry, Aphra—it's just been a hell of a week."

"And seems likely to continue hellish," agreed Spector. "I'm sorry, Miss Marsh, I didn't realize you were so old-fashioned."

"It's not a problem outside," I said. I didn't want to mention how even a whiff of the smoke sometimes set my lungs aflame. It was probably only my own fears and memories, given that Caleb didn't seem to suffer from his own cigarettes.

Still, I excused myself. The two of them might appreciate the time alone, and I wanted to find out what Trumbull knew about recursive exponent wards.

Inside, I realized that Dawson might need deniability as much as Spector did. Perhaps he'd find an excuse to pull her away. I took Audrey aside into the living room, hoping that Caleb might catch hints of our discussion and make his own judgments about what his lover would wish to know.

"It sure sounds like he wants us to check up on Barlow's guys," she said when I'd finished telling her about my conversation with Spector. "The question is whether we want to."

"I'd certainly like to know what they're planning," I said. "If we can learn something that will force them to leave campus, so much the better."

"You know I'm not afraid of a little trouble. But this is riskier than our raid on the library. There could be real legal consequences if we got caught—or a bunch of mad FBI agents if they figure out who ratted on them."

"I know what it is to be on the state's bad side," I told her. "They don't wait for provocation."

"Provoking them doesn't help, though."

"Not knowing their plans can be worse. If they're after what it sounded like the other day, it could be bad for a lot of people, not just us." I paused, inhaled. Audrey wasn't the enemy. I wasn't even sure whether she really disapproved. "Are you against the idea, or just playing devil's advocate?"

She laughed. "A little of both. Sometimes you feel safer if everyone else is a little nervous too."

I sat on Trumbull's stuffed chair and rubbed my forehead. My skin felt stretched and painful. "I've been nothing but nerves since Barlow caught us. Worse since Peters accused my people of—whatever betrayal he thinks we had the freedom for. If we're found going through their things, they'll have more ammunition against us, and that does scare me. Sometimes it's all I can do not to catch the next plane to San Francisco, or run back to Innsmouth and beg the elders to solve this, whatever it takes." The words fell from my lips like cursed gems in old stories: even with Audrey it was a hard confession.

She squatted beside me, put her hand on my knee. "Hey, it's okay. We're going to make this work." But she also asked, curiously: "Could they do that? Solve the whole thing?"

I shook my head. "No more than parents ever can. They might be able to help with the books, if the Yith won't stand in their way, but I already know the limits of their ability to oppose the state."

She sucked on her lip. "My parents can usually solve any problem, as long as it can be solved by throwing money at it. Not always worth the cost, though."

"Throwing money, the elders could do. There's a lot of gold in the ocean. I don't see how that helps here, though."

She sighed. "Me neither. And I'm sort of glad we wouldn't have to ask my folks, if it came to that." She stood and gave me a hug. "On the other hand, I can promise that if they try to grab a Winslow, they won't find it easy to make everyone shut up and look the other way. And if they come after you guys again, I'll call in every favor we have in every newsroom that owes us one."

"You'd do that? I mean—" Realizing that she might take my doubt as an insult, I changed course. "Do you think that would work?"

"Papers are always looking for a good scandal. From what you said, in the '20s they managed to make you look like the scandalous ones— but Daddy knows how to point reporters in the right direction, and so do I."

I leaned back to look at her, trying not to feel jealous. I ought to be grateful that we now had friends who carried such influence. Hadn't Caleb said we'd do better with connections outside the town?

Before the raid the Marshes too had freely exercised their influence, albeit within a smaller sphere of privilege. Perhaps if we'd endowed a building at the university, or funded charities beyond the town's borders . . . but avoiding the outside world's attention had seemed safer. We had always recognized that some problems could not be solved with gold.

"Thank you," I said. "It means a lot, knowing that there's someone who'd try not to let us be forgotten, this time."

She smiled, a little sadly, and leaned against the arm of the couch. "Don't worry. You're pretty unforgettable." She shook her head and let the smile spread. "This kind of planning really is borrowing trouble. I can distract Dawson so you can talk to Trumbull. She'll know how to make this work if anyone does. Do you normally run midnight raids every night?"

"Only since you got here."

Caleb stuck his head into the living room, and snickered as he caught this last. "Deedee's gone outside to do something with Spector. I don't know if she's decided what, yet."

"Thank you for eavesdropping," I told him.

"You're welcome."

Trumbull followed him in and settled on the couch. "Mr. Marsh seems to think we should speak without representatives of the government present. I'm listening."

As succinctly and unemotionally as I could, I laid out what Spector hadn't quite suggested, and my reasons for thinking the risk worthwhile.

Trumbull considered for a minute. At last she nodded. "I don't like having those people here. Not only are they irritating me personally, but they also threaten to actively interfere with our work. I'll come along, and help as I can in getting around their protections. I should be able to do considerably better when I've had time to prepare." Her expression darkened. "But there is only so far I can risk myself. If things go badly, I won't stick around to get captured again."

Caleb bared his teeth. "We'd expect nothing more, Great One."

She smiled back, amusement mixed with an odd sort of fondness. Of course she wouldn't be offended. "Recursive exponent wards—could he mean fractal wards? There's something that doesn't come up often in this era. If they've developed an early variation, I ought to see it in any case."

"How do we handle that kind of ward?" I asked.

"It depends on the specific equation used, but generally one creates a countering equation to camouflage oneself as a part of the ward." She went into a more technical explanation that I didn't follow even slightly. After a minute she interrupted herself, hissed through her teeth in exasperation. "Never mind. I'll take care of that part. I have no idea how your species survives at this level of mathematical sophistication."

"We manage," I said stiffly. Caleb was glaring at her, and I hurried on: "Aside from sophisticated and dangerous equations, what else can we expect to find? Not people, I hope, if we go late enough."

"Ordinary locked doors?" suggested Caleb.

Audrey raised her hand. "I have bobby pins."

"That sounds helpful," said Caleb. "Although I still have the keys from Deedee—let's try those first."

I heard footsteps and held up my hand even as I recognized the echoing tap of Charlie's cane. He came in a moment later and settled himself on a spare chair. He cocked his head at me and raised an eyebrow. Neko followed, and sat demurely with her tea.

"We're planning a break-in." I sighed. "Another one."

"That will hopefully go better than the last?" asked Charlie. "No wonder Ron—Mr. Spector—and Miss Dawson left in such a vaguely explained hurry."

Trumbull looked at him a long moment. "Actually, you could be useful."

He bowed in his seat, eyes narrow, and doffed an imaginary hat. "I often think so."

"Some of the protections we might encounter—variations on those common in this era, I mean—are easier to get through if one individual remains outside, linked with those who enter. Your pre-existing connection would be ideal."

I watched him for concern, but he nodded. "Better than waiting around for the alarm to go off again."

"We should decide what we're looking for," said Audrey. "With this kind of thing, you want to get in and get out, not poke around and hope you find something important before someone pokes back."

"The missing books, for a start," I said.

"Assuming there *are* missing books," said Neko.

"There are," said Trumbull. "The librarians wouldn't have gone along with any charade on that count."

We talked further, but that was the gist of it. Get through ordinary locks, overcome whatever defenses Barlow's team had created, find what we needed, and retreat. When we snuck into the library, I'd been nervous. Now, my mind was ablaze with fears: of capture, of threats to my friends, of a bullet in the back of my head—or worse, Caleb's. And behind the fear of all the ways this could go wrong, fear of what could happen if we failed or did nothing.

Innsmouth sacrificed fewer sons to the First World War than most towns, but I'd grown up knowing of its horrors. The weapons of the most recent conflict were worse. Now another war loomed, and whatever Barlow learned would be shared with the generals. The horrors would be no less if both sides made use of them. Still worse weapons might well be conceived by science. Those were beyond my control. But the magical ones, and Barlow's role in creating them, I could perhaps do something to stop.

CHAPTER 23

We joined Spector for dinner at the faculty spa, where we talked of inconsequential things. I attended as well as I could to the conversation at Barlow's table, but they were similarly discreet. Spector excused himself afterward, and Dawson did not appear on the path as was her usual wont.

"Do you trust him?" Caleb murmured as we walked back to Trumbull's place.

"To do what?" The day had been relatively warm, and the glitter of renewed ice crusted the walks as night fell. I kept a careful eye on Charlie.

"To keep backing us if we're caught. This could be awfully convenient for him."

"Given that he's sworn we're trustworthy, it's only convenient if we're not caught." I broke an icicle from a bush as we passed, let it transmute to the comfort of cold water against my tongue. "I think he's a good man, or at least trying to be good. I think he has a sense of honor. I also think he's being pulled in more directions than he'd like." Charlie stumbled, and I jerked in response before I realized he'd caught himself. I hoped Spector would want to protect him, rather than get him out of the way as a potential embarrassment. I thought I knew the man well enough to expect the former, but frightened people do foolish things. "I think we need to do this for our own reasons, not just his."

Entirely superstitiously, we decided to leave at 1:30 a.m. rather than repeat our timing at the library. As before, we spent the evening together in meditation and preparation—save for Trumbull, who joined us only to help with the anchoring spell that would draw on our connection with Charlie. I felt Dawson dimly through the confluence, and hoped she would consider that connection a deniable sort of knowledge.

The campus lay quiet as we set out. The students were past the rowdy exultation of their reunion, but not yet stressed enough by the semester's workload to seek late-night outlets. Laughter drifted from distant dorms, but otherwise there was only the quiet crunch of feet over thin ice and the scrape of Charlie's cane. Trumbull carried a small hand telescope and measuring instruments, intended as an excuse to dismiss casual queries.

On our last visit to the administrative hall, I'd kept my eyes on the ground. The brick edifice was less gothic than the church and library, but still had a looming quality to it, pretending a more ancient vintage than it could actually lay claim to. The college arms were carved in stone blocks on either side of the door: keys crossed over a book, and the motto "QUOD REVELĒTUR OCCULTUM EST." The words implied that the keys would open the book, but in the image they seemed rather to stand as guards, blocking the way.

The building's windows were all dark. The door, if not ancient, appeared as old as the university, a monument of oak planks and iron bands. The lock appeared promisingly old-fashioned as well. Caleb tried the handle with a shrug (it was indeed locked), then compared options on the key ring. In the distance, one of the university's guard dogs barked. We stilled, but it did not come closer. Caleb only had to test three of the skeleton keys before one turned. Tumblers clicked softly and the door swung open, well-oiled. Charlie retreated with Trumbull's scope in hand, promising to wait and assuring us that his coat and gloves kept him shielded from the cold.

We stepped inside and locked the door behind us. Audrey flicked on a small flashlight. Its beam stabbed the dark hallway, making me flinch.

"Can't you get by without that?" asked Caleb.

"Still can't see in the dark. I'm sorry, I tried."

"All right," I said, "but be careful. Once we're in a room with windows, we don't want to attract attention."

"Teach your grandma to suck eggs?"

I thought of my grandmothers, and forbore response.

Neither Trumbull nor my brother needed reminding of the way to Barlow's office. We walked swiftly, though I winced at every echo of our footsteps. At the door, I knelt to peer through the crack underneath. All appeared dark save for a faint glimmer from windows beyond, and no sounds emerged to suggest someone working late by moonlight.

Trumbull held her hand before the door, traced sigils as she murmured to herself. The words were old and strange, and folded in on themselves in ways that I could not entirely comprehend. After a moment I was no longer sure whether I heard or felt them. My skin, too, was made of words, or of numbers, endlessly and blindly twining around each other. They fed on each other's tails, birthed new numbers in carnal equations. The draft from the door prickled against the in-curling geometries that I had become.

"Try the lock," she said.

Caleb fumbled with the keys, but after a couple of tries found one that fit. Audrey turned off her flashlight. Caleb waited a moment to turn the handle while our eyes adjusted. The still-crawling numbers did not interfere with my vision, and whatever wards Trumbull had detected did not block our entry.

Once I passed the threshold the strange sensations faded. All was much as we'd left it, save that the chairs to which they'd tied us had been restored to other locations. The sliver of waning moonlight limned everything with a sallow glow.

I went immediately to their bookcase. Three years in the bookstore had given me a quick eye for changes to a shelf, but I saw no additions to the titles I'd noted before, and nothing that looked like it came from the library's restricted section. It was all theoretical texts and modern math, mostly in English. I did note a few titles missing—perhaps taken to their hotel for late-night study. And it occurred to me now, in the midst of our trespass, that they might sensibly have done the same with stolen volumes.

Across the room, Trumbull made a little huff of discovery. Joining her, I saw a notebook crowded with diagrams and equations and notes, written in English but marred by unfamiliar terminology.

"What's that?" I asked.

"Proof that they're trying to learn the art of body switching—and making progress, in spite of some severe gaps in comprehension. There are ideas here, in their most recent notes, that strongly imply access to *On the Sending Out of the Soul,* but I doubt it would constitute proof to anyone not extremely well-versed in the literature."

"We should take it," suggested Caleb. "Set them back in their studies. Though they'd still have the book."

Trumbull hefted the notes thoughtfully. "*On the Sending Out of the Soul* is an important work, but crude, as are most human works on the topic. There are key insights in these notes that they may not have duplicated elsewhere." She flipped through. "They seem to have some concept of how to overcome geographic separation, though they aren't quite there yet. Impressive. Human magic so often treats spatial distance as an inflexible barrier."

I looked at the notebook with renewed respect, as I might a venomous jellyfish. "It would make a difference, then, if we took this. They could use these ideas to start wars, or massacre millions."

"Most ideas can be used for that purpose by most sapients, given the opportunity." She examined the notes again, eyes darting quickly over the pages. "So very frustrating. They've almost begun to reach true understanding on a technical level—but their comprehension of the art's obligations is nil. Petty creatures."

"Then let's relieve them of the burden." Caleb held out his hand. His lips twitched. "It'll make a fine addition to your collection, don't you think?"

She put the book firmly back on the pile. "Take it, and they'll seek twice as hard for spies, and keep their hold on the library until they regain confidence in their understanding. Which could be a long time. We need the infestation removed from campus, not fully entrenched."

"We need them not to start another World War!" I said. Audrey shushed me frantically, and I held back further exclamation. Trumbull gave me a cool look. Of course, she knew precisely how many more such wars would be started, and the tallies of the dead. "I know we're not likely to have world peace any time soon," I said more quietly. "But I intend to do what I can."

"You may not," she said firmly, "render this age's best repository un-usable. Not if you want your own people's library preserved."

"I don't want it enough to sacrifice millions of lives." Half nauseated, half elated, I tried to reach for the book. I expected her to try and block me, but found myself simply unable to touch the notebook: as if it sat under still water, it wasn't quite where I put my hand.

Audrey stepped around us and, with a grimace of effort, picked it up. "This is not the Maltese Falcon," she announced. I must have looked confused at her apparent non sequitur, for she added: "Got to take you guys to the Belvedere sometime—terrific second-run movies. This is not a one-of-a-kind artifact holding all their knowledge and power. They're researchers—human researchers, who work in teams and worry about fires—they're going to have notebooks full, and they won't have brought them all to Miskatonic. We need to stop *them*, not steal one notebook." She put it back on the pile.

"Thank you, Miss Winslow," said Trumbull.

"Save it. Just because it *isn't* Crowther Library versus more lives like my brother's, don't think I didn't see you make that trade."

"I didn't know you had a brother," I said, foolishly.

"I don't. Haven't for about four years."

We stood awkwardly for a moment. Then Trumbull said, "Let's see if we can find anything that *is* of use, and leave before someone catches us arguing."

"Suits me," said Audrey stiffly.

I put a hand on her wrist. "I'm sorry for your loss."

"Thank you."

I glanced back at Trumbull, now returned to her browsing. "It must drive her crazy that you can resist her. I don't know how you do it."

Audrey shrugged. "She telegraphs. I know what someone trying to manipulate me looks like, and I don't appreciate it. Especially when they're so smug."

"I don't like it either, and it doesn't help."

She shrugged again. "Well, if it isn't secret rock powers, maybe I can teach you something."

We searched the room. There were plenty of fascinating items—I examined the interrogation talismans at length, despite the discomfort—but nothing from the narrow range that either university administration or federal government might object to. I reluctantly classed the expedition as a failure, though if nothing else it helped us better understand our foe. If Audrey was right, we'd eventually need to confront them directly, and we'd need that understanding to have any chance of stopping them.

I knew it was possible that we couldn't stop them—that they would have their desired arts, and their wars to follow. Trumbull's presence was a constant reminder that every human civilization, every earthly race, eventually reached some peril that could not be overcome.

At last we regrouped. We surveyed Barlow's domain, checked and checked again for signs that might tell of our entry. Trumbull renewed her counter-ward and, skins crawling with impossible numbers, we left.

The moment I stepped into the hallway, I realized what I'd been missing. "Wait, I've figured it out!" Audrey shushed me, and I lowered my voice again. "I know where it is."

"Where what is?" said Caleb, and "Where?" asked Audrey. She

turned on her light, but let it dangle, tracing little infinity signs on the floor.

"The evidence." I was already moving, and the others hurried to keep up with me. I struggled to turn my moment's intuition into a logical explanation. "Of course they wouldn't keep anything that could get them in trouble with the university in that office—everyone knows they're there; there are probably administrators in and out all day. But I think I know where they'd go to be more discreet."

"Oh, I follow," said Audrey. In fact she ran ahead of me, swinging into the stairwell. I went after her, down concrete steps into the less public passages of the building's underbelly. Trumbull and Caleb hurried behind.

Here we found not well-polished floors but dust and cobwebs, bare bulbs of considerable vintage, doors with rusty hinges. In the back of my mind I felt Charlie noticing and echoing my excitement. And further still, the faint whisper of Sally's heart and breath, racing as if in response to my own thoughts.

Audrey and I halted together before the same door.

"How do you know—" began Caleb. But I was already pushing it open.

To reveal a room illumined by witchlight, etched with diagrams like a sea of interlocking gears—gears made of numbers that pulsed and twined like those Trumbull had placed on my skin. I wished I still had that protection, but already I walked toward the particular gear that called to me, still half-believing that it held precisely the thing I sought. *I don't like being manipulated,* I thought, but it didn't help. Audrey, likewise in thrall, stepped into a gear of her own.

The strange call vanished as soon as I stood within. My head cleared, but invisible shackles held my legs. At the room's shadowed edge, beyond the great sea of enmeshed equations, I saw that we were not alone. Barlow, his secretary Mary, and Peters were there—and alongside them, Sally and Jesse. All five stared at us with shocked expressions.

Sally found her voice first. "Audrey? Miss Marsh? What are you doing here—I swear, I wasn't breaking my promise, I just wanted to learn—please—"

Mary slapped her across the cheek. "Be quiet. We need to find out what's going on here, and we can't afford panic. If the equation is bringing in *people,* something's very wrong."

Jesse, who'd been kneeling at the diagram's edge, stood slowly. "It's not. Or at least not human people. Audrey, what did she do to you?"

"Started to teach me magic. What the hell are you doing here?"

"Learning magic." He eyed me, walked around the edge of the room to get a better view. "Your new mentor's not human. I wasn't sure whether she forced you to stay with her, or whether you'd just gotten caught up in something bigger than you could handle. But with what happened to Leroy, we needed power of our own. These guys started asking us questions, and we found out we had some interests in common."

"I'm human," I said, picking the accusation most immediately worth responding to. "Just a subspecies."

"Are you?" asked Mary. "It said so in the files, but I didn't take them seriously."

"Amphibious," said Barlow. "Supposedly. And certainly more loyal to her immortality-granting ocean gods than to any country. What about that one?" He jerked his elbow at Audrey.

"I'm human," she said. "Just a subspecies. Will you please shut down this goddamned spell?"

"Which looks," came Trumbull's voice from the doorway, "absurdly unsafe. What by all the gods do you think you're doing?" Twisting, I could see her and Caleb. Caleb looked ready to charge across the floor, and I made shooing motions. I wanted him to run for Spector, but he didn't seem inclined.

"It's an inventory equation," said Barlow. "It's meant to track down and sample any exotic power sources that might be available within a given range." He turned to shuffle a stack of notes. "The sensitivity appears to be higher than predicted. I do apologize, Miss Marsh—

I didn't intend to detain you a second time. Although perhaps I should have. You seem to have come from very close by. What were you doing, skulking about the administration building after midnight?"

I gritted my teeth. "Trying to find out whether you were doing something dangerous. Which you were."

"Certainly. Dangerous to our enemies." He narrowed his eyes and shifted his weight; I could tell he would have preferred to come closer. "If you consider yourself an enemy of the United States, I think we'd better talk after I finish the inventory. Unfortunately, the equation is difficult to interrupt before it's run its course." He looked up to nod at the others. "Miss Trumbull, Mr. Marsh. I'm afraid we're somewhat occupied at the moment, but if you want to leave now . . . well, your unwillingness to answer a few questions will be noted. This will take another hour or two; perhaps you'd prefer to come around the side and join us—I understand you have some background in more traditional esoterica. You might be interested to see what we've accomplished here." And he clearly wanted to see their reaction to it.

Trumbull, who'd been listening to his suspicions with an expression of increasing disapproval, did not approach. "Are you mad? Your 'equation' is a nonspecific summoning and binding, however unorthodox—it'll drag in one of everything it can reach. There are things that don't bind as easily as two mixed-race humans."

"Really, miss, there's no need to be hysterical."

"She's a *professor*," said Audrey. "And she knows more about esoterica, traditional or otherwise, than you'll ever—"

One of the gears—less a gear, up close, and more an amorphous globule edged with numbers—began to pulse brightly. Then another, and then the whole room burst into a haze of actinic light. It ought to have been cacophony, but I heard nothing other than Trumbull's startled hiss, abruptly cut off. I tried again to move, but the spell bound me fast. Something rushed past, cold as space and carrying silence with it. Memory flared of the thing I'd encountered during our own ritual— now I knew I'd only glimpsed it at a distance. It surged against me and I felt the touch of a nameless need deeper than hunger. I choked on something that was not air.

My connection with Charlie flared, all fear. But even fear made a spot of warmth, a little space where I could draw sudden, painful breath. I still heard nothing, though I could make out vague shapes moving beyond the light.

I had another connection in this room, beyond the confluence. My hands were unbound, though moving them brushed the edges of my bubble of warmth and air, and my fingers came back hoared with frost. When I pulled up my sleeve, it was a moment before I felt the fabric against my fingers. I touched the sigil on my arm. *Sally. Sally, let me look.*

I doubted my words would get through, but I hoped she'd sense the intention behind them. And it worked: for a moment, I saw through her eyes. Sally pressed her back to the wall, painted concrete rough against her hands, trying to stay as far as possible from the morass of color that overflowed the edge of the diagram. Then there was light, and our connection flickered, dimmed—did not go out, but I felt her paralyzed terror only at a great distance.

The cold haze began to tighten around me, pressing inward. Caleb and Audrey and Charlie felt far away, and Dawson impossibly distant. I hurled signals into the void: fingertip flutters, tiny patterns of breath. I knew now that no one could answer with aid; I only wanted to be noticed and remembered.

Iä, Shub-Nigaroth, tell my grandfather . . .

And then the light started to shrink—or to pull into itself, retreating and compressing into lightning-bright pinpricks. I forced my lids closed over huge, dry eyes. The light flared painfully even through that protection and then, at last, vanished. I rubbed my eyes, felt my tear ducts loose a little precious fluid to soothe them. I opened them cautiously.

Illumination bloomed, pale and painless: Audrey's flashlight. She shone it around, found Trumbull on the floor beside Barlow, scribbling furiously with chalk. Then I had to cover my eyes again, if only for a moment: Caleb had found the wall switch.

Trumbull threw the chalk to the floor. It shattered, and the suddenly returned sound echoed from the walls. I stumbled as my bonds dissolved.

"You are abominable creatures," she said, rising to face Barlow. "Do you think you can play trial and error with this kind of thing? Your own lives and sanity are yours to risk, for whatever they're worth. But you very nearly wiped out three hundred years of work!"

Barlow took a step back. "What are you talking about?" He glanced at the diagram, with its strange asymmetries now subtly altered, and frowned.

"You interfered," said Peters. "You were deliberately trying to sabotage—"

"Keep silent," she snapped, and then smiled as he did. "Well, you've burnt out your little amulet, if nothing else. All of you hold a moment."

I thought perhaps I ought to intervene—but the urge was not a strong one. Our captors stood dazed as Trumbull looked them over. A part of me watched avidly, delighted to see them at her mercy. And a larger part hoped that she would take advantage—that whatever interest the Yith held in my people's existence would inform what she did next.

"Ah," she said to Jesse. "You raided the library, but they took the excuse to steal what they wanted for themselves. And made better, or worse, use of the materials than you could have hoped to on your own. Somehow you thought their mentorship a route to safety. You are an idiot." Over her shoulder, to me: "He distrusts you because you wouldn't mate with him."

"Thank you; I had figured that part out myself." I recalled his cheerful insistence that he'd accepted my refusal, and felt my urge to intervene wane still further.

Trumbull glanced at Sally, still pressed against the wall, and dismissed her. She passed on to Peters. "An intelligent brute. Terrible combination, all too common."

Barlow was next. "Loyalty and curiosity. A rarer combination. A pity that you direct your virtues toward such petty ends—and that you aren't nearly as intelligent as you want to believe yourself."

Then she turned on Mary. "Now you, you're more interesting. You might have been one of Miss Marsh's pupils, under better circumstances. Or a researcher in your own right in fifty years, without tailoring your studies to the agendas of imbeciles. A pity: I hate to see intelligence wasted. But we cannot afford you repeating such experiments; Miskatonic must stand for a few years yet." She cupped Mary's chin, locked eyes. For a moment Trumbull's body sagged, jerked away—then returned to its accustomed posture of confidence. Mary gasped and pulled back. She put her hand to her chin, touching it gingerly.

Trumbull looked around. "It would be best if you recalled this night well enough to learn more caution. But I see you rewriting your memories already—better then to know only that your 'equation' failed spectacularly, and leave us out entirely." I realized, with mingled regret and relief, that her concern was all for their dangerous experiments; their suspicion of the people of the water, the threat of their politics, hadn't even registered. And I didn't dare speak up, lest I disrupt her work.

One by one, she took their heads in hand and met their eyes. No sign of body switching this time, simply a moment of contact. When she got to Sally, she snorted. "You've already effaced the whole thing for yourself. Some minds are truly incapable of correlating their contents."

At last she stepped back. "Well. Clean up and go home. Or curl gibbering in a corner; I'm sure it will serve the world just as well." To the rest of us: "Are you coming? Or do you want to stay here and wait for something else to try and eat you?"

Audrey glanced at Sally. "But—"

"She'll do better if you leave her mind to scab over on its own," said Trumbull. Audrey looked uncertain, but followed. Caleb and I did likewise. I wanted to be out of that room.

Trumbull began muttering to herself. By the time we left the building, she was cursing audibly in Enochian. Or so I supposed: not all the expletives were ones I recognized.

"What did you do to Mary?" Caleb asked, cutting through the stream of profanity.

"Gave her alexia," she said. "She's the smartest of them, and did much of their design, for all Barlow styles her his secretary."

"And now she can't read?" I asked, horrified in spite of myself. If it worked, though . . .

"It's easy enough, on a human brain—though the process does make it more vulnerable to later lesions." She glared at us. "I swore I wouldn't put myself in danger, and instead I find myself defending the local archive from outsiders. I'm losing all sense of scale."

"We're glad you stayed to help," I said. And, thinking that might not be enough: "As you said, they risked destroying three hundred years of work."

"And in defending three hundred, I risked millions of years of memories. I will answer for that, you may be sure."

Charlie hurried up to us. "Are you all right? I thought I saw—what was that?"

"Outsider," said Trumbull.

"Do you remember what I said about trying to summon gods?" I asked.

"That it's a bad idea; other things are likely to answer."

"Yes. Apparently no one ever told Barlow. Or Mary, I suppose." Trumbull's suggestion that Mary might have made a good student felt strange. I imagined a woman like Audrey, already grown and forced into the box of a powerful man's expectations, discovering a talent for magical research.

Dawson came running around the building. She flung her arms around Caleb. "You absolute idiot—what were you doing?"

"Failing to get any useful evidence," he said. "What are *you* doing here? Aren't you supposed to be back at Dean Skinner's place, pretending you don't know where we are?"

"I figured you might get in trouble and I ought to pretend from a little closer. But when you got in trouble, I had no idea what it was, or where you were—idiot!"

He pulled her close, and they walked with arms linked, murmuring insults. Trumbull looked at them, muttered something about mating practices, and stalked ahead.

"We still don't know how to get them off the campus," I said to Charlie and Audrey. "I don't think we can try something like that again—they're too eager for evidence of sabotage. And it sounds like they weren't even the ones who stole the books—they just haven't turned in the perpetrators."

"I'm really mad at Jesse and Sally, but I don't want to get them in worse trouble." Audrey shook herself. "My head hurts. Let's find out if Trumbull keeps aspirin in the house, and then see if sleeping on it helps. Maybe we'll have a great idea in the morning."

CHAPTER 24

Neko met us, found the aspirin, opined that we illustrated every possible reason to avoid practicing magic, and pro forma invited Audrey to sleep in our room again.

I woke shivering in the early morning, to find Neko and Audrey sitting on the other bed, talking quietly.

"Were you having nightmares too?" asked Neko. She patted a free spot amid the sheets, and I struggled free of the dream's paralysis to join them.

"Shub-Nigaroth's laughter," I said bitterly.

"What's that mean?" asked Audrey.

"It means," said Neko, "that it's not practical to fear everything in the universe that's scary."

"Essentially, yes," I said. "So She probably thinks it's funny that I now have nightmares about being *cold,* too."

"I'm so sorry," said Neko, and hugged me tightly. I leaned against her, trying to forget the airless chill of my dream.

"You too?" I asked Audrey.

"My dreams were different," she said, turning her head away. Audrey, stripped of her usual manic confidence, seemed a worrisome and vulnerable thing.

"Different how?" I tugged on the sleeve of her nightgown, and she let herself be drawn back to our mammalian warmth.

"It was a good dream. Sort of."

"Oh, those," said Neko.

Audrey flopped back on the bed. "I read too much about the Mad Ones, the other day. I dreamed that we were in that basement, unable to move, listening to Trumbull talk about how dangerous the spell was, and I just—just turned into smoke or energy or something. It was easy. And I floated over and started doing things to Barlow and Peters, to make them stop. It wasn't like the spells you've been teaching us— I only needed to think about it to break them, and I felt so smug that I'd saved everyone. And then I started doing the same thing to Sally—" I held her while she sobbed. Between her gasps I caught the word "monster," repeated.

Neko held her too. "No, you're not, you're not—Audrey, look at me. Look at me." At last Audrey did pull back and turn, sniffling. Neko went on. "Only the way we all are. You know those horrible movies, with the Japanese villains all white guys in bad makeup?" Audrey nodded, shakily, and I got the feeling that she'd liked some of those movies better than we had. "I have dreams where they come and get us out of the camps. Or where I'm one. Sometimes you look for strength where you can find it, even if it's horrible."

"But that's different. The Mad Ones really *are* down there some-where, right now, eating slaves and mutilating prisoners."

"And men of the air are up here," I said, "mutilating prisoners and killing millions in wars and trying to summon brain-eating entities for power, and probably eating things I don't want to think about too. And Trumbull's people sacrifice kids for immortality. And my people, under the water, preserve every stupid idea humans have had since we first lit fires. We're all monsters, or related to monsters, one way or another." I wrapped my arms around my knees, still shivering. "I'm sorry, that wasn't very reassuring."

"No, it kind of was." She sat up, rubbing her eyes.

"Salt water?" I asked, and Neko laughed. "What?"

"You're predictable, that's all. Audrey, she wants to wash your tears into a jar so you can give them back to the ocean. It's actually weirdly comforting, too."

Audrey laughed shakily. "Sure, why not. It's not like anyone else wants them."

I got up and padded out to the kitchen. The dining room was dark— thankfully Trumbull wasn't working late tonight.

I showed Audrey how to use the salt water. She dipped her fingers, wiped her eyes, then dipped her fingers back into the cup I'd found. I set it aside on the sill.

"Trumbull's asleep," I said. "I wonder if she's having a bad night too."

"Do Yith dream?" asked Neko.

"I've no idea. I'd expect them to have a fair amount of control over it, if so—but she really was scared."

"She wouldn't have acted so angry if she wasn't," said Audrey. "I'm glad she stuck around to save us, even if she was a jerk about it afterward."

"So am I," I said. "I hope she's human enough right now for sleep to do her some good. Whatever happens next, I suspect we'll need her help to get through it." And persuading her to grant that help—if it were possible at all—would probably be my task.

~~~~~~

I'd just fallen back asleep at last—or so it felt—when a pounding on the front door shocked me awake. I lay still a long moment, caught between waking and dreaming, before I realized that it was 1949, and this couldn't be the soldiers who'd demanded entry twenty-one years past. *It's January 27th.* The anniversary of my father's death had passed yesterday, unnoticed in the tumult.

The knocking paused and started again, and it occurred to me that if Trumbull's amnesias hadn't taken, this still might be soldiers. Neko sat up, wide-eyed. We both started throwing on clothes. Audrey rolled over, and I nudged her.

"Oh god, my head. What's going on?"

"We don't know," I said grimly.

We hurried into the hall to see Trumbull in a bathrobe and an extremely irritated expression. She opened the door, and Spector rushed in. Charlie followed more slowly a few yards behind.

"What on earth is going on?" Spector demanded. He stamped snow off his feet and glared. "Barlow insists that someone sabotaged one of his experiments last night. He's convinced you did it even though he didn't see anyone and won't say how it happened. And he says his secretary is 'damaged,' as if she were a piece of equipment. He swears he'll have me disciplined for recruiting a 'team of moles,' and Mr. Day insists he didn't *see* anything."

"Sabotaged?" Trumbull went from irritated to livid. "*Sabotaged?* Fhi-grlt Ngwdi'ygl!"

I pulled Spector aside, not sure if *you're lucky to be sane* had been a statement or a threat. Charlie pushed the door open, took in our various expressions, and moved to stand beside me and Spector.

"It's a long story," I told Spector, "But they came close to 'sabotaging' the whole campus, and Trumbull stopped them."

"Ah." There was a long pause, then with a sort of weary hopelessness he asked, "Evidence?"

"None. I'm sorry."

"God damn it. Well, he knows damn well all he has is a hunch, so they're turning everything upside down looking for proof of their supposed saboteur, and they told me point-blank that they didn't think I'd be much help. It's obvious he thinks that if he looks everywhere else and doesn't find anything, he'll be able to get permission to go after my team directly. Through proper channels this time."

"What are they doing now?" asked Audrey.

"Questioning more people, combing the library collections for something—I don't know what. Searching faculty offices. They may even go through the student dorms and faculty housing just to prove they've been thorough, I don't know. Eventually they'll make it over here—and I'm sorry, they may well get permission to question you again."

Trumbull grimaced. "I still have to teach a class this morning. Are you all planning to spend the whole day sitting around my house again?" If the question wasn't hint enough, the glare that accompanied it was.

"I'd like to head back to Hall for the day," I said. Audrey nodded vigorously, and there were general murmurs of agreement, even from Neko. "Or will that look too suspicious?" I asked Spector.

"Everything looks suspicious to them right now," he said. "Frankly, I'm damned if I'll sit around waiting for him to get to me. I've made all the calls I can, and no one wants to talk with me who wasn't listening already. Clearing out and letting them make a public mess all on their lonesome . . . isn't a great idea, but it's the best I've got. You can explain more about your night on the way."

"Where's Caleb?" I asked belatedly, suddenly worried for him.

"He never came back to the guest dorm," said Charlie.

"We need to pick up Miss Dawson, but . . ." Spector trailed off. I felt a surge of relief, both at the reminder of where Caleb had likely gone, and at Spector's apparent understanding.

"He'll make it," I assured him. I closed my eyes and reached through the confluence in Caleb's direction. It was getting easier. I felt warmth, even breaths, a measure of calm that those of us sleeping here had not been granted. I pushed a little of my still-slowing pulse in his direction, and hoped it would be enough to wake him.

Spector's car was meant to fit six in a pinch, and Dawson was our sixth. We drove around the side of Skinner's house, out of view of the front door. Spector literally looked the other way, and a moment later Caleb ran around the corner. He peered dubiously in the window at the crowded seats. I pushed open the door and leaned out. "Climb on in, brother dear!"

After some experimentation, we ended up scrambling around so he sat next to Dawson with me on his lap.

"Why do you guys do that?" asked Dawson.

"Do what?" asked Caleb. He put the lie to his innocence by ostentatiously ruffling my hair. "Sister dear?"

I poked him in the ribs.

"It's sort of a joke," he said. He reddened, but his tone turned more serious. "In the camps, some of the guards believed we all married our siblings. Playing along made them look stupid."

"And helped convince them that they didn't want to touch the girls," I added.

"I know that sort of joke," said Dawson. She leaned against him, giving Audrey a hair more space.

A guard at the side gate made us roll down our windows. He smirked, but nodded to Spector and let us pass. His eyes were restless as he turned back to his watch, and he fidgeted with his cigarette.

"All right," said Spector. "Let's hear it."

"Are you sure you want to know?" I asked.

"No. But it sounds like I can't afford not to."

I told him about the previous night, glossing over our break-in but making up for it with the details of Barlow's subterranean sanctuary.

"You know," said Spector, "I thought most of their claims about what they could do were parlor tricks. Or just exaggeration."

"They send you out to deal with the freaks," said Caleb. "Do you mean to tell me you didn't believe in magic?"

"I believe there are a lot of things about the universe that we don't understand yet. We've seen hints about transdimensional mathematics— some work done right here at Miskatonic—and ESP for almost twenty years now. But a lot of things in the original Innsmouth files were made up whole cloth from malicious rumor. Demon-summoning rituals seemed of a piece."

I sighed. "Most of them probably were. But there truly are entities that don't mean humans well—they don't mean us harm, either, but their natures are such that they'd need to work hard not to destroy us. They just don't care. If someone makes a crack, they come through for their own purposes, and the destruction follows."

"Ah. But you sent this thing home—or Trumbull did."

"As far as I can tell." I shivered—even thinking about the sound-devouring cold was enough to make the air feel thin around me. I took a deep breath. "I have no idea if Trumbull sent it home, or just elsewhere, but she seemed confident that she'd shut down whatever was pulling it through."

"I suppose she'd know more about it than the rest of us."

"If she weren't there, I don't think we'd be alive now. Depending on how much of that thing there was to come through, I wouldn't bet on anyone in Morecambe County."

Spector's grip tightened on the steering wheel. "I guess that must happen, sometimes. There are enough stories about vanished towns."

"I don't suppose," I said, "that kind of risk would be enough to get them recalled. Or fired. Or tried for treason."

He laughed. It sounded strained. "Even with evidence . . . it might get them pulled back and given a stern lecture. It might also get them sent off to continue their research under more controlled circumstances. There are people who appreciate that kind of power."

"Sure, it's powerful," said Audrey. "As long as you don't mind standing at ground zero while you set it off."

"That doesn't always stop people," said Spector.

~~~~~

We picked up bagels in Kingsport. Their warmth did a little to suppress my memory of the previous night, and to combat the fatigue that still fogged my mind. The library was just opening as we arrived, and we settled gratefully into our usual spot.

We were more grateful when Edith Birch brought us, along with the usual stack of Kirill's notebooks and references, additional texts and notes. The books themselves, as we examined them, appeared fairly pedestrian—several well-known fakes, a few impressively obscure fakes, a sprinkling of works that were legitimate but common. But the notebooks . . .

They weren't anything we'd sought, but they were fascinating. Generations of girls like Audrey, like Mary, even like Sally, had encountered some hint of the art—in Hall's scant collections, at Miskatonic's open classes, from boyfriends' coyly dropped hints—and become obsessed with something outside their permitted knowledge, beyond the strictures that bound them to safety.

It shouldn't have shocked me. Charlie had come to me with that same desperation for deeper knowledge, and Audrey too in her own way. But magic and the elder tongues had for so long represented freedom to me *because* they were a piece of home. They were comfort and safety, even as they offered glimpses of things that could never be comforting or safe. And so it took these dozens of voices—desperate diaries, efforts to reinvent ancient knowledge from nothing again and again—for me to truly understand that they were stretching outward in desperation while I stretched inward. That there were people, beyond the few I knew, who might actively seek to understand the strange rather than destroy it in revulsion.

Might even come to its aid, when we were ready. I realized that I was shaking.

I stood and paced around the table, trying to get my body and emotions back under control. I rubbed my arms against the draft, wondering if last night's adventure had permanently altered my tolerance for cold. I hoped the effects would fade with time, or with distance.

"Are you okay?" asked Charlie.

"Yes." I forced a smile. "I just thought of something. Not important, just personal."

"That's great," said Audrey. "I hope you'll tell us about it when you're ready, but in the meantime I've still got a headache, so . . ."

"Sorry," I said, and sat down. I returned to the notebooks, full of new curiosity about their creators' lives and thoughts. About whether any of them had caught more than a glimpse. About people who, found at the right time, might have been friends and allies and students. About chances lost.

And that was Sally, too. And Leroy and Jesse. When they saw me— when Leroy and Sally saw the elders—they might have been scared, might have acted foolishly, but they also saw the proof of their deepest yearnings. If I hadn't been so frightened myself, if I had seen beyond the elders' treatment of them as dangerous outsiders, if I had *understood,* I would have realized that they could never let it lie. Sally and Jesse had broken into the library, had accepted Barlow's offer of mentorship, because I'd shown them magic—and then given them nothing beyond the demand to keep it a secret.

I set the journal in my hands aside, and paged through others with less attention as I considered my error and whether there might still be some chance of repairing it. Then a name scrawled inside one cover— at the bottom of the stack, perhaps placed there by Birch through an odd sort of protective instinct—brought me abruptly back to our current troubles.

Not wanting to hold this alone, I tapped Caleb on the shoulder. He put down his half-accurate primer to see, and his mouth made a little o.

"What did you find?" asked Spector.

I held the book up. "The name on this journal is Asenath Waite."

"You've mentioned her before," said Audrey. She leaned forward, then winced and rubbed her head.

I never had gotten around to explaining Asenath to her. I supposed it was time. "Asenath's name is on the notebook—but it's her father, Ephraim, who wrote the notes. He was the last perpetrator of body theft tried in Innsmouth. In absentia, of course. The man who shot him, after he jumped bodies again, is in an asylum outside of town. But discovering Ephraim took a long time, and he—as Asenath—went to school here." I sighed. "I expect someone must have sent her—his—papers here afterward. That librarian who's been so helpful was a friend of hers. I haven't wanted to tell her—I don't see that it would do much good."

Audrey let out a low whistle. "Yeah. I guess—I don't know. I feel like I'd want to know, but I probably wouldn't, actually. What's he have to say, then?"

I dove into the book, reluctant but feeling a sort of duty. Hall's librarians took care with personal journals, and there were others in the stack by the same hand—but we soon discovered that Ephraim recorded all but his most innocuous thoughts in a mix of R'lyehn and Enochian, and often supplemented linguistic security with mirror writing and personal shorthand. I was the only one with the skill to make any sense of it.

Even putting aside his crime, Ephraim Waite was not a credit to our people. He obsessed over the supposed defects of his stolen body, convinced that his every failure reflected the limits of the female brain. His evaluations of his fellow students were crude and dismissive—though beneath that, there were hints that he appreciated their company and drew comfort from it. He even saw a little of their potential, in spite of himself. And he never tried to corrupt them for his own use. As I read further, I discovered such reluctance was far from his universal habit.

Ephraim knew that the Yith carried out their tasks with the aid of scattered cults, whose service they repaid with tidbits of knowledge. Not having so remarkable a mission to spark loyalty, he bought his own worshippers not only with carefully tailored scraps of esoterica, but with the assurance that their basest urges were the will of the gods.

I swallowed nausea and suppressed another shiver—and almost glossed past a line in his description of a group working in the outskirts of New York City:

> *Volkov, a strong and ambitious man, could make a good high priest. V. eager to learn the arts, though perhaps too independent-minded. He hopes to return home when the current troubles pass, assuming they ever do. He constantly reminds me that his name means "wolf" in his native Russian. Must find some way to remind him that wolves are pack creatures—and make a dog of him.*

I nearly spoke up immediately, but restrained my tongue. The implications were obvious, but what I should do about them was not. Here was a Russian who might well have brought the rituals of body theft back to Moscow—perhaps to buy immunity from his country's "troubles." If this was the Russians' key to learning that art, it had been taken long ago, long enough that Barlow's searches for a spy on campus became absurd. And knowing the danger's source might make it easier for Spector's people to watch for intruders. At the least, they could make it more difficult for any one person to do great damage.

And Spector trusted me, had brought me here because whatever our political differences, he believed I'd let him know about any true danger.

But if we had clear evidence that the Russians had gained the art, all the more cause for Barlow and his masters to desire it for themselves. Another argument for their views, at the expense of Spector's moderate faction. Even Spector might be persuaded that the research was a necessary evil. And if the Russians truly had learned from one of my people, however apostate, it would be held against us.

Words spoken cannot be effaced, but silence can always be filled. I wanted to think this through before I said anything. I turned the page, read on of unrelated outrages.

As I read of a particularly heretical ritual performed in the wilds of New Hampshire, another bout of shivers wracked my body. This time, when I wrapped my arms around myself, I found the spot of deeper cold on my forearm.

I stilled. For the first time that day, I attended to the source of my fear rather than trying to suppress it. And found, at the other end of the link wrought by my grandfather, a mind fighting for focus and trying desperately to ignore the germ of ice growing in its depths. A flash: Barlow pacing his office while Peters stood by the window and Jesse read aloud to Mary, and I—*Sally*—tried to focus on taking notes from Mary's dictation. The words faded in and out; I struggled to fill in the gaps. They already believed I was stupid and hysterical; they'd kick me out if I couldn't be useful.

"Audrey!" I said.

She looked up and glared. "What?"

As gently as I could, I asked: "Your headache—has it changed at all?"

"I wish it had. I'm trying to concentrate."

The others looked up, caught by my urgency. I went on: "Is it *cold*?"

"It feels like I've got frostbite on the inside of my skull."

I put down the book and stood. My chair scraped against the floor, and Audrey winced. "We have to go back to Miskatonic. Now."

Spector was already standing, gathering his notes. "Tell us."

"Trumbull's banishment wasn't complete. There's a piece of that creature stuck in Miss Ward's mind—and maybe in yours too, Audrey. I'm sorry."

Audrey swallowed visibly. "We'd better get her to finish her work, then." She touched her head, brought her hand down to examine as if expecting it stained by frost or blood. "What will it do?"

"I don't know." I helped Charlie up. "But I doubt it's just going to lie there."

"Me too." She took a deep breath. "I haven't just been snapping because of the pain. Something feels . . . it feels like I'm supposed to be angry."

Audrey was one of the strongest people I knew, determined in the pursuit of her goals, able to push through all manner of attempts to control her—but it was likely that her ancestor's experimental whim had left her vulnerable in peculiar corners. If my neglect had pushed Sally and Jesse into an alliance with Barlow—had led directly to last night's mad risks—then this contagion, too, was on my hands.

We stepped outside and found the weather grown fierce. While we huddled in Hall's illusion of safety, storm clouds had begun to disgorge sleet; it blew into our faces on a biting wind. We traveled as swiftly as Spector dared drive.

CHAPTER 25

The gate guards looked preoccupied as we approached. At first I thought them simply inconvenienced by the storm, but as we drew closer I saw by their emphatic gestures that they were arguing with someone. Thinking of people likely to carry on arguments in the middle of a blizzard, I hoped it was Trumbull. It was urgent that we find her as swiftly as possible—and then Sally. We pulled alongside.

Spector rolled down his window and asked, "Boys, what seems to be the trouble?"

One of the guards turned, started to answer. He was interrupted by the figure in a heavy coat who pulled down his scarf to reveal himself, disappointingly, as Dean Skinner.

"Miss Dawson," he said. "You're back, good." He frowned, looking perturbed by her spot in the back seat, well-surrounded. But he moved on to Spector. "You—can't you do anything about these imbeciles?"

"They're not my imbeciles," said Spector. "Didn't you invite them to campus?"

"I cooperated—same as I did with you and your . . ." He trailed off, barely sparing a grimace of distaste for me and Caleb. "But you haven't fabricated reasons to shut down the library, or started interrogating everyone in my program! I want them out!"

"Entirely understandable," said Spector. "I'll tell my supervisors you said so—and you ought to tell the college board."

"It doesn't bother *them*—they don't need to use the library every day, or worry about whether classes are being taught properly. And if *you* could stop interfering with my professors' duties, that would help too." His breath fogged the air in short, angry puffs, quickly dispelled.

Spector sighed, "I'll see what I can do." Window resealed, he said, "That's something, anyway. Friendliest he's been since we got here."

Dawson's tone was wry. "If there's one thing the dean hates more being on a leash, it's people who slip *his* leash."

Spector took the turn into Trumbull's drive slowly, and still we skidded a little. I helped Charlie up the walk. Snow burned cold against my skin, and I was shivering violently by the time we got inside. The others, save for Audrey, shed coats and scarves I'd never bothered to put on. She rubbed her temples and grimaced.

"I hope she's here," she said. "I really don't want to go back outside."

Trumbull wasn't downstairs. "Maybe she's in the math building," I said. "But if they're questioning people, she wouldn't want to be there at all. Let me check the study."

The cold washed over me again halfway up the stairs, and I leaned against the banister until the wave passed. I felt stiff, queasy. *Iä, Dagon, remind my body that the cold water is home.*

No response. As ever. I continued upward, seeking the closest thing to a god I'd likely ever get a useful answer from.

Perhaps it was better for my opinion of the gods that they stayed distant.

I knocked on the study door. I heard no answer, and considered the relative risks of interrupting Trumbull's work against the delay of seeking her elsewhere. For once, her preferences were not high among my concerns. I opened the door.

I stared for a moment, then threw myself to the floor—where Trumbull lay, eyes closed, head propped on a cushion.

"Charlie! Neko!" I checked for breath, found it slow and even. "Caleb!" Her pulse was regular. At my shout she rolled her head against the slate and murmured words I couldn't make out.

Footsteps pounded the stairs, and Caleb and Neko appeared. They crowded through the doorway, Audrey and Spector and Dawson close behind. Charlie's cane sounded behind them.

"What happened?" asked Audrey. She, also, knelt to check breath and pulse. "Did it get her, too? Is she fighting it?"

"No." I looked up, and took in fully what peripheral awareness had already hinted. The desk had been cleared, the walls stripped of diagrams. The strange machine was gone as well. "I think she went home."

"She—that cowardly bitch!" Audrey shoved the sleeping body, and I grabbed her arms.

"That's not her," I said.

Neko put her hands on Audrey's shoulders. "Breathe. We're all monsters here."

After a moment Audrey relaxed in my grip, though I could still feel the tension underneath. "Yes. Sorry." She leaned back, and I released her wrists to grip her hands instead. She gripped back, tightly as any ordinary woman of the air could manage.

Under our joined hands, whoever now occupied Trumbull's body moaned. I let go and motioned the others back. She continued to stir; Neko mouthed "water" at me and slipped out.

Her eyes flickered, and a familiar voice muttered, "Where did I put those notes?"

Then her eyes flew wide, and she screamed. She scrabbled away from me, and I put up my hands. Needing something to appease her long enough for more complete explanations, I said, "Professor, it's okay. You fainted, and I found you." Seeing that the others were now well within her field of vision, I added, a little feebly, "We found you."

She took us in and frowned—as I suppose anyone might at finding themselves surrounded by strangers of diverse and dubious aspect. She masked her alarm swiftly, recovering an aplomb worthy of her body's previous tenant. But when her glance fell on the window she drew a sharp breath, and her whole frame went tense. She stood slowly, walked to the glass with equally careful measure.

"Why is it snowing?" she asked, as if demanding of a child why broken seashells were strewn about the parlor.

I looked at the others, but their expressions told me this was my task. "Professor, do you remember where you've been for the past six months?"

"I've been here, obviously." But her hands gripped the sill hard enough to pale the joints.

"I need to tell you something that'll be difficult to believe." I caught my breath as another shiver hit me, thankfully a lesser one. "And I hope you'll believe me anyway, because we're in considerable difficulty and you—if you don't believe me, it'll make everything harder."

"Speak," she said. Neko returned, handed her a glass of water. She frowned again, but drank and seemed steadier for it.

I decided to start with the basics, or at least the immediately verifiable. "It's January 27th, 1949. For the past half a year, another being has inhabited your body—a researcher from another time, another species. You'll have spent about five years in her body, many aeons in the past. Some memories will eventually come back to you, but it's unlikely that you'll ever recover most of it. I'm sorry about that."

She put the glass down on the desk, stared at its clean surface a long moment. "You're clearly mad. But it's also obviously winter. Have I been in some sort of fugue state?" A look of horror passed over her face. "Who's been teaching my classes?"

"She has. I mean, it has. The Yith. I don't gather anyone here knew you enough to tell the difference. Although I'm afraid she may have skipped today's sessions."

She laughed: a looser laugh than Trumbull's—the other Trumbull's—supercilious amusement. But there was an edge to it. "Dean Skinner certainly wouldn't notice a replacement, unless he actually liked the creature. How does this marvelous story explain what you're all doing in my office?"

I looked down, and steeled myself for introductions and explanations. But Spector stepped forward and offered his hand. She took it automatically. "Ron Spector. I'm with the FBI—I brought Miss Marsh,

Mr. Marsh, Mr. Day, and Miss Koto to Miskatonic for a research project. Knowing the school's prejudices, I neglected to mention that half of my team were of the female persuasion, and I'm afraid Dean Skinner demanded that your, ah, predecessor play hostess. I can get them into a hotel if you object, though I'd prefer to do so after the storm. Miss Dawson is an employee of Skinner's who's been helping us, and Miss Winslow here is a student of Miss Marsh's who goes to the Hall school."

Trumbull eyed his badge. "That's quite the menagerie. And you believe this nonsense story?"

"I've seen some pretty strong evidence in the past few days, yes."

"Professor," I said. "I'm not an expert in these things myself, but I understand there are theories of multidimensional geometry—you *are* a specialist in multidimensional geometry, yes?"

"I most certainly am." She drew herself up and glared.

I hastened to add, "I meant, as opposed to being an expert in some other mathematical area. Tr—the woman—the entity, I mean, who was in your body this morning, she also studied multidimensional geometry."

"Ah. Yes, there are geometrical proofs that, combined with some extremely dubious branches of psychology and folklore—and a degree of intoxication—suggest the possibility of mental travel through time and space. The men in the department are prone to speculating about such things, but I've always considered them fantasies for people who don't find the math itself sufficiently enthralling."

I remembered the painted dreamscape in the living room and wondered how much of her dismissal was cold skepticism—and how much that such ideas, admired as flights of creative theory in the men of the faculty, risked accusations of mysticism in a woman.

Cold seeped through the window, and I wrapped my arms tightly. I had no fallback from my plan to beg Trumbull's help, but it felt important to make *this* Trumbull understand. If nothing else, a multidimensional geometry expert might still be useful. And there was a chance that, buried in her memories, we might find some clue what we ought to do next. "Perhaps—I could show you some of our magic. Not direct proof, but enough to show we're not making this up out of whole cloth."

"I know how stage magic works. I'm not impressed, and I think I want you out of my house."

Audrey had been pacing the study's limited free space like a caged lion. Now she bent to retrieve a sheet of paper from beside the desk. "Here," she said to Trumbull. "I think she left your schedule."

Trumbull plucked it from her grasp. "This is not my handwriting."

"I promise you," said Audrey. "I don't know the details of your classes."

"She left class notes?" asked Caleb. "That's remarkably thoughtful, by her standards."

"What's all this in the margins?" She held it out, pinched between thumb and forefinger as if it carried some unknown contagion.

I looked. "It's Enochian. *What kind of species withholds basic calculus until its young near adulthood? Compress section on matrices and insist on a more reasonable pace of learning.* That sort of thing. It looks like notes to herself—she must have left the sheet she made for her own reference."

"Isn't Enochian one of those obscure dead tongues they obsess over in the folklore classes?"

"It may be that," I said. "It's also the Yith's native language. And I use it for liturgical purposes, but that's neither here nor there."

She set the schedule firmly on the desk, and pinned it with the water glass. "If you try to pull a penny out of my ear, I *will* throw you all out into the storm."

I began drawing the diagram. Some time in the last few hours the slate had been washed clean, its previous palimpsest erased. Presumably the cultist who aided Trumbull's return had wanted to be thorough. "The Inner Sea would be best"—among other things, it was the only ritual I felt adequate to perform right now—"and might even help a little with our problem. At the very least, those of us in the confluence can support each other a little more. It's risky, though, strengthening our connection under the circumstances . . ."

"If I can help, I'll do it," said Caleb. Charlie nodded, as did Dawson after a moment of hesitation.

"Thank you," I said. I continued drawing, and focused on keeping my hand steady. "I can use Trumbull's—the other Trumbull's—alterations to protect the professor."

"What do I need protecting from?" Her tone was sharp, but she watched the diagram unfold with interest.

"As I said, we're in considerable danger. Last night we had to deal with . . . it's hard to explain. Another entity, less comprehensible and less interested in our well-being than the Yith who had your body. It left a piece of itself in Miss Winslow, and in—someone else I'm connected to. I'm afraid this would be difficult to explain all at once, even if you believed me about the basics. But you shouldn't be at risk from the ritual. Mr. Spector, Neko, if you want to wait downstairs, this shouldn't take more than half an hour or so."

"If you think the risk is reasonably small," said Spector, "I feel like I ought to observe. I've read plenty, but I'm beginning to realize how much I've missed."

I paused my drawing. "Mr. Spector, this is a sacred ritual. You may wait downstairs, or you may participate. You may not stand by the door and take notes."

He hesitated. "Does the ritual involve prayer?"

"To gods foreign to your own? No, it's not religious. It's just sacred."

He squared his shoulders. "All right, then."

Neko hovered in the doorway, and at last stepped in. "Just this once."

"Are you sure?" I asked. "You've never wanted to before."

"I'll admit, I'm kind of curious. And I'm already stuck with the trouble."

Caleb refilled the salt water. I drew my knife—Yith-Trumbull's apparently having been removed along with most other overt traces of her presence—and showed our newcomers where to sit and what to do.

I started the chant as we each bled into the water. The rhythm of the familiar syllables warmed me, and I tried to pass a little of that warmth down the link to Sally. It was hard not to clutch it close, even knowing her pain for the source of my own.

There was a taint in the river of my blood, stagnant in the midst of torrent. It glowed and pulsed, never quite there when I tried to examine it directly. Around it the water grew cloudy and slow.

As I looked more closely I found thin threads, almost invisible, stretching out and away. I examined one, cautiously. It hummed beneath the touch of my mind, and I caught another glimpse of Sally, shivering, trying to concentrate on her note-taking as sound faded in and out. Barlow speaking to me sharply, my twitch of guilt and fear as I tried to focus.

I could do little about what had already spilled into my blood, but the threads were slender, fragile and finite. I could easily break the spell that my grandfather had set in place. Not only for me—the whole confluence would be safer if we could focus on Audrey alone.

They said that it was safest to leave me here.

I let the threads be and joined with the rest of the confluence, already flowing together. Spector and Trumbull and Neko, if I had done my work right, were well isolated. Unless they knew how to reach for us, as the Yith had, they would be safe in their own waters.

Charlie and Caleb and Dawson suffered only hints of disturbance—here and there amid their streams I winced at a flash of cold. But Audrey's blood had grown strange. The cold thing had entered her more deeply than me, and burrowed into the soft mud and silt that ought to have been her natural protection. Where the glow pulsed out, something else clustered around it: tiny spots of absolute darkness that absorbed all attempts to perceive detail. They ate at the glow. Not fast enough, for it still swelled and bubbled from the burrows where it had fastened, but they ate. And as they ate, they grew. No more than half of what ran in her veins remained mistakable for ordinary human blood.

There was a certain hypnotic fascination to it. But I drew back, broadened my focus. I pushed strength into Audrey, and the simple reminder of our presence. Charlie and Caleb and Dawson did the same, and I hoped there was enough that I needn't feel guilty redirecting a little to Sally.

The connection persisted as I pulled back to the study. Neko looked relieved when she saw me wake. I ought to have checked first on Trumbull or Spector, but it was my sister's opinion that my eyes sought.

"Well," she said, leaning back on her hands. "I see what the fuss is about."

"Going to try it again?" I asked.

"Maybe someday. Like I said, it's not what I want to spend all my time on—but I'm glad I tried it. Are you guys okay?"

"That's a complicated question," I said. "Mr. Spector, are you well?"

"Apparently so." His brow was furrowed, but he didn't seem inclined to share and I let him have his privacy.

Finally I turned to Trumbull. "Well?"

If her mask had slipped, it was back now. But she said: "All right. Suppose we posit that you're not as mad as you sound."

I shivered. "That's better than nothing."

"Tell me again what's going on."

I summarized the situation as best I could—the outlines of our research, Spector's colleagues and their dangerous studies, the Yith, the barely-averted disaster that had caused her to flee. The cold that ate at Sally and Audrey.

"So she returned to her own time . . . and sent me back here to handle this intruder in her stead?"

"I don't think that she—it—expected you to handle it," I said. "I wish I could say otherwise. The Yith retreat when they think a situation is beyond what they can, or should, deal with. And they're usually better equipped than whoever takes their place."

Her lips quirked. "Very reassuring."

"Could your family help?" Charlie asked me.

I'd been thinking about that. "I don't know. But they're probably our best option right now." Snow pattered against the window, almost drowned out by the wind that rattled the glass. Snow would cover the sand, wind send the waves surging toward the dune and crashing over Union Reef. But the cold thing wouldn't wait for the storm's end. "We need to try and get Miss Ward first. She's doing worse than any of us."

"Who are your family?" asked Professor Trumbull. "Why do you think they can help?"

I yearned to go back to San Francisco, where I didn't keep needing to explain myself. "Are you from around here?"

"I grew up in Kingsport—though I went to Pembroke. I don't trust people who spend their whole lives in the county, especially professors who've never left except to hare off to Antarctica or some such for a few months."

"What do you know about Innsmouth?"

"Aside from it being a ghost town? Rumors that I would have dismissed until a few minutes ago. Are you a hybrid fish monster, then?"

I sighed. "I'm from an amphibious branch of the human race. I'm not a hybrid anything. We prefer 'Chyrlid Ajha' or 'People of the Water.' Or 'Deep Ones,' though that's a bit poetic for everyday use. We live a long time, after metamorphosis. Not as long as a Yith, but Archpriest Ngalthr or my grandfather are likely to have a lot more experience with this kind of thing than I do."

"Can they help me remember?" There was an urgency in her voice that I hadn't heard before.

"I don't know. But they'll certainly have worked with people who hosted Yith. They'll know what can be done, if anything can."

She leaned forward. "What do they look like?"

I blinked; my eyes felt like ice cubes. "My family?"

"The Yith."

"Oh." I had a picture in the children's text downstairs. I'd show it to her later. "No one knows what their original bodies looked like. But the one you would have been in . . . wrinkled, conical forms, about ten feet tall, and moving on a sort of a rippling base. Four limbs coming out of the top, with pincers on two of them, funnels for eating on the third, and the head on another. Three eyes on the head, and tentacles for picking things up. I can show you illustrations."

She closed her eyes. "I can almost picture it. But I don't know if what I'm picturing is real."

"Maybe the elders can tell you." I stood and went to the window. The blizzard showed no sign of abating, and even the draft made me ache. Warmth, still flowing from the others, held it back a little. I closed my eyes and felt along the less comfortable connection. There was direction to the fragile threads. "We need to go by the library. And then drive to Innsmouth. I don't think this can wait for better weather."

"I don't think so either," said Audrey. She sounded steady, but through the confluence I felt the chill within her, and the darkness around it.

"Do you drive?" I asked Trumbull. "I don't know how we're going to fit everyone otherwise."

"It's been a while." She frowned. "It was two days ago. Or feels like it. Except that it doesn't at all. But yes, I drive. I hope my . . . guest . . . kept the gas tank full." She looked around the room. "Miss Marsh, where is Emily?"

"I'm sorry," I said. "Who's Emily?"

"My maid. She should be here."

"Trumb—your guest—didn't keep any servants. She said something about letting a maid go who she worried might notice the change."

"Damn it! How—" She opened the door and peered out into the hallway. The missing woman failed to materialize. "Never mind. I'll find her again once the storm's passed."

"I'm sorry," said Caleb. He shrugged. "The Yith don't tend to maintain relationships. Among the people of the water, friends and family know to wait, but when people don't understand what's going on . . . it's good you didn't have a husband or children."

"No," she said. "I didn't."

Dawson elbowed Caleb, who muttered an abashed apology.

Trumbull shook her head. "Let's go find your missing friend."

I tried to hold Audrey back a moment before we went downstairs. "Your blood . . ."

She pulled away. "Let's talk about it later. Little enough to be done, anyway."

The other Trumbull could have told us whether the void-specked cells were normal—an ordinary immune function shared by all the people of the rock, kept in reserve against need and likely to retreat when done—or whether they were a product of whatever experiment had created her bloodline. Whether the darkness and anger could be cautiously encouraged, or whether they would consume her as easily as the outsider.

I found a spare coat, somewhat ragged, at the bottom of Trumbull's winter chest. Even driving from faculty row to the library, we went slowly through icy streets. Frozen sandbars covered the sidewalks; if Trumbull had a late afternoon class, it would have been canceled.

The library's front path was equally treacherous. Barely six inches had fallen, but the wind made it uneven: two-foot piles in some places, and others where our boots scraped bare stone. The gale blew droplets of cold against my stinging eyes and lined them with frozen tears.

We found a little shelter in the overhanging stone of the entryway. Spector knocked heavily, then tried the door. It was locked. Caleb fumbled in his pockets for the keys, but the door creaked open and one of Barlow's guards examined us with displeasure. Behind him, three more put out cigarettes and frowned at our interruption. Dim light filtered through the foyer's stained glass, marking them in strange colors.

"I'm sorry, sir," said the guard. "Mr. Barlow left explicit instructions that he wasn't to be disturbed."

"We've discovered something that might help with his research," said Spector.

The guard shook his head. "I'm not going to argue with him, and neither are you. Orders, sorry. It's a mess out there; you'd better get back inside until the storm passes." And he shut the door again.

Audrey glared. "That was useless. Idiots!" She kicked the threshold and turned her glower on the rest of us. "Well, come on. They still don't know how we got in the first time." She began trudging in the direction of the side entrance. I prayed they hadn't thought to guard that as well. My face was growing numb, and I felt as if my thoughts were doing the same.

Snow drifted high against the library's east side. We scraped it away with gloved hands and pulled the door open enough to slip in. No guards awaited us. The service passage was still cold, but shelter from the wind came as an intense relief.

"Why does anyone live in New England during the winter, if it feels like this to them all the time?" I demanded as I stomped snow from my shoes.

"I couldn't begin to tell you," said Charlie.

"You get used to it," said Audrey. She pulled off her gloves and rubbed her cheeks. "Worse today, though. It's easier when you can stay inside."

My connection with Sally was a compass, not a map. But I suspected they'd ensconced themselves in the restricted section. We followed our old route upward.

After a few minutes Trumbull said, unprompted, "I'd appreciate it if you called her something else. Whenever you say, 'Professor Trumbull did such and such,' it's very distracting. And unpleasant: I didn't do any of those things."

"I'm sorry," I said. "I'll try to remember. We can call her 'the Yith.' But she never gave us any name other than yours."

"It's—" She stopped abruptly in the middle of a narrow corridor, held her hands out claw-like. "I know it. I know it, but I can't pronounce it."

Audrey looked at her sympathetically. "Amnesia really isn't as useful as some entities seem to think."

"Have you ever heard of Atlantis?" asked Caleb.

"You've mentioned it before. Please tell me *some* mystical nonsense is actually nonsense?" said Spector plaintively.

"Some is," said Caleb, "and there was never a place *named* Atlantis. But there really was an island city-state built on anachronistic knowledge from a poorly executed Yithian memory wipe, and they really did destroy themselves with ill-considered use of that same knowledge."

Spector shook his head. "I don't think knowledge needs an esoteric origin to be dangerous."

The restricted section was well-lit and well-insulated: a bright if not warm spot at the library's heart. On the second level of the stacks, a door stood open. We found Barlow's people there, in one of the rooms set aside for studies that wanted no witness.

Barlow came swiftly to his feet as we entered, hand moving toward the gun under his jacket. "Ron, I can't believe you'd bring these people here now, of all times."

Spector gave him an exasperated look. "I'm here to help." The familiarity made me wonder what background they shared beyond their political disagreements. Surely the agency's few experts in supernatural matters must sometimes be required to work together more directly.

"You've made it clear you won't even admit to yourself that you're harboring saboteurs. And you," he added to Trumbull. "I'll have your head for playing with the guards' minds again. There's no other way they'd have let you by."

"We came in the back door," I told him. "And we came now, of all times, to help. As Mr. Spector said."

Barlow nodded at Peters. Before I could decide how to react, Peters rushed forward and grabbed me. He twisted my wrists tight behind my back and pressed his other arm against my neck, forcing my chin up so I could feel my pulse thudding against his skin.

I went still, every muscle tensed against the instinct to fight. I could break his hold, but not without hurting him. Not without the consequences that would bring. I sought Caleb's eyes and willed him to stay where he was. He, too, had frozen, but I could see joints flex, gaze dart in search of a moment's opportunity. I shook my head a fraction, felt Peters tighten his grip in response. I swallowed, hard: a soldier had grabbed me and our father had leapt to stop him—and died with another soldier's bullet in the back of his head.

Spector held up his hands. "Don't make this mistake again, George. You're searching at random; we can make a difference. My people aren't responsible for your problems, and you have two women hurt."

"Two?" Barlow surveyed his team. There were only the two women on it.

"I'm fine," said Sally, glaring at Audrey. She didn't look fine: her skin was wan, her muscles locked painfully against the shivers that threatened to overwhelm her. But if Barlow noticed, he didn't acknowledge.

Mary rose from her chair and approached Spector. She looked him up and down, secretarial camouflage abandoned. "What do you know about what happened?"

I swallowed against the pressure on my windpipe. "*I* know that it doesn't take sabotage for an experimental ritual to go very, very wrong."

Peters's grip loosened a fraction, and Barlow nodded. "Let her talk. I want to hear *everything* she has to say." He eyed Trumbull, and I knew that with more agents here, he'd have happily grabbed us all. I glanced at her as well: where her guest would have glared back and made some cutting remark, she'd masked her expression entirely, save that her pupils had gone wide.

I was tempted to forgo Trumbull's deception. This wasn't Atlantis, and I wanted to say something that would shake them out of their paranoid arrogance. Shouldn't they know how close they'd come to destruction? Shouldn't they know how we'd discovered their disastrous summoning, and that the disaster was their fault and no other's?

But Barlow didn't believe he was doing something safe. He simply believed it necessary. And if he knew about the Yith, he was precisely the sort to seek out their other representatives around the world, and drag dangerous knowledge from them by whatever means he could muster. And, if he were truly foolish, try to keep them from sharing it with others.

I closed my eyes, breathed as deeply as I could, and tried to think beyond my father's blood and Peters's grip on my wrists. I needed to focus on what we were doing now: Audrey and Sally's lives and sanity, and perhaps my own, depended on it. But I knew how to be honest, and how to be silent, and neither seemed wise. If Audrey weren't so distracted, what would she say?

"We picked up on what you were doing last night," I said. "We came to find out who was running an unshielded summoning, but when we got close enough it grabbed us as well. We found you in the basement of the admin building. Something else came through. You don't remember any of this?"

"No, of course not," said Barlow, but his eyes grew distant and worried.

"Is this your explanation for why letters look like gibberish to me this morning?" asked Mary.

"You use math and language in your rituals, don't you?" Peters tightened his grip, and I tried to keep my voice calm and reasonable. "They can rebound against you, if you don't know exactly what you're doing. There are reasons the traditional methods are so rigid. And even those carry risks."

"They aren't 'rituals,'" Peters interrupted. I felt his breath against the back of my head. "No more than a new kind of engine, or psychotherapy. Set up a machine or a pattern of actions, and get a certain result from the universe."

"Call it what you will," I said, "it went wrong. As any machine can. That wasn't our doing, I swear by all the gods. We helped shut it down. But the thing you summoned—'inventoried'—left a piece of itself in Miss Winslow. And we think in Miss Ward as well. You really don't remember?"

"No, we don't," said Barlow. He turned back to Spector. "I can't believe you would drag your . . . collection . . . here, to give us fairy-tale excuses. This is absurd even for you."

Mary held up her hand. "Mr. Barlow, they could be making this up entirely, but it's more plausible than it sounds. Some of the energies we work with aren't entirely compatible with ordinary human psychology. It's why so many less careful researchers end up in asylums."

"Are you telling me you believe this? Mary, I know you're shaken up by what happened, but I thought you had a better head on your shoulders."

I saw some response rise in her face, wiped away before she turned to face him. "I'm saying it's plausible, that's all. It's also plausible that their 'help' was real, but did more harm than our inventory would have if left to run its course."

"I wish that were true," I said.

Spector spoke up. "Whether or not you'll take our help, please listen to your assistant. Let Miss Marsh bring Miss Ward to work on the problem our way, and you can work on it in yours. What really matters is that one of us solves it."

Ignoring him for the moment, Barlow came over to me. He stopped too near, close enough that the bitter scent of nervous sweat wafted over me. His breathing came too harshly and deeply; he clearly fought as hard as I did to keep himself under control. But at last he gave a quick, tight nod. "We've no evidence that would justify an arrest to the Bureau—not yet. We don't have time to find it right now. But don't think we've forgotten about you."

Peters released me. I rubbed feeling back into my wrists and forced myself to step away slowly and calmly. Safely among my allies again, I looked back at Sally. It was her decision, I reminded myself, that was most urgent now—more important even than whether Barlow believed me a traitor. "Please come with us, Miss Ward. We can help." I touched my forearm, meeting her eyes. *You tell everyone you're fine, but you aren't suffering in silence. This doesn't harm only you.* I saw her notice, saw her consider.

But Mary looked at me with cold eyes. "Don't," she said to Sally. "They're confident enough, but their superstitions may still have caused the trouble last night—and can only do worse now." She went to Sally, bent over her chair, put a hand on her shoulder. "Are you hurt? Truly?"

Sally nodded shakily. The admission cost her; the shakes continued as she bent over, allowing them at last to show.

Mary's voice was soothing and determined. "I may not know everything we need to do right now, but I promise you I know how to do the research. I'll find out what happened to both of us, and I'll find a way to fix it. We promised to help you learn what you needed to know—and we will."

"I promise you'll be okay," said Jesse. Sally looked up at him, plastering on a smile.

"Good, that's settled." Barlow was clearly discomfited. "Ron, take your people and get out of here; you've made enough trouble."

"I wish you'd trust me," said Spector, only a hint of anger in his voice. "Have you forgotten Geilenkirchen, too? We needed to take those 'superstitious' ideas seriously then."

"Geilenkirchen was entirely theoretical work, and you know it. Hitler was working from the same sources we found, and he never learned anything of substance. If he had, we'd have seen a land invasion on U.S. soil—or worse. The difference between us is that you've finally started taking the theory seriously, but you haven't learned which parts are nonsense."

I met Sally's eyes one more time. "Miss Ward, please. If we don't do something about this, and soon, you could die."

She looked hesitant, but shook her head. Mary moved between us. "We'll take care of it here."

I wanted to drag Sally with us, pull her through the barbs of doubt that Mary had planted. But Barlow and Peters were armed and just barely willing to let me go. I could break the threads that connected us and leave her to her chosen fate. I should.

Only I had yet to see her make the choice.

"We'll be with my family," I said. "You know where to find us."

CHAPTER 26

Beyond the campus, Arkham kept the roads well cleared—but outside of town they were only sporadically plowed. I sat beside Trumbull, my brother and Dawson in the back seat, gripping the armrest and trying not to second guess a skill I lacked entirely. Headlights tunneled through the darkening snowfall, occasionally picking out the answering lamps of Spector's car ahead.

"I hope your family keep their houses warm for us mortals," said Trumbull.

"We used to," said Caleb. Dawson took his hand, and he pressed his face against the glass. I felt an echo of its slick coolness, a comfort filtered through my brother as it wouldn't be to me. The car slipped sideways, and my grip tightened, but Trumbull righted us with a grimace and a muttered imprecation.

The trip to Innsmouth, which had taken a scant hour the previous week, lasted past dusk—or what seemed dusk, with the sky well hidden by cloud. As we closed in, the road's poor repair forced us to slow further. No gulls heralded us, no scent besides salt spray and the pervasive smell, crisp and clean and utterly hostile, of the snow.

The construction crews had abandoned the town for the day, leaving the streets thick with snowdrifts. Spector and Trumbull forced the cars through.

Storm-swamped, Innsmouth looked more alien. I could no longer find familiar angles or imagine neighbors still hiding beyond collapsed porches. I could scarcely believe in rebuilding where the elements had so long and so successfully manifested their whims.

I shuddered as we pulled to a stop by the abandoned waterfront market. So long as we'd pressed through the weather, it had been easy to tell myself all would be resolved once we arrived: that I'd be able to hand over the burden. But we got out, and still I felt the confluence around me, at once both cloak and weight. Still I felt slender threads stretching between me and Sally—and suspected my grandfather would not hesitate to cut them himself and relegate her to the cold.

We scraped snow from a collapsed stall with gloved hands, and found a few boards beneath the top layer still dry. These we dragged over the dunes, and Spector and Caleb went back for additional tinder as Dawson and I stacked the foundation of a small bonfire. The tide was going out—not normally a propitious time for summoning, but surging waves kept the ocean close. As they retreated, they left a flat damp area up against the dunes. Here a fire might be tended and ritual diagrams maintained for a few hours.

Caleb struck a match and touched it around the edges of the interwoven boards. When they were crackling he held a cigarette to the flame, and lifted it to his lips. Then he shook his head and ground it in the sand. "It still hurts. Even after all this time. I'm not going to do that to you."

"Thank you," I said. "If it hurts, why do it?"

He shrugged. "I thought I was dying. Why avoid the pain? After that . . . punishing yourself gets to be a habit. And besides, it annoyed Trumbull—the Yith, I mean."

The summoning diagram hurt to draw. Not only physically, as the wet sand shocked me with unaccustomed cold. But the twining, pulsing equations of Mary's spell intruded into my thoughts. Again and again, I checked my work for infection by those strange forms. I feared that instead of calling my elders for aid, I would draw in some other thing that waited eagerly for the access so recently denied. Or worse, I would call both together.

"Check my work?" I begged Charlie. He put an arm around me and I swallowed tears. He looked over the spellwork, pronounced it good. I swallowed the irrational conviction that my oversight had bled into him through the confluence.

Our fire leapt into the newborn winter night, and snow surrendered its form to enter the circle of warmth. A gust threw the flame sideways. I stumbled back; the borderland was thin between burning and freezing.

Still, my bones warmed for the first time that day, and I pulled off my gloves. I couldn't imagine shedding my coat, but I could face the night with more equanimity. Perhaps we humans were all creatures of flame, having gathered together around it long before we separated into our kinds.

I took the bowl, brought from Trumbull's house, and left the fire's respite. Snow whirled against me, and the waves growled above the sound of the storm. I could just catch the glint of their whitecaps: ever-changing tendrils of a thing the storm barely touched. I knelt at the water's edge, dipped the bowl during a lull between waves. The water sang to my blood, but its cold stirred the unearthly thing that pulsed there. Frigid filaments stretched eagerly into my damp fingers. Defiant, I licked my knuckles before retreating and tasted not the plain table salt from Trumbull's kitchen, but the complex medley of minerals and shed life found only here.

I spilled a little water on the diagram, passed it around so that we might cleanse ourselves. This I had not done at our first summoning, but today I needed it. Then the knife, and blood in the sigils. There was just enough, this time, to show faintly on the wet sand. I threw a pinch of blood-touched sand on the fire, bringing it with us into the calling. I felt the warmth pierce a little deeper.

We chanted, weaving our voices around wind and wave and snow.

The summoning rose, tasted us and knew us, passed on into the depths. And then we fell silent, and it was time for the hardest part of the ritual. We waited.

Back at Miskatonic, Barlow paced and read aloud, glaring every time Mary interrupted with a question. Sally still took notes, now joined by Jesse, who caught what she missed when hearing faded. Peters read to himself, a scowl on his face. The cold seeped back in.

"It's your turn to tell a story," I said to Audrey.

She looked up, eyes dark in the firelight. "Now?"

"Trum—the Yith was right. It's an old tradition, and it helps. Besides, would you rather sit here in silence wondering how long they're going to take?" I could have asked any of my companions, but I hoped the request would distract her, perhaps even help her hold against the things that fought to consume her.

"All right, fine." She rearranged herself, brushing sand off her skirt. She took a minute, but at last settled with her chin propped on her fists. "Once upon a time . . . do you guys say that? Or is it too easy to find someone who remembers the time?"

"We say 'It is written in the Archives.'"

"That's the same thing the Yith said."

"Yes," I said, "but when they say 'It is written in the Archives,' they mean 'I read this a while back.' When we say 'It is written in the Archives,' we mean 'Once upon a time.'"

"Well. Once upon a time," she repeated. Then: "No, I can't. Not tonight. I'm sorry." She pulled herself to her feet and ran away from the fire, down the beach. I shared a quick, startled glance with the others before going after her.

The snow closed in quickly, though I could still feel a scrap of flame where I'd spread our mingled blood. Audrey hadn't gone far—I found her a little way along the sandbar where the dunes pressed forward to meet the storm surge. She stood shivering, clutching herself tightly, letting the edge of the surge crash over her leather boots. She gasped frigid air, held the breath behind gritted teeth, released it and waited long for the next as if suffering some mortification. I touched her forehead, still bare despite all her layers. She winced, but leaned into my touch and after a moment began breathing more evenly, if a bit too quickly.

"All the stories I know are lies," she said. "And I can feel it in me, growing stronger. I've been able to feel it all day, the dark thing, whispering and shouting and trying to change me and it's doing it, I can feel it. And I can feel the cold thing too, and it's winning, I can feel it winning—I don't even know how much of me will be left by the time it takes over."

My heart sped to pace her rising panic. I found some corner of calm I hadn't known I still possessed, and pushed it at her. "You can do this. I know you can. I've seen you keep Trumbull out, for the gods' sakes."

"Trumbull was different. She's . . . slippery. Meant to move from body to body without catching on anything. These things are inside me; the dark thing is a part of me. It's them, it's the Mad Ones trying to make me one of them."

"Trumbull said the madness wasn't heritable."

"Trumbull said they might have put in anything, during their *experiments*. It slept until something triggered it, but now it's making me like them. I feel so angry at everyone, and I keep pushing it away, and it keeps coming back stronger and stronger. When you asked for a story I wanted to hit you—I wanted to, I don't even know, *break* you. Like in my dream. I don't think I could, and I'm glad, but suppose that changes too? I learn so quickly." She pulled back from my hand. "You should cut me out of the confluence."

"Audrey, no!"

"You'd all be okay without me bleeding into you—you'd be able to help Sally get better. She may be an idiot, but if you can get the cold thing out of her, she'll still be a good person."

"You're family."

"You've barely known me for a week."

"Yes," I said. "But I *know* you. We won't leave you to face this on your own."

She crossed her arms. "You're being an idiot. You're so much more important than me; you're literally the last woman of your people who can still have babies. Your elders will tell you the same thing. They'll kill me out of hand if they think I'm a threat to you."

I stared at her. "You think that? Is that why you ran off?"

She lurched as if on the verge of some violence, but pulled herself back. "No. It's why I came."

"Audrey . . ." I didn't dare touch her; she seemed as if she might bolt at any moment. "They won't. They wouldn't. They know what we have."

"I didn't expect comforting lies from you of all people."

I squatted, making myself small. I dipped cupped hands into an in-rushing wave, dashed cold salt water against my eyes. It hurt, but it cleared my head. "Audrey, please believe me. The universe is a danger-ous place, with little comfort to be found. I'll do all I can to prevent it, but you *could* die of the cold, or of the dark, or of the void-touched storm. My family aren't always nice, and they do what they must to protect their own. But they know that when the universe doesn't care, someone has to. If we don't care, we lose ourselves, even without Mad Ones changing our blood."

She laughed bitterly. "If everyone thought like that, Christians would still be getting gobbled up by lions."

I'd read of such things in a history class, but didn't want to argue the difference between self-sacrifice and holding on to something worth defending. It didn't seem like it would help. I licked my lips. "There are animals that feed solely on Christians? Why didn't anyone tell us?"

That got the desired laugh, less bitter. "You need to learn more about the last two millennia." She squatted beside me, and with an abrupt sweep of her arm splashed water on her own face. "Ow. That does kind of help."

"Let's go back to the fire. No sense arguing over what the elders will do when they'll be here soon enough—and no sense trying to talk me into something I'm never going to do."

"Fine. Throwing a fit just made me colder, anyway."

By the flames, Caleb was explaining to Trumbull more of what she'd missed. Dawson sat near him but, eyeing Spector, did not quite touch. Charlie nodded at us with a worried expression, but no one was forward enough to ask for a report.

The first time we'd called the elders, the day had been calm and bright, and roiling waves heralded their arrival. This time—with the waves already high and the wind howling—they appeared silently in the flickering half-lit shadows around us.

Trumbull gasped and pushed herself back from the fire, and a dozen scaled heads swiveled to stare at her.

"You've found trouble quickly, Aphra Yukhl," said my grandfather. I leapt to my feet and threw myself against him. Salt-damp arms enfolded me.

At last I pulled myself away. "I'm glad you came. I don't know what to do. We've gone from trying to retrieve our books to trying to keep someone else from misusing them dreadfully, and . . . and we've been hurt."

Grandfather held my chin and looked at me carefully, examined my companions over my shoulder, then lifted his head to sniff the storm. "The Yith fled home, I gather."

"Yes." Trumbull rose to join us and extended her hand. I caught only a slight trembling. "Hello. I'm Dr. Catherine Trumbull. A pleasure to meet you."

I moved aside and Grandfather took her hand in his larger one. "Obed Marsh. A great honor."

"We have rituals, don't we?" I asked. "To help people returning from the Archives? Some sort of guidance?"

"We do," said Archpriest Ngalthr. He bowed and introduced himself to Trumbull. "There is also a book, *On the Rise and Fall of Stones,* which you might find useful. But first it seems we have a more urgent situation. Tell us, child."

He gestured to the campfire, and the rest of us made room for the archpriest, Acolyte Chulzh'th, and my grandfather. The remaining elders stood guard against whatever might come out of the storm.

Spector twisted half around to see Jhathl standing post behind him; she nodded and bared a sharp-toothed smile. Spector nodded back and after a moment's hesitation turned firmly to face us. Snow hissed to steam against the leaping flames.

I introduced Spector and Dawson as trustworthy representatives of the government, and then once more explained how we'd come to this point. With Trumbull, I'd had to cover everything, but could give only the barest outlines. For the elders, there were parts I could easily gloss over, others where I shared all the detail I could recall, hoping they might pick up on some clue of which I'd been unaware. Archpriest Ngalthr quickly proved himself attuned to my story's subtleties, though not in the way I'd desired.

"Hold," he said. "Do I understand that you've decided to rebuild the spawning grounds?"

I'd intended to bring that up in private. "Yes."

Grandfather—now sitting between myself and Caleb—put his hands flat against the wet sand and closed his eyes. "Thank the gods. I am glad you thought better on it."

I bristled internally, but kept it to myself. He had a right to be relieved, to have opinions on the spread of his own blood. "We had many reasons to do so," I said. "But we must deal with this other trouble before it's possible."

The description of Mary's summoning ritual, if nothing else, diverted the conversation.

"Are they mad?" demanded Chulzh'th.

"So Professor Trumbull—so the Yith suggested," I said. "We were fortunate to have her there, and more so that she stayed long enough to end it rather than fleeing immediately. But she took their memories, and did something to the brain of their best magical theorist that made her illiterate. Their confusion is making matters worse, but telling them about the Yith wouldn't improve matters at all."

"She did—illiteracy?" Chulzh'th sounded exasperated. "I never heard the Yith were idiots."

"I've seen this before," said Ngalthr. "She'll have lost not only letters, but even the ability to draw a lion or a skull as a sign to warn of danger. To the Yith, those who cannot create and understand permanent symbols are scarcely beyond brute animals. The most terrible possible fate, and an absolute barrier to further work."

"Humans are less easily discouraged," said Grandfather. "Someone will read to her, write for her. She'll only become more determined to break through the mysteries that have scarred her."

"Perhaps," said Chulzh'th. "They claimed her as their secretary. They may not want to admit the importance of her lost skills. It takes a man of imagination and confidence to acknowledge such genius in a servant."

"Mr. Barlow has more imagination than you might expect," said Spector.

Grandfather leaned forward, long fingers steepled. His talons clicked gently. "His team's experiments are not blasphemous, merely foolish. But people are likely to die of their foolishness, and the question becomes how many they'll destroy alongside themselves. Or how many can be saved, if we stop them quickly."

"We'll not start another war with the surface over this," said Archpriest Ngalthr. "Opening the outer gates is dangerous, but it isn't the only way to destroy at such a scale."

"They endanger the spawning grounds," said Grandfather.

"So would a war."

"It certainly would," said Spector. "Much as they annoy me, you may *not* try to kill my colleagues. I have been doing my very best to argue for a *more* cooperative relationship with the Aeonist communities, Deep Ones included."

"We're supposed to be cooperating to stop dangerous cults," I said. "Whatever they do or don't worship, right now Barlow's group fits that description. Why haven't you sent me to infiltrate *them*?" I said it sarcastically, even as it occurred to me that he'd done precisely that. "Never mind. I won't make you say it. Grandfather, we have a more immediate problem. The outsider that the Yith banished left something behind.

There's a piece of it in Audrey, and another in Sally—and it's reaching into me. I don't know how to get rid of it."

Ngalthr scowled. "That is the risk of a panicked banishment. Let me see. Aphra Yukhl, I can examine them most safely through you."

Audrey sat very still as I held out my arm, let Ngalthr cut another stinging sigil. My awareness was shallow this time, but grew sharper as I sensed the expanding core of ice within Sally, the cold and dark battling within Audrey. And realized that I ought to have warned him . . .

Ngalthr sniffed deeply and then leapt up, hissing at Audrey. She leaned back, baring her throat. "Well, go on then."

Neko pushed herself between them. "Ngalthr-sama, don't. She's no more a monster than the rest of us."

"When did you learn?" Ngalthr asked me.

"The Yith figured it out a few days ago—after our last visit. She said the madness wasn't heritable." Ngalthr visibly relaxed.

Audrey drooped. "It is now," she said. Neko put a hand on her shoulder.

"Do you recognize the thing in her blood?" I asked.

"I've only dealt with the Mad Ones once," said Ngalthr. He shuddered, a ripple of light against crest and scales. "Not enough to recognize the scent on your last visit, but it's grown stronger. I've never looked directly at their blood." He flexed his claws. "Not with my inner sight." He put his skin once more against mine, and I felt his minute examination as he probed through our shared connection. Chulzh'th crept close and placed her smaller hand beside his. Together they covered my entire forearm. Their scent, salt and fish and cool musk, mingled with burnt wood and the crackling immediacy of the stormy air.

At last they sat back. "I've never seen anything like the way your blood is fighting," said Ngalthr to Audrey. "But the outsider, that is a known danger. And, unfortunately, a tenacious one."

"Is it a risk to the rest of the confluence?" asked Audrey. Her voice shook.

"Perhaps. But except for what's come into Aphra from Sally, the outsider hasn't truly spilled over yet. Should it defeat you, it might attempt
to use your body for its purposes, for whatever time it could maintain your living form. It could not do so for long: they are blind, probing things, trying to manipulate laws and senses that they cannot
comprehend."

"Can you do anything about it?" she asked.

"I know what to do for a man of the water," said Ngalthr. "Unfortunately it is a dangerous process, and depends on the sufferer having
both finely developed magical skill, and great endurance of the body.
Two scarcely-trained children of the air—or of the air and rock—are
unlikely to survive."

"I don't care," said Audrey. "I'd rather die than have either of those
things take me over. I don't want to hurt anyone."

Ngalthr crouched before her. He touched a claw to her forehead.
"I am not in the habit of torturing young girls to death."

She took the claw between her fingers and moved it down to her
neck. "No need. Aphra has a knife, if you're squeamish."

"No!" I said. I checked my waist to confirm the blade still securely
sheathed there. "Stop doing that—if the archpriest doesn't have an answer, we'll come up with something, but we're not giving up on you."

Ngalthr retrieved his claw. "I know this is hard, child," he told her.
"You have a few hours yet, before you must choose between death and
surrender."

Grandfather turned to me. "You carry a less personal link, however."
He took my arm, and I pulled it back. "Aphra Yukhl, we need no
longer fear that she'll betray us."

"Without me, she'll fall to the cold."

"Then let her! You risk more than just yourself."

"We have a few hours yet to choose between death and surrender."
I stood. "Give me the time to think this through. I'm going for a walk,
and no one is killing anyone before I get back."

Away from the heat and light, I looked back to check on them.

I heard murmurs, but the fragile peace appeared to hold for the moment. That was good. Though the cold inside reached eagerly to meet the lesser chill without, I needed to be away from the fire's complexities, alone with the ocean and the storm and my own confusion and fear.

I'd seen for myself, over and over, that there are pains and ends that cannot be avoided. There should be no shock here. And yet I'd known too, when I said that I'd mourned too much to risk children, that I'd never grown inured to the pain.

As much decision as there was to make, it wasn't even mine. It was Audrey's and Sally's to deny or accept, to surrender or fight to a more dreadful and protracted defeat. But Audrey still looked to me. And I had no answer to give her.

I knelt and dug my fingers into wet sand, felt the granularity of shells and stones ground fine by the relentless waves. I traced lines that added up to no spell, and sifted foolish ideas. Draw the cold thing into me (somehow, miraculously) and endure the treatment that Audrey and Sally could not. Find some other Yith (tonight, on whatever continent they made their current abode) and demand access to magic that no human had ever been permitted. Pray, and receive an answer.

Each idea was more impossible, more hopeless. And yet, I wasn't ready to give up. As Grandfather had reminded me, humans were not sensible that way.

I thought of sand and storm and ocean, wind and wave and fire. Ways of reaching out, fighting, holding to what we wanted.

The suggestion taking shape in my mind didn't solve our problems. It didn't save Audrey or Sally, didn't retrieve our books or lever Barlow's people from the library or stop their deadly experiments. And yet, trembling with cold where I could once have stood naked in the gale, it was all I could think of.

CHAPTER 27

"Could you ease the storm?" I asked Ngalthr. "Just here, around us? Or is it too strong?"

"I can soften the tempest," he said. His gills flared briefly against a gust of snow, closing tight when they found only open air. "You are too sensitive to the cold tonight. This isn't safe for you."

"The outsider's making me cold," I agreed. "That will pass soon enough one way or another. But that's not the reason. I celebrated Winter Tide with Charlie this year, on the West Coast." The archpriest nodded approval, and I went on. "But it isn't the same. I don't know that it will *help,* but looking at ourselves under the stars, seeing where we are . . . either it might make it easier to think of something or . . . or it could be a cleansing, if . . ." I looked at Audrey, who nodded as well. "If there's no way to save Audrey. If we can't do anything else, we can bear witness. Do something other than be scared."

"I'd like that," said Audrey, thin-voiced.

Ngalthr dipped his head. "The timing of the ritual isn't the most important part; it's good that you understand." He wiped the sand clean of the summoning, and began sketching the more complex sigils for the Tide ritual.

Chulzh'th came up behind me as I watched. "You'll make a good acolyte, when you come into the water."

"You do me honor." The compliment gave me little comfort. But it made me wonder abruptly how I might remember this night's crisis in a hundred years. *Would* I be an acolyte, learning to face such things with equanimity? I might be more like my grandfather, preaching and ranting to foreigners on land, and given wary respect in the water for deeds done outside convenient titles. I knew little of deep city politics, but enough to be aware that Grandfather never sat easily within any bounds given him.

"What are we doing?" asked Spector.

I started guiltily. "An actual religious ritual. Is that going to be a problem for you?"

"As long as I don't have to pray . . . is there anything I can do to help?"

I smiled, in spite of the cold. "Just watch. And think, and talk. The Tide is more a way of looking at the world than any specific action."

He nodded. "At the Jewish New Year, there are a few days between when the old year ends and the new begins, when we're supposed to meditate and make amends. Like that?" I nodded.

Ngalthr stepped back from his diagram and gestured for silence. When he got it, he tilted back his head and lifted his arms to the sky, silhouetted against the fire. He chanted, a thundering bass that merged with storm and ocean, vibrating in my chest and loosening the ice there. It wrapped around me, a voice out of memory to make me shiver with awe and huddle close in gratitude. I closed my eyes, their corners wet and not with snow.

The chant pulled me from myself, let me feel the wind and snow and clouds as another, stranger body. And I could feel, too, Ngalthr among the elements—not trying to control them as I had in my first attempt the previous month, nor surrendering to their patterns as I'd done more successfully. I could see now that what worked on a few clouds would have torn me apart on a night like this. He embraced the storm, coaxed it, negotiated as one might with a horse or some powerful but potentially cooperative predator. Or as if one could make a confluence with the uncaring Earth itself rather than mortal individuals.

Gradually, the wind died down. Snow fell, but slower and more gently. A single slender crack opened amid the clouds, letting through a hint of the starlight beyond.

Ngalthr sat, inhaling deeply. The other elders, too, settled around the outskirts of the fire, except for two who remained standing watch against the empty dunes. My awareness fell back to my own fragile body, half-burnt and half-frozen by a night grown marginally less inimical. My breathing eased, and some of the tension ebbed from my shoulders.

"Now what do we do?" asked Audrey.

"Look to the stars," said Ngalthr. "Pray. Confess. Listen to the cosmos, and to each other."

I did as he bade, leaning back in the sand to watch the sliver of infinity that we had opened. Cool light spilled through, magnified to visibility as it reflected through the falling snow. Above, hidden, the moon lay crested by sunlight and shadowed by the Earth. Most of the sun's other worlds lay empty this aeon, but some had once borne life native or invasive, and others would bear it again. Distant suns, too, attended worlds that bore or would bear life, and stranger minds waited at the void's edge. Darkness and cold would take them all, and the stories of most would not survive their own suns.

No meditation on cosmic humility could keep me from caring whether Audrey died tonight. I turned my gaze away from the stars, and moved to sit beside her.

"I'm sorry I got you into this," I said.

She tilted her head to the sky. "Don't. I got myself into it. I chose, and it's not like you didn't warn me what it would cost."

"I said magic would make you aware of mortality. It's not supposed to speed things up."

"You also said the universe wasn't under our control." She laughed dryly. "My family will be so mad. They might sue the school, I guess. Winslows put on such horrible funerals—everyone goes to church, and then they stand around catching up on who got what job and who got married. How do your people handle it?"

I wanted to tell her that it wouldn't happen, that she'd live, but we'd already had that argument tonight. At least for the moment she didn't seem inclined to hurry it along. "We used to go to the temple and say the Litany, and offer prayers for the dead to each god. There's a cemetery up at the far end of the gorge, and we'd go there for the burial, and tell stories about the person, and a scribe would write them down in the temple book. Or on something else to be transcribed later, if it was raining. We're supposed to pass the funeral records on to the Yith, if we can find one and get them to pay attention for long enough. But contact is unpredictable—it never happened when I was a kid, so the only memories preserved from that time period will be anything she found at Miskatonic."

"Well," said Audrey. "I can't complain that I won't be remembered in the Archives. Rudely, I hope."

I laughed. "The record of how much we annoyed her will outlast the Earth." It was weirdly reassuring. "And the saltcakes."

She sighed. "This is helping. I'm still cold, but I'm not as angry. I feel like I should . . . do something. Should I talk to Archpriest Ngalthr? You're supposed to talk to priests when you might be dying. I never liked talking to the Christian ones, though. Is he going to try to baptize me or anything?"

"There are rituals that involve immersing yourself in sea water, but this isn't one of them. Yes, you should talk with Ngalthr."

She went to kneel before him. I wanted to hover, to hear what wisdom he might have to impart, but I recognized an odd sort of territoriality. I had, after a fashion, been priest to the confluence. Whether or not I had any predilection for such a role, I had no training, a contrast more apparent in the presence of real clergy. Seeking a distraction from my mind's petty grumbling, I went to check on the others.

Spector and Charlie spoke quietly with Grandfather and Trumbull, though Spector looked up long enough to say, "Yom Kippur involves less weather magic."

"I'm certain you have your own miracles," said Grandfather, and they returned to their discussion.

Caleb was talking with Neko and Dawson, who waved me over to join them.

"How's she doing?" asked Neko.

"Better," I said. "In mind, if nothing else."

"That's something. This would be nice—ridiculously cold, but nice—if I wasn't so worried about her. I wish she'd stayed out of it."

"She doesn't," I said.

"I've been trying to think of a solution," said Caleb. "It feels like we ought to be able to find a way around this, if we could only come at it from the right direction."

Dawson touched his arm. "You can't, always."

We'd worn that circle bare already. "I never asked you," I said to her, "why you wanted to study magic. It's a traditional question."

"Caleb said. It seems a bit nosy."

"I know. That's why I didn't ask you earlier."

She looked down. Caleb reached for her, but dropped his hand when she didn't welcome the proffered touch. She said: "I want something that can't be taken away, if someone gets displeased with me."

I thought of several things to say, but instead simply bowed my head.

"It's a good reason," said Caleb. He hesitated. "Not that it's up to me to say so. I want to give you things, but I don't want you to have to worry about me taking them back."

Her eyes crinkled, corners folding out into lines etched by past amusement and bitterness. "You're a sweet boy."

The cold, which had ebbed with the ritual and the fire's heat, stabbed through me then. A line of ice from brain to heart, stiffening spine and lungs. I saw a book grasped between aching hands, a flash of silent, worried faces—and then all sensation from Sally cut off save for that line of cold, and threads of desperation reaching in search of heat and air and light.

I must have gasped, for Grandfather jumped up, grabbed me, and swung me so close to the fire that it nearly singed my skirt. I faltered against him but managed to regain my feet, and found that he'd startled me out of my paralysis. He pushed up my sleeve, touched the fading scar of the sigil, and scowled.

"Enough of this," he said. I realized what he was doing and for a moment I gave in to my fear—of the cold, of the desert heat that seemed its kin, of dying alone in their grip—and I simply leaned into my grandfather's touch. He dragged his claw across my forearm, and the threads started to snap.

"No!" I forced back the fear and shoved him away, almost stumbling into the fire. But I managed to push him off balance; he fell and rolled as Caleb scrambled out of the way. Both stared at me in shock.

I wanted to prostrate myself, beg forgiveness, but that would imply surrendering to his judgment. It was unthinkable, by my childhood standards, to do otherwise for an elder. The guards, who'd turned at my shout, lowered their spears cautiously.

"I'm sorry," I said. "She'll die without me holding her up. She'll die *now*." I could feel her, something still human clinging to the remaining threads, drinking the heat that trickled through. "I can give them a few more hours."

Ngalthr rose swiftly and grasped my arm, though I tried to pull away. He was faster than Grandfather, and I had no chance to surprise him. Once he had me I wasn't foolish enough to struggle. "Child, we need you," he said. "Have you never learned to tell when a drowning man is beyond saving?"

"You said you could save a man of the water," I said. "I can take the risk, and the pain, to give her a chance."

"No!" Grandfather was back on his feet, and with Ngalthr on my left arm I couldn't keep him from grasping my right. I pulled my left a little closer to my body, protecting the sigil as best I could. He went on. "I won't see you hurt that way. You're being foolish, and there's nothing to be gained by it. Her family has more children than all our people together—your life is not your own to gamble frivolously."

"I'm not being frivolous," I said. I tried to articulate my stubbornness, things I hadn't known until they were tested. I didn't even like the girl. "I am a Marsh. I will do things worthy of that name, not huddle in safety for the sake of bearing offspring. And if someone falls under my power—however little that power might be—I'll use it to protect them. Some things matter more than whether Caleb and I become the last children of Innsmouth. For the sake of all the generations under the water, not just you who know and care for me, I'll preserve the family's name over our numbers."

Obed Marsh stared at me a long moment, and I tried not to flinch under his unblinking glare. Then he dropped my arm and stepped back. "I think you're making the wrong choice. But I'll grant you three hours. If your enemies can work miracles in that time, they'd best show you the gratitude you'll be due."

I felt cautiously along the link and decided that in three hours—if Sally were still there to hold on to—I could have the argument again. "Done." Archpriest Ngalthr nodded approval and released me. I rubbed my arm. Now that the rush of emotion was past I could feel the ice once more, strong and spreading.

The others swarmed me: Neko and Audrey and Charlie all anxious to see whether I was well. Caleb and Dawson hung back—Caleb glancing nervously at Grandfather. I closed my eyes and tried to recenter myself.

"Aphra," said Audrey, "let's try something."

I opened my eyes. "What should we try?"

"You're really good at running into danger," she said. She stretched, looked to the line of starlight still jagged across the clouds. The wind, though still gentled by the elders' hold, had picked up again. "But you're not much for the really crazy gambles that can make the danger interesting."

I thought that danger was too often dull, and crazy gambles rarely considered just how much there was to lose. But that wasn't the world Audrey had managed to make for herself, during her nineteen years alive and free. Daring, I said, "I'm not mad enough, you mean."

She nodded. "The archpriest said running away doesn't suit my nature. He's right. If I'm going to die, I'd rather see what my ancestor gave me. The stuff in my blood—it's the only thing we've seen that can fight the cold. Maybe there's something we can do to make it stronger, or share it, or control it better." Her audacity flagged a moment. "Just promise that if it does take me over, you won't stop them from doing what they have to. Or argue with them, or hold it against them."

I took her hand and bowed over it, touching her knuckles to my forehead as if she were the archpriest. "I promise."

We made a place for ourselves close to the fire, glaring away those who tried to hover. In the midst of the Tide, there was no need to nest ritual within ritual: concentration was all we needed to bring the confluence into focus.

Audrey's blood had become a coruscating miasma of cold light and consuming darkness. Even the little that my mind still interpreted as water, it saw roiled with mud.

A shadow fell over me, and Chulzh'th settled alongside us. "That was brave. And right."

"Thank you," I said. Then: "We're working."

"I know. I thought you might want help from someone who's studied this for longer than a year."

"Aphra's been studying for a year and a half," said Caleb. We made room.

It didn't work. Audrey's defenses responded to none of the spells Chulzh'th knew for controlling the body: they were not wounds to be healed or illnesses to be fought back, nor the common guardians of human blood. They acted as part of her when treated as invaders, and as some strange other thing when treated as her own. We couldn't draw them out to defend Sally, and we couldn't limit their reach within the body they claimed.

The cold spread, likewise unresponsive. My hands felt made of ice. I tried not to let it show.

Two hours and fifty-two minutes later by Audrey's watch, a shouted "Hallo!" echoed over the dunes. The guards came to attention, raising spears and tridents.

"It's Mary!" I cried. Irrational relief blotted out pain, and I ran toward her voice, calling to assure her that we were here.

At the dune's peak I slowed to see what awaited us. Mary stood beside a dark car, directing someone who leaned over the back seat. As he straightened, I could see that it was Jesse, bearing Sally's limp weight in his arms. The rest of their team was nowhere in sight.

Audrey appeared beside me, clapped a hand over her mouth, and ran down toward them. Two of the guards and Chulzh'th also crested the dune.

"No threat," I told them, hoping it was true. I hurried down with the elders at my heels.

"This is your doing," said Jesse as I arrived. Then he caught sight of the elders and jerked back, almost dropping Sally.

I darted forward and caught her side, her weight briefly on my wrists before he regained his balance. At the touch of my skin against hers I felt a warming, and she moaned softly. Startled, I touched her again, felt her senses flare against the cold. I scooped her from his arms, and she lolled against me.

"I know," I told him.

"No, the blame is mine," said Mary. I turned to look at her and she met my gaze. "Before she went unconscious, she told me to take her here. I thought I could fix this. I was wrong. I'm sorry. You said that your people would know what to do."

I bowed my head. "I was wrong too. They know a treatment, but they can't use it on men of the air."

She closed her eyes, but only for a moment. "I'll speak with them—perhaps together we can come up with something." A humorless smile played on her face. "And if you really are working with Russia—or with demons—helping us would allay suspicion."

I let it pass; there was too much else going on and I couldn't find the energy to argue. "You came. The others . . . ?"

"Will forgive me in the morning, I hope." She nodded at Jesse. "Mr. Sadler, thank you for guiding us here. If you want to go back to Miskatonic or wait in the car, you're more than welcome."

Recalling his smug explanation of why their ritual had caught me, I couldn't help glaring in spite of my remorse. I wasn't being entirely fair, and realized it even as I spoke. "Or you could come back to the beach with us, and tell my grandfather how after I rebuffed your advances, you decided that uncontrolled summoning spells would make a fine revenge."

"That had nothing to do with it—I was trying to protect Audrey."

"You didn't," said Audrey. "Go home and go to sleep."

He looked at the elders again.

"I'll come," he said. "I'll help how I can. But please don't tell your grandfather. I said I was sorry."

"I know," I said.

I started up the dune, and discovered immediately that pushing someone away in anger was one thing, but carrying a girl nearly my own weight up a shifting slope was beyond my strength. Chulzh'th took Sally, lifting her easily as she climbed. Mary and Audrey followed, and Jesse scrambled after us.

I led them back to the fire. "Archpriest Ngalthr," I said, formally. "Allow me to introduce Mary . . . I'm afraid we've never met properly; I don't know your family name."

"Of course you don't." She held out her hand and the archpriest took it, claws closing around her like a father holding the hand of a small child. "Mary Harris, FBI. I understand you have a method of curing Miss Ward that's impractical in its current form."

"She would die. Both because she is a woman of the air, and because she is untrained." Chulzh'th came close, and Ngalthr pressed the back of his hand to Sally's brow. She whimpered quietly. "And because she is already gravely weakened. Thrice dead, and in pain more terrible than she suffers now. This is your doing."

"I know. I'm trying to fix it. Please tell me about the treatment."

Grandfather stalked over to join us, and I moved automatically to stand between him and Sally. "So you can attempt it yourself?" he growled. "The results would be far worse in untrained hands."

She looked at him coolly, but a hint of anger leaked into her voice. "So that I can try and determine whether there's some less harmful principle that can be abstracted out. As I'm currently unable to so much as write out an equation, I will be dependent on you to implement any treatment I can suggest. I hope you'll judge it on some basis other than whether it's been tried before. Please tell me what you would have done, if you thought she could survive it."

"We don't discuss these things with outsiders," said Grandfather.

"Please," said Mary. "I'm trying to save a child's life."

"Two," said Audrey.

Mary glanced at her and flushed. "Two lives. If there's something I must do to make myself clean, or to avoid profaning sacred secrets by hearing them—"

"Your profanity is beyond question," said Grandfather, "but irrelevant. If there were ever any core of truth to the blood libels that destroyed our children, they came from misrepresentations of such desperate methods."

"If there's a chance she could come up with something—" I said.

"As she did with the summoning? First you risk yourself to preserve the illusion that you can save someone already lost; now you would risk all of us."

"The summoning may have been foolish, but she's created new arts that do work." I neglected to mention the specifics. "I've seen them."

"No," said Grandfather.

"Yringl'phtagn," said Ngalthr warningly. "It is a small chance, but would you prefer rumors of killing children, or children dead in truth because of your fear?" He looked to the clouds, then to Mary. "You have entered a place of sacred ritual. Honesty and plain speech are sacraments of the Tide. I will answer your question, and you will listen."

For the first time, Mary looked nervous. "All right."

"Outsiders, such as the thing you summoned, cling to this world by taking the place of your own self. Their presence drains vital power from mind and body, destroying both. If they know what life is, or that they have displaced it, we have never been able to tell.

"Detached from their host, they are unable to survive the laws of this universe. We have blades, enchanted to cut both body and mind. These we must use at the points where the outsider clings. The longer they have infected their host, the more such points there are." Mary watched Ngalthr intently as he spoke. Grandfather looked away, though his glance stole sometimes in my direction. The archpriest laced sharp-clawed fingers together and went on:

"To survive such a cleansing requires physical endurance and the ability to heal quickly. But it also requires mental training and focused will. The mind, when attacked, instinctively flees from the flesh—and in doing so carries a part of the outsider to safety. Only someone trained in the arts of mental travel can deliberately hold fast to their body, experiencing all that it suffers—and ensuring that the outsider remains present and vulnerable to be cut away. Fail, and the body dies while the mind drifts anchorless, still bound to the outsider, until both dissipate into the void."

I shivered, imagining it: staying with the pain, allowing it, knowing that I could stop it and must not. I might well have to, if I put off my separation from Sally much longer. Or if I had miscalculated our existing connection.

I could understand why my grandfather was less willing than I to risk such a sacrifice.

Mary waited a moment, still watching intently. "Is there more?" she asked.

"That is all of the method," said Ngalthr. "There is much ritual built around the essentials. It gives the person something to hold on to other than their own pain. There is a room in the catacombs of our temple designed for such purposes—not a necessity, though it saves time and the risk of error. But the core of it is the cutting, and the endurance."

She stood and paced. "Mind and body," she said, half to herself. "That part's easy enough, and you could reduce—what if you used anesthetics? And had a modern surgical theater to minimize bleeding, sterilize everything, and sew up the wounds afterward?"

Chulzh'th looked thoughtful. "The medical techniques . . . would help, in part. But the harm to the body is what forces the outsider loose. And"—she flexed her fingers, careful not to let her claws pierce Sally's side—"it would be hard to keep gloves whole."

"I can wield a blade," said Mary. "If I have guidance."

"Drugs to dull pain have been tried," said Ngalthr. "But most by their nature loosen the mind from the body. If the mind is not there to feel the pain, the outsider remains untouched as well."

"Damn." Mary continued pacing. "I don't know that I could talk Kingsport Congregational into giving the lot of us a private surgery at 1 a.m., in any case. Damn."

"I'll try it," said Audrey abruptly.

Ngalthr frowned at her. "Child, I said *no*."

"I don't have Aphra's strength, but I have more endurance than most people. I'm doing a lot better than Sally is, and that's down to whatever this . . . thing . . . is, in my blood. It might help me survive. And I may not be trained in mental travel, but I learn fast. I'm already stubborn enough to hold on when people are trying to push me out." Her eyes slid sideways to Trumbull, but with Mary present she didn't specify. "And I'm dying, anyway. I'm not afraid of it hurting a bit more."

"I have done this before," said Ngalthr. "And I will not do it to you."

"Audrey," I said. "The thing in your blood—" Turning to Mary. "Audrey has something in her blood—we don't know what it is, but it looks like—pieces of void that try to eat up the invader. It hurts her too, but it's why she's doing so much better than Sally. We were trying to find a way to share it, and get it under control, but we couldn't figure it out."

"Really?" Mary turned on her. "How did you come by it? What do you know about how it works?"

Audrey shrugged, beyond shame. "I had ancestors who were supernaturally crazy and liked running crazy supernatural experiments.

But I don't know anything about how it works, because their experiments were a few generations back and they didn't leave any notes."

Mary raised her eyebrows. "You're talking about the Mad Ones? Or some seventeenth-century enthusiast in Providence or Salem?"

"The Mad Ones Under the Earth." Audrey pronounced it with melodramatic relish. "You know about them?"

"I may take the classics with a grain of salt, but I've read them." She looked at the elders. "Possibly a larger grain than I should have. Tell me everything you can about this protection of yours."

Audrey, and those of us who'd seen her blood, did what we could to explain it—what it looked like to the inner eye, its effects, everything we'd tried to bridle it.

Mary held her hands out, flexed them as if trying to grasp something. "I could . . . there are equations that describe the body and mind. The ones I used for the inventory spell were too general, obviously, but they could be made more specific—perhaps specific enough to summon and control a part of the body."

"Or the cold itself?" I asked.

"If we knew more of its nature. A gift from the Mad Ones would be far easier, if only because they're human. But I can't work out the equations. I can't do them in my head, and I can't write them out."

Trumbull stepped forward. "Can you walk me through them?"

"I can try." The two of them fell into technical jargon.

Ngalthr knelt to scratch a symbol in the sand. "Do not use this for summoning. It is the basic symbol for the K'n-yan—for the Mad Ones."

"That's an equation?" asked Trumbull. "Wait, yes, I see . . ."

I wondered what a mathematician might learn during a sojourn at the Archives, and how much might filter through the memory blocks, given impetus. I watched their work, hoping to better understand the logic that connected diagram and equation, formalized symbol and ever-changing reality. But the more I listened, the more it seemed to me that something was lacking.

There's a logic and a predictability to magic: things we know we can do, tools we've practiced well. But there are also—not limits, precisely, but knowledge more distant than we'll reach before the sun goes dark. It's likely, though beyond our ken and concern, that there's knowledge too far for the Yith to reach before the universe itself fades. Beyond those limits are things that, if they even distinguish comprehension from chaos, see us as numinous, nameless horrors—as we do them.

That humility is what allows us to work, when we must, at the edges of understanding. Define your work solely with equations, I suspected, and it would have no room for those edges. But my way, and the elders' way, had already failed. And though Mary and Trumbull grew increasingly energetic in their discussion, I heard no hint of a breakthrough. Any hope of bringing us all through the Tide, whole, must draw on all our strengths.

What did I have to offer, aside from childhood memory and two years' study?

Memories of survival. Stories told around fires, or under covers behind guards' backs, shared across languages and cultures. Friends and family who'd reached across barriers of understanding. The confluence, water and rock and air flowing together in our mingled blood.

I moved closer to Mary and Trumbull, and when they paused said, "We're connected. Charlie and Audrey and Caleb and Miss Dawson and I through common practice, and Sally here." I rolled up my sleeve so they could see what remained of that link. "All three kinds of humans. Can we do something with that?"

"Maybe," said Mary, and "Suppose—" And Trumbull said, "If you define—" and they were back to their jargon, of which I caught only the suggestion that our link might fill an otherwise indefinable gap in some larger structure with which they struggled.

The cold in my spine began to spread once more. Chulzh'th sat by the fire, listening, Sally across her lap. I joined her, touched my skin again to Sally's. I felt the pulse of warmth, as before, but weaker.

"You're going to lose her," said Chulzh'th quietly.

"I know."

"You should cut the link."

"Not yet." I glanced at Mary and Trumbull, just as they rose from their consultation. They looked hopeful, and worried.

"How quickly could you find one of those knives?" Mary asked Ngalthr.

"There's one in Y'ha-nthlei, beyond the reef. It would take almost two hours to retrieve. There used to be one in the temple, and it may be there still. But I've already said I won't use it on them."

"You won't need to, not directly. Miss Marsh is right—we can use the connections that already exist between her and the other two, work through her strength and probably Miss Winslow's as well, to break the cold from all of them."

Grandfather understood a second before I did. "No! You won't risk my granddaughter that way!"

"If there's a chance of saving them, I'll do it," I said.

"You will not." He paced toward me. I backed away, hand over my forearm—and he whirled to drag Sally from Chulzh'th's grasp. Awkward under the girl's weight, Chulzh'th tried to pull her away. But Grandfather held Sally's arm long enough to scratch on it some sigil I could not see. I felt the last thread snap, the cold drain from my spine.

"Grandfather!" I shouted, at the same time that Archpriest Ngalthr called his name and wrenched him back from Chulzh'th and Sally. One guard, looking extremely nervous, stepped between him and Audrey and raised her spear. I stored my gratitude; for now I dropped to my knees beside Sally. Chulzh'th passed her to me, stood and stalked to Grandfather.

"Did you learn nothing from watching me lose my temper?" she demanded. "You'll answer for her death."

"I know. But I only have two grandchildren."

I pressed Sally's wrist, but my fingers were nearly numb and I couldn't find her pulse. I held my hand near her nostrils, felt the warmth of her exhalation. A pause, then more warmth. Another pause, another breath. And then nothing.

I kept my hand there for what seemed an aeon. More words passed between Grandfather and the others; I didn't hear them. I laid Sally's body on the sand, and looked up at him.

"I'm still cold," I said.

I couldn't tell whether it was actually true: whether the shivers that flooded my body were remnants of the outsider, or the memory of those remnants, or simply anger—as much at my own traitorous gratitude as at him. In that moment, I didn't care: it was enough to see his protective straining, held in check by Ngalthr's claws around his arm, drain away.

Jesse picked up Sally's wrist, looked in horror at Grandfather. "You killed her."

"She was already dying. I was trying to save my granddaughter."

"He'll answer for it in our courts," said Ngalthr. "Right now we'll do what we can for the living."

Audrey ducked under the guard's still-raised spear, lowered herself beside us, touched Sally's forehead. There were tears in her eyes; she ignored them. "Jesse, later. We have to deal with it later, we have to deal with this now."

"He killed her."

"He kept Aphra from saving her. We don't know if that would even have worked. And there's nothing to do about it. If you want to throw yourself at a giant fish-guy with three-inch talons, can you please do it tomorrow? By then I'll either be dead, or better enough to deal with mourning you, too."

"I'm not going to hurt the boy," said Grandfather. Ngalthr released him, and he too dropped to the sand beside us. Jesse inched back, but Grandfather simply touched Sally's brow. "I'm sorry, Aphra. I wanted to keep you safe."

"I'm not safe."

"I know that. Do what you must; I'll witness it in penance."

I sighed, and wiped away tears I would not ignore. Beyond penance, having him there would be a comfort, though I wouldn't say so now. I turned to Mary. "What you were planning—will it work without a man of the air?"

"No—we'll still need someone to take the part Sally would have played," Mary said. "One person for each type of human, each type of strength. I could do it."

"You couldn't," said Trumbull. "You need to be able to focus on the ritual, and on whether our design is doing what it's supposed to." I saw Jesse swallow and glance at Audrey—could see him trying to make himself say something before Trumbull continued, "Besides, it would be best to use someone already bound to her."

It was no surprise, then, when Charlie pulled himself up. "I'll do it." Dawson didn't argue, nor ought she have.

Caleb and Neko walked beside me as we made our way the few blocks to the temple, his arm around my shoulder and hers squeezing my hand. I squeezed back and leaned against him, though I wanted to urge them elsewhere. It was some sort of paradox, to yearn for their presence but also wish them not to see. Grandfather concerned me less, though I knew it would hurt him as well to see me in pain. Perhaps I did think it some sort of expiation.

"You don't have to watch," I told Neko, reluctant even as I said it.

"Is this something you're going to have nightmares about?" she asked.

"Probably."

"If you're going to wake me up in the middle of the night about it, then I should be here now."

CHAPTER 28

Chulzh'th carried Sally again; Jesse walked beside her. As we left the beach, the line of starlight slid shut. The wind picked up, and I lifted my face to the snow. The storm might have lost its momentum, but it hadn't forgotten itself.

The temple was only two blocks from the dunes. I hated to see it silent and empty, hated more to cross the threshold, where the wooden door hung off its hinges, and smell dust and mildew in place of incense. Audrey's flashlight found cobwebs, layers of dirt, detritus blown in and pews and lamps scattered and broken. Figures of gods had been toppled, or looted from now-empty pedestals.

Ngalthr found and lit an old-fashioned torch, and led us down narrow stairs into the catacombs, trailing pungent smoke. As a child I'd entered rarely, but the subterranean warren had been a place of adventure. You could get in trouble for exploring the catacombs, but turning a corner might unveil anything from an ill-made statue of Nyarlathotep to a collection of century-old brooms. As the archpriest led us through the winding maze, I realized that even on those sojourns I'd seen little of their extent.

"These chambers were intended to hide all Innsmouth and much of Y'ha-nthlei, if needed," said Grandfather. "But they did little good when danger actually came."

"The soldiers attacked the temple first," said Caleb. "No one could have fled there."

We stopped at a line of stone platforms, carved with stylized figures of elders and long, sinuous fish. Chulzh'th placed Sally's body on one. To the side, an archway opened onto a larger room. Ngalthr entered, lit candles still in their sconces, and set the torch in a holder.

The room was made all of black stone, traced with veins of gold. Diagrams and symbols and passages of Enochian etched the walls and floor. In the center stood an altar of the same material. I approached, cautiously, and saw the shallow indentations in the top, carved to hold a human body. Tatters of a cushion rotted at the head, and scraps of leather bonds clung to the iron rings that must have anchored them.

No bonds remained whole to buttress my will. I would simply have to keep still.

Ngalthr felt at the base of the altar and pulled loose a block of stone. When he stood, he held a knife. He offered it to me, and I examined it. The handle was gold, worked in stylized figures of gods and waves. The blade was plain and functional steel, folded so that tiny rivulets glinted across the surface. It was an old technique, one that I had seen only in the work of elders and in a sword belonging to an old man who lived near the Kotos. He'd brought it with him from Japan, and secreted it somewhere prior to the war.

Interesting how such distant cultures had discovered the same way of strengthening metal. And easier to consider the coincidence than to think about what that metal was for.

Trumbull examined the room's carvings with clinical eyes, discussed necessary additions and alterations with Mary, and decided that the room itself need not be modified. They called me over, along with Charlie and Audrey. Mary pulled pen and ink and a small brush from her bag; after further discussion Trumbull used the brush to paint our faces and arms. I took a deep breath and undressed first. Ngalthr would need me to do that anyway, soon enough, and I didn't wish to increase our risk by smudging Trumbull's work. Spector at least would find this uninteresting, I hoped, though he looked away delicately. I looked at Jesse and did not blush or smirk. He met my gaze briefly, then ducked his head.

"Do we, ah, need to . . . ?" asked Charlie. He'd removed his jacket and pushed up his sleeves to make a larger canvas, and was already shivering. I was pleased to find that while I could still feel the crypt's chill, it was not so deep or distressing as it had been. Then I felt the shame of my comfort.

"Shouldn't be necessary," said Trumbull, tracing a long equation down her arm. Focused on her work, her face held a little of the detached quality I'd grown accustomed to. "Though Miss Harris thinks some of the physical effects may carry through the link, so if you're wearing anything you especially don't want to bleed on, you might remove it."

We began.

There is courage, different from that which armors warriors, in lying down before a knife. There is, I think, yet another sort in wielding the knife. Archpriest Ngalthr met my eyes as I lay back on the altar. I was afraid he might apologize, but he didn't. The stone curved subtly against my bare skin: I found where I was meant to lie easily. The cool solidity sank into me, until I felt no more able to move than the altar itself. My heart beat fast; my breaths came deep and long. Outlined by air and stone, I felt keenly aware of all my body's surfaces.

Firelight echoed in sparks from the carven walls, from the skin and scales and clothing of those who stood around me. Ngalthr and Mary began chanting: Ngalthr the familiar words of the Inner Sea, Mary something stranger, half in English and half in the jargon she shared with Trumbull. My awareness of the room and my own skin grew sharper—but overlaid on them came Charlie's skin and Audrey's, the blood that coursed within each of us, and the energies that bound that blood together. Fainter impressions followed of Caleb and Dawson, and I knew with regret that we would not be able to fully spare them.

But Mary's equations did what we couldn't alone. The darkness flowed over Audrey's banks and spilled into the rest of us. It made me feel angry and strong and confident—and beneath that frightened at an anger and confidence nothing like my own. In turn, some of the strength of my own blood spilled over into her and Charlie. It sent their rivers foaming to rapids, and made a place of clear water within Audrey's tumble of light and void.

And in that tumult of mixing blood, I could see clearly that some of the pulsating, airless cold still remained in me—my own contagion, not only an echo of Sally's. If I had cut her loose on my own, earlier, would I have spared myself this? But I couldn't regret staying with her.

And it didn't make the work harder, that I must bear this for myself as well as for Audrey. It only meant that if I failed to save her, I would have my penance swiftly.

The chant ceased; our strengthened connection settled into place. Then the elders began singing. They'd moved to the edges of the room so that music wove around me from all directions. The words were familiar, though it had been long since I'd heard them: a chant offered to the sick, the dying, the grieving. The Litany of the Peoples of Earth was a part of it, but so too were prayers to all the gods, and something that was nearly a prayer to the listener—to be strong, to be patient, to endure, to wait and change.

The ancient words were comfort, a reminder that pain too was ephemeral. But I felt Charlie's heart lurch, and knew how they sounded to his ears: harsh and alien and ominous in the progression of archaic tones. The elders sung in swooping altos that bubbled on the low notes, and in basses so deep they vibrated bone. I braced myself, clinging to the sound, hoping it would be enough.

At the first cut, I screamed. It was not only physical pain, where the knife bit into me below my collarbone. I saw my father lying still with blood seeping over half-formed gills. Twelve again, weak and terrified, listening to my mother's prayers in the back of a van full of prisoners.

Before the knife pulled away I forgot that it would end. Then I heard the chant again, felt Charlie's determination and fear and Audrey's strange dark defenders, remembered that I must not run. But too, I felt Charlie gasp, heart painful in his chest. I pushed a little of my own blood over its boundaries, trying to share endurance I wasn't convinced I had.

Ngalthr's face, when I dared look, was grim. I had the luxury of screaming; he did not. I watched the knife descend and did not close my eyes, for his sake. Pain blossomed across my forehead, and blood. This time there was no memory, only a wash of heat that limned the cold within me but did nothing to lessen it. Desert and drought, and the sun burning away the last of the oceans. I would be reduced to ash; I had to flee. And there was a dark place I could go, far away, where I could hide.

But amid the burning I felt Audrey's protective void, free of heat or cold or doubt. I had promised to stay here. I reached for it, knowing her defenses were dangerous but unable to care about anything beyond the pain and the fear and the holding on.

The blade lifted. I gasped, and bit down hard on my tongue so I couldn't beg Ngalthr to stop. That pain was barely perceptible. I closed my eyes, focused my will on not begging, not running. Yet when I felt the knife brush my belly, I thrashed and could not force my body still. I heard crying, recognized it for Neko's.

Cool, sharp-tipped hands grasped my arms and held them fast. I opened my eyes and saw Grandfather, his own eyes shut, but there and doing what was needful. I could not shame him. I relaxed my muscles, bit by bit, beneath his grip, and forced the rest of my body to follow. I closed my eyes again, and this time when the cool metal touched my navel, I controlled my reaction well enough that Ngalthr found his target. And screamed again as he did so.

Where the knife touched my mind, I saw Audrey fallen, still and cold as Sally. Charlie, withered and wrinkled and forgetting my name, screaming to see me as an elder. Neko, Caleb, Grandfather, piles of beloved, empty bodies. I clung to those I knew hopelessly lost, and stayed beside them as I had promised.

Cut after cut, fears and memories and exquisitely specific doubts and pains stripped utterly of context. But when I opened my eyes, when I could, I saw Grandfather still there, and Charlie and Audrey on either side. Audrey leaned hard against the altar, gasping, and Charlie stood bent and rigid. They held my hands so tightly that it would have hurt, if I were still capable of noticing such a pedestrian discomfort. I clung to them, and to myself: because I had promised, and because their shared strength gave me an anchor, and because the one fear that remained constant was of how much worse it would hurt if I turned away.

The knife bit hard into the join of neck and shoulder, and I felt myself falling into endless void, knowing at once that I had lost control and would drift forever fading, and that I must continue to hold where I was certain I'd already let go. And in the midst of that paradoxical terror, I felt the cold loosen its grip. Hooks that had dug fast into me, into Audrey, slipped.

Another cut, and I became convinced that Ngalthr had erred, that it would be me cut loose from my body and the cold left to take up residence. It would convince everyone that it was me, lead my friends to death and ruin. I tried to pull away, to stop it, but firm hands held me down. As Ngalthr lifted the knife, the cold went with it, pulling away from me and from Audrey like a withered scab.

Ngalthr gasped—we all did, I think—and he held the coruscating light on the tip of the knife, well away from the living humans around him. The chant changed, became more rhythmic and aggressive. The mass dimmed, pulsed, dimmed again, and flickered out at last.

I lay in the suddenly darkened room, pulse pounding, realizing slowly that I did not need to brace for the next cut. A broader awareness returned, beyond the lessened pain and the hands that had held me throughout: the stone now warm beneath me and sticky with my own blood, the smell of sweat, the remaining sting of myriad cuts, cold air that now seemed a balm, murmurs from the edges of vision.

Charlie leaned on the altar, drawing shaky breaths. Audrey eased herself down against the cool stone; through our link I felt it solid against her back. I tried to sit up, found that it was a bad idea and lay back again. Chulzh'th appeared with a damp cloth and began cleaning my wounds. I felt absurd for flinching where it stung. I managed to turn my head, and saw Caleb and Dawson and Neko.

"You okay?" Neko asked, voice squeaking a little on the question.

I laughed shakily, found that I could manage that though it hurt my throat. "I will—" I coughed, and pain shot through my chest. I swallowed hard, and Chulzh'th handed me the salt water she'd been using to wash me. I drank it greedily, and managed to say: "I will be. Give me a minute."

"Aphra?" Audrey's voice echoed too loudly. "I think we still have a problem."

CHAPTER 29

Through the link I felt it: the gift of Audrey's ancestor, trium-
phant over the outsider, rising to take the space it had been
granted. The dark strength was greatest in the woman who
bore it, but it swirled too in me and Charlie. I felt an anger and a strange
joy that belonged to none of us as individuals. My pain, I realized as I
looked more closely, had fed the Mad Ones' creation even as it worked
against the cold. The k'n-yan, all the stories said, drew pleasure and
power from exotic tortures. Though this pain had been to a purpose
and endured willingly, it had been terrible enough, and strange enough,
to feed any such need.

"What's going on?" asked Mary.

"My little pets helped," said Audrey. "But now we can't put them
back in their box."

Mary looked frightened. "The equations—the ritual was supposed
to take care of that. If it didn't work—"

"It didn't," said Audrey. I could sense her anger spilling in a growing desire to share the pain we'd just been through, pain it now started
to remember as a malicious attack.

This would not keep while Trumbull and Mary tried to recalculate.

"I know what to do," I said. In truth, "know" was a very strong word,
but it grabbed Audrey and Charlie's increasingly distractible attention
and helped me suppress the anger in favor of unearned confidence.

I tried again to rise, and this time found sitting possible if vertiginous. Grandfather let go my wrists and did not argue. I looked down at myself, found raw red lines beginning to scab over but still tender to the least touch or movement.

"Good," said Charlie. "What?"

"Help me stand."

Audrey and Charlie helped me to my feet, and Caleb and Dawson and Neko hurried forward to offer additional hands. Spector hovered just out of range, seeming torn between feeling he should help and realizing that this was beyond his powers. Ngalthr, too, kept his distance, head bowed. I looked around for Jesse, found him standing still by the door, watching Audrey with frightened eyes.

"This was too much like the Mad Ones' arenas," I tried to explain. "The differences would only matter to us. We need to remind them that we're not under the earth."

Archpriest Ngalthr looked up. I tried not to let the knife draw my eyes. "Ah. Yes, I see," he said. "That could work, perhaps." I focused on the "yes" rather than the doubt. I pushed myself to my feet, leaned heavily on Audrey.

"You want your clothes?" she asked.

"Not now. We need to go outside."

"And therefore you should have clothes."

Anger overwhelmed me, ridiculous in the face of such a tiny argument. "Not. Now."

We filed out: Audrey helped support me on one side and Caleb on the other. Chulzh'th knelt briefly beside Sally's body, whispered a prayer. "We'll come back afterward," she said to Jesse. "Do you want to stay here and keep vigil?"

He looked around at the crowd, and at the catacombs. "No. I'll come."

I felt stronger even as we walked. Scabs still pulled where I moved too quickly, but Ngalthr had not exaggerated our endurance. By the time we got outside, I no longer needed support to stand. I spread my arms to the snow and the cold, and found that they no longer hurt me. That was good, given what I planned.

Looking at the symbols still inked on my outstretched arms, I saw another problem. "Miss Harris—the ink you used, will it come off in water?"

"With a little scrubbing, yes." She wrapped her arms around herself. "In D.C., they don't like it when you come into the office painted up like some savage."

So I'd have a minute. I just needed to figure out precisely what I'd use it for.

Back over the dune and down to the water. The wind had picked up, and though the tide had receded waves still crashed high on the beach. I placed Charlie and Audrey just out of their reach. "Focus on the connection between us," I told them. "And with me, especially; I don't know how long I'll be able to keep it going."

The underlying, permanent connection of the confluence would help. This would have been harder, with Sally in Charlie's place—no, I'd just have had to bring her into the confluence. And I'd have come to love her as well as I now did Audrey and Dawson. I recalled the strangers in the sandwich shop, all the possible intimacies passed by.

I walked into the water. I raised my arms high to protect the symbols painted on them, though it probably looked like I was being dramatic. I forced that self-consciousness aside, and focused. A few hours ago the water's cold would have set me shivering. Now, along with the scent of salt and stormwrack, it told me that I was home. I curled my toes in the sandbar, felt it ooze between them. A wave rolled past, lifting me and setting me down a foot away, tossing salt-spray against my eyes. I dug in my toes, licked my lips, and reached out. To Audrey and Charlie, watching nervously from shore—but also to the water itself.

You cannot control the ocean. The ocean transforms constantly, moved by a thousand currents; the ocean endures. But you can send your mind into it. It is a vast body, and will swallow you whole if you don't stay anchored. I remembered what I'd seen as Ngalthr reached into the storm. Not control, and not surrender. An invitation.

I invited the water into my mind. Only a crack—all I dared—and still it tore me from all sense of balance. I flailed against it, instinctively, then forced myself to mental stillness. What was in me now was vast as a storm, but far smaller than the ocean itself. It washed into the river of my blood, and I reminded it where the banks were, directed its flow where it would cleanse rather than destroy. I sent it washing over into the rest of the confluence.

This is my strength. This is my protection. It is older and stronger and cleaner than the new-forged tools of the Earth. I make it yours, too.

Under the wash of salt water, the dark tide receded—first in me, then in Charlie, then finally at its source in Audrey. This was nothing it had been created to fight. It seethed and pushed, but slowly drained away into whatever wellspring within her had birthed it. It did not disappear. Awakened, it was a part of her, and I suspected it would be always. But it fell away into quiescence, and left her blood the muddy roil it had been when I first saw it. Only a few glints of darkness remained to show that the protection—and the strength, and the danger— still remained, waiting.

The connection between us started to fade, and I had time to think, *Oh, my arms must have gone underwater,* before I became entirely aware of my body: not only my arms, but all of me surrounded by ocean. I'd lost my footing; no sandbar told me what direction to kick. My lungs burned.

Strong arms wrapped around me, and I felt myself held and lifted. I gasped sweet air, turned my head from an approaching wave, saw that it was Grandfather who'd pulled me up.

"Thank you," I managed. He stroked silently toward the shore, and seconds later set me back on the sand.

He put his hands on my shoulders and gazed at me. "Aphra Yukhl, later we must discuss how one makes such risks less completely foolhardy."

"It worked," I said breathlessly.

"Yes. And if it had not, you wouldn't be in a position to make that argument."

"We needed to do something in a hurry, and no one had a better idea."

He snorted. "I'll tell you several stories that start that way. Later."

"Yes, Grandfather."

CHAPTER 30

I t is written in the Archives that, once upon a time, the gods looked out on a universe barren and unthinking save for themselves. And they tested and experimented until they sparked matter into a form that might, one day, be capable of thought. And Shub-Nigaroth, mother of fear, looked on the first life and said: it will fail, but for now it is good.

Spector gave me a blanket from his car—unnecessary for warmth but welcome for my recovering modesty—and lectured me about hypothermia. Charlie fussed as well, though not before pointing out to Spector that cold wasn't as much of an issue for me as sharp objects. I settled back and let them bicker; it would take both their minds off the night's events. I felt strangely well. The ritual had been one of the hardest things I'd ever chosen to do—but I had chosen it, and survived, and saved myself and Audrey. I had not been helpless.

Professor Trumbull and Mary Harris made their way over. "Miss Marsh," said Mary, "could you please explain what you just did?"

"In equations?" I thought about the logic of it, how the ocean might be a grand sigil for all that stood opposed to intentional cruelty. I doubted I could articulate it well enough to satisfy them. "No. I can feel the shape of it in my head, but what I did tonight—I was guessing too fast to describe it properly."

"I have discovered a truly marvelous demonstration of this proposition," said Trumbull. Mary laughed; I didn't ask.

"Miss Harris," I said. Then I hesitated. "Your team came to Miska-tonic to learn magic for waging war."

She glanced at the others, and I wondered if I ought to have taken her out of earshot, but she said slowly, "You really aren't the ones who shared those things with the Russians, are you?"

I pushed Ephraim Waite firmly to the back of my mind. He'd for-sworn our laws and our community, and would only be amused if he knew his crimes laid at our feet. "I've said that before, and it's true."

She nodded. "I don't know if Mr. Barlow will listen to me. But I've seen a little of Innsmouth tonight. I don't think you're loyal Americans—but I don't think you're traitors, either. Not that kind. You'd turn your backs on our troubles, but I don't think you'd give to someone else what you never gave to us."

I drew myself up. "There's only so much we can care about a coun-try we'll outlive—and that tried to destroy us only a few years ago. But our people fought in the First World War, and in the wars before that back to the Revolution. If we aren't willing to protect a place, we leave."

She nodded again, more firmly. "And that's what we're trying to do here—learn what we need to know to protect the United States. No one wants another war, but we need to be prepared."

Now, I felt a wash of helplessness. We might know how to cleanse tainted blood, but we had never found spell or word to dissuade a state when it wished to do harm.

Then again, Mary was not the state, but one person who might be reasoned with—and whose cooperation and advice might do what we could not. "Have you seen, now, why we have laws and rules about which magic is permissible? That it's not merely superstition?"

She smiled wryly. "I've seen that I need to take more precautions in my research, if that's what you're asking. And that Mr. Spector may be right about consulting with outside experts. Tonight has certainly been educational."

"Thank you," said Spector. "I've been trying to tell Barlow that for years."

She sighed. "He cares very deeply about American security. And he's very confident in his judgment—justifiably so, most of the time."

"You know," said Spector. "I could use a new secretary. I might even be able to push through a raise—to something more like what an agent makes, given the types of material she'd probably have to deal with."

"If I hear about anyone looking for a position," she said, "I'll let her know."

Spector looked like he wanted to argue. Instead, he said, "We need better relations with the Deep Ones. If nothing else, think about the naval advantage."

"I've been thinking about it. That was quite the storm, earlier."

"The elders don't normally take sides in the wars of the air," I said. "But this *is* where we live, for now, when we're on land and free." Spector winced; Mary did not. "My father was too old, but I had uncles and cousins in the First World War. One of them was in the Navy; I know he got his ships through some hard weather. We can help—but there are laws older than this country that need to be followed."

She gave me a penetrating look. "Are you in a position to make treaties for your people?"

"No. Are you?"

She laughed. "Not in the slightest. But Mr. Barlow listens to me, even if it doesn't always look like it, and other people listen to him."

"There are people in R'lyeh who listen to Archpriest Ngalthr. And others who listen to my grandfather."

She nodded. "What are these laws? Aside, one presumes, from avoiding overly general inventory equations."

Mary craned her neck as Ngalthr slipped up beside me. I continued: "I know you've been doing research into body theft. It's not the most dangerous of arts, but it is the most destructive of trust, and of individual lives. And it's forbidden."

"Which is what Upton came up against, I recall—I suppose that's reassuring, after a fashion. If it's true, it certainly makes it less likely you'd spread it around." She paused. "Atomic bombs and outsiders in the world, and you worry about people jumping bodies?"

"We 'worry' about all those things," said Ngalthr. "We act against such crimes as fall within our domain, or we ensure the price is paid. If you find saboteurs or spies using such arts, we will gladly help you against them."

She nodded, and didn't press him on what he had not said: that the crime was no more forgivable in potential allies. "One can only follow so many lines of research at once. If I had a more promising avenue of study to offer my superiors . . ."

Ngalthr—a priest, but also often a mediator of R'lyeh's millennia-spanning political squabbles and compromises—nodded somberly. "We might be able to suggest a few possibilities."

Later, he pulled me aside, and spoke softly so that the men of the air couldn't hear. "Do you trust her promises?"

I hadn't yet slept, though fatigue was beginning to creep into my bones. I had been talking to Audrey and Jesse, listening to their stories about Sally and wishing I had a notebook. It took me a moment to realize that he was talking about Mary. "I don't know her well enough to judge. I wouldn't try binding her to it magically, though; her team would take it badly."

"One day, your family will learn that other people are not blind."

"I'm sorry, Archpriest. It's been a long night. I truly don't know— I think she's honorable, but I don't think she worries about following set rules and promises so much as what she thinks is right. And her judgment hasn't always agreed with mine."

"Well. We'll try this. We will watch and wait, and if need be we'll move the spawning grounds yet again. Innsmouth will do for now, though. We'll retrieve gold from our stores; it should be sufficient for you to buy back some of what's rightfully yours."

Even tired, I could imagine the advantages of a small fortune. Mis-katonic might not sell us our books, but the construction companies working on the outskirts of town were likely motivated by more straightforward greed.

"Archpriest. There's something you should know." A glance told me that Spector and Mary and Dawson remained elsewhere. The plash of waves would cover our words. "I found Ephraim Waite's journals at Hall. One of his cultists was exiled Russian nobility. And not pleased with his exile."

Ngalthr hissed softly. "You haven't told them."

"I was trying to decide whether I should." I hesitated. Speaking would make the choice real. "There are things they'd be able to do to protect themselves, however small, that would work better if they knew where the threat originated. But I think even Spector would feel he had to tell his masters. They've tried to blame us already, even without the details. With them, the paranoia would become even worse than it is now—and probably more destructive than any number of saboteurs and spies."

"The dangers of paranoia are much of why that art is so strongly forbidden. Yes, your judgment is good. Keep silent for now, and let me know if you learn of a reason to speak."

Hiding Ephraim's secret would be far from a perfect protection. Barlow hardly seemed to need evidence to suspect us, and we still didn't know who had visited Upton scant months before. The answer to that, when it came, might well spark its own paranoia. But for now, this was what I could do.

Spector's trust in me, ultimately, couldn't weigh more heavily than the unknown lives saved or lost by my decision.

Dawn, scarce stronger than moonlight, whispered behind the overcast as we drove back to Miskatonic. Mary drove Jesse home, bearing Sally's body. She would tell Barlow what had happened, or most of it, but the public story would be that Sally, distraught by her boyfriend's hospitalization, had wandered out into the blizzard and frozen to death. She deserved better, but it was a tale people would accept all too willingly.

I didn't ask Mary for details about how they'd have her found, or how they'd explain the sigils still scarring her arm.

I supposed some secretarial duties were more pleasant than others.

Audrey and I had spoken more with Jesse. He was exhausted—as we all were—but had agreed to cooperate with the story. I hoped his unbound promise would hold. At least Audrey seemed to have persuaded him that she kept company with me by her own will.

There was one more person who must hear the truth. Trepidatious and feeling out of place, I followed Audrey and Jesse into Leroy's hospital room.

He was awake and sitting up, though his skin still looked waxen. As soon as he saw us, he asked, "What's wrong?" And then, "Where's Sally?"

"Sally's gone," said Jesse, his voice thin.

"How?" He looked at me. "Why are you here?"

"I was there," I said softly.

"Aphra tried to save her," said Audrey. I bowed my head, not brave enough to protest the claim.

"Like you did me," he said reluctantly. "Did your family . . . ?" He trailed off, eyes flicking to Jesse.

"He knows about them," I said. "He was there too. And no, not my family this time. Not . . . not for the most part. Jesse, perhaps you ought to explain the first bit, since Audrey and I weren't there."

"Um." Jesse took the single wooden chair, and sat, gingerly, beside Leroy. "After Sally told me to talk to Aphra about what happened to you, we decided we needed to know more. We were obviously getting into the kind of thing we've always talked about, and we needed some sort of power to protect ourselves, and to be able to stand up to whatever happened. So we snuck into the library."

"Without me?" Leroy's enthusiasm was immediate and automatic. He flinched even as he spoke, but didn't try to deny his reaction.

"We found some restricted books that looked good. We thought we were doing all right, until the alarm went off . . ." He continued through their encounter with Barlow's people, the federal team's willingness to provide cover for their own ends, their offer of mentorship in exchange for shared texts.

Aside from the need for a precipitating burglary, it was much how Charlie and I had started working together. At that time, I could hardly have claimed more experience than Mary—only a better awareness of my own limits.

Up through the start of the inventory ritual, it seemed clear that Leroy would have happily gone along with every bit of their plan. At that point, however, Jesse was forced to admit amnesia and hand the narrative over to me.

I summoned once again the half-lie we'd told Barlow: that we'd noticed the odd ritual in progress and been caught up in it when we came to investigate. "Then something else answered the summons. We've been calling it an outsider—one of the things that doesn't belong in our universe, but waits for someone to make a crack in the world. It was . . . cold. And hungry. Professor Trumbull managed to banish it before it could spread, but it left a bit of itself in Audrey and Sally. And in me, through the connection that my grandfather made."

It hurt to tell the story, and yet it was also strangely relieving. I *could* speak of it, could explain things that at the time had felt beyond words, could turn them into something human. Leroy listened intently, but glared when I told him, not trying to gloss it over, what my grandfather had done and why he had done it. Glared harder when Audrey insisted that it had probably been too late to save Sally anyway.

"We don't know," I said. "We can't know."

"The ritual was hard for me, and I was doing a lot better than she was. I'm not excusing your grandfather, but I'm a lot more upset with Miss Harris for not bringing her to us earlier."

I went ahead and described the ritual for Leroy's benefit. When I explained why we'd been able to make it work, he looked at Audrey with mingled horror and fascination.

"Yes, yes, I know," she said. "I'm descended from a bunch of murderous crazy people. I bet you are too, Mr. I'm-Related-to-Charlemagne."

"Probably, but they never did anything like *that*."

"My relatives could tell you stories about British magicians," I said.

Distracted, Leroy turned his attention back on me. "Your family aren't healthy to be around."

While I was considering my response, Audrey said, "Healthier than Barlow's people. Especially if you don't try to poke them in the eye."

"He attacked me!"

"She's a girl, you moron. And you threatened her!"

"Enough," I said. "Chulzh'th lost her temper, and she knows it. If you're going to admit I saved your life, then you should know that she did too—I panicked and did the healing ritual wrong, and she helped me get it back under control."

"Ah." Leroy sat back, quelled. He looked at Jesse a long moment. "I don't know what to do about this. You're right, that we need . . . something. But if your spooks can't be trusted, I don't know where we can learn."

"You could study with us," I said. "I should have offered earlier. I'm sorry."

The looks the boys turned on me then made it clear that, however much they might be pressed into keeping our secrets, they weren't ready to treat me as a fellow human. My own reactions were a tangle: anger at their judgment, relief at the excuse to avoid further intimacy, shame at my relief.

"I hope you find your own way," I said. Then, apprehension twisting into the tangle: "Just, by all the gods, please don't try to summon anything you haven't already spoken to. It's not an effective route to power."

Audrey nodded. "In general, if you think what you're about to do might destroy Arkham, tell me first so I can grab anything I've left here."

"Are you still talking to us?" Jesse asked her.

"Sure. Just not studying with you. Call me if you change your minds."

I returned to the Innsmouth beach a few days later, with Neko and Spector and the confluence, to wait while elders brought up treasure from Y'ha-nthlei: mined nuggets, jewels and coins salvaged from centuries of shipwreck, and a few pieces of the worked gold jewelry so loved by R'lyehn artisans. These were not for trade; I bent my head as Grandfather placed one around my neck. It was heavy and cool, a thick bas-relief of elders and exotic cephalopods prostrate before gods.

"From your grandmother," Grandfather said. "She could not come yet from the central ranges, but sends this and her love."

I'd met Grandmother only a few times during my childhood. On land, before I was born, she'd kept house and raised her children well, but while she loved Grandfather she never loved such domesticity. After her metamorphosis she'd joined one of the exploratory companies that mapped the ever-changing floor of the Atlantic. That she'd heard already of my survival, quickly enough to send such a message and such a gift, was a small miracle.

Grandfather offered another necklet to Caleb and then—acknowledgment a miracle of another sort—smaller pieces to Audrey and Charlie and Dawson and Neko. Dawson handed hers back to Caleb, and smiled brilliantly as he clasped it around her neck.

I knelt to examine the more ordinary treasure. There's something diverting about boxes full of gold, in spite of the small number of problems against which they're useful. Judging from the others' reactions, it was one of humanity's shared peculiarities. Perhaps it's that their use is easier and more pleasant than so many other methods of solving problems.

"So," I told Dawson. "Turning Innsmouth back into a town is going to take a lot of work. And we'll need to hire people to do much of it."

"Or," said Spector, "as I mentioned a few days ago, I could use a secretary."

Dawson looked between us, then out over the ocean. The day was calm, with the sun showing through thin clouds. A few patches of snow tipped the dunes. "I don't know," she said. "I'm kind of fond of Massachusetts."

"Outreach to Aeonist communities is one of my responsibilities," Spector said. "It would help to have someone here who knew the place."

"Let me think about it."

I suspected she would take her time; it was a pleasure to have options, when such luxury could be found.

"Charlie had an idea," I told Ngalthr. Charlie looked at me, startled; his insight probably wasn't the part of that conversation he remembered best. "Over the centuries, some of our people have taken lovers from out of town who left, and whose mist-blooded children never returned to the water. Some of their descendants must be out there, now; if we could find them they might help us strengthen Innsmouth."

"And sire or bear children more likely to come into the water? Yes, I see that."

"Anything you might know about who left, or where to find their descendants, would make it a lot easier to invite them home."

"Yes." Ngalthr hummed to himself, deep in his chest. "Our historians will have information that may be of use. More might be found in the journals now at Miskatonic. We must decide what to do about those."

"About that. Trumbull—the Yith, I mean, who called itself that—suggested before it left that it was growing less pleased with Miskatonic's archival services."

"Is that what they're doing there? I always did wonder. So it offered to remove our collections—to where?"

"To Innsmouth. If we build a library to their specifications, of course."

He gave a bubbling laugh. "Of course. An ideal outcome . . . assuming it held to that judgment when it returned home, and the rest of its people agreed."

"Assuming." I looked out over the ocean, back at the dunes hiding ruins we hoped to rebuild. "I'm reluctant to depend on the Great Race's benevolence, just now. But I can't think of any other options."

He knelt and sifted coins between webbed fingers. "Miskatonic will not sell, not to us nor any agent of ours. But it's possible they could be bribed. You might offer to endow a reading room, for example. With conditions."

"My family knows lawyers who do that sort of thing," said Audrey. "I could help find someone."

I thought about it. I disliked Miskatonic: their arrogance, their treatment of Trumbull, the highhanded way that most of the students interacted with everyone around them. If the people of air must hold our books, my preference would be to share them with the Hall School. To remain dependent on Miskatonic's approval, no matter if it came more easily, would gall. But even were Mary to chivvy her team out of the library tomorrow, I saw no practical way to free our collection.

Of course, within bounds, generous donors might set conditions as they pleased.

"You've got an idea," said Audrey.

"I was just thinking—if we did this, we needn't just demand access for readers from Innsmouth. We could make it open to Hall students as well."

"Entrance to the library whenever we asked?" A smile spread on her face. "That'd be a sweet thing. Big donation, though."

I gave the boxes a significant look.

"This is no great portion of the water's treasure," agreed Ngalthr. "There is much we cannot do, but where gold is concerned you need only ask for what is required."

I thought about it: a hole forced through Miskatonic's bulwarks. A place on their campus where they could not bar the wrong kind of people. Such an incursion might grow, if cultivated over time. *Perhaps we might endow a professorship as well.*

I started to smile.

Audrey eyed the boxes thoughtfully, but her own smile faded. "I almost died, but I took the risk willingly when I started studying. And Sally . . . I don't know if she thought about it, but she would have risked her life to get at this stuff. But the other people on campus, in town, that Barlow's ritual could have hurt—I hate to say it, but the more people who can read those books, the more easily a few idiots could ruin things for everyone."

I wanted to deny it. It was a truism that magic wasn't for power, that there were easier ways to hurt and kill. But whatever magic was *for*, Barlow's people had misused it, and easily. As had the Yith, in their own way, and Ephraim, and probably his "wolf," too.

"We could keep some of the books restricted," I said reluctantly. "Caleb and I can figure out which ones really are dangerous—and you can warn us if we aren't being imaginative enough." It wouldn't stop Barlow's people from making up their own mistakes—but it wouldn't help their kind along, either.

Even letting outsiders at the foundational works was a risk, I supposed. But then again, those were the works that taught us what *not* to do, and how to go on safely. And more, they were a cautious window between us and men of the air—a risk that might help them see us as people rather than monsters or faceless traitors. Safety beyond gold, if it worked. I hoped it would be worth it.

The night before our return to San Francisco, Neko and I made dinner at Trumbull's house. Skinner had rebuked her for missing her Thursday classes, but she'd otherwise managed to pick up the semester's threads with minimal interruption. She'd also started to examine the traces her guest had left in the mathematics building.

". . . and she scribbled notes in every book in my office."

"The Yith are known for their marginalia," I said. "Pick up a little Enochian, and you might discover some interesting research tips. And probably rude comments about famous mathematicians, too."

"That might be worth some study." Her lips quirked. "These salt-cakes are delicious. Odd, but delicious."

"Thank you." I decided not to mention her guest's opinion on the matter.

"I could help with the translation," offered Audrey. After much discussion, we'd decided that at the least she ought to finish out the year at Hall. It would give her time to ease her friends' concerns, and to come up with some reasonable story for her parents. And if worse came to worst, she could study with Caleb and Dawson in Innsmouth. We'd correspond, and Charlie and I would fly out as often as we could—but I wasn't ready to leave San Francisco yet.

"That would help," said Trumbull. She gave Audrey a searching look. "They don't give me an official slot for a research assistant, you know."

Audrey shrugged. "It'll be unofficial, then. It's not as if I've learned much from the things I'm *supposed* to be doing."

After dinner, Charlie and Spector stepped outside to smoke—and, I presumed, to discuss their own impending returns to California and D.C. They had worn each other's scents most mornings, of late.

"Come up to my study?" Trumbull asked me quietly.

I followed her up the familiar stairs. The room was starting to show her own character, new books and papers spread on the desk. She'd kept the floor slate, and pale chalk-marks suggested that she'd been working through a few equations.

She leaned back against the desk and rubbed her temples. "I've been dreaming about it. Even the memories that come when I'm awake feel a little like dreams. I'm never sure whether I can trust them."

"Human memories are never trustworthy," I said. "If I had to guess, these are probably no worse."

"Has anyone ever told you that you're extremely un-reassuring?"

"I'm sorry," I said.

She sighed. "Don't be. You're probably right; it doesn't help to doubt them. It's not as if I can check. I have a favor to ask."

"You saved Audrey's life," I said. "Ask it."

She hesitated. "I've gathered that your people live a long time."

I nodded. "If nothing kills us."

"Have you ever heard of a place called Fángguó?"

It took only a moment to recall. "Yes. It hasn't been founded yet, but we've heard of it from the Yith and their returned captives over the millennia. It has a lot of names—'Fángguó' isn't as common as 'Cān Zhàn,' or 'the Protectorate'—but it all seems to be the same place. No one knows precisely when it will rise, or how quickly it will fall. It's believed to be in China, or some colonial extension of theirs."

She let out a breath I hadn't noticed her holding. "Good. I thought it was in the future, but I could have misremembered, or misunderstood. They don't use our calendar, you see. I had a friend, among the other captive minds, who came from there. Zoeng Saujing." She wrote it out for me on the slate, and I imagined the two speaking through clacking pincers in cone-shaped bodies, bent over tablets to find a shared alphabet so that they could learn each other's true names. "We were very close. I've written out a message. Would you deliver it?" She handed me an envelope.

It was a small favor. And it felt like doing my part for the Archives, as well, to carry such a message across millennia. "By the time the paper crumbles, I'll have it memorized. And I'll find her for you."

"Thank you." She paused. " 'Her'? We were in very different bodies; how could we even know?"

"Chinatown's not far from where we live in San Francisco. Saujing sounds like a woman's name." Which Trumbull clearly hadn't intended me to know for some time. "Of course, names evolve, over time. One of my great-great-great-aunts still mourns a Dunwich man by the name of Beverly."

She shook her head. "No, you had it right. It's not as if you won't meet her. I hope. Will you still deliver the message?"

"Of course." As gently as I could, I asked, "Your maid Emily . . . ?"

She shook her head. "Not interested in any apology I can offer."

"I'm sorry."

"Even in bits and scraps, I can remember how much I loved the Archives. The purity of the conversations, people from all of history judging each other on nothing but our minds. Even little as I recall now, I wouldn't want to give that up. But I wish I could get my . . . guest . . . in the same place for one conversation. I'd have a few choice words for her." She handed me an envelope and a single sheet of densely written paper, eyes averted.

She'd filled the bin beside the desk with crumpled stationary. I wondered when in the night those memories had come back, how quickly she'd risen. "If you want to add to this at any point, let me know. I have plenty of texts memorized; I've room for more."

I read the letter over later, in the safety of the guest bedroom. I didn't show it to Neko or Audrey, or tell them what it was. It was intimate, explicit—and honest about being half of a correspondence that could never be reciprocated. It loved, it mourned, and it promised to move on. Trumbull was not one to sacrifice her possibilities here and now for the sake of a lifetime pining, and she expected the same of Saujing. I folded it and put it back in the envelope.

"Are you looking forward to going home?" asked Neko.

"Oh yes," I said. Apologetically, to Audrey: "I'll miss you and Caleb and Dawson, and I'll come out as often as I can. But I miss Mama Rei and Anna and Kevin. And the store. And the hills and the fog, and being able to see the mountains from the beach." And I missed what was, still, a place of healing for me. I wanted very much to see Innsmouth reborn, and the walls of Miskatonic cracked open. And I would. But I still needed more of what San Francisco had to offer.

"I miss them too," said Neko. "But I was thinking. You're looking for these mist-blooded people, to try and bring them back to Innsmouth. Someone's going to have to travel to meet them. I could help."

"Is that what you want?" I asked. "Even after everything that's happened, you still want to keep traveling?"

"I kind of hope my next trip will involve fewer desperate midnight raids. And better food that we haven't cooked ourselves. But yes, it's what I want."

I hesitated, but chose bluntness. "Traveling who knows where, looking like you do. It won't be easy."

She propped her elbows on the windowsill. The night was clear, and the waxing moon gave enough light for people other than me to see by. "Barbed wire keeps you in one place. I'm not going to do that to myself, even to stay safe. I won't go alone—you'll need someone who can show off more of what Innsmouth has to offer, in any case. But I can help."

"Yes," I said. "You can."

My family had grown, and I wanted to keep them all safe. But it wasn't my place to deny them the rain.

~~~~~

Spector saw us off at the airport. Charlie sat and read while we waited for the plane, carefully not looking up. Neko pressed her nose to the glass, watching the great mechanical birds wander their paved nests. Before the camps, this would have been impossible: the cross-country trip requiring days by train. Now a government check or Innsmouth gold could purchase a flight. The Yith, at home, were supposed to have flying machines available for any who cared to see distant lands and the tops of clouds; I wondered whether Trumbull could say how they compared to ours.

Spector took a drag on his cigarette. The air was thick with smoke and the plane would be the same; I breathed shallowly and reached through the confluence for hints of other, easier breaths. "I don't know whether to apologize for bringing you out here," he said.

I looked at him in surprise. "Don't. It's been a hard month, but we've gotten a lot that we needed from it. Or . . . is there something I should know?"

He shook his head. "No. I was hoping you'd get some use out of the trip; I suppose I just hadn't bargained on how much." He pressed the stub into an ashtray; his fingers twitched as if seeking something else to hold. He glanced at me sideways and lit another cigarette. "I wanted to remind them that I could be useful—and that you could too. I didn't consider Barlow, though. He doesn't agree on either count, but when I left he was caught up in a different project entirely." He lowered his voice. "I'm more worried than I was before about what a body snatcher could do—on either side. Seeing the trick in action has that effect, I guess. It's dangerous, and I hope Miss Harris manages to draw them off. If she does, though, they won't forget that you had something to do with that. They weren't there with us. They won't understand what happened, and they'll want to keep an eye on you."

I laughed bitterly, and suffered through the coughing that followed. "Somehow I don't think we can avoid that, no matter what happens." I thought of Ephraim's journal, and swallowed. "Fear is going to have its way, regardless. In some ways, it doesn't matter who has an ability like that, or even if anyone does. Once people are on guard for it . . . they'll find what they're looking for."

"I see that. The past few days I've caught myself watching people, trying to see whether anyone walks like an inhuman monster. Or a Russian, or a fugitive Nazi. Like someone who isn't used to their body." He shook his head. "Witch hunts. Always a good distraction from real problems."

"And we both know where they'll look, when they want to find witches."

He sighed. "Some of these people, I don't think they see a middle ground between perfect loyalty to us, and perfect loyalty to someone else. You've got people speaking up for you—that's the best I can offer. That, and trying to find more chances for you to prove yourself." Before I could respond, he added, "And yes, I know that's a mixed blessing."

I suspected he knew that from experience. Clearly he still needed to prove himself, and his loyalty, regularly. It seemed unlikely that either of us would ever be allowed to stop.

EPILOGUE

In San Francisco, the nightmares changed.

I hadn't slept easy for twenty years, and had resigned myself to mixing these latest troubles with my more practiced unconscious ruminations. Perhaps I would see the camp guards wielding Ngalthr's ritual knife on my mother as she died, or flee from burning desert prison into cold vacuum.

Instead, all my older fears were pushed aside. As soon as I closed my eyes, I found myself sitting alone on an empty beach. Dunes rose beside me, high as mountains, and the ocean lay still and waveless to my other side. I walked between them until I was exhausted, but I knew with absolute certainty that I would never see another living creature. I'd find no end to the solitude: there was no place to flee or seek, and no one looking for me on either side of that boundary line.

No meditation could make these visions lucid, or even let me recognize them as imaginary while I dwelt in them. And though my studies told me that the human mind only dreams sporadically throughout the night, these lasted the full span of my supposed rest.

When I confessed the dreams to Charlie—and they felt very much like a dreadful transgression—he listened solemnly, saying nothing until I had finished. He walked over to the workroom's bookshelf, ran his hand across the familiar titles.

"Mine are of the store," he said at last. "Looking in book after book, and finding every page blank. I was hoping you'd know what to do."

"Void," I swore softly. I had prayed that the dreams were only my own fevered imagination. But prayers are rarely answered.

"It's the confluence, isn't it?" he asked. "It doesn't work the way it's supposed to, this far away."

"I think so. We could go back and ask the archpriest if there's any way to make the connection more flexible, but I don't think he'd know. We didn't usually travel all that far, before. And in the water, distance is a different thing. We could ask him to break it."

"No! I mean, is that what you want to do?"

I shook my head. "I want to live where I will, in the place where I need to be. But it would be worse to give up the family we've just started to form. The Kotos . . . what we've been through, we're family no matter where we are. And I could come back for a few days, here and there. But the confluence, much as we love each other, needs this connection."

He rested his hand on the workroom door. He didn't have loving family here, as I did, but he had friends and the business he'd built up over years. "That's how I feel, too. I guess everything has a cost. It would just be nice to have some advance warning."

I rose, embraced him, said nothing. He didn't need me to tell him how the universe worked.

"I wanted to go back to Innsmouth, eventually," I told Mama Rei. "But not like this."

She put down her sewing and patted the couch cushion beside her. I gave up my pacing and sat, leaned against her side, let her hold me. "You need to be with your family," she said.

"I know. I wish they didn't live on opposite sides of the country."

"Yes." Mama Rei's father had sent her to school in Osaka when she was young. She never talked about missing the family who hosted her there, and she didn't now.

I realized I was crying. I sniffed and rubbed my eyes. Right now, I didn't want to get up, away from her, even for the sake of finding salt water.

"Aphra-chan," she said. She leaned her forehead against mine. I felt the faint creases of her skin, and smelled familiar, familial sweat. "Don't mourn. We're here, and you'll visit when you can. Perhaps we will even fly out ourselves; it must be a more interesting journey than the one over the Pacific. You've told me how much happens under the waves, but it is hard to tell from aboard a ship." I giggled in spite of myself, and she stroked my hair. "Home is where your family is. You have a lot of family, and they will all miss you, but they will all wait for you."

"I love you. You're much more patient than Grandfather."

She laughed. "I will come and meet him, and find out."

"I'd like that."

I imagined it as I packed—as on too little sleep and dreams that sapped our waking energy, Charlie and I crated the store's inventory for shipping to the newly leased building in Arkham. If the Kotos flew out—perhaps they would fall in love with the New England spring, with my worrisome and exasperating blood relatives, and decide to stay.

But they had roots here, people and food and the culture of the city that held them fast—as those things would have held me, if I'd had my way. And even if they chose, absurdly, to give all that up, I still had connections in water and air, among different places and peoples, that would never mesh easily. Even if I hadn't chosen the strictures that now forced my hand, I had chosen to open myself to those intimacies. The vulnerability, the mourning, everything I had to learn from their disparate experiences, were things I had accepted with every conversation offered and every request granted.

I had not been helpless when I made those choices. And though I dealt with their consequences out of necessity, I was not helpless now.

ACKNOWLEDGMENTS

This book owes its greatest debt to Howard Phillips Lovecraft, who invited everyone to play in his sandbox—even the monsters.

After I wrote "The Litany of Earth," I thought I was done. I'd said what I needed to about Lovecraft and being a monster; it was time to move on. When people started asking for more, I figured it was just a nice way of saying "I liked it." But the requests kept coming, and I started explaining to anyone who'd listen why the story didn't need a sequel.

My second thanks, therefore, are to everyone who pushed for more of Aphra's story until I talked myself around and figured out what else I had to say. Eager readers are the best inspiration I can think of—please don't stop asking.

An excellent agent does too many things to easily list. Cameron McClure speaks fluent publisher, marketer, and author, and translates lucidly between dialects. In getting *Winter Tide* ready to shop around, she helped me level up my editing skills, a push that I badly needed. She has been, and continues to be, a pleasure to work with.

Carl Engle-Laird believed in Aphra enough to make "Litany" his first slush acquisition for Tor.com. He gave my little novelette the red carpet treatment, from an intense (and intensely needed) line edit through hand-selling it to anyone who came close enough to listen. I was delighted to work with him on the novel as well. The book you now hold is far stronger for his encouragement, editing, and squeefulness.

Jo Walton and Ada Palmer drew attention to "Litany" with early and high-profile reviews. Ada's "non-review" is a remarkable work in its own right, and all that any author could hope to have said about their writing. My Yith owe much to her discussion of Petrarch and Diderot; the whole book owes much to the bar she set with her praise.

Jo has provided empathy, honesty, and high-level writerly geeking since well before I even thought of Aphra. As a salonière and hostess, she facilitated this book's birth in very practical ways. In her Balticon hotel room, I awoke worrying that "the next Aphra novelette" looked like it might actually be a novel—she gave me tea and assured me that it was okay to have a novel. Six months later at her home in Montreal, fortified by more excellent tea, I finished the draft at 4 a.m.

Elise Matthesen, professional muse, provides Aphra's jewelry.

I have the best beta readers. They provided structural advice so scary and correct that every round of editing involved a large component of just doing more of what they told me to. Lila Wejksnora-Garrott picked up on themes I didn't even know I had. Kathryn McCulley's snarky comments made me giggle—a powerful antidote to editing anxiety—and showed me which bits actually worked. Anne M. Pillsworth represented the faction of Lovecraft lovers, reminded me that readers can't read minds, and helped ensure that deviations from Mythos canon were deliberate. Marissa Lingen spoke for the faction that loves Lovecraft not; she also encouraged me to move romantic relationships out of my head and onto the page. Allen Berman gave all-around useful commentary and represented the faction that doesn't read Lovecraft at all—feedback well worth printing out the book's very first hard copy.

Anne is also my Best Co-Blogger on Tor.com's Lovecraft Reread series. Thanks to her and our community of commenters, I've had excellent company in my efforts to assimilate the whole Mythos for easy deconstruction. They are all delightfully cyclopean, perhaps even rugose. There are not enough places, online or otherwise, where one can comfortably critique Lovecraft's racism, wax enthusiastic over the architecture of Y'ha-nthlei, and geek about historical understanding of plate tectonics—all flame-free.

The problem with historical fantasy is the history—for giving mine some resemblance to actual events and experiences, I'm indebted to many libraries and used bookstores. My reading list was long, but I want to make particular mention of George Takei's *To the Stars*. While it's not exactly a standard historical reference, his child's-eye-view portrayal of the Japanese American internment, and the community's postwar recovery, were invaluable touchstones. (While I'm at it, I'll also thank him for his kindness to an eleven-year-old Trekkie who managed to get the date of the costume contest wrong at her first con—also an important contribution to my writing, in that I stayed with fandom rather than getting scared off.)

My followers on Twitter and Livejournal patiently answered hard-to-look-up questions like "I know people smoked everywhere, but libraries?" and "Even in the rare book room???" The past is another, smellier country. Finally, the docent at the National Japanese American Historical Society in San Francisco's Nihonmachi provided helpful guidance on postwar cuisine along with a variety of other research materials. All errors—of which I'm sure there are many—are my own.

My parents' stories of growing up in the '40s and '50s helped color Aphra's world. If I'd known that writing about a gay Jewish New Yorker who works for the government in the '40s would evoke so many details about my great-uncle Monroe—very clearly a relative of Ron Spector's—I would have done it a lot sooner.

I hope my in-laws will forgive my borrowing a few names, since I didn't ask permission. Lovecraft populated the Miskatonic Valley with Uptons; the Skinners and Trumbulls and Crowthers followed naturally. The real ones are all very nice people and none of them are in fact possessed by eldritch abominations.

Householdmates Jamie Anfenson-Comeau, Shelby Anfenson-Comeau, and Nora Temkin provided moral support throughout the writing process, appropriate admiration of cover art, and dramatic exclamations that they "knew me when" every time an author copy appeared in the mail. Bobby, Cordelia, and Miriam do not facilitate the writing process, but do inspire it—and are delightful in many other ways as well.

First and finally, my wife, Sarah, is alpha reader, continuity checker, patient listener to artistic wibbling, seneschal, child minder, epigrammatic problem solver, and source of potent slash goggles. I could not have written this book without her.

ABOUT THE AUTHOR

RUTHANNA EMRYS lives in a mysterious manor house on the outskirts of Washington, D.C., with her wife and their large, strange family. She makes homemade vanilla, obsesses about game design, gives unsolicited advice, and occasionally attempts to save the world. Her stories have appeared in a number of venues, including *Strange Horizons, Analog Science Fiction and Fact,* and *Tor.com. Winter Tide* is her first novel.